W9-BSS-451

RAVE REVIEWS FOR
RICHARD LAYMON!

"I've always been a Laymon fan. He manages to raise serious gooseflesh."
—Bentley Little

"Laymon is incapable of writing a disappointing book."
—*New York Review of Science Fiction*

"Laymon always takes it to the max. No one writes like him and you're going to have a good time with anything he writes."
—Dean Koontz

"If you've missed Laymon, you've missed a treat."
—Stephen King

"A brilliant writer."
—*Sunday Express*

"I've read every book of Laymon's I could get my hands on. I'm absolutely a longtime fan."
—Jack Ketchum, author of *Off Season*

MORE PRAISE FOR RICHARD LAYMON!

INTO THE FIRE

RICHARD LAYMON

LEISURE BOOKS NEW YORK CITY

A LEISURE BOOK®

July 2006

Published by

Dorchester Publishing Co., Inc.
200 Madison Avenue
New York, NY 10016

ISBN 0-8439-5732-8

The name "Leisure Books" and the stylized "L" with design are trademarks of Dorchester Publishing Co., Inc.

Printed in the United States of America.

Visit us on the web at www.dorchesterpub.com.

INTO THE FIRE

CHAPTER ONE

"You were it. Do you know what I mean? There was never anyone else, not for me. Do you know when it was, the first time I ever saw you? Sally Harken's thirteenth birthday party. I hardly even knew Sally, since we didn't go to the same school. The only reason I got invited to her party, my mom and dad were friends with Sally's parents. I didn't want to go, can you believe that? They had to make me go.

"And then you walked in. I'll never forget it. You had bangs that hung down almost to your eyes, and those blue eyes shining out, and those white teeth. You wore a white blouse. It had short sleeves, but you had them rolled way up high on your arms. And you had the cuffs of your shorts rolled up, too. The shorts were blue denim, and looked brand-new. The legs must've been too long to suit you, so you turned them up. It was like you were all cuffs. Cuffs and smooth, tan skin.

"Speaking of cuffs, how are you doing?"

Pamela, sitting in the passenger seat with her cuffed hands resting on her lap, stared out the window and didn't answer.

"Are they too tight?"

They *were* too tight. The sharp edges of the bracelets dug into her wrists, and her fingers tingled. But Pam didn't want Rodney to fool with them. "They're fine," she said. She wanted him to leave her alone.

"You sure?"

"Yes."

"Anyway, that's when I fell in love with you. We were thirteen, and you walked into Sally's party and . . . it hurt me to look at you, you were so cute and beautiful and . . . you had a freshness, an innocence, something like that. And you also had that twinkle in your eyes. A kind of glint. You've still got that. Not at the moment, of course. But it'll come back. Once you get used to things, it'll come back.

"Of course, you lost most of that freshness I was talking about. It's a shame. Everyone loses it, though. Maybe it goes when you start in with sex. Or maybe it's when some special sort of dream dies in you. Who knows? You kept it longer than most girls. You still had it in your junior year. Your first year as a varsity cheerleader. Oh, God, the way you used to look . . . that pleated skirt, that sweater. When you jumped, the sweater would come up just an inch or two above the top of your skirt, so there'd be a little strip of bare skin showing. I used to watch you at the games, and want to kiss you there. I knew just how it would feel, and how it would smell.

"Anyway, that freshness thing was gone when we started our senior year. Even without it, you were . . . wonderful. But a different kind of wonderful. Not so much like an innocent, eager kid, more like a woman. And you sure hadn't lost that sparkle in your eyes. It's sort of as if, everywhere you look, you're seeing things that amaze you. And like maybe you're hoping to throw in a quip.

"Of course, too, you just got more and more beautiful. I couldn't believe it when I saw your picture in the newspaper. The picture sure didn't do you justice, but it about tore me apart. To look at your face again, after so many years. I thought to myself what a fool I'd been, depriving myself of you, making do with a string of gals that were nothing but lousy imitations of the one and only *you* I longed for in my heart. They were available; that's all they had going for them. They hadn't gone off to some damn college halfway across the country, like some people I could name. So I just had to make do with them. I tried to make them look like you. Silly, huh? I made them wear a wig that looked like how you wore your hair. I dressed them up like you, too. And I called them Pamela. Sometimes, when I tried really hard, I could sort of trick myself into thinking they *were* you. It wasn't an easy trick, though. Mostly, I was just disgusted with myself. You know? That I'd let myself get so obsessed with you and couldn't let it go and had to trick myself with a bunch of crummy substitutes.

"So when I saw your picture in the paper, it was like a sign that I oughta quit all that and go after the real thing. So that's just what I did.

"Bet you must be wondering what took me so long. They ran that picture six months ago, didn't they? And it gave your husband's name, and even the address of the newlyweds' home. So why did it take me six months to show up and claim you? Is that what you're wondering?"

"I'm wondering what you did to those girls."

"Oh, mostly the same as what I plan to do to you. Except for one difference, which is that I'm going to *keep* you. I've bought us a house. It's a fine little place where nobody'll ever bother us. It'll be our home. We'll have a wonderful time."

"Did you kill them?" Pamela asked.

He smiled. "I put them out of their misery."

"Oh, God."

"I guess one might say it's your fault. All those girls *and* that husband of yours, all of them died because you went on your merry way just as if old lard-ass Rodney Pinkham was a nobody. Should've paid me more attention, maybe. Should've maybe *dated* me."

"*Dated* you? You never even asked!"

"You would've laughed in my face."

"I've never laughed in *anyone's* face!"

"Bet you called me Piggy behind my back."

"I didn't."

"*They* all did."

"I never heard *anybody* call you Piggy behind your back."

"Liar."

"If you wanted to go out with me so badly, why didn't you just *ask!*"

"Told you why."

"I might've gone out with you. You didn't have to *kill* people. My God . . . how many were there?"

"Including your husband? Oh, sixteen."

It numbed Pamela's mind. Fifteen girls had died because of this man's obsession with her?

Not just Jim.

She'd thought it couldn't get any worse than last night. *It can always get worse*, she realized.

"It's not all that many, fifteen," Rodney explained. "I mean, it *sounds* like a lot when you just blurt it out like that. But what you've gotta remember, it went on for five years. That only averages out to three a year. That's not so many. Would've been plenty more, except you went and got yourself married and they ran your picture in the paper. Now that I've got you, the rest of it's gonna stop. I mean, why would I want them when I've got you? You're all I ever wanted."

He turned his head and smiled at Pamela. It was the way he had smiled ever since she'd known him: an odd, quick lift of the upper lip that showed not only his front teeth but the gums above them. The crevices between his teeth always used to be packed with crud from old meals, and all the snacking in between.

Which was one of the reasons everyone had called him Piggy. They'd called him Piggy not only because of his obesity, but also because of his tiny eyes and his filth and body odor and the remains of food decorating his clothes and teeth.

Pamela had always figured that the nickname was an insult to swine everywhere. She preferred to call the creep Rotney, because everything about him seemed rotten, repulsive. Hoglike. Among her friends, she'd said terrible things about him. She had always been kind *to* him, though.

Maybe that had been a mistake. Not hurrying away whenever he approached, the way most kids used to do. Smiling at him. Talking to him. Treating him like a human being, even though his disgusting appearance and sour smell had sometimes made her eyes water. A couple of times, she had actually gagged in the middle of chats with him. Wanting to spare his feelings, she'd claimed it must've been something she ate.

Maybe she *should* have avoided him, laughed at him, called him Piggy or Rotney to his face. If she'd been really bad to him, maybe none of this would've happened.

All those girls . . . Jim.

Went away Jim, came back Rodney.

That was how it had seemed, anyway.

The room had been dark last night except for the light from the television. Pamela was in bed, propped up with pillows, watching the tail end of the eleven-o'clock news and waiting for Dave to start. Jim had gone off to the bathroom. He seemed to be taking longer than usual. Pamela hoped he was shaving. He usually shaved before bed if he planned to fool around. The VCR was already set, so they would be able to watch the tape if they missed some of Dave's show.

When she heard Jim's footsteps outside the room, she drew the top sheet up to cover her bare shoulders. She wanted it to be a surprise that she had dispensed with her nightshirt. Jim walked into the bedroom. He wore his paisley bathrobe, the same robe he'd been wearing ten minutes ago, but he had *grown*. He looked as if he'd somehow swollen up—grown taller, spread out until he was so fat that his robe wouldn't shut all the way. The front of his belly bulged through the gap and looked like uncooked bread dough. Only for an instant did Pamela's mind stumble with confusion about the sudden change in her husband.

Then she realized that the man in Jim's robe wasn't Jim. He reached for a light switch.

The bedside lamps came on and made the room bright. Pamela recognized the man in Jim's robe. She hadn't seen him in five years, not since high school graduation, but he hadn't changed very much. His smile was *exactly* the same—a lift of the upper lip. Same piggy eyes. He raised his arms and spread them wide. "My dear! Have you missed me?"

Pamela could hardly breathe. She felt as if a mallet were pounding her heart. She wanted to call out for Jim.

But Jim had to be dead, didn't he? Dead.

Rodney took a step toward her.

She whipped the sheet away and flung herself over and squirmed across Jim's side of the bed, reaching down for the nightstand drawer. She grabbed its handle. Jerked it open. Drove her hand down inside the drawer toward the SIG SAUER .380 that Jim kept there for emergencies.

Before she could touch the pistol, Rodney kicked the drawer shut. It slammed on her forearm. As she cried out, her arm was grabbed and jerked out of the drawer. Rodney shoved it up high on her back, driving her face into Jim's pillow. Then he climbed onto her.

The weight of his body mashed her against the mattress. The robe must've come wide open. She could feel his bare, greasy skin all down her back and rump and legs. With her face in the pillow and his massive weight on her back, she couldn't breathe. She couldn't scream. She could hardly move. She fought to suck air into her lungs, but failed. *This is it*, she thought. *Oh, Jesus, I'm gonna die.*

When she woke up, she was surprised to find herself alive. And spent the next several hours wishing she were dead. Rodney finally dragged her out of the bedroom. At the bathroom, he showed her Jim's body. Then she watched him set the house on fire. She remembered being carried outside in Rodney's arms, but nothing after that.

She came awake in the passenger seat of his car. The sun was low, and in her eyes. Her hands rested on her lap, shackled together with handcuffs as if she'd been arrested by the police. She ached almost everywhere. In some places she felt raw pain. Rodney must've dressed her. She couldn't remember it, though. It seemed as if she'd still been naked on her way out of the house.

She wore a green pleated skirt. It was very short. It reached only halfway down her thighs, and she could feel the upholstery of the car seat against her bare rump. She also wore a gold pullover sweater. It had a crew neck and long sleeves. The wool felt heavy and hot. It was scratchy against her skin. All the outfit really needed was a big, green felt. J sewn to the chest of the sweater, and it would be a pretty fair replica of the varsity cheerleader costume she'd worn at Jackson High. Rodney seemed unaware that she'd awakened, so she closed her eyes again and pretended to sleep. She thought about what had happened last night.

Jim was dead.

At twenty-three, Pamela was a widow. She'd been beaten and half suffocated. In his grunting, hog-man voice Rodney had promised to do so many things to her. He mentioned some of them. With gloating relish. *Dirty fucking pervert!*

What if I just throw myself out of the car? Probably bust my head open, but that might be better than going on. At least it'll be over and done with. In some ways, the idea appealed to her. But she knew that she wouldn't hurl herself out of the car—not while it was speeding along at sixty. *Not gonna kill myself. No way, no how. I'm gonna live through this.*

Right. That's what they all think.

She had no confidence that she could live through this, but she knew she would try. She would be patient and wait for just the right time to save herself. And so she sat motionless, head down, eyes shut, cuffed hands resting on her lap. For a long time Rodney drove along in silence.

Maybe he thought she was sleeping. Maybe he was preoccupied with plans or fantasies.

When he finally started to talk, the words came out in a heavy rush that seemed to have no end.

"You were it. Do you know what I mean? There was never anyone else, not for me."

Then he fell silent, and she wondered: *When he stops the car, what's he going to do to me?*

CHAPTER TWO

"Now that I've got you, the rest is gonna stop. I mean, why would I want them when I've got you? You're all I ever wanted." He turned his head and smiled at Pamela.

She turned her face away from him. She stared out the window. All she could see beyond the edge of the road was desert. Not a desert of sand, but of hard gray ground that looked like a mixture of dry mud and gravel. She knew the brush was mesquite. The stubby trees were yuccas. Some of the cacti were prickly pear, cholla, and saguaro. The saguaro looked like giant men with their arms raised in surrender. But she didn't see any men out there. The only animals in sight were a few hawks or buzzards floating across the sky on widespread wings. Except for the road, the area seemed to be a wasteland. There was bound to be civilization ahead, though. At the very least, a service station. Rodney hadn't stopped for gas yet, so he would have to get a fill-up soon.

I'll make my break when he stops for gas, she thought. She wondered if he had a gun. He might've taken Jim's pistol out of the drawer. He might've had a gun of his own, last night, when he broke into the house.

For all she knew, he might be armed to the teeth.

She hadn't seen any guns on him, but that didn't mean much. The little .380 could fit in a pocket of his pants.

I don't want anybody getting killed. But I can't let him take me to his hide-

out, she told herself. *Have to make my getaway before that. What if his next stop is the hideout? Maybe he found a place that he could reach on a single tank of gas. Or maybe he has a couple of jerri cans stowed in his trunk.*

Pamela suddenly found herself peering past Rodney at the gas gauge. The red needle pointed to E. She felt a lurch of fear. *Take it easy,* she told herself. *My angle makes it look worse than it is. It's not really on empty yet. We've probably got twenty or thirty miles to go. We could be in a city by then. And if we do run out of gas here in the middle of nothing, it might give me a chance to get away.*

"Am I going too fast for you?" Rodney asked.

Apparently he thought she was staring at the speedometer. "I'm worried about the gas," she said.

"We're fine."

"Will there be a gas station pretty soon?"

"Nope. Nothing between us and home."

Home. Coming from him, the word made her feel sick. "Will we have enough gas to reach it?" she asked. "Our home?"

"Sure. We oughta be coming up on the turnoff in another fifteen miles, and then it's only twelve to go."

"That's almost thirty miles."

"Twenty-seven." He looked at her and raised his upper lip. "We might have to go the last bit on fumes. Maybe even on foot. It won't matter, though, long as we make it to the turnoff. We can always walk from there, if we have to. Nobody'll come along and bother us. It's just an old dirt road that doesn't go anywhere. It goes to our house, and noplace else."

"What about a gas station?" Pamela asked.

"We don't need one."

"I do. I have to use a restroom."

Rodney looked very interested. "Number one or number two?"

"Number one."

"Ahhh. You don't need a restroom for that."

"Where am I supposed to go?"

"Anywhere you like. Except the car."

"Then you'd better pull over."

"Wait till we get to the dirt road."

"I can't."

"Sure you can."

"I'm telling you. I have to go *now*." She saw him glance at the rearview mirror. Apparently the road behind them was as empty as the road ahead. Rodney stepped on the brakes. As his car slowed down, he steered to the right. The tires bumped down off the pavement. The ride became bumpy, and the tires made crunching sounds on the rough surface of the shoulder.

After a few seconds, the car stopped.

"Don't move," Rodney said. He shut off the engine, pulled the ignition key, and swung his door open. Hot, dry air swept into the car. He climbed out. His door thunked shut. Pamela watched him walk toward the front of the car.

In spite of the heat, she felt loose and shivery inside.

I'd better just pee and let it go at that, she told herself. *I don't have to do anything crazy.*

If I don't do something crazy, he'll have me. He'll get me to his place and that'll be it.

As he walked past the front of the car, he watched her through the windshield. He had an eagerness in his tiny pig eyes. Sweat glistened on his nose.

He's planning to watch.

Rodney turned and came toward her door. Reaching into the left front pocket of his pants, he pulled out a small black pistol. The SIG SAUER. He'd taken it after all. He opened the passenger door.

"What're you gonna do, shoot me?"

"That'll be up to you."

"I won't try anything."

"Hope not."

"Will you take the cuffs off?"

"What do you think?"

"Please?"

"You must think I'm pretty stupid."

"What are you scared of? What could I possibly do to you? My God, you're twice my size. And you've got the gun. So just take the cuffs off me, okay?"

"No-kay. Come on out."

Pamela scooted to the edge of her seat. Rodney was staring at her legs. Keeping them together, she turned sideways and swung them out the doorway. She used her cuffed hands to stop her skirt from climbing too high when she squirmed forward.

Rodney laughed. "Who you trying to hide it from?"

Ignoring him, she stretched her legs down. She couldn't quite touch the ground, so she scooted off and dropped the rest of the way. The ground felt rough and hot under her bare feet. She stood up straight in the V of the open door.

The heat of the desert sun was so great that she felt as if she were standing in the midst of a fire—a blaze that seemed only moments away from igniting the hair on her head, the shoulders of her sweater. Her body suddenly ran with dribbles and trickles as if her skin were melting.

"My God," she muttered.

"Soon as you're done with business," Rodney said, "we'll climb back into the car and be on our merry way. In air-conditioned comfort, such as it is."

"Better than this."

"You're the one who wants to pee."

She hobbled clear of the open door. Rodney threw it shut. Squinting against the afternoon brightness, she looked for a place beyond the roadside where she might have some privacy.

None of the nearby cactus plants were high enough. There was a good-sized organ-pipe cactus, but it was at least a hundred feet away. She'd destroy her feet going that far.

This isn't about peeing, she reminded herself. *It's about escaping. If I can get to that organ-pipe, I'll have that much of a head start.*

Unless he comes with me.

She squinted at Rodney. He was grinning at her, enjoying her discomfort. "Could I borrow your shoes?" she asked.

"What do you want shoes for?"

"So I don't kill my feet. I want to go over there." She pointed at the cactus. It was tall and green. It looked like a saguaro, but it had no arms.

"What do you wanta go over there for?"

"To relieve myself."

"Forget it. Do it here."

She shook her head.

"Do it."

"No. Somebody might come along."

"Think so?"

She swiveled her head from side to side. Nothing was approaching from either direction. But the highway had dips and bends. "What if I start to go, and a car comes?"

"Isn't gonna happen. And so what if it does? They get a free peek, so what? If they stop and try to mess with us, I'll blow their heads off."

Facing him, she stiffened her back. "I'm not going to do it here. Just let me go over to that cactus. I can get behind it and nobody'll be able to see what I'm doing."

"What a kick. You care? After last night?"

"Yeah, I care."

"Okay, okay. What the hell, why not? Anything for my honey."

"How about shoes?"

He coughed out a laugh. "Anything but that."

"Just let me borrow your shoes for two minutes, okay?"

"What am I supposed to wear?"

"You can sit in the car."

"What's this, fantasyland? I'm going with you."

Of course he is, she thought. *What did you think, he'd give up his chance to watch?*

"Go on," he said. "I'm right behind you."

She started walking toward the cactus. She moved slowly, picking her way with care to avoid stepping on any of the shiny bits of broken glass that littered the roadside, then keeping her distance from the prickly pears and cholla. In spite of her care, bits of rocks poked the bottoms of her feet. She winced when they stabbed her. She kept her teeth gritted. Sometimes the scorching heat of the ground made her hiss. But she kept on walking all the way to the organ-pipe cactus.

She stepped behind it.

Rodney halted beside her. "Did you notice?" he asked. "Nothing came by."

"Really," she muttered. She didn't care.

"Could've saved yourself all that hurt."

She looked back at the road. It still appeared to be empty in both directions. The only car was Rodney's. It sat there hunched in the sunlight like some species of metal beast. A beast with a foul, rancid soul. Just biding its time, waiting for them to come back so it could bear them away to Rodney's den.

I'm not getting back in.

"Come on and do it," Rodney said.

"Not with you watching."

His lip slid up. "Get outta here. You forgetting about last night? I saw all your itty-biddy bits and pieces."

"That was last night; this is today."

"Lift your skirt and squat, honey."

Squinting into his eyes, she slowly shook her head from side to side.

Rodney laughed softly. Then he pressed the muzzle of the pistol against the bridge of her nose. The feel of it made her eyes ache as if she had crossed them.

"Do you want to die?" he whispered.

"No."

"Do you want me to hurt you so bad that you'll *wish* you were dead?"

"No."

"Good." Rodney took two steps backward. Keeping the pistol aimed at her face, he sank to a crouch. "How about doing me a cheer?" he said.

"A *what?*"

"I was gonna wait till we got home, but I wanta see you do one now."

"A cheer?"

"A good one. Pretend it's a night game at good old Jackson High, it's fourth down and goal to go, and our guys just *gotta* make it."

"My feet."

"You're the one who had to make us stop. You're the one who had to walk all the way out here barefoot so you could have the privacy of a cactus. You wreck up your feet, whose fault is it?"

"I can't do a cheer with my hands cuffed."

"Sure you can."

"Not a good one. You want me to jump, don't you? You want me to make my skirt and sweater fly up. That's the idea, isn't it? Well, I can't really make them fly unless my arms are free."

His tiny eyes stared at her. "The only problem," he said, "is you'll try to run away if I take off the cuffs."

"No, I won't."

"Yes, you will. I'm not an idiot. Do I look like an idiot?"

"Where would I run to? We're out in the middle of nowhere."

"You might run to the car."

"You've got the gun."

"That's very true." His eyes narrowed to pink slits. "Have you ever been shot?"

"No."

"It hurts. If you make me shoot you, it'll hurt *a lot*. Because I won't kill you. I'm not going to ruin it all and kill you, no matter what you do. But I'll shoot you just enough to stop you so you can't get away. And it'll hurt. And that'll only be the *start* of the pain for you, because I don't like traitors."

"I won't try to get away," she said. "Okay?"

"Better not."

She raised her outstretched arms.

Rodney stood up. He switched the pistol to his left hand. With his right he dug into the front pocket of his pants. He came up with the leather key case that had been swaying under the ignition during the trip. One-handed, he flipped it open, shook the keys, and took hold of the key he wanted.

Pamela stood motionless while he unlocked the cuffs and removed them. He slipped the cuffs and key case into his pocket as he stepped backward again. Then he crouched and nodded up at her.

"Ready," he said.

She nodded. She took a deep breath. She stood at attention. Then she clapped her hands four times. *Smack, smack, smack, smack.* With each clap she took a big step backward. After the fourth she halted. Legs together, shoulders back, chin up. She tried to make herself smile. And her eyes filled with tears as she suddenly thought about Maui. She had run through most of her best cheerleader routines for Jim during their honeymoon there. They'd had a picnic lunch—and a couple of beers—on a hidden beach they discovered along the road to Hana. Afterward they'd taken a stroll along the beach. She'd done a few cartwheels on the sand and Jim's enthusiasm had prompted her to give him a major show. Her only audience was Jim. Halfway through, she'd taken off her bikini. Jim had looked stunned, ecstatic, watching her prance about naked—leaping, kicking high, twirling, doing handsprings and flips. At the end of her performance she'd thrown her arms around him, exhausted and gasping. While she hung on him, he'd pulled down his trunks. Then he'd clutched the backs of her thighs, lifted her, and lowered her slowly, going up into her high and deep.

Pamela sniffed. With the sleeves of her sweater, she wiped the tears from her eyes.

"Whatcha waiting for, crybaby?" Rodney said. "Let's go." He clapped four times.

Smack, smack, smack, smack.

"We got *pep!*" Pamela shouted. She kicked her right leg high and clapped. "We got *steam!*" She kicked up her other leg and clapped. "We are the boys on the *Jackson team!*"

She leaped, throwing her hands overhead and flinging her legs out high to the sides. The jump tossed her skirt up and slid the sweater up her midriff.

Thataway. Give him what he wants.

She landed with a harder jolt than she expected.

Rodney, squatting close to the ground, looked sweaty and a little stunned—as if he had trouble believing his luck. He was silent for a few seconds. Then he applauded.

"Go, Pam, go!" he called. "Let's have another one!"

She shot her fists into the air and shouted, "Our team is red-hot!"

"Yeah!"

She twirled, making her skirt rise high as she shouted again, "Our team is red-hot!" She halted, facing Rodney. Clapping hard and stomping her feet, she yelled, "'Cause we got killer instinct—and they do not!" She ran at Rodney yelling one long "Yaaaaaay!" as she dived into a handspring, did another handspring and another, her skirt and sweater flying up and down to let Rodney see more than he had ever seen at any football game, letting him see it all as she kept on yelling, "Yaaaaaay!" and flipped her way closer to him. Landing just in front of him, feet together, she cried out, "*Team!*" She clapped once more, then shot both fists into the air and kicked with her right leg.

The kick was meant for Rodney's face. He gasped. Flinched backward.

CHAPTER THREE

Pamela watched her bare foot flash up past Rodney's face, and knew she'd missed.

Oh, God! I blew it!

Her leg kept rising.

I'll be high-kicking when he shoots me.

But Rodney wasn't shooting, not yet. He was tumbling backward, arms flung out, the gun pointing off to the side. As his back hit the ground, Pamela reached the top of her kick.

She brought her leg down, lunging forward at the last moment to stomp Rodney's knee.

He cried out.

She dropped with both knees onto his belly. It was big and soft. A hog belly full of meat and cheese fried in grease. Her knees sank in halfway to the ground. Rodney's eyes bulged. Air exploded from his mouth and nose, blasting out spittle and snot.

His left hand came up, clutched the sleeve of her sweater.

His right hand started to rise with the pistol.

Pamela dropped straight forward. The sweater in Rodney's grip stretched and pulled off her shoulder, but couldn't keep her away. She fell onto him, her belly on his face. He pressed the pistol against her ear.

She grabbed his wrist and forced his hand away. He didn't seem to have much energy. The smell of fried food belched from his mouth.

He writhed beneath her. His face felt like a soccer ball under her belly. A soccer ball with a hard, jutting chin—with breath that seeped through her sweater and felt like hot water against her skin. That smell of grease would seep into the material. Stay there. Maybe even seep into her skin.

She wondered if she could smother him this way. Just stay on his face till he died.

It would be a good way to get him—suffocate him with the very body that had been his obsession, the body that he'd killed Jim for, the body that he intended to use and hurt and soil so badly.

Kill him with it!

His face pushed up at her belly and he began to snap, chin jerking up and down, teeth clamping shut on her sweater, biting and biting, going for her. Pamela sucked in her belly. He went after it, snapping. His spit soaked through fabric to her flesh.

As she started to push herself up, he nipped her skin through the sweater.

"Ahhh!" she cried out.

She got away from his teeth, but he sat up, snapping. Her left hand was busy trying to keep the pistol away. With her right she grabbed his face and tried to push it down. His face kept coming at her, forcing her hand backward, lifting her until she was perched on her knees and starting to slip down the hill of his stomach. She was only moments from falling.

"No!" she yelled, and dug her thumb into his eye. His body jerked rigid and he shrieked.

Teetering on her knees, Pamela lunged for the pistol. Before she could reach it with her right, his hand jumped out of her grip. He smashed the pistol against her cheekbone.

She toppled sideways.

As she fell, she thought, *Blew it again. I'm dead meat.* Her shoulder struck the ground. The blow seemed to shake her whole body. She felt sharp bits of gravel digging into her arm and hip and the side of her leg. But only for an instant, because she was rolling. Her back slammed the ground, and she skidded.

The moment her skid stopped, she lifted her head and looked at Rodney. He was curled on his side, left hand cupping his face as if he hoped to catch whatever might spill from his eye socket. His right hand swayed, trying to aim the pistol at her. He made a high-pitched humming noise.

"Would you like another cheer?" Pamela gasped as she sat up. "I'll do you another cheer." She leaned forward, drew in her legs, and got her feet underneath her. "Which cheer would you like?" She stood up. The pistol kept pointing at her, but Rodney didn't seem able to hold it steady. "Do you want my favorite?"

Without waiting for an answer or a shot, she clapped her hands and started marching backward as she chanted, "U! G! L! Y! You ain't got no al-i-bi! You *ugly*! You *ugly*!"

The gunshot kicked up dirt beside her right foot. Grit whipped the side of her leg.

She put her back to Rodney and broke into a sprint. With the next shot, dirt exploded from the ground a few yards ahead of her and off to the left.

Two down, five to go. *Just keep missing! Please keep missing!*

She dodged a cluster of prickly pear, then poured on the speed again: chin tucked down, back hunched, arms pumping, legs kicking out, reaching. . . .

But never far enough. Never fast enough.

She huffed for air. Sweat poured down her body. She knew she had to be running faster than she'd ever run before, but it seemed so terribly *slow*. A plodding pace. No more than a trudge!

Not fast enough to outrun a bullet. Not by a loooong shot.

But Rodney was blind in one eye, had to be in awful pain, and maybe he wasn't such a great marksman in the first place. He had already missed her twice at fairly close range. And she was a lot farther away from him now.

Why isn't he firing? She looked back.

He was on his feet, chasing her, pistol in his right hand, his left hand clenched into a fist and jabbing forward as he ran. One side of his face was an eyeless slick of blood. Pamela heard herself let out a whimper.

I'm not gonna get away, she thought. *He's gonna keep coming and keep coming till he gets close enough, and then he's gonna use the gun on me.*

That's what he thinks. He's fat and out of shape and hurt bad. I can outrun him till hell freezes over.

If I don't keel over from heat prostration, she thought. *If my feet don't bleed me dry.*

She glanced at the ground behind her. She was leaving spots of blood on the desert floor. *He can follow those till hell freezes . . .*

Maybe she could make it to the car.

What good would that do? she wondered. *He's got the keys.* She didn't even know anymore where the car *was.* The highway was off to her right; the car didn't seem to be there. Looking back over her right shoulder, she spotted it far off in the distance.

Good thing I don't have the keys, since I'm running away from the damn thing!

She considered changing direction and making a run for the road; a car was sure to come along sooner or later. Anybody seeing her would know she needed help, and would probably give it to her. But if she went for the road, Rodney might run for his car. It wasn't *that* far behind. He could just hop in and chase her down with it.

Better not go any closer, she thought. She twisted around to make sure that he wasn't gaining on her. He was sprawled on the ground, far back. Pamela stopped running. Standing still, she gasped for breath and wiped the sweat out of her eyes.

Rodney looked as if he'd flopped facedown. He didn't seem to be moving at all.

All right! Pamela turned away from him and poured on the speed. She ran hard, dodging cacti and mesquite, sometimes leaping over rocks that got in her way. Rodney, she supposed, had been brought down by the heat and too much exertion and the pain or shock of losing his eye—but he would probably recover soon, and come after her again.

At the edge of an arroyo, she stopped to catch her breath. The slope was fairly steep. She wondered if she should try to climb down, or slide to the bottom on her rump.

Slide, she decided. *You don't want to lose your footing and take a header.*

She bent over and clutched the sides of her skirt. Then she looked back to see if Rodney was after her yet. And couldn't see him at all. Suddenly scared, she turned around and stood on tiptoe. No sign of him.

Maybe he's still down, she told herself. *I just can't see him because of all the rocks and bushes and stuff.*

Off to her right, a cluster of rocks jutted up from the floor of the desert to a height of about twenty feet. She hurried toward them. They seemed to be farther away than she'd first supposed. Farther away, and higher.

As she ran, she began to think she was making a mistake. She should've kept on running *away*. This detour was stealing her advantage. Rodney might be up and gaining on her—closing in with every step she took toward this damn pile of rocks. But she'd already come this far. So far no sign of Rodney.

At last she reached the foot of the rocks. She was breathless, worn out, sodden with sweat. But she didn't pause to rest; she began to scurry upward. When she was halfway to the top, she decided that she was probably high enough for a good view. She crawled onto a slab of rock that looked fairly smooth and didn't have much of a slant. She sat on it, knees up, feet against the surface to keep her from sliding down.

Hands cupped around her eyes, she squinted off across the desert.

After a while she spotted Rodney. Still sprawled on the ground.

Sighing, she wiped the sweat off her face.

For a while she simply watched him and savored the knowledge that she was safe. Rodney was down. He was far away. As long as they both stayed put, he couldn't hurt her. She looked at the road.

Nothing was coming.

Why did they even put it here if nobody uses it? she wondered. *Put it here just for Rodney.* Then she thought, *Maybe so.* The idea spooked her a little. "Just kidding," she muttered. A road bound for nowhere. *That's ridiculous*, she told herself. *It's not some sort of a phantom highway; it's just out in the middle of nowhere and probably goes between a couple of podunk towns nobody ever goes to, so it doesn't get used much.* Somebody would be along sooner or later. Pamela tried to remember if she'd seen any other vehicles since they'd made the turnoff onto this stretch. None that she could recall.

What if nobody does come along? she wondered. *I'm safe here. That's what counts. He can't get me. Just oughta make myself comfortable and wait things out.*

Her sweater felt like a heavy, damp coat. She pulled it off and sighed. The breeze was hot and dry against her skin, but it felt wonderful.

She folded the sweater and sat on it. The thick wool pad made a good cushion.

Rodney still appeared to be lying motionless out there. She checked the road. Still deserted.

If somebody does come along, she thought, *it won't do me any good. Not while I'm up here. He probably won't see me, and I sure can't get down to the road in time.*

That's okay. I'm fine right here. For now.

But the sun felt awfully hot, so she tugged the sweater out from under her rump and draped it over her head. Some of it hung down her back; some of it shrouded her face. She lifted the part that hid her face, and held it up with both hands to make a sunshade.

She gazed out from under it. Rodney was still sprawled on the ground. Had he moved at all since going down? She didn't think so.

Maybe he's dead?

Maybe he's not.

With her sweater off and her arms raised, there was nothing to stop the dribbles of sweat that ran down her body. They slid all the day down to the waist of her skirt, tickling as they went. Every so often, when the itching became intolerable, she let the sweater flop down over her face and used both hands to rub herself.

Relieving the itches felt wonderful. But she hated to do it because she couldn't see Rodney while the sweater covered her face.

Each time she lifted it, she was afraid that he might be gone.

He isn't going anywhere, she finally told herself. *He's all done chasing me.*

But is he dead? She was pretty sure that a poke in the eye could be fatal—if you got in deep enough to hit the brain. Had she jabbed her thumb in enough for that? She doubted it. But if the poke hadn't killed him, maybe he'd been dropped by a heart attack. A big, fat guy like him running around the desert, fighting with her, getting plenty of shocks to his system from all the damage she'd inflicted . . . not to mention he'd probably been exhausted to start with. Driving for hours. Awake all night, first killing Jim, then wearing himself out with taking Pamela captive, then burning the house. She'd spent much of the night hoping he would be knocked dead by a heart attack. *If he is dead now,* Pamela thought, *I can get hold of his car keys and drive away. But if he's not dead and I go for the keys . . .*

She let the sweater flop in front of her face. Using both hands, she rubbed her itchy sides and belly and breasts. Her skin felt hot and slippery. With the sweater down, her face seemed to bake. She lifted the sweater and sighed at the good feel of the breeze. *The car has air-conditioning. But what if Rodney's faking?*

He can't be faking the eye. If he isn't dead, he's messed up very badly. I'd have to be nuts to go for his keys.

She waited. She watched Rodney. She watched the road. More and more often she found herself staring at Rodney's car. Imagining herself sliding into the driver's seat, slipping the key into the ignition, and taking off. Leaving Rodney behind. Heading for a town just up the road (there must be one), while cool air poured onto her from the vents.

Only one way to make it happen, she told herself. *Go for the keys.*

He'll kill me!

Only if he can.

CHAPTER FOUR

Pamela went for his keys.

First she pulled the sweater on. The heat of it made her grimace. But she kept it on, and made her way down from her perch on the rocks.

She hobbled over the burning ground.

I'll take his shoes, too, she thought. *His shoes, his keys, his shirt.*

A nice, lightweight shirt with short sleeves. But she remembered that it had gotten all bloody because of his eye, so she decided against taking it.

Just his shoes and keys, she told herself. Finally his body came into view. Pamela made her way toward it, limping, wincing each time she set down a foot. When she was only a few yards away, she stopped. She stood motionless and gazed at Rodney.

Is he breathing? Not that she could see.

Maybe this is exactly what he's been waiting for, she thought. *He knew I'd come back for the keys if he stayed still long enough. And now I've done it. Walked straight into his trap.*

He lay facedown, his head turned to the right, both arms up and bent at the elbows. His right hand, on the ground a few inches from his forehead, still held the pistol. His grip on the pistol didn't look tight. As if he'd fallen asleep with the gun in his hand. *Maybe that's what he wants me to think?*

To shoot her, Rodney would need only to raise the pistol off the ground, move its barrel a couple of inches, and pull the trigger.

Slowly and silently, Pamela circled around him. Finally she was standing a distance beyond his feet. She stood motionless and watched him while she tried to catch her breath.

If he was going to shoot me, she thought, *he would've done it when I was in front of him. Wouldn't have let me get behind him like this.*

But I didn't go very close to him. Maybe he didn't know I'd shown up. Maybe he still doesn't know I'm here. But he'll know when I try for his stuff. Unless he's out cold or dead.

To get the car keys, she would need to reach into the right front pocket of his trousers. Squeeze her hand in between his thigh and the ground. He would feel it. And he would feel it when she tugged off his shoes.

Maybe he isn't feeling anything?

Pamela took a small step and crouched. Reaching down between her knees, she wrapped her fingers around a clump of rock. She tried to pick it up, but the rock was embedded in the dirt. So she shook it and jerked it, and soon worked it loose.

She lifted it.

The rock was about the size of a steam iron, and heavier. Raising it to shoulder height, she walked slowly toward Rodney. She stopped near his feet.

What do I do now? she wondered. *Drop it onto his back and see if he says, "Ouch"? Brilliant idea*, she thought. *He says, "Ouch," then turns over and shoots me.*

She could think of only one smart thing to do: bash his head in.

Don't try to do it by throwing the rock, either. Keep hold of it, dive onto his back, and bust his head open before he knows what's happening.

I can't do that, she thought. *Oh, yeah? Why not? The dirty bastard murdered Jim. Not just Jim, but all those girls. And don't forget what he did to me. He kidnapped me and shot at me. It's self-defense if there ever was a case of self-defense. On top of which, the dirtbag deserves to die!* She hurled herself at Rodney.

When her rump dropped onto his back, he let out a grunt. Not dead! *Not yet!*

Pamela hoisted the rock high, ready to slam it down against back of his head. He made a quiet whimper. She hesitated. *Do it!*

But he wasn't trying to fight, wasn't even trying to grip the pistol. He was just lying there making little whimpery sounds.

Then he murmured something.

She hissed, "What?"

"I give."

He gives? That's what a kid says wrestling with his brother!

"*You* give?" Pamela blurted. "You *give?* When you killed my husband!" *He wants to quit. Like this is a game that just got too rough.*

"Please," he murmured. "Don't . . . don't hurt me. My eye!" He started to sob.

Do it, she told herself. *Just do it. Get it over with.* But she couldn't force herself to strike.

Wait till he tries something. That way it won't be so much like a cold-blooded killing.

"If you move a muscle," she said, "I'll kill you, so help me God."

"Don't . . . Please. I'll do . . . anything."

"Let go of the gun. Take your hand away from it."

His fingers trembled and opened. His hand slid off the pistol.

Pamela wanted to pick it up, but her right hand was holding the rock. She switched the rock to her other hand, then leaned forward and reached out past Rodney's shoulder.

Her fingertips were about to settle on the pistol when he grabbed her wrist. She swung the rock at his head, but he was already bucking beneath her, already jerking her arm by the wrist.

She felt the rock connect with him. The blow made him cry out.

It didn't stop him.

Pamela hurtled headlong past his shoulder. She landed on her side, skidding. He let go of her wrist. She rolled onto her back, hoping to start a quick series of rolls that would put her out of reach.

But she was still on her back when his fist came down, hammering her belly. Her breath exploded out. She *had* to keep rolling and get away from him, but all she could do was hug her belly and bring her knees up and try to suck air into her lungs. Then her arms were pinned to her sides by Rodney's knees. He was sitting on her chest.

"Get off! I can't breathe!"

He hunched down so that his face loomed over Pamela's face.

"Look!" he gasped. "What you . . . did to me." He hunched lower.

His empty socket looked like a bloody gash. It dripped onto Pamela's cheek and nose. His upper lip twitched. He altered his position slightly, and the socket dripped toward her right eye. She shut her eyes fast. She felt warm patters on her right lid. Rodney made laughs that sounded like choking noises.

Then something went into her mouth. It knocked against her upper teeth, thrust against her tongue. She opened her left eye. He had thrust the pistol into her mouth.

"Blow your . . . fuckin' brains out," he muttered.

He shoved the barrel deeper. It pushed against her uvula, and she started gagging.

She didn't hear the gunshot. Not at first. What she heard first was a sound like a mallet smacking meat. Rodney's head jerked up, and she caught a glimpse deep into his forehead through a hole the size of a shirt button. *Then* she heard the gunshot. It sounded like distant thunder echoing through a canyon of clouds. An instant later, gore spouted out of the hole in Rodney's forehead. It arched past Pamela's face, then curved lower and splashed her straight between the eyes as he crumpled forward.

CHAPTER FIVE

Pamela didn't know why the ground was vibrating underneath her, or what the loud, windy, roaring sound might be.

She wondered where she was. She wondered what day it was.

Then she suddenly remembered that Jim was dead, and her whole life seemed to collapse into bleak rubble. She remembered about Rodney. She supposed she was in his car, maybe stretched out on the backseat, and he was probably driving her the rest of the way to . . .

No! She'd seen a deep hole in the middle of Rodney's forehead. *He's dead*, she realized.

She opened her eyes. She was stretched out on a seat, all right. But not the seat of Rodney's car.

Pamela was in a bus—on one of those long, cushioned benches where people sit just behind the driver, facing the aisle. The windows above the back of the seat were covered with yellow fabric that muffled the sunlight and gave the air a murky, golden hue. The air felt warm, but not terribly hot. She guessed that the bus's air conditioner must be going.

She turned her head. The long seat across the aisle was empty.

Lifting her head, she looked down at herself. She still wore the cheerleader sweater and skirt. Most of the sweater was caked with blood so thick that very little of its original gold color was visible. It was neatly arranged, however, and so was the skirt. Somebody must've taken care to straighten her clothes after placing her on the seat.

Apparently someone had also cleaned her face. It had a freshly washed feel. Exploring it with her hand, she found no trace of stickiness. Not on her face, and not in her hair. Her hair felt slightly damp. She checked her hand. There was no blood on it.

Someone had done a good job of washing her, at least from the neck up.

Looking past her feet, she saw a couple of passengers in the first row of forward-facing seats. A man and a woman. They sat rigid and stiff in safety belts that crossed their chests and laps. They both seemed to be gazing straight forward. They were dressed very well to be on a bus in the middle of the desert: the man in a jacket and tie, the woman in a flower-patterned dress.

This must be a charter bus, she thought. Maybe taking a church group on some sort of an excursion.

Got lost on their way to the Grand Canyon? Besides, religious groups don't usually go around putting bullets into people's heads.

Then just who shot Rodney?

Pamela doubted if she'd been saved by either of these two people. They sat there like a couple of statues.

Pamela nodded a greeting at them, but they didn't respond. She turned her head. Across the aisle from the couple sat a kid. Maybe their son. About eight or nine years old, he wore a ball cap, blue jeans, and a T-shirt. Pamela tried to read his T-shirt. Parts of a few words were hidden under the chest strap of his safety belt, but she pieced together a message that seemed rather odd: *I've been to Pits—it IS the Pits. Pits, CA, pop. 6.*

Though the boy seemed to be dressed like a normal kid, he sat rigid by the covered window, arms at his sides, face forward, and didn't move.

"Hi," Pamela said, hoping that her voice was loud enough to be heard over the noise of the bus.

The kid didn't even look at her.

Real friendly people, she thought. Probably a religious group, a bunch of holier-than-thou fanatics. Maybe they were practicing a vow of silence.

Yeah, but somebody shot Rodney. Somebody saved my life. She sat up. Turning toward the aisle, she lowered her legs. The bottoms of her feet felt stiff and sore, so she eased them down gently against the floor. The rubber mat on the floor felt cool and smooth, a little gritty. She waved at the kid.

He ignored her.

So she turned her head to the left. Just past the armrail of the seat where she'd been lying, a metal partition rose from the floor to about the height of her shoulders. She supposed it was there to shield the back of the driver's seat, though the top of the seat showed—and so did the driver's head.

He didn't wear a hat. His black hair was cut so short on the back and sides that his scalp showed through. The close trim made his ears seemed way too large. On top, his hair stuck straight up like the bristles of a brush. "Hello," Pamela said.

He didn't answer.

"Driver?" she asked, raising her voice.

"No talking, ma'am," he called without looking back. He didn't sound angry, just like a man stating a plain fact.

"What?" she asked. "What do you mean, no talking?"

"No talking to the driver while the bus is in motion. Company policy."

"Oh. Okay." She supposed it must be a safety rule. "Sorry," she added.

"No problem."

She wondered if the bus company also had a rule against standing up while the bus was in motion.

Soon find out.

Leaning forward, she reached out for the shiny tubing of a support pole. She clutched it and pulled herself off the seat. Pain soared up from the bottoms of her feet. She stood hunched over, clutching the pole, her mouth torn open in a silent outcry. The worst of the pain didn't last long. She straightened her body. As she took deep breaths, she noticed that the window shades across the aisle appeared to be strips of yellow blankets. They were secured to the windows with broad, silvery strips of duct tape. *Real classy,* she thought. *What sort of bus is this? Probably one of those rattrap death machines without any brakes you hear about when they crash in the mountains on the way to a revival weekend or Bible camp or something.*

And the pilgrims got to heaven a little sooner than they expected. Amen.

Maybe we are on our way to Bible camp. If we don't crash and die first.

Moving only her head, Pamela looked toward the front of the bus. The brightness from the windshield made her squint. Ahead of the bus was a two-lane road through the desert.

The same road she'd been traveling with Rodney? She couldn't tell. But it sure looked like the same desert.

She could see the driver's face in the rearview mirror, but sunglasses hid his eyes. She nodded a greeting, in case he was looking at her. He didn't react.

At least he's not ordering me to sit down.

With his sunglasses and flattop and the lean, rough features of his face, he looked like he ought to be a motorcycle cop.

A cop moonlighting as a church bus driver. That'd be a good one. Might explain what happened out there with Rodney.

"Hello?" Pamela said.

The face in the mirror turned slightly. As patiently as before, he explained, "I can't talk just now, ma'am. Not while the vehicle is in motion. It's for the safety of everyone aboard."

"Okay. Sorry."

The hell with it, she thought. Then she stepped to the center of the aisle, turned away from the brightness of the windshield, and peered toward the back of the bus. In the hazy yellow glow, she saw that many of the seats seemed to be occupied. She guessed that there must be fifteen or twenty passengers.

None talked. None moved, except for rocking and shaking a little with the motions of the bus.

What a lively crew, Pamela thought.

With so many passengers, however, there must be at least one who would open up and tell her what was going on.

Grimacing and flinching with every step, she hobbled down the aisle. The pair in the first seat didn't even turn their heads as she approached them.

What's the matter with these people? A few paces away from them, she saw what the matter was. She halted.

She moaned.

She grabbed the nearest support pole to hold herself steady, and heard herself mutter, "Isn't *this* wonderful? Isn't *this* just what the doctor or-dered? What the hell is *this*?"

The couple hadn't been ignoring her, hadn't been snubbing her, hadn't even known she existed.

"Dummies," she muttered.

The kid across the aisle was also a dummy. So were the two women sitting side by side in the next row of seats. They looked like a pair of mannequins heisted from a department store. Maybe they'd been model-ing casual wear at JC Penny. Both wore colorful outfits that looked cool and comfortable: knit pullover shirts, Bermuda shorts, knee-high socks, and white tennis shoes.

Nobody sat across the aisle from them, but behind them was a male mannequin dressed in a pin-striped suit and tie.

From where she stood, Pamela could see at least a dozen more passen-gers scattered here and there among the seats. Some sat alone, others in pairs. None moved.

They're all dummies. Every last one of them. She felt goose bumps scurry up her body. They started at her knees and crawled up her legs and but-tocks. They raced up her spine to the nape of her neck. Her arms and breasts went prickly. Her nipples squirmed and grew stiff. Her scalp crawled. Her legs began to shake.

Stop it! she told herself. *It's not that big a deal! Last night was a big deal. Rodney was a big deal. This is nothing. It's creepy.*

That's the thing, she thought. *It's no big deal, but it's too damn weird. Creepy, eerie, spooky. Like something out of an old* Twilight Zone—*but no big deal.*

No big deal, my ass I'm the only real person on a busload of dummies!

Maybe I'm dead, she wondered. *Nice thought.*

Maybe Rodney killed me, after all, and this is some sort of soul-bus taking me wherever it is that souls get taken to. Like the train in that song—the one that's "bound for glory." Only this isn't a train; it's a bus. The glory bus.

"Bull," she muttered.

I've gotta stop scaring myself, she thought, *and find out what's really go-ing on.*

She looked over her shoulder at the bus driver. *Won't say much, but at least he's real. My old buddy, Charon. Ferryman of the dead.*

"Cut it out," she muttered, and faced the rows of mannequins. "There's got to be a logical explanation," she whispered, and felt a smirk come to her face. "Right," she said. "Sure. That's what they always say, 'Gotta be a logical explanation.' Yeah, a logical explanation, all right— *el shitto has hit el fanno;* that's the logical explanation."

She decided to take a closer look at her fellow passengers, so she continued toward the back of the bus. As she hobbled along, she spoke softly to them. "Anybody here *not* a dummy? Speak up. Anybody want to offer me a logical explanation as to what you're doing here? Nothing about me being dead and on my way to hell, please. And I don't want to hear that the driver's a lunatic, either. Understood? Perhaps he's a traveling dummy salesman? How about it? Anyone? How about you?" she asked the final passenger.

This one wasn't sitting up like the others. He was stretched out on the long seat at the very back of the bus. Approaching him, Pamela could see only his legs. He wore dark trousers, and his feet were crossed at the ankles. The back of the seat in front of him blocked the rest of her view.

"Hello?" she asked. "Cat got your tongue?" *What if this is a real person? Fat chance,* she told herself. Then she stepped past the last seat back and looked down through the murky yellow light and saw that she'd made a good guess: the figure lying on his back, feet crossed, was a real person. She figured out who he was when she saw his bloody shirt. Then she recognized the neat round hole in his forehead, and the pit where his eye should've been.

He looked as if he'd been laid out to dry, a while ago, after being dipped headfirst into a vat of blood. Pamela gagged. She turned away from the body. She began staggering down the aisle, hurrying past row after row of mannequins.

He brought Rodney! Why did he bring Rodney? What's going—

A sudden braking of the bus shoved Pamela forward. About to fall, she stretched out her arms and grabbed seat-back handles on both sides of the aisle. From behind her came a thudding sound. She looked back. Rodney had been thrown to the floor.

The bus continued to lose speed for a while, then made a right turn that thrust Pamela sideways. She kept her grips on the seat handles and stayed on her feet through the turn.

Now the bus was on an unpaved road. Pamela saw the strip of rough dirt through the windshield. And she felt it. The floor shuddered under her sore feet. The whole bus bounced and lurched and vibrated. It shook so hard that she thought it must be falling apart. She pictured it leaving a trail of pieces to mark its passage: a tailpipe, a hubcap, a muffler, a drive shaft.

From what she could see through the windshield, the terrible road seemed to be leading toward nothing except more mesquite and cacti and brush, ravines and jagged, dry piles of rock and a mountainous area that looked just as desolate as the desert. *Not taking me to a town*, she thought.

Maybe he's got a house out here, same as Rodney. A fun house where he's gonna have the same kind of fun with me Rodney planned. She twisted her head around. Rodney was still on the floor. His body seemed to be trapped, facedown, between his seat and the legs of the seat in front of him.

Going nowhere.

The feel of the floor pounding against her feet made Pamela want to cry.

Gotta sit down.

She belonged on the long seat near the front of the bus. That was where someone—most likely the driver—had put her, so that was where she ought to be. Besides, it was a good distance from Rodney's body. When she let go of the seat handles, however, the lurching bus tossed her forward. She landed on her hands and knees in the middle of the aisle.

She supposed she could *crawl* to the front. *The hell with that*, she thought.

She climbed onto the nearest empty seat. This entire row was clear of mannequins. Across the aisle, a couple of bundles were piled on the seat. One of them appeared to be a sleeping bag, while the other was a large fabric satchel with handles. *The driver's stuff*, she supposed. *He must sleep on the bus. Maybe it's his home, and he lives on it with his dummy collection.*

Now, he's collected me.

He saved my life, she reminded herself. *Someone did, anyway. And the driver seems to be the only person around who might've done it.*

She guessed it was possible that her rescuer had shot Rodney and vanished, that the bus had come along later and there was no direct connection between the two events.

That didn't seem terribly likely, though.

The driver almost *had* to be the one who'd saved her. Leaning on the armrail, she peered up the aisle. All she could see of the driver was the back of his head.

What if he's not a good guy? she wondered. *He's prowling around the desert with a bus full of dummies and probably some sort of high-powered rifle.* Pamela hadn't seen the rifle, but he must've fired it from awfully far away; the bullet had struck Rodney a long time before she'd heard the crash of the gunshot. *The guy has to be weird,* she thought. *But he saved me. Maybe he can have me. Let's face it, what's he doing on a dirt road like this? He should be driving me to the nearest town, not deeper into the desert.*

"This doesn't look real good," she muttered.

CHAPTER SIX

They were in a canyon when the bus finally stopped. The driver reached out to his right and shoved a handle, opening the front door. Then he shut off the engine.

To Pamela, the sudden quiet seemed enormous.

The driver stood up and turned around. Pamela stared at him.

She felt scared, but weary. They'd spent at least half an hour on the rough dirt road. She'd worn herself out with wondering about the driver, imagining all the things that he might want to do with her, and trying to figure out the best course of action for herself.

Her most recent conclusions: he might or might not intend to rape or murder her; she shouldn't try to attack him or escape until she knew more; by then, it might be too late; she could sit tight and see what happened; he might be a friend; if he turned out to be a bad guy, she would fight him to the end.

He started walking up the aisle. *Oh, God, here he comes.*

He wasn't a large man, like Rodney. Medium height, and slim. He wore a gray short-sleeved shirt. It was tucked into blue pants that were cinched around his waist with a black leather belt.

A bus driver's uniform?

Why isn't it all rumpled and sweaty and bloody? Pamela wondered. *It would have to be, if this is the guy who hauled Rodney into the bus. Not to mention hauling me in. But his uniform looks neat and clean, as if he's done nothing more than sit behind the steering . . .*

Almost here. Get ready.

He walked past Pamela as if he didn't notice her. She couldn't believe it. She twisted in her seat to watch him. At the back of the bus, he crouched and took hold of Rodney's ankles.

Go!

She lurched out of her seat and raced down the aisle. The nearest exit was the side door, just ahead and down a stairwell to the right. But it was shut and might give her trouble, so she ran past it. Dashed for the open front door. Each footfall made her wince with pain. She gritted her teeth and tried to run faster.

"Don't fall and hurt yourself," called the driver.

When she reached the front, she glanced back. He wasn't even watching her. He was still at the rear of the bus, bent over, dragging Rodney's body into the aisle.

Doesn't he care that I'm getting away? Maybe not. Maybe he doesn't care because he knows I can't really escape. Nowhere to go.

We'll see about that, she told herself, and charged down the steps and leaped off the bus. The desert heat slammed down on her.

Here we go again, she told herself. She started running toward the nearest high ground, a rocky butte not too far away. If she could get up there, she might be able to pull a disappearing act among the boulders and crevices. At the foot of it, she looked back.

No sign of the driver.

She couldn't see inside the bus because of the makeshift yellow curtains on the windows, but the side door was still shut, and he wasn't at the front door yet. She didn't know whether the bus had an emergency exit at the very back. She hadn't noticed one back there, but she'd been awfully distracted at the time because of Rodney's body.

School buses usually had an emergency exit at the rear, and this looked like an old, medium-sized school bus. It wasn't painted like one, though. Only the curtains were yellow. The rest of the bus—what Pamela could see of it—was painted a dull gray color that reminded her of how a lake looked on a gloomy, overcast day.

It had a word painted in black above the windows, where the name of the school district had probably once been.

PEQUOD

Terrific, Pamela thought. *I've been captured by Captain Ahab.*

She turned away from the bus and hurled herself at the rocky slope. She scrambled upward, climbing higher and higher, huffing and sweating, her throat clenched because of the pain soaring up from her feet.

"Be careful you don't hurt yourself," the driver called. "I didn't shoot this feller just to have you fall and crack your head open."

Stopping at the top of a boulder, Pamela put a hand against a steep wall of rock and turned sideways. She was surprised to find herself so high above the floor of the canyon.

The driver was just outside the front door of the bus, bent over and walking backward, dragging Rodney's body by the wrists. The head, faceup, wobbled from side to side between the straight arms. The body skidded along on its back. The feet shook and bounced.

"What're you doing?" Pamela called.

Not bothering to look up, the driver answered, "Gotta dump him." Beyond the front of the bus, he started dragging the body uphill. "It'd be a sight easier if you gave me a hand," he announced. "Not that I'm complaining. I killed him, after all—my duty to deal with his mortal remains. But a helping hand'd be appreciated."

"Where are you taking him?"

"Up yonder." He dropped Rodney's arms, then tilted back his head. Pamela supposed he was looking at her, but she couldn't see his eyes because of the sunglasses. Raising an arm, he pointed in the direction he'd been dragging the body. "Yonder there," he said. "I'll just give him the old heave-ho down the glory hole."

"What were you going to do with me?" Pamela asked.

"Take care of you, I reckon. Take you on down the road, soon as I'm done with my business here."

"How do I know you won't . . . do something to me?"

"What do you mean, *hurt* you?"

"Yeah."

"Why would I want to go and do that?"

"Some men do."

"You mean like him?"

"Yeah."

"Look what I done to him."

"Why'd you do it?"

"You want to gab, come on down so I ain't gotta yell." With that, he picked up Rodney's arms and resumed dragging the body. Pamela watched him labor with it. She shook her head. Rodney was a lot bigger than him. It had to be a tough job, struggling uphill with a heavy body like that on a hot day like this.

He shot him for me. I'd be dead right now.

"Hold on," she called. "I'll come down and help."

"Much obliged." He dropped Rodney's arms, and sat himself on a nearby rock.

I must be out of my mind, Pamela thought as she began to make her way down from the rocks. *He's out of his, for sure. But he did save my life. And he seems pretty much okay except for the fact that he drives around the desert with a bus full of dummies. Maybe there's a good reason for that,* she told herself. *Right. A logical explanation. Even if he is nuts,* she thought, *maybe I can stay on his good side and he'll treat me okay.*

Near the bottom, she leaped the rest of the way to the ground. The hard earth smacked her wounded feet. She cried, "Ahhh!" and hobbled over to the bus. She leaned against its side, propped a foot across her knee, and inspected the damage. It was filthy, scratched, and bloody. She supposed her other foot was just as bad, or worse.

"Go on in the bus," the driver called, "and grab yourself some shoes." He was still sitting on the rock.

"Really?" Pamela called.

"Just take 'em off a passenger. I'll wait."

"Thank you!" She hobbled to the open front door and limped aboard, then stopped. The key was in the ignition. She stared at it.

I'll never get another chance like this. She glanced out the windshield. The driver, sitting on the rock near Rodney's body, wasn't even watching. His head was turned away and tipped back as if he might be admiring the scenery.

Did he leave the key here on purpose? she wondered. *Maybe it's a trick or a test or something. To see if I try to make a getaway. Maybe he's just careless, forgot to take the key with him. Or maybe it's his way of telling me that I'm not his prisoner.*

Who knows?

The hell with it, she thought. *I told him I'd help with the body, so that's what I'll do.*

She limped down the aisle to the seat behind the boy dummy. Both the young female mannequins wore knee socks and white sneakers.

The driver hadn't said anything about taking socks. Would he mind?

Pamela pulled the shoes and socks off the nearest figure. Sitting on the aisle floor, she put them on. The socks felt almost as good as bandages. When she stood up her feet still hurt, but they felt protected. The socks' arid soles made a springy cushion for them.

Would the driver get angry if she borrowed more? The rest of the mannequin's outfit, for instance?

The plaid shorts and lime-green polo shirt looked cool and fresh. And clean.

She felt miserable in the clothes she had on. They made her sweat. They made her itch. The sweater and skirt were not only heavy and hot, but filthy. And covered with Rodney's blood.

Besides, they'd been a gift from him.

An imitation of her high school cheerleader costume, put together by Rodney so he could get himself all turned on.

He had dressed her in it. Maybe he had dressed his other victims in it, too. Some might've been wearing it while he did horrible things to them. Perhaps some had even worn it after they'd been killed—the inside of the sweater and skirt touching their dead skin.

Pamela wished she hadn't thought of that. *Now I have to get out of this stuff.*

She spotted the driver outside, still sitting. He seemed to be paying no attention to her or the bus. She crouched slightly, and couldn't see him anymore. Staying low, she unfastened the Bermuda shorts and drew them down the mannequin's legs. Then she unbuckled the safety belts, pulled the figure into the aisle, and stripped off its knit shirt. Standing, she glanced at the driver. He still sat on the rock. So she tugged her skirt down. Squatting, she pulled the sweater off.

Pamela looked at herself. A lot of bruises and scratches and weals, but they didn't concern her. What concerned her was the blood. She supposed that nearly all of it was Rodney's blood. It must've soaked through the sweater. She didn't want it getting on her clean clothes. Quickly she turned the cheerleader skirt inside out. She used the skirt with both hands to towel off her skin. The blood was damp, maybe kept moist by her sweat, so she was able to wipe off most of it. Then she tossed the skirt aside and slipped into the bright-green polo shirt. Holding the mannequin's shorts, she stood.

The driver was sitting on the rock, head down.

Pamela stepped into the shorts, pulled them up, and fastened them. A bit loose, but not enough to matter. She tossed the old sweater and skirt onto an empty seat, then walked toward the front of the bus. Though her feet still hurt, this was the best they'd felt in a long time. The best *she'd* felt. The clothes were light. They seemed to float against her, not wrap her in heat and load her down. She wished there'd been undergarments to wear. This was like being half-undressed. The shorts were certainly better than the skirt had been, but the clinging knit shirt made it very obvious that she wasn't wearing a bra.

She supposed she could find something to wear over the shirt. *Too hot around here, already. The hell with it.* She climbed down the stairs and stepped to the ground.

The driver raised his head. "Look at you," he said.

Pamela grimaced at him. "I grabbed a bit more than just shoes," she said. "I hope that's okay. I mean, my stuff was horrible, and—"

"You take whatever you want, girl. You're welcome to it."

"That's really nice of you. Thanks."

This guy isn't going to attack me, she thought. *He's nice. Except maybe he's just in a calm period right now between his fits of homicidal frenzy.*

No, no, no, she told herself. *He's okay; he's fine.*

As she approached him, she held out her hand. "I'm Pamela," she said.

He stood up. He took her hand and gave it a small squeeze. His grip felt solid, but restrained. "Pleased to meet you," he said. "My name's Sharpe. Walter Sharpe." He released her hand. "You call me Sharpe."

"I go by Pamela, mostly."

"Howdy, Pamela."

"Howdy, Sharpe."

"That outfit there, it sure looks better on you than it did on Fran."

"Fran?"

"The gal you took it offa. Fran Lowry."

Oh, wonderful—he's got names for them.

"Well, time's a-wasting," he said. "What's say we dump this ol' boy? Pick an arm."

Pamela chose the left arm. She lifted it by the wrist. Sharpe, at her side, picked up Rodney's right arm. They began walking backward, dragging him.

"I want to thank you for, you know, saving me. He was about to kill me."

"Figured he weren't up to much good."

"He murdered my husband last night."

For a few moments Sharpe didn't say anything. Then he shook his head. "That's a real shame. I'm sorry to hear it. My God, he made a widow outta you. Makes me double glad I put that bullet through his skull."

"We'd only been married for six months."

"A real shame," Sharpe said.

"He showed me Jim's body." Pamela was a little surprised to hear herself telling Sharpe about such things. Dragging Rodney and telling her secrets. "It was . . . in the bathroom. He showed it to me on the way out . . . when we were leaving. Jim was on the floor, but . . ."

The memory suddenly made her retch and double over. As she heaved, she saw through teary eyes her vomit cascading down onto Rodney's face.

"That's all right," Sharpe murmured, gently patting her back. "Get it all out. You'll feel a whole lot better, you just dump it all out on him."

When she was done vomiting, she remained bent over with her hands on her knees. Her vision was blurry with tears. Her chest hurt. Her throat and nasal passages felt scorched.

"Here," Sharpe said, "I got a hanky for you."

"I'll . . . mess it up."

"You need it more than me."

He held a red bandanna under her face, so she took it. She wiped her face and blew her nose, then straightened up and stepped a couple of paces backward. Rodney's face was carpeted with colorful, chunky glop.

Last night's pizza.

Jim had phoned Pizza Guy to order it for home delivery. Pepperoni and sausage, thin crust, with extra cheese. They'd eaten it in the living room on TV trays, drinking beer and watching a tape of the previous night's *Letterman* show. Jim's last meal. His last *Letterman* show. His last everything.

Pamela started to weep, but then she saw how Rodney's open mouth was full to the brim.

She suddenly lost interest in crying.

She turned away and gagged. It hurt her in the chest and across her back. She wondered if she'd somehow damaged herself with all the vomiting. She concentrated, trying not to gag again.

Just don't think about the puke in his mouth. She gagged all over again.

"You okay?" Sharpe asked.

"No," she gasped.

"Don't look at him. Tell you what. You just stay here and take it easy. I'll see to this feller."

Without looking around, she nodded.

"Good thing he's already dead," Sharpe announced. "If he weren't, he'd likely be wishin' he was."

Pamela laughed. She couldn't help it. Just a small laugh. It hurt, but not as much as the gagging.

She heard Rodney being dragged away. Then she felt guilty about making Sharpe do all the work, so she hurried after him.

Keeping her eyes on him, she said, "I'll take a hand."

"You don't have to."

"I just won't look at him."

So Sharpe turned an arm over to her. She clutched its wrist with both hands. Side by side, she and Sharpe trudged backward, dragging the body. She stared off to the left to avoid looking at Rodney.

"Where did you say we're taking him?" she asked.

"Up to the glory hole."

"The glory hole?"

"Used to be a lot of mines 'round these parts. Some of the pits, they just got left behind, open and all, when the ore played out. I found this here glory hole a few years back. I doubt much of anyone knows it's here, 'cept me and maybe a couple of old prospectors."

"Do you live somewhere nearby?"

"Yup. In nearby bus."

Don't ask! But she couldn't seem to help herself. "With the others?"

"That's about the size of it."

Don't, don't, don't! "With . . . Fran and . . . uh . . ." she said. She turned her head the other way, forcing herself not to focus on Rodney, and looked at Sharpe's face. "Who are they?"

"Well, they ain't so much *whos* as they're *whats.*"

"Oh. Okay. *What* are they?"

He turned his head and smiled at her. "You telling me you don't know?"

"Well . . ."

"They're *store* dummies," Sharpe said, and looked over his shoulder.

"Well, I know *that.* But . . ."

"Better hold up, we're here." He let go of Rodney's arm.

Keeping her gaze away from the body, Pamela crouched and set the other arm on the ground. Then she stood and turned around.

"That's it there," Sharpe said, nodding.

The hole just a little farther up the slope from them looked like the mouth of a cave.

A vertical cave. Pamela walked slowly toward it. Sharpe stayed by her side.

"You don't want to get too close," he warned.

A few strides more, and Pamela suddenly found that she *couldn't* walk any closer to the hole. Her legs, going shaky and weak, seemed to know they were near enough. They stopped her. She had an urge to back away, but she fought it. Bending her knees slightly, she stood her ground.

Sharpe stopped beside her.

"It's a hole, all right," she said.

"Goes straight down," Sharpe told her.

"Very far?"

"Far enough."

"It seems like . . . a horrible place to leave someone."

"No more than what I reckon he deserves. 'Sides, he's dead. He won't know no better. You just stand pat, and I'll take care of him."

Sharpe went to get Rodney.

From where Pamela stood, she could see only partway down the mouth of the hole. The far wall of it was bright with sunlight. She supposed that the sunlight must peter out, farther down—get dimmer and dimmer until there was none at all—blackness. Sharpe stepped past her. He was bent over and trudging backward, dragging Rodney by the wrists.

"Be careful," Pamela said.

"Yup."

He kept walking backward, closer and closer to the edge of the glory hole.

"Sharpe!"

His head lifted, but he didn't stop.

"Watch where you're going!"

"Oh, don't worry about this ol' boy."

He was only about two paces from the pit, and still backing up.

"Damn it, Sharpe! You're gonna fall in!"

At the very rim of the pit, he halted and let go of Rodney's wrists. He stood up straight. He grinned at Pamela. "No need to fret. I ain't exactly a novice at this."

"Would you *please* get away from the edge!"

"Sure." He stepped over Rodney's body.

Pamela took a deep, trembling breath.

Standing over Rodney's feet, Sharpe turned his head toward her. "I already emptied his pockets for him, back on the bus. Anything you want before I give him the ol' heave-ho?"

"I don't think so."

"Well, then." He lowered himself to his knees, clutched Rodney around the ankles, and pushed. The body started scooting headfirst toward the pit.

Pamela looked at Rodney's face. Much of the mess must've slid off, but he still had gobs of vomit clinging to his face. It still filled his open mouth. It covered his one eye, and was packed in the socket where his other eye used to be. She imagined cold pizza hurl trickling down his throat. Thick, cheesy lumps of it.

Pamela swallowed hard and looked away.

He deserves it, she told herself. *He deserves everything.* When she looked again, his head was over the hole, tipped way back. His shoulders were at the edge.

Sharpe kept shoving.

Rodney's arms flopped into the hole. Soon his back was bent so much that he looked as if his spine might snap. Sharpe let go of the ankles.

Rodney's feet kicked toward the sky. Heels up, he plunged straight down and vanished.

"Jesus," Pamela muttered. A moment later there came a thudding sound.

Sharpe stood up. "What was the feller's name?" he asked. "I like to know their names."

"Rodney Pinkham."

"Mind if I say a few words over him?"

"Whatever you want."

"Much obliged." Cupping both hands to the sides of his mouth, Sharpe lowered his head and called, "Good riddance, Rodney Pinkham. Rot in peace."

CHAPTER SEVEN

Norman nearly always locked his car before leaving it. This time he decided not to bother.

Norman climbed out, shut the door without locking it, and stepped to the gasoline pump marked REGULAR UNLEADED. After filling his tank, he walked no more than fifty feet to the gas station office. No waiting. Stepped right up to the counter, gave his pump number, handed over a twenty-dollar bill, accepted his change, and headed for the door.

In and out, just like that.

Away from the car for two minutes, maybe less.

But on his way to leave the office, Norman thought about the container of Wolfbane teriyaki beef jerky he'd noticed on the counter while paying for the gas.

The label on the tall, plastic jar had caught his eye: *Wolfbane—you'll howl for more.*

He loved teriyaki jerky.

He'd never heard of Wolfbane.

All the best jerky was the kind you'd never heard of, the kind you found in out-of-the-way places like gas stations in small towns you were passing through on your way home from college.

Only a stride from the door, Norman halted. *Screw my diet*, he thought. *One or two jerkies in the great scheme of things aren't going to make any big difference.* So he returned to the counter.

Ahead of him was a woman buying a pack of cigarettes. It didn't take her very long. When she left, Norman stepped up to the counter. "Guess I'll have some of this jerky," he said.

"Help yourself," the clerk told him.

Norman opened the clear plastic jar and took six strips of Wolfbane teriyaki beef jerky. The clerk held out a paper sack, and he slid them in. Then he screwed the lid back onto the container.

He paid.

More than twelve dollars, but when did good jerky ever come cheap? Finally he walked out the door.

When he looked at his car, he thought he'd made a mistake. This couldn't be *his* red Jeep Cherokee. It was a popular model and color. Another must've pulled in.

One with a man in the passenger seat. Norman looked for his.

There wasn't another Cherokee on the gas station's lot. There wasn't *any* other car. Besides, this one was stopped at the pump where he'd filled up. And it had his license plate number.

He suddenly felt cold and crawly in his bowels. *It's mine, all right.*

He should've locked up. He *always* locked up. But this was a nice little town on the Oregon coast, where you'd have to be paranoid to lock your car when you were just leaving it for two minutes to pay for your gas.

Would've only been two minutes, he reminded himself, *except you had to have the jerky. Just had to have it.*

One or two jerkies in the great scheme of things won't make any big difference. Right.

Just if some jerk climbs in your car while you're buying the damn things.

Now what? he wondered.

He took a deep breath, let it out slowly, and walked toward his car. The guy in the passenger seat smiled and waved at him. Norman decided not to approach the passenger door. He went to the driver's door instead. Breathing hard, shaking, angry, and scared, he swung the door open. He ducked slightly and peered in at the stranger.

At least he hasn't got a gun, Norman thought. *Thank God for that, anyway.*

The man didn't have any visible weapon at all.

He turned toward Norman, gave him a smirk and a nod, then lifted an elbow and rested it on the back of the seat.

Though he couldn't have been much older than twenty-one, he looked as if he'd stepped out of the 1950s. Like he thought he was the Wild One or James Dean or Charlie Starkweather or Elvis or something. His blond, greasy hair was swept high. His blue eyes had a movie-tough guy nonchalance. His sideburns stretched down to his earlobes. He wore a white T-shirt that hugged his muscles, and faded blue jeans. Below the cuffs of the jeans, Norman could see a pair of black motorcycle boots, complete with side buckles.

"Hello," Norman said, trying to sound calm.

The guy winked at him. "Hello, good buddy."

"Uh . . . you're in my car."

"And a very fine vehicle it is. My name's Duke." With that, he swung his right shoulder forward and extended his hand past the steering wheel.

Norman kept his own hands at his sides. "I think . . . maybe you'd better get out."

"Figured you'd give me a lift."

"Well . . . I don't think so."

"Why not?"

"Because."

"Because why?"

"Please," Norman said, "just get out. I'm not going anywhere till you get out, okay? I'm sure you can find somebody else to ride with."

Duke seemed somewhat amused. "But I want to ride with you, big fella."

"Come on. Get out. Please."

"What am I hurting? Just let me ride. . . ."

"Look, you don't want to make me do something, do you? Do you want to make me go back in the office and have them call someone?"

"Like the cops?"

"I guess so. I don't want to get you in any trouble, but you're in my car. What am I *supposed* to do? I can't go driving off down the road with a complete *stranger* in my car."

"Told you, I'm Duke."

"But I don't *know* you. For all I know, you might be some sort of a . . . a criminal or something."

Duke smirked. "Do I look like a criminal to you?"

Damn right you do, he thought. But he didn't dare say it. "I don't know. Are you on your way to audition for *Grease* or something?"

Duke let out a quick laugh. "Hey! That's a good one! *Grease*. I seen that movie. The Olivia! The Newton! The John! What a babe! Is she a babe or what?"

"Yeah," Norman muttered. "She's a babe."

"But you're not saying I look like *her*. You're saying I look like the guy. Travolta."

"I'm not saying that. I'm just saying I wish you'd . . . It's not even my car. It's my father's car, and he's really strict about not giving rides to strangers."

"You do everything your daddy tells you?"

"Look—"

"How old are you, anyhow? Wait, let me guess. Sixteen?"

"Very funny. Get out, okay?"

"You're a college boy, right? Going home for spring break."

"So what?"

"Ah, I'm right. I'm always right. How come you aren't on your way to Palm Springs for the big spring bash?"

"I don't go in for that kind of stuff."

"Surprise, surprise. Bet you live off your old man. He pays for everything, right? You drive his car. You do whatever he says. Him or mama. You never worked a day in your life, and you've never gotten in a single little bit of trouble."

Screw you, Norman thought.

"Haven't gotten into much fun, either, I bet."

Norman glanced toward the office, but a gas pump blocked his view. *Great. They can't even see what's going on. Won't even see if I get a flick knife in my guts . . . if he's got a flick knife, that is. But with his looks, he's bound to have one. Maybe slipped down the side of one of those motorcycle boots.* He thought for a moment; then an idea cheered him. *Another car's bound to come along pretty soon*, he told himself. *Then Duke might just sidle away.*

"Got a girlfriend?" Duke asked.

"None of your business."

"Didn't think so."

"Get out of my car, okay? Please?"

"You could learn a lot from a guy like me. Course, you already know that, don't you? That's how come you're so scared."

"I'm not scared."

"You're scared of everything."

"I am not."

"That's your main problem."

"You don't even know me."

"Don't kid yourself. What's your name?"

"That's my business."

"See that? You're scared to even tell me your name. What do you think, I'll look you up sometime? Drop in on you?"

"I don't have to tell you anything."

"It's probably some sort of sissy name. What is it, Melvin?"

"No!"

"Elroy?"

"None of your business."

"Susie?"

"It's *Max*!"

Duke smiled. "Max. As in Maxwell. Knew it."

"As in Mad Max," Norman said. He wished he hadn't just blurted out the first name he thought of that didn't sound geeky.

"Okay, Max. Here's the deal. I've got your registration in my pocket."

Norman opened his mouth. He didn't know what to say.

After a moment he said, "No, you don't."

"Oh, yes, I do." Duke patted a front pocket of his jeans. "Is your old man named Kenneth?"

Norman moaned. He heard himself murmur, "God."

"No, your dad ain't God. Sorry to disappoint you on that score, Maxwell."

"Give it back," Norman said.

"If I give it back, how will I be able to look you up and drop in on you?"

"Hey. Please." Tears suddenly came. They made his eyes feel hot and blurred his vision.

"Aw, don' cwy."

"You'd better give it to me!"

"What'oh baby dooo?"

"I'm gonna get the cops on you! I swear! If you don't hand it over by the time I count to three, I'm gonna call the cops."

Duke smiled, nodded.

Norman wiped his eyes, but more tears came. He could feel his chin jumping up and down.

Don't start bawling!

"One," he said.

"Two," said Duke.

"Two and a half," Norman said.

"Two and three-quarters."

"You'd better give it! I'm warning you!"

"We're just a wee bit nervous about saying 'three,' aren't we?"

"Am not!"

"Cool your jets, pal. You can have it back. All I want's a ride, know what I mean? I don't want you throwing fits."

"I'm not throwing fits!" He sniffled, then wiped his eyes again.

Duke jammed his right hand down inside the pocket of his jeans. He plucked out the registration slip. "This what you want?"

Norman nodded. Duke reached past the steering wheel, the paper pinched between his thumb and forefinger.

He won't really let me have it, Norman thought. *When I go for it, he'll jerk it away.*

Norman went for it fast. Grabbed it and tugged. It came free.

Yes!

Quickly, he tucked it into a rear pocket of his shorts.

"What do you say?" Duke asked.

"Thanks," he muttered. He took a deep breath, and his lungs seemed to tremble as he inhaled.

"I'm not such a bad guy," Duke told him. "How about that ride?"

Norman shook his head. "Just get out now, okay? I'm not asking again. If you don't get out right now, I'm gonna—"

"Wait."

"No more waiting. Cut!"

"Thirty-two nineteen Avenida del Sol, Tiburon."

Norman shriveled inside.

"I got it right?" Duke asked.

Norman stared at him.

"What about the cops, Maxwell? You suppose they've got some sorta technique that'll wipe that address out of my mind? 'Cause if they don't, I might just end up dropping in. Know what I mean?"

Norman just kept staring at him. He didn't know what to do.

"Get in the car, Maxwell. Let's blow this one-horse town." Duke grinned. "It'll be fine. I'm not gonna hurt you. Give me a ride where I want to go, I'll climb out, and that'll be the end of it. No midnight visits to thirty-two nineteen Avenida del Sol, Tiburon."

"Promise?" he asked. He had a feeling that someone else was asking the question, but he knew it came from him.

"In." Duke patted the driver's seat. Norman obeyed. He pulled the door shut, set the sack of jerky on his lap, fastened his seat belt, and slid the key into the ignition. He twisted it, and the engine kicked into life.

"Where do you want to go?" he asked, his voice distant and hardly familiar.

"The coast highway's fine by me. You were heading south, weren't you?"

"Yeah."

"South's fine by me."

Norman drove away from the gas station. Soon he left the town behind. Duke found a country music station on the radio and turned the volume high. That was good, because Norman didn't want to talk to him. He wanted to get rid of him, but he felt trapped. He wished he had never stopped at that gas station. That wasn't the mistake, he realized. You can't exactly avoid stopping for gasoline. The mistake was leaving the car unlocked so the bastard could climb in and make himself at home and get his paws on the registration. That was mistake number one. Mistake number two was buying the jerky. He thought about how nice it would be to go backward in time and try again.

Do it the right way. But he had done it the wrong way and ruined everything. *At least I've got the jerky*, he thought. Steering with his left hand, he reached down with his right and opened the sack. He pulled out a long, dark strip. Duke looked at him.

"Want one?" Norman asked.

Duke reached out and took it from his hand. "You're a bud."

Norman drew another strip out of the sack. He clamped it between his teeth and ripped the end off it. The slab in his mouth felt very firm. But not hard and dry, like some jerky. As he chewed, the meat softened. His teeth squeezed out rich, sweet juices. He moaned with pleasure.

"This ain't bad," Duke said.

Norman moaned again. This was, by far, the best teriyaki jerky that he'd ever tasted.

"What's this stuff called?" Duke asked.

"Wolfbane teriyaki beef jerky."

"Wolfbane?"

"'You'll howl for more.'"

Duke tossed back his head and howled.

Norman smiled.

Maybe this guy isn't so bad, he thought. *Hell, can't be all bad if he goes and howls like that over my jerky. He probably is a cool guy if you get to know him.*

Are you nuts? Norman asked himself. *This guy as good as kidnapped you! Yeah, but he hasn't done anything. So far, so good. And the jerky is incredible.*

"You can have some more when you're done," Norman told him.

"Don't mind if I do. You're okay, Max. You know that? You're an okay guy."

"Thanks."

"I think we're gonna get along real good." Duke reached out and gave his thigh a couple of solid, friendly slaps.

"It's Norman, actually."

"What's Norman?"

"My name. It isn't Maxwell; it's Norman. I sort of lied about it before."

"Why'd you want to do that, Norman?"

"I guess I was afraid you'd make fun of it."

"Norman ain't a bad name."

"Thanks."

CHAPTER EIGHT

Norman drove past the girl who was walking backward along the side of the road, her thumb out.

"You gotta be kidding me," Duke said.

"What?"

"Passing up a babe like that? You some kind of a fag?"

"No!"

"Pull over!"

"I don't pick up hitchhikers."

"This one, you do. What are you, nuts? Didn't you look at her?"

"Yeah, but—"

"Don't be a loser all your life."

"It's stupid and dangerous to pick up hitchhikers," he blurted.

"Don't worry; I won't let her hurt you."

"Very funny."

"Pull over."

The southbound side of the road had no breakdown lane, and its shoulder was narrow. It was bordered by a low steel guardrail to keep cars from flying off the coastline cliffs.

"There isn't anyplace to pull over," Norman said. He glanced at the rearview mirror. "And I can't just stop. There's a truck behind us."

"U it."

"I can't just U it."

"Why not? Nothing coming. Do it."

"Are you nuts?"

"Show some *hair*, Norman!"

Norman wasn't sure what that meant, but he liked the sound of it. He checked the traffic. Then he hit the brakes. As his speed fell, the truck bore down on his rear. Its horn blasted. He whipped the steering wheel and cut hard to the left. The Jeep swung toward the middle line. Crossed it. Skidded. Found traction again in the northbound lanes and kept turning. Though the right-side tires went off on the gravel, he knew he had control. He'd made it!

"Thataway to go," Duke said.

"Thanks." He started to steer back onto the pavement.

"This is good enough. Just stop here and we'll wait for her."

That sounded fine to Norman. He pulled the rest of the way off the road and shut off the engine. He felt happy with himself for doing the U-turn so well.

"There she is," Duke said.

Norman spotted her. She was quite a distance away.

"Nobody better pick her up before she gets here," Duke said.

She swaggered along the road as if she owned it. A big denim bag, suspended from her shoulder by a strap, swung beside her hip.

Cars, trucks, and a couple of big recreational vehicles drove past her, and all of them had to swing wide. Norman wondered if he, like the other drivers, had veered to go around her. He couldn't remember doing it. His mind must've been on something else.

"That babe's got balls," Duke said.

"I doubt it," Norman said.

Duke laughed. "Hope you're right, Normy! What a waste that'd be, huh? 'Cause it sure looks like the rest of her's top-drawer."

"Yeah," Norman said.

"You don't think so?" Duke asked.

"She looks fine."

"What a babe. Give the horn a toot."

Norman beeped the horn. The girl didn't break stride, but her head turned. Duke waved. She made a quick nod, then stopped and faced the highway and watched for a break in the traffic.

Norman didn't like the looks of her. Even from this distance he could see her eye makeup and flashy lipstick. Though she appeared to be no older than eighteen, her hair was white. A bleach job, Norman figured. And he didn't like the way it was cut so short. The pixie style was meant for slim, delicate girls. Not someone like this.

She had a wide face with blunt features. Her shoulders and hips were very broad. Her arms and legs were thick—not quite fat, but so heavy and solid that it seemed crude of her to show them off by wearing such skimpy clothes.

Her tank top exposed her arms entirely, and left her shoulders bare except for narrow straps. It was so tight that it hugged every curve and bulge. It didn't reach down far enough to meet the waistband of her jeans, so Norman could see her skin there—and her belly button.

She wore the blue jeans low on her hips. They were faded almost white. The legs were cut off at the crotch, and the side that wasn't blocked from sight by the denim bag had a slit going halfway up. Norman supposed she must have a matching slit on the side, though he couldn't see.

He wondered if the slits were meant to be sexy. Maybe they were just there to make room for her thighs.

Her stocky legs were bare to midcalf. That was where the boots began. Dirty white cowgirl boots with high heels and pointy toes.

Hasn't she ever looked in a mirror?

If she's "top-drawer," Norman thought, *I'd hate to see what's in the bottom.*

An RV the size of a railroad boxcar came roaring down from the north. It angled across the centerline to give the girl some space. She vanished. The wind of the passing RV shook Norman's Jeep. When he could see again, the girl was running across the highway.

A very controlled, measured run. As if she felt that running was required, but wanted to show that she was in no great hurry.

One hand, in a loose fist, swung forward and back. The other clutched the shoulder strap of the denim bag that lurched and swayed by her hip. Her breasts seemed small for someone with such wide shoulders and full hips. She looked as if she had a couple of oranges trapped inside her tank top. They leaped around quite a lot.

"Look at 'em go," Duke said.

"What?"

"What do *you* think? Man, I wouldn't mind sucking on one of those."

Before quite reaching their side of the road, she stopped running. A couple of casual strides, and she stepped off the pavement. She turned and walked straight toward them. Smirking, swaggering, swinging her hips.

"What a piece of work," Duke muttered.

"A piece of work, all right."

"You're a fag, all right."

"Am not. And look, don't do anything . . . weird. Just leave her alone, okay?"

"Oh, yeah. Right. Want her for yourself, huh?"

"I'm a fag, remember?"

"Yeah, we both know better than that. Tell you what." Instead of telling Norman anything, he swung open his door and climbed out.

"Howdy!" he called to the girl.

"Howdy right back at you, guy."

"Your chariot awaits." He patted the top of the Jeep. "We'll let you sit up front. Give me your bag, there."

"Thanks." She lifted the strap off her shoulder and swung the bag toward Duke.

He caught it. Climbing into the front seat, she smiled at Norman.

Her eyes were on him, so he couldn't check her out the way he wanted to.

"Hey," she said.

"Hi."

She smelled fresh and clean, a way that made Norman think of a breeze coming in off the ocean. Duke shut her door. He opened the back door, then flung himself in and set her bag on the floor.

"Thanks for stopping," she said to Norman.

"Glad to help."

Duke's face appeared between the seat backs. "They call me Duke," he said.

She turned her head, and her nose almost touched his. "That's a dog's name, ain't it?" she asked.

Duke let out a howl.

She laughed and mussed his hair. Then she pushed his head out of the way. "Now, who are you?"

"Norman."

"Norman," she said, and slipped her hand up the short sleeve of his shirt. Her fingers curled under, nails lightly scraping his upper arm. Goose bumps scurried over him. He squirmed.

He gave her a nervous smile. "What's your name?" he asked.

"Boots."

"Boots?" Duke said. "What kind of a name is that?"

"You're someone to talk, aren't you? *Duke*."

"I guess we oughta get going," Norman said, and started to check the traffic. When an opening came, he swung out, made a tight U-turn, and stepped on the gas.

Duke leaned forward. "Where you going, Boots?" he asked.

"Noplace much."

"You must be going *somewhere*," Norman said.

"Nope. I just follow my boots. Get it?"

"I guess." .

She picked up her right leg and crossed it over her left knee.

She was looking at her foot, not at Norman. So he stared at the raised side of her thigh. It looked pale and very smooth. He wondered what she would do if he reached out and put his hand on it.

Not about to find out. No way!

She wiggled her boot. "See how it's pointing? Down the road. That's where I'm going now. With you guys."

He glanced again at her thigh, then forced himself to look out the windshield. "Don't you have some kind of a destination in mind?" he asked.

"What for?"

"I mean, aren't you trying to *get* someplace?"

"Anywhere I am, that's fine with me."

He smiled at her. She smiled back.

Her eyes give me the creeps. And it's not just the makeup, he told himself. Something was wrong with the eyes, themselves. In a way they looked like perfectly normal brown eyes. They had no physical defect that he could see. But they seemed to have an emptiness.

Cow eyes, Norman thought. *Cow eyes and a pig face.*

Cut it out. She's not so bad. Maybe she's just dim-witted or something.

He returned his gaze to the road, but his mind stayed on Boots.

Why on earth, he wondered, *does she want to use all that makeup?*

Maybe to hide the emptiness. Instead of hiding it, though, the gaudy makeup seemed to highlight it. Like an elaborate frame around a blank canvas.

Bull. She's some sort of low-life white trash. Probably thinks gobbing her eyes with that stuff makes her look glamorous. Bet I could screw her.

Who'd want to! She's creepy, repulsive, and probably diseased.

I oughta try and get rid of her, he told himself. *Her and Duke. What am I doing with these creeps in my car? Get rid of them both. And soon, before they pull something.*

"I've got an idea," he said. "Since we aren't in a big hurry to get anywhere, why don't we stop for a while next time we come to a decent stretch of beach?"

Duke clapped him on the shoulder. "Good thinking. Let's do it."

"Can we have a picnic?" Boots asked. She sounded as if she'd always wanted a picnic. But never had one.

"Sure," Norman said. "We'll have a picnic on the beach."

"Let's stop and pick up some stuff," Duke said. "We'll have us a real party—beer, the whole nine yards."

Boots clapped her hands. "This'll be *wild.* Oh, you guys are the greatest!"

Her enthusiasm made Norman feel a little sad. The whole point of the picnic was to get her and Duke out on the beach so he could lose them. But here she was, acting like a waif who'd been cheated out of every picnic ever promised.

Probably never had a Christmas, either.

She'll get her picnic on the beach, he told himself. *I won't ruin that for her. Snacks, a few beers. Then Duke'll probably start putting some moves on her . . . and it's "So long, been good to know ya."*

The gas station where they stopped for their picnic supplies had a full-size convenience store. Instead of pulling up to a pump, Norman swung into a parking place near the front door.

With any luck, he might miss out on the picnic after all. He shut off the engine, then reached into his back pocket and took out his wallet. He removed a twenty-dollar bill. He held it toward Boots.

She plucked it free. "Twenty buckaroos!"

"Why don't you go in and pick out whatever you want?" He looked over his shoulder. "What sort of beer should she get?"

Frowning, Duke scratched at one of his sideburns. "Can't go wrong with Bud."

"Maybe you should go in with her." To Boots, he said, "You aren't twenty-one, are you?"

"I've got a license says I am."

"You can help her pick something, Duke."

Duke reached between the seats and squeezed Boots's shoulder. "You got something you want me to *pick*, darling?"

Grinning, she tilted back her head. "Wanta pick my nose?"

God, Norman thought. *She's a regular Dorothy Parker.*

She and Duke both seemed to find the exchange hilarious. Norman shook his head. He had to smile, but only because they were being so moronic.

After they'd settled down, Norman said to Duke, "While you're in there, why don't you see if they have any of that Wolfbane jerky?"

"'You'll *howl* for more!'" Duke blurted, and howled. Boots joined in with a howl of her own.

These two are meant for each other, Norman thought.

But then Duke said, "Let's *all* go in."

"Yeah!" Boots cried out. "That way we can *all* pick what we want." She waved Norman's twenty-dollar bill. "I'm buying!"

As he entered the store with his laughing companions, he supposed it was just as well he hadn't been left in the Jeep. He *would've* sped off— and missed out on the picnic.

In a way he was looking forward it.

He looked forward to it even more when Boots stopped in front of a sunblock display.

"Let's get some of this," she said.

"Okay."

"I like the oily kind," she explained.

Norman and Duke looked at each other.

With their help, she picked out a coconut oil that promised "a full, rich tropical tan" but not much protection against the sun.

Roaming the aisles, they came upon a section with beach gear: plastic buckets and shovels, beach balls, goggles and snorkels, and a small assortment of towels and swimsuits.

"Do you have . . . something to wear?" Norman asked.

Boots nudged him with her elbow. "I got me a *fabu*lous little bikini. Just you wait!" She winked at Duke, and he winked back at her.

Oh, man. Norman thought.

Turning to Duke, he asked, "Need anything?"

"You mean like trunks? You kidding me?"

"Maybe we should get some beach towels," Norman said. "Even if nobody goes in the water, we can use them to sit on."

"And lay on," Duke added, glancing at Boots. They each chose a towel.

After wandering through the rest of the store and picking out what they wanted, they went to the counter.

That was where the jerky was. While they waited in line, Norman studied the labels on the containers. He couldn't find any Wolfbane, so he decided against buying jerky here.

They bought the towels and suntan oil, two cold six-packs of Budweiser, packets of presliced hard Italian salami and sharp cheddar cheese, a box of Ritz crackers, sacks of Cheetos and onion-flavored potato chips, and a package of chocolate-covered Oreo cookies.

When Boots saw the total price, she made a face and waved the twenty-dollar bill at Norman. "I don't think this'll do it," she said.

"Not even close," Norman admitted. As he slipped his MasterCard out of his wallet, Boots shrugged and stuffed the twenty down a front pocket of her cutoffs. He raised his eyebrows.

"I'll keep it warm for you," she said.

CHAPTER NINE

Norman drove slowly past a sign that read, BEACH PARKING. He steered onto the unpaved lot. Except for a couple of cars, a van, and a small RV, the lot was deserted. He could see several people scattered about on the long stretch of beach. The sky was almost cloudless. The Pacific looked deep blue, the curling ridges of the incoming combers as white as snow.

"Oooh," Boots said. "This is so *fabulous*. I just can't hardly wait to sprawl out in the sun. Now you guys run along and set up the picnic, and I'll just change in the backseat and catch up to you in a little bit."

"We better stay and guard you," Duke said, smirking.

"Yeah," Norman said. "It might not be safe."

"You guys." She shook her head. "Shame on the both of you. You're just angling for a peek."

"Us?" Norman asked. He smiled and hoped his disappointment didn't show. He wanted very badly to stay—to stand "guard" outside the Jeep and sneak glances at her while she stripped buck naked in the backseat.

She knows that's what we want, he realized. *Maybe she isn't as stupid as she looks. Or sounds.*

"You guys just go on and take all the goodies with you, and I'll be along in a minute."

"Let's go, Norm."

He frowned over his shoulder at Duke. "Are you sure it'll be safe to leave her alone?"

"Aah, nobody's around. Come on."

"Don't go and worry about me," Boots told them. "Any fool tries to jump on me, he's gonna die screaming."

The words shocked Norman. "Jeez," he said. "You're a mighty tough little thing, Bootsy girl."

"I ain't so little, but I'm plenty tough."

"We better haul ass, Norm, 'fore we make her mad." Then he reached over the seat back and mussed her hair.

She laughed. "Quit it!"

After raising the windows, Norman shut off the engine. He pulled out the ignition key and stuffed the key case into the front pocket of his shorts.

Then they all got out of the car. After the sacks were unloaded, Boots climbed into the backseat. Duke started to shut the door for her, but she stopped it with her foot.

"You want me to smother to death in here?" she asked. "Norman rolled up the windows, you know. It's not that I'm *fond* of having a door open while I strip down bare-ass, but I sure don't aim to *bake* to death."

"Roll your window down," Duke told her.

She thumbed the switch. Nothing happened. "See? I can't."

"It doesn't work when the key isn't in," Norman explained.

"See," she said to Duke.

"So, put the key back in," Duke told Norman.

"I can't. Not if I'm leaving. You know? Somebody might steal the car."

"Not with me in it," Boots said. "I'll just lock up and bring you the key when I'm done."

"I don't . . . uh, think that'd be a very good idea."

"He's scared you'll take it," Duke said.

"Me?"

"No," Norman said. "It's not that."

"Like hell it's not."

"I'd just be awfully nervous. I mean, somebody might come along and . . ." He shrugged. "Anyway, it's my dad's car. If it was my car, you know . . . but it isn't."

"Norman's a very nervous guy," Duke pointed out.

"I could *stay* until you're ready," Norman offered. "I could just sit in the front seat, you know, and run the windows for you. And I wouldn't have to *look* at what you're doing back there. I could even do something like cover the rearview mirror, if you want, or—"

"Cover the mirror with what? Your underpants? Never you mind about that," Boots told him. She didn't seem angry. Smiling, she flapped a hand at him. "You just take your keys with you and go on. I'll be just fine here with the door open."

"I'd *like* to help."

"I know. That's all right. Everything's dandy. You guys, get!"

"Come on," Duke said.

Arms loaded with the sacks from the store, Norman and Duke turned their backs to the Jeep and headed for the beach. Norman had an urge to look over his shoulder, but he fought it. What was the point, anyway? He wouldn't be able to see anything, not with Boots in the backseat.

As they walked onto the sand, he said, "Don't you think we should've stayed?"

"Nah. She knew we wanted to get our jollies watching her strip. She just don't trust us enough yet. For all she knows, we might be the sort who'd jump her."

Norman forced himself to smile. "If we did that, she'd make us die screaming."

"Tough little bitch. Love it. You get a look at her eyes?"

"You mean the makeup?"

"I mean the whole nine yards, buddy. She's not a gal you'd want to piss off, if you know what I mean. What we gotta do is play along with her. She'll loosen up once she gets to know us. Before we know what hit us, we'll be fucking her lights out."

"You think so?"

"I know so."

"Jeez."

"You bet."

Not me, Norman thought. *I'll be jumping in the Jeep and taking off, first chance I get.*

They walked a distance farther before Duke said, "Here looks good to me."

"Me, too," Norman agreed.

They were about fifty feet from the water; the sand was dry and soft. They put down the sacks, spread out the towels, and sat down. Right away Duke peeled off his T-shirt. He had a very good tan, for April in Oregon. *He's probably been traveling around.* Norman thought. *Out in the sun a lot. Lifting weights, too.*

On his left upper arm was the tattooed slogan, BORN TO RAISE HELL. *Figures.*

The only real surprise was that a guy like Duke didn't have more tattoos. He must've decided that BORN TO RAISE HELL said it all.

Unless he's got them somewhere I can't see them. Norman decided to keep his own shirt on, at least for now. A cool breeze was blowing, so he didn't feel hot in spite of the bright sun. And he knew he wouldn't look good shirtless next to Duke. He had no tattoo, no tan, and no prominent muscles. He did remove his shoes and socks. He looked at Duke's heavy black motorcycle boots. The side buckles gleamed silver.

"Are you a biker?" he asked.

"Not anymore. Not since I totaled my Harley."

"You had a Harley."

"You gotta be kidding. What else is there?"

"Hondas . . . ?"

Duke sneered at him. "I look like the kinda guy'd get himself caught dead on a rice rocket?" He tossed a can of Budweiser to Norman, and took one for himself. They popped open the beers. As they started to drink, Boots came striding toward them.

"Whoa, mama," Duke muttered. Norman stared at her.

She smiled and waved. He returned the wave. *Doesn't she know how awful she looks?* Her shoulders and hips seemed even broader than he remembered them—her arms and legs thicker. She also had a bit of a paunch. She had no business wearing such a skimpy bikini. It was black, which made her skin look very pale and pasty. As she swaggered closer, Norman saw that the bikini was knitted. Its top looked tired and loose. Limp strings held triangular patches of black yarn across her breasts. The patches bobbed and jiggled and swayed as she walked.

Black cords swooped down over her hips to pull at a V of yarn that came up from between her legs.

"Bitchin' bikini, babe," Duke said.

"Yeah," Norman added. *Hideous!* he thought.

"You like?" Boots asked. Stopping in front of them, she flung up her arms and cocked a hip. "Ta-dahhh!"

Her top was too small and too loose. Half an inch of skin showed under each breast. Before Norman could get a good look, however, she turned around.

Black cords were tied in bows behind her neck and back.

"Ta-dahhh!" she proclaimed again, and swished her butt to one side.

Her cheeks were wide, white, and smooth—and mostly bare. A couple of cords slanted down from her hips. They met a slim patch of yarn that went down the center. Through the tiny holes in the knitting, Norman glimpsed her crack. His heart thudded.

If the front's like that . . .

Boots continued her slow turn. Seconds later, she was facing him again.

Oh, my God, Norman thought. The view ripped his breath out and pumped heat into his groin. He didn't want to be caught staring, so he forced himself to look at her face.

"Very nice," he said. "Is it . . . is it homemade?"

She beamed. "How'd you *guess?*" Not waiting for an answer, she pranced over to the third towel. She sat down on it cross-legged, one knee pointing at Norman and the other at Duke. Duke tossed her a beer.

As she snatched it from the air, Norman watched her breasts. There was no doubt about it; her nipples actually jutted out through loopholes in the knitting. Their tips were sunlit and pink as tongues.

I've gotta stop looking, he told himself. *Gotta. Gotta!* He raised his beer. The top of the can flashed in his eyes. It blocked his view of Boots while he drank. When he lowered the can, he tried to hold his gaze on her face.

She was smiling, her attention on the beer that she was about to pop open.

She really is ugly, Norman thought. *Very piglike.*

She tilted back her head and drank, so he dropped his gaze to sneak a look between her legs.

Doesn't she know? he wondered. *My God, it's sticking out like she's got it mashed up against a tiny little chain-link fence.*

She knows, all right. She has to know. She's just some sort of weird pervert or nympho or something. Or maybe she doesn't know, or doesn't think it matters. Any way you slice it, Norman thought, *she's definitely not operating with a full deck. She wears a thing like that in front of us. Why the hell didn't she let us watch her change? She's showing off everything she's got, anyhow.*

She's nuts, that's why.

"You lookin' at me?" she asked.

He couldn't believe it. She'd caught him! Heat surging to his face, he met her eyes and shook his head.

"No," he said. "I wasn't looking at anything."

"You were, too."

"No. Honest."

Duke smirked. "Busted."

Suddenly grinning, she said, "Well, don't." She reached out and gave him a playful slap on the knee. "Ain't polite to stare at a lady's cooz."

She burst out laughing, and so did Duke. After a moment or two Norman joined in. He wasn't amused, but he laughed with a mixture of relief and nerves. And gratitude.

She isn't so bad, he thought. *Most gals would've torn me apart for doing something like that.*

Most gals don't wear a bikini like that.

She doesn't mind me looking, he told himself. *That's the thing. She likes it. She wants me to do it.*

All the more reason to get the hell out of here.

He took a few more swallows of beer, then set his can on the towel by his hip. He shoved it to make it stand upright.

"I'm getting pretty hot," Norman said.

Duke and Boots laughed about that.

"Yeah, yeah, yeah," he said, grinning. "Anyway, just watch my beer for me, okay? I'm gonna get into my trunks, after all. You guys can go ahead and break out the food, if you want. I'll be right back." He got to his feet and stepped off the towel. "Either of you need anything from the car?"

Boots shook her head. Duke waved him off.

"Right back," he said, and started toward the parking area. Halfway there he had a strong urge to glance over his shoulder. *Don't! You'll blow it. Duke'll come running. Just play it cool. Walk slow. Don't look back.*

He listened, but he didn't look. He heard the squeal of seagulls, the rush of the surf, but he didn't hear anyone coming.

What's to hear, footsteps in the sand? The click of a flick-knife spring?

They aren't coming, he told himself. *They bought my story. Hook, line, and sinker.*

Maybe.

Then he was so close to the Cherokee that he knew he'd made it.

Unless they're right behind me . . . He'd heard that gals like Boots made trophies out of fellas' gonads. He shriveled up tight.

As he reached into his pocket for the keys, he turned toward the driver's door and swiveled his head.

They were both still sitting on the towels! Not even looking at him!

Head down, Duke was reaching into a grocery sack on his lap. Boots appeared to be watching him.

I made it!

Norman unlocked the door, swung it open, and climbed in behind the wheel. Hand trembling, he slid the key into the ignition. A buzzer sounded. The noise made him cringe, but he told himself that Duke and Boots couldn't possibly hear it. They might hear the door thud shut, though, so he left it open.

Don't close it till the engine's going, he told himself. *You'll be outta here before they can even get off their butts.* On the beach, Duke took something out of the sack.

A brown bottle. The coconut oil. *For a full, rich, tropical tan.*

Norman felt a tightness in his throat. He'd wanted to be there when she slicked herself up with that oil. Wanted to watch, and smell it, and maybe give her a hand.

Boots took the bottle of oil, but didn't open it. Instead she set it on the towel by her side.

Of course, Norman thought. *She's gonna wait till I get back. She doesn't want me to miss the show.*

Little does she know . . . He started the engine. Their heads turned.

"Sorry," he muttered. He shifted to reverse. Duke and Boots stayed sitting on their towels, staring at him.

They aren't even gonna try to stop me, he realized. *It's like they don't even care.*

Why should they care? Three's a crowd, right?

That isn't it, he told himself. *The thing is, they know there's no point. They can't possibly stop me. They wouldn't stand a chance. That why they aren't trying.*

As he started to back up, Boots raised a hand overhead. The same hand that had patted his knee after she caught him looking. It flapped up and down, waving good-bye.

CHAPTER TEN

Pamela sat up. She'd spent long enough stretched out on the seat, some-times gazing up at the ceiling of the bus, sometimes sleeping. She didn't mind the sleeping. But she was wide-awake now.

If she stayed on her back, she would start dwelling on Jim and Rodney—*Rotney!*—and all the terrible things that had happened. Or she might start wondering about Sharpe again. What was his problem? Where was he taking her?

She sat up, swung her legs off the seat, and gently placed her feet on the floor. Leaning forward, she peered out the windshield.

Still in the middle of nowhere.

It looked nice out there now. The bright, hot glare of the sun had mellowed. The pavement, the whole desert landscape, was awash with a rosy glow.

Must be almost sundown, she thought. Her mouth was dry.

Sharpe had given her a plastic bottle full of water after they'd finished dumping Rodney's body. She'd been sipping at it off and on. Between drinks, she'd kept it trapped between her hip and the seat back. It must've rolled against her rump when she sat up. She could feel it there now.

Reaching behind herself, she picked it up. She twisted off the cap and took a drink. Her stomach growled. She looked at Sharpe. From where she sat she could see only the top of his head. So she stood up. Wincing with each step, she limped across the aisle. She swung around and dropped into the seat. Now she had a side view of Sharpe. She took another sip of water.

"Where are you taking me?" she asked.

He didn't so much as glance her way. "No talking to the driver while the bus is in motion, Pamela."

"Oh, give me a break."

"Company policy."

"*What* company? This is *your* bus, isn't it?"

"Sorry."

"Okay, okay." She sighed. Turning her head, she gazed down the aisle. Back there the bus was dim with murky golden light. She could make out the blurred shapes of the mannequins. They seemed to be bouncing and swaying a little with the motions of the bus.

She faced Sharpe. "Is it against the rules if I chat with the other passengers?"

This time his head tilted back. Checking her out in the rearview mirror. She saw the reflection of his face. He still wore the sunglasses.

His thin lips didn't smile. "They don't say much," he said.

"What are you doing with them?"

"Driving 'em."

"Why?"

He shook his head.

"None of my business?"

He didn't answer.

"You've got to admit," she said, "it's pretty strange."

"Quiet, now," he said. "That's too much talk already."

"I'm a little hungry, you know."

"Can't be helped."

"You don't have any food in here?"

Again he shook his head. "We'll be stopping by and by. Now cut out the talk."

"Okay." She settled back in the seat, sipped water, and wondered what he meant by "by and by." To her, it meant "soon." But maybe it didn't mean that to Sharpe.

Maybe it's like, "In the sweet by and by." She tried to sing the old hymn in her mind.

"*In the sweet by and by, we will come to that beautiful . . .*" Something. Shore? Cross? Sky?

That sort of "by and by"—the hymn sort—didn't seem to mean "soon" at all. It had to do with when you're dead; she was pretty sure.

Terrific, she thought. *We'll all just gather at the river.*

"I know," she said. "Those things aren't mannequins back there. They're just former passengers you starved to death. Petrified passengers."

He didn't look at her, but his back seemed to stiffen slightly. A jaw muscle bulged.

Uh-oh, Pamela thought.

"Just kidding," she said.

He acted as if he didn't hear her. His back remained rigid, and the muscle in his jaw stayed knotted.

"I'm just hungry," she explained. "I didn't mean to say anything wrong."

His head lifted slightly. "Never mind," he said. Moments later he raised an arm to point out a roadside billboard. "We'll stop there," he said.

The big white sign had red lettering.

MAKE A PIT STOP AT PITS
IT'S REALLY THE PITS
PITS, CA, pop. 6

Pamela had heard of Pits, but she couldn't remember. *No. Wait. The T-shirt on the kid.*

She peered down the aisle at the boy dummy. His T-shirt looked dark and rusty in the gloom, and she couldn't make out the words. She was sure, though, that they were about the same place as the billboard. Pits, California, population six.

Leave it to California, she thought, *to have a town with only six inhabitants and still make a big deal out of it.*

At least one of them apparently had a sense of humor. The kid bought his T-shirt there, so . . .

The kid did not buy his T-shirt there. The kid is a dummy, he's never bought anything anywhere, period.

Sharpe must've bought the T-shirt, she told herself. *Or he got hold of it one way or another. The same with the clothes on all the other dummies . . . and me.*

She felt a corner of her mouth stretch. *I'm just one of the gang. Sharpe's gang. With one minor or significant difference, depending on how you look at it.*

She shook her head and wondered how she'd digressed to such a level.

The T-shirt on the kid. Sharpe must've gotten it at Pits, which meant there had to be a store—some sort of gift or souvenir shop. And a place like that was almost certain to carry food.

A whole assortment of snack food would probably be sold at a place with souvenir T-shirts for sale. Pamela longed for an actual meal, but anything would do: potato chips, popcorn, pretzels, peanuts, candy bars, jerky. And a good, cold beer to wash it down. Though a soda would be fine. Probably could get beer at a gift shop.

A few minutes later they drove past another billboard.

IT'S THE PITS GAS! FOOD! FUN!
ONLY TEN PITIFUL MILES TO GO
PITS, CA, pop. 6

Things are looking better and better, Pamela told herself. The place wouldn't advertise food if you couldn't get an actual meal there. A cheese-burger, for instance. Or a hot dog. Maybe pizza. And only ten miles away.

About fifteen more minutes, at the speed Sharpe seemed to be driving.

Pamela spotted another billboard in the distance, and watched it grow until she could read it.

IT'S NOT PITTSBURGH
IT'S JUST THE PITS
COME SEE OUR
PALACE
THE EIGHTH WONDER OF THE WORLD!!!
PITS, CA, pop. 6

Soon another billboard appeared.

ASK TO SEE OUR PITS
FREE LOOKS
JUST ASK!

FIVE MILES TO GO
PITS, CA pop. 6

Smiling, Pamela shook her head. *Ask to see our pits? What does that mean?* Next came the best of the billboards.

EAT! EAT! EAT! THE PITS CAFÉ, BREAKFAST, LUNCH, DINNER
DOWN-HOME COOKING
PLUS OUR FAMOUS BOTTOMLESS PIT OF COFFEE!!!
PITS, CA, pop.6

A real café! Thank God, Pamela thought. But she suddenly realized that she wouldn't be able to pay for a meal. She had no money.

Or anything else.

She had nothing at all of her own. She'd been naked when Rodney attacked her. Later he had dressed her in the costume he'd brought with him. He'd dragged her out of the house without her purse. And now she was wearing clothes from one of Sharpe's mannequins.

She didn't even have her engagement and wedding rings. At the bathroom door last night, Rodney had pulled them off her finger. "We don't want *these!* They're *his*. He can *have* them." One at a time Rodney had hurled the rings at Jim's body. The engagement ring had hit Jim in the forehead and bounced into the bathtub behind him. In the tub, it made a sound like a coin clinking and rolling around. The diamond wedding ring had landed with a quiet little *plip* sound on the intestines bulging out of the slit in Jim's belly.

Pamela pressed a hand against her mouth. Her eyes watered. *Why did I have to think about that? Get used to it.*

I am getting used to it, she thought. *Must be. I didn't throw up this time. Didn't even gag.*

But she did feel ashamed of herself. For the past half hour or so she'd been thinking about almost nothing except where and when she would get her next meal.

Jim's dead. He's never going to eat again. And I'm worried about being a little hungry. What the hell is the matter with me?

I'm alive, she reminded herself. *What am I supposed to do, give up eating?*

"I don't have any money," she said. Before Sharpe could respond, she hurried on. "I know I'm not supposed to talk to the driver while the bus is in motion, but I'm starving and we're almost to this café and I haven't got a dime on me. But I want to eat. Okay? I mean, I *will* be able to pay you back. It just might take a while. I've got a bank account and credit cards, but I don't have anything *with* me. Rodney didn't exactly let me pick up my purse while he was dragging me out of the house last night. And also he burned the house *down*, so there went everything. Like my checkbook and credit card. But I'm not poor. I have a job. I can pay you back if you'll buy me something to eat. Okay?"

His head lifted slightly. "It'll be on me."

"That isn't necessary, but—"

"I saved your life, so I reckon you're family now. I take care of my own."

"Well, thanks," she said. She wasn't sure about having Sharpe consider her "family." Before she could give it much thought, however, Pits came into sight beyond the windshield. *It really is the pits*, she thought.

What she saw was a roadside conglomeration consisting of a rundown gas station and a small café surrounded by a vast parking area that seemed to double as a junkyard. There were a few old mobile homes scattered about the rear. Between the gas station and the café, but back a short distance, was a fenced area that appeared to be a graveyard. On a rise beyond the graveyard was a Victorian house that looked as if it had been uprooted from a movie studio backlot, where it might've been used decades ago as a setting for haunted-house epics.

That must be the palace, Pamela thought. "What a dump," she said.

"Home, sweet home," Sharpe said.

"I thought you lived in your bus."

"That's right." He slowed down, then steered off the pavement. As he rolled toward the gas station, an old geezer near the pumps saw him coming and waved. Sharpe tooted the horn. A moment later a woman in a white dress came running out of the station's office.

Sharpe drove past the pumps, then swung to the right and eased into an empty space that seemed to be just the size of the bus.

Looking over his shoulder, he said, "Welcome to Pits, popo six." Then he reached out and worked the chrome handle of the door lever. The entrance door wheezed open.

Pamela leaned forward, ready to stand.

But she stayed in her seat when the woman leaped into the doorway and bounded up the steps. Sharpe climbed out of the driver's seat. The woman took a quick look at Pamela, then threw herself into Sharpe's arms. They stood at the front of the bus, embracing each other. Sharpe seemed to be returning the hugs in a fairly perfunctory way—gently, but without much passion, as far as Pamela could tell.

He ought to be a little more enthused, she thought, *having a gal cling to him as if he were a long-lost lover who'd just returned from the wars.*

While he did little more than stand there with his arms around her back, the woman moaned, kissed him over and over again on his mouth and cheeks and neck, ran her hands up and down his back, caressed his face, and stroked his hair, all the while squirming and rubbing herself against him.

Finally she separated herself from Sharpe. Flushed and a little breathless, she straightened her dress and turned toward Pamela.

"Hi," she said.

"Hi."

"Sorry about that. I don't usually . . . I haven't seen him in a while."

"No problem."

Sharpe still had an arm across the woman's back. He squeezed her shoulder and said, "This here's Lauren. Lauren, meet Pamela."

"Nice to meet you," Lauren said.

"Same here."

Very nice to meet you, she thought.

Even though Sharpe had saved Pamela's life and hadn't abused her in any way, he was definitely strange. Being alone with him had kept her uneasy. So the very presence of Lauren was a relief.

And it was very good to find that he had a woman in his life.

Wasn't after my bod, after all. All that worry for nothing.

"Welcome to Pits," Lauren said.

Pamela stood up as she approached. They shook hands. Lauren had a sturdy grip. She looked sturdy, but also delicate: tall and wide shouldered, though extremely thin; thick hair the color of straw; amazing eyes of forest green. Her face, bony and hollow checked, was saved from looking cadaverous by the tawny glow of her skin. Her complexion made her seem more like an athlete than a corpse.

Pamela guessed that she was no older than thirty. And probably descended from hippies, by the looks of her granny dress. The white garment was buttoned up the front almost to Lauren's throat, short-sleeved, shapeless and loose, and so long that it reached down almost to her ankles. *All she needs is a flower in her hair.*

Stop that, Pamela told herself. *She probably wears a dress like that because it's nice and cool. Just the thing for dwelling in the middle of a desert. Same goes for her sandals. At least she's not barefoot.*

Fixing her deep green eyes on Pamela's eyes, she said, "You've been through some tough times."

"That's for sure."

"Well, you'll be fine now." She smiled. "You've been saved."

CHAPTER ELEVEN

"I'll show you around," Lauren said, "and then—"

"We better get some grub in her first," Sharpe broke in. "Take her on over to the café, and I'll be along by and by."

Smiling, Lauren said, "Come along."

Pamela followed her down the stairs at the front of the bus. When she stepped to the ground, pain shot up from her feet. She sucked in air, hissing.

"Your feet?" Lauren asked, frowning.

"They're a little racked up. But I'm fine."

"I know just the thing. Wait here." She started to hurry away.

"It's fine," Pamela protested. "I don't need anything."

"Yes, you do. This'll be just the ticket." A moment later Lauren disappeared around the corner of the gas station office. Pamela limped after her, embarrassed, wanting to tell her not to bother with whatever she had in mind.

And almost collided with the old geezer she'd seen earlier by the pumps. As she stepped out of the bus's shadow, he came around the corner.

She gasped and jerked to a halt.

"Howdy do." He gave her a big grin. His gums were interrupted by a few brown, twisted teeth.

"Hello," she said.

My God, she thought. *What is this guy?* A few terms came quickly to mind. *Old-timer. Prospector. Mule skinner. Desert rat. Snake rustler. Sand bandit.* The only thing that looked worse than his dental situation was his cowboy hat.

The ancient, filthy hat sat crooked atop his head, its brim turned up in front. It might've been a good hat at about the time of the Alamo's fall. In the years since, it had apparently been slashed, shot, stomped, kicked, burned, and drenched thousands of times with the old coot's sweat . . . or worse. It was decorated with so many stains that Pamela couldn't even guess at its original color. She imagined that the sorry old hat, if caught in a rainstorm, would likely have yellow runoff.

Not much of the old man's face showed. Most of it was hidden behind his wild gray hair, his heavy eyebrows, his thick mustache and beard. His eyes showed. They were squinty, with blue irises and bloodshot whites. His nose showed. It looked like a strawberry that had been kicked around on a dusty road. His lower lip was cracked and peeling.

The guy's a walking ruin, she thought. But she had to change her mind about his age. He wasn't exactly the old coot that she had supposed. Probably in his middle fifties. With the exception of his hat, his clothes looked reasonably clean, but heavy and hot. His plaid flannel shirt had long sleeves, and Pamela could see the neck of a faded red T-shirt he was wearing underneath it. The shirts were tucked into his blue jeans. His belt had a big silver buckle. On his feet were a pair of scuffed and dusty black cowboy boots.

Giving Pamela an odd, lopsided smile, he lifted the hat off his head. "Name's Hank," he said. "Honorary mayor of Pits, chief guide, man Friday, you name it and I'm it. Hank."

"I'm Pamela."

"Ye're a dish." He winked.

"Thanks."

"A real hot tuh-matuh."

"Well . . ."

He narrowed an eye. "Show you my pits?"

Trying to smile, she shook her head. "Not right now."

"It's my job. Chief guide. How about the Dillinger Death Car? Wanta see her?" He pointed at the rusted ruin of an ancient automobile near a far corner of the lot.

"Is that it?" Pamela asked.

"Yessirree. Wanta see her?"

"Maybe later."

"Don't miss her."

She couldn't help but smile. "Is that really the Dillinger Death Car?" It certainly looked like a vehicle that might've been around back in the thirties.

"You can see the bullet holes," Hank said, and winked. "The baby's *peppered* with 'em."

"Are you trying to trick me?"

"How d'ya mean, there?"

"You're talking about *John* Dillinger?"

"None but."

"I don't think he was in a car when he was killed."

"Ya don't, huh?"

"I think he was standing outside the Biograph Theater in Chicago."

"*Haw!*" Hank reached out and clutched her shoulder. "Can't fool *you!* Nosirree! You're a smart cookie; yes, you are! I like you."

"Thanks."

He leaned in close to her. As if sharing a dark secret, he said, "You got no idea how many plug-fuck ignoramuses come along here and *believe* every dang thing I tell 'em. *No idea!*" He cackled. Then he stepped back, scowled, and nodded. "That ain't no *Dillinger Death Car.* It's the *Jesse James Death Car!*"

Surprised, Pamela found laughter bursting out of her. She was even more surprised to find herself reaching out and slapping Hank on his shoulder. A puff of dust rose off his shirt.

"What's your name!" he demanded. Hadn't he already asked?

"Pamela."

"Pamela! Good for you!"

"Well, thanks."

"Ya gonna stay?"

She shrugged. "For a while, maybe."

"Good deal! I stayed. Aim to keep stayin', too, till the day I go toes-up, and then I'm gonna have 'em plant me over yonder on Boot Hill with the dogs and monkeys. Been here since 'seventy-two."

"That's a long time."

"You betcha!"

Lauren came riding around a far corner of the gas station office. She was on the front seat of a bicycle built for two.

"Hank!" she called out. "Have you been bothering the lady?"

He cackled. "Making a plug-fuck nuisance outta myself, and you know it."

Lauren pedaled toward them, a big smile on her face. "Hank is an inveterate bushwhacker. We keep him around to scare the children off."

"Haw!"

"Are you one of the 'pop. six'?" Pamela asked him.

"You better betcha, baby!"

"Which are you?"

He winked. "Some folks take me for number two."

"You're terrible!"

"Ain't I?"

Lauren stopped her bike just beyond Hank. She put her feet on the ground and held the bike steady by its front set of handlebars. "Climb on aboard, Pamela, and I'll pedal you over to the café."

"Well . . . okay." She limped toward the bike's second seat. "Nice to meet you, Hank."

"You know it!"

Laughing, she shook her head.

Hank stepped backward, out of the way. He leaned against the rear of the bus and watched her mount the bike.

"Don't be no stranger," he said.

"See you around, Hank. Mayor Hank."

He guffawed so loud she thought he'd up-'n'-out one of his lungs.

"Ready?" Lauren asked. "Here we go."

They both pushed at the ground to get the bike rolling. Then they put their feet on pedals and started to pump.

"Beats walking," Pamela admitted. "I was afraid you might show up with a wheelchair or something."

"Nope."

From behind them came a raspy, almost tuneless voice singing, "Mademoiselles got derrieres, whoop-de-doo. Mademoiselles got . . ."

Cheerfully, Lauren called over her shoulder, "Put a lid on it, you raunchy old sidewinder!"

"*Pardonez moi!*" Hank yelled.

Lauren glanced back at Pamela, smiled, then faced forward. "He's about as addled as they come," she said.

"I sort of like him."

"Well, I'm glad to hear it."

"Is he really the mayor of Pits?"

"He's pretty much whoever he says he is, I guess."

A dusty old pickup truck swung off the highway and rolled slowly across the dirt. It seemed to be heading for the café. Lauren raised an arm and waved. The driver tooted his horn. He stopped in the midst of fifteen or twenty other vehicles that were scattered about near the café: an odd assortment of cars, trucks, vans, and even a couple of motorcycles. Some looked fairly new and roadworthy, but quite a few didn't seem to be in much better shape than the Dillinger/James Death Car.

Lauren dodged several as she and Pamela pedaled toward the café.

They glided very close to the remains of an old Pontiac. It had no windows. Pamela felt heat come out of it. A smelly heat that made her think of melting rubber. On the dashboard was a plastic Jesus.

The plastic Jesus looked almost new.

Parked near the front entrance of the café was a Toyota Land Cruiser, its cargo space loaded with luggage.

They steered past it. Then Lauren swerved away from the café door, braked, and lowered her feet to the ground. She held the bike steady while Pamela dismounted. After that, she leaned it against a stucco wall.

The man from the pickup swung the door open for them. He looked like a younger version of Hank, but with better teeth, whiskers instead of a full beard, and a fairly good-looking outfit comprised of a cowboy hat, plaid shirt, blue jeans, and boots. Smiling, he lifted his hat.

"Thank you," Pamela said as she entered.

"Mah pleasure, ma'am. Howdy, Lauren."

"Howdy, Wes. This is Pamela. Sharpe just now brought her in."

Wes followed them into the café. "Reckon ye're a lucky gal," he told her. To Lauren, he said, "She's what, the seventh?"

"Yep."

"Sharpe's got himself a long ways to go."

"Afraid so."

"Pleasure to meet ya, Pamela."

"Nice to meet you, Wes."

He sauntered toward the counter.

Pamela saw four other customers at the counter. A family with two kids sat at one of the booths, an elderly couple at another, and a group of four teenagers at a corner booth. There were several wooden tables scattered about the area between the booths and the L-shaped counter, but they weren't being used. "Would you like a booth?" Lauren asked.

"That'd be fine."

Lauren led her to one at the front of the café. They slid in across from each other. The table between them had a green Formica top, and looked clean. A couple of menus were propped up behind the napkin holder. Lauren took them and handed one to Pamela.

"We've got good food, here. Terry's a whiz in the kitchen. Sharpe brought him in, and he stayed. Our vittles were mighty poor till he showed up."

"Has Sharpe brought in *everybody?*"

Smiling slightly, she shook her head. "Terry's the only one who's stayed. He didn't have anywhere better to go, and found out he liked it here."

"Wes said something about me being the seventh."

"There were six before you."

"Six what?"

"People Sharpe has saved since he started the mission."

"*Saved?*"

"Like you." Lauren turned her head and smiled at the approaching waitress. "Nicki, I want you to meet Pamela. Sharpe saved her today."

"Hey, great!" Nicki beamed. "He's moving right along."

"I'll be an old lady in a wheelchair," Lauren said.

"No, you won't!" Nicki set down the water glasses and reached a hand toward Pamela. "Pleased to make your acquaintance," she said as they shook.

Nicki looked as if she belonged in a ski lodge, not in a café in the middle of the Mojave Desert. Her blond hair had a braided ponytail behind, and a thick curtain of bangs in front. The bangs hung almost to her pale blue eyes. Her face had a Nordic look, in spite of its dark tan.

She wore a knit pullover shirt similar to the one that Pamela had taken from the dummy in the bus. Nicki's was white, not lime green, and had her name in red stitches above her left breast. It appeared to be a few sizes larger than Pamela's, too. Filled with mounds and curves and slopes.

Around her waist was a blue apron with pockets for her order pad and tips. It hung down like a very short skirt, ending just above the cuffs of her shorts. The shorts were bright red. They looked snug around her thighs.

"Ready to order?" she asked.

"Give us a few more minutes," Lauren said.

"Can I bring you something to drink while you're deciding?"

"Do you have beer?" Pamela asked.

"You bet." She flashed her white teeth. "All we got's Bud, but that suits most folks."

"That's fine."

"One for me, too," Lauren said.

"You got it." She headed for the counter.

"She seems nice," Pamela said.

"A good kid. But she drives Terry crazy. He's got it really bad for her, but she won't have a thing to do with him."

Pamela felt a quick shiver. *Rodney and me.*

"A thing like that can be dangerous," she said.

"Keeps the place lively." A corner of Lauren's mouth tilted upward. "We'll have to make up some sort of billboard about this place being a 'passion pit.' You just wouldn't believe all the lust and unrequited love we've got around here."

Shaking her head, Pamela made a wry half smile of her own. "That's how I got here, I guess. A guy had the hots for me and wouldn't let it go. Killed my husband," she added quickly.

The last three words were enough to shut her throat and fill her eyes with tears. Across the table, Lauren blinked. She pressed her lips together. They formed a tight, straight line. Leaning forward, she reached out and squeezed Pamela's hand.

"Nothing bad'll happen to you here. We take care of one another, and you're welcome to stay just as long as you want."

CHAPTER TWELVE

Pamela cried softly, head down, trying to stop. Hoping everyone in the café wasn't staring at her. Lauren kept hold of her hand, and said nothing.

Nicki showed up with the beer. She set two frosty glass mugs on the table. Then she put a hand on Pamela's shoulder. Pamela looked up at her.

"Whatever it is," Nicki said, "I'm sure sorry. You gonna be all right?"

"She's been through some rough times," Lauren said. "That beer's bound to help."

Nodding, Pamela murmured, "Thanks." She sniffed. With the back of her hand she wiped her eyes. "I haven't . . . had a chance to look at the menu."

"No problem."

"Do you like burgers?" Lauren asked.

Pamela nodded.

"Get her a Pits Burger Deluxe and chili cheese fries. Same for me."

Nicki let go of her shoulder and started to turn away. Before she could leave, Pamela said, "I don't . . . have any money." She sniffed again. "Where's Sharpe?"

"He'll be along."

"He said he'd pay."

"Don't worry about anybody paying," Lauren told her. "I own the joint."

"The café?"

"Everything."

"Oh. Neat." She lifted the heavy mug and drank some beer. The beer was very cold.

"We like it here," Lauren said.

"Pop. six?"

"That's me, Hank, Nicki, Terry, Wes, and Sharpe when he isn't on the road." Lauren lifted her mug. It left a wet ring on the tabletop. Most of the frost had melted, leaving the mug clear and dripping. But a few small white patches slipped down its sides like the last remnants of snow sliding down a car's windshield. When she lifted the mug toward her mouth, the bottom of it dripped onto the front of her white dress. She didn't seem to notice.

With the rim at her lips, she sucked at the frothy head. Then she tipped the mug up and drank.

In a way she seemed too willowy and ethereal to be drinking a mug of beer. A delicate glass of white wine might've been more appropriate. On the other hand, a hefty mug of beer seemed just about right for the Lauren, who was weathered, gaunt, and earthy. Somehow she seemed two different people rolled into one. One delicate, fey, spiritlike. The second the outer shell: made tough by life, strong enough to fight back if fighting was required.

Lauren set the mug down on the table, smiled at it, and rubbed the back of a brown hand across her lips. "You're welcome to stay," she said. "You can sleep in Mosby's trailer. He hasn't got any use for it."

"Well . . . thank you. I don't know."

"Sharpe won't be going anywhere tonight, if that's what you're wondering about. He'll probably stick around for a day or two—longer, if I have any say in things." She raised her eyebrows. "Are you in a rush to get home?"

"He burned it. Rodney. The man who killed my husband. The house is gone. My home. Everything." She stared at her beer, and struggled not to start crying again.

"Pamela? Do you have family?"

"In Chicago." She took a drink. The mug dripped onto the front of her pullover. The drops felt like ice water. "I don't want to go there. My job . . . I work in L.A."

"What do you do?"

"Just . . . I'm a teacher. A substitute."

"Oh, dear God. A sub in Los Angeles? That must be about the nearest thing to hell on earth."

"It's not much fun. It's a way to work into a . . . a real teaching position. You know, you get your foot in the door. Jim had a good job, though, so . . . I don't know what I'll do, but I've gotta go back. I mean, that's where I live, and guess I'll have to find an apartment or something."

"It doesn't sound as if you've got much to go back to."

"Well, not much."

"Sharpe'll drive you back to L.A. when he's ready to go, if that's what you want. But there's no law that says you've gotta go with him. You can stay here just as long as you want. I'd recommend it for a while, anyway, after what you've gone through. It's peaceful here. It's a good place for getting over troubles."

"Thanks. I don't know. . . ."

"Play it by ear. But figure on staying tonight, at least. I always keep Mosby's trailer up in case of company."

"Okay. Thanks." She looked out the window. Long shadows stretched across the dirt lot in front of the café. "Where do you suppose Sharpe is?"

"Oh, he'll be in my trailer taking a shower, I guess. That's usually the first thing he does when he comes back."

"He told me he lives in the bus."

"His bus doesn't have a shower."

Pamela glanced at Lauren's hands to double-check. No rings. But she supposed that didn't prove anything; Lauren didn't seem to be wearing any jewelry at all.

"Are you and Sharpe married?"

"Afraid not."

"But you're. . . . something?"

"I guess we're something, all right."

Pamela waited. When Lauren didn't go on, she decided not to push. She drank some more beer instead. The mug dripped chilly water onto her again.

She put the mug down.

Across the table, Lauren sat motionless, one hand on her own beer mug, her eyes lowered and blank with a stare, her straw-colored eyebrows drawn together just enough to carve a pair of small grooves into the skin between them. *It's my fault,* Pamela thought. *I shouldn't have asked about Sharpe. I must've hit a sore spot.*

Bumbled right into it.

Should've known better.

One of those "unrequited love" things she was talking about, probably.

"Are you okay?" Pamela asked.

"Huh? Sorry. What did you say?"

"Is something wrong?"

"No. No. I wonder what's keeping the burgers." She flashed a smile at Pamela. "Maybe I'll have to give someone the boot."

"It hasn't been so long."

"But you must be starving." She peered off across the café, eyes narrow. "Ah, here they come now."

Turning, Pamela saw Nicki hurry around the end of the counter with a big, loaded tray.

"I'm going to marry Sharpe," Lauren said.

Pamela looked at her, surprised.

She nodded, smiling. "Soon as he's done with his mission. By then, of course, I'll probably be an ugly old hairless hag . . . and too old to have babies." As she spoke the last part, her smile trembled and her eyes suddenly brimmed with tears.

Nicki arrived and began to unload the food. "That's two Pits Burger Deluxes, chili cheese fries . . . Lauren?" Nicki crouched slightly and peered into her boss's eyes. "What's the matter, honey?"

"Just the usual."

"Damn that man."

"Don't say that. He can't help it."

"He sure can, too, help it. Jesus H. Christ, there's no excuse. The dead don't mean squat. Somebody oughta tell him that."

"He has to do it."

"Bullshit, if you'll pardon my French."

Lauren fixed her red, wet eyes on Pamela. "He saved your life, didn't he?"

"Sharpe? Yes."

"What sort of danger were you in?"

"Rodney . . ." She looked at Nicki, then back at Lauren. "He was going to kill me. He killed my husband last night."

"Oh, God," Nicki muttered.

"And he . . . threatened he'd do a lot of things to me. Anyway, then he kidnapped me. He wanted to take me to a place in the desert, but I sort of escaped. Almost. The thing is, he finally got me down on the ground and stuck a pistol in my mouth. I'd hurt him bad. He was going to kill me. I mean, he would've pulled the trigger in about one more second. And suddenly he got shot in the head. Sharpe shot him right in the middle of the forehead."

"Wow," Nicki said.

Lauren simply nodded. Then she turned to Nicki. "See? It's not exactly bullshit. If it hadn't been for Sharpe and his mission, Pamela'd be food for buzzards about now. Instead, she's about to partake of a Pits Burger Deluxe."

"Well," Nicki said. "I know. It's just maddening, though, that's all."

"I've noticed," Lauren said.

Nicki shook her head at Pamela. "It's not that I'm not really glad he saved your life. I mean, that's great. But he's just so obsessed, and here's poor Lauren who loves him like crazy, but off he goes anyhow just as if he didn't give a rat's hairy behind, if you know what I mean, and one of these days he'll probably wind up getting himself killed . . ."

"Stop it," Lauren told her.

"Well, it's just so *maddening.*"

"Don't you have some other customers you might want to go and bother, Nicole?"

She rolled her eyes upward. "Well, I *suppose* so."

Lauren reached out and squeezed her forearm. "Get out of here, okay?"

"Somebody oughta pound some *sense* into that lunkhead, that's all."

"Go."

"I'm going, I'm going." She stepped backward with the empty tray. "I'm just saying he oughta think about *you,* for a change, and quit—"

"Hey!"

"Okay, okay." She gave a shrug at Pamela, smiled at both of them, then turned around and hurried off.

Lauren was next to shrug at Pamela. "Better dig in," she said. "All this talk, our food's gonna get cold."

"Yeah."

"Eat it."

Pamela looked down at her meal. A Pits Burger Deluxe and chili cheese fries.

The fries were hidden completely beneath thick blankets of chili and melted yellow cheese. So much steam curled off the concoction that Pamela knew she'd be risking a mouth burn if she didn't wait a few minutes before taking a taste. She turned her attention to the Pits Burger.

The bun was nearly as large as the plate. Its top was brown, shiny, and striped with dark grill marks. Lettuce leaves and curls of onion stuck out beneath the bun's top, but only here and there, not enough to hide the crispy edges of the hamburger patty.

Edges that dripped with cheese.

"It sure looks good," Pamela said, and had to shut her mouth quickly to prevent drool from spilling out.

"Just wait'll you sink your teeth in," Lauren said. "The patty's partly sausage, by the way. It's my recipe. A mixture of ground beef and sausage."

"Ah. Sounds great."

She needed both hands to pick up her Pits Burger Deluxe. The bun felt slippery and crisp under her fingertips. Afraid of losing it, she tightened her hold before biting in. Warm juices and cheese spilled down her palms and wrists.

She opened her mouth wide and took her first bite. Her teeth crunched through the bun, lettuce, and onions, then sank into the meat. A wonderful assortment of sweet, tangy flavors filled her mouth.

Moaning with pleasure, she began to chew.

CHAPTER THIRTEEN

When Boots bit into her hamburger, red juice dribbled down her chin.

"Are you sure that thing's done enough?" Norman asked.

Chewing, she turned her burger around and showed it to him. The inside of the patty looked like a raw, bloody wound. The sight of it disgusted Norman.

"You oughta have them cook it some more," he said. "You could catch a disease or something."

"This is just how I like it," Boots said, her words muffled. She opened her mouth wide. It was full of mushy, partly chewed burger.

Norman looked away.

Boots laughed. "You're funny," she said. She ran the back of her hand across her chin to stop the dribble. When she lowered her hand, her chin was shiny.

She's so repulsive, Norman thought.

Right. But here I am.

Back at the beach parking lot, hours ago and fifty miles north of where they now sat eating supper, he'd had a perfect chance to get away from her and Duke. He could've driven off and never seen either of them again. But what had he done? He'd shut off the engine, gone to the back of the Cherokee, and searched through his luggage until he found his swimming trunks.

In the backseat, where Boots had changed into her tiny little knitted bikini, he'd taken off his shorts and underwear and put on his trunks. Then he'd hurried back to where Boots and Duke were sitting on their beach towels.

"Thought you were gonna split on us," Duke had said, smiling.

"It crossed my mind. I just couldn't drive off and leave you two stranded. Thought it would've been a dirty trick."

"Like we don't *know* how come you came back," Boots had said. Tongue protruding between her lips, she'd somehow made her breasts hop and shake inside the flimsy bikini—without apparently moving the rest of her body.

"That isn't why."

"Like fun."

"Glad to have you back, bud," Duke had said. "It don't matter how come you stuck; just matters you done the right thing."

The right thing, my ass.

The one thing certain to Norman, as he'd sat down on his towel and picked up his beer, was that sticking with these two had *not* been the right thing. It was probably the least right thing he'd ever done. He *should've* driven away.

He'd come back to them only because of Boots, because of her knitted bikini, because of what he'd been able to see through its loopholes.

And because he'd wanted to be there when it came time to work the suntan oil into her sun-heated skin.

Sitting across from her now in the diner, he shifted uncomfortably as he remembered.

Soon after his return to the beach, Boots had squirted the coconut oil onto her palm and spread it on the front of her body. It had a strong, sweet scent. Her hand had slipped underneath the bikini—both the top and the bottom—and Norman had been able to watch it through the meshwork of black yarn. Watch it slick her skin with shiny oil. Watch it linger inside the bikini, fingertips roaming and stroking as she glanced from Norman to Duke with her lazy, blank eyes.

Done, she'd sprawled on her back. Legs apart. Hands folded beneath her head.

Gleaming in the sunlight from face to feet. He was sure he could see her—

"*What?*" Boots asked, lowering her hamburger.

"Nothing."

"Tell." She smiled, but she didn't look amused. "You're thinking about me, aren't you?"

"Yeah, I guess so. About the beach."

"I knew it." She took another bite of her hamburger. After a few chews, she said, "Probably spoiled yer eyes, you was staring at me so hard."

"Well . . ."

"I was gonna let you do my back, but then you went and walked off. How come you walked off?"

I was about to explode, that's why. "I just felt like taking a walk," he said.

"Duke was kinda rough. He kinda hurt me. Hope he didn't leave no bruises."

"Well . . ."

"I kinda like it when it hurts. Don't like bruises, though. I got me real delicate skin, in case you didn't notice. I bruise easy. Burn, too. Sunburn? Wonder if I got me a burn out there today."

With the hand that wasn't holding her hamburger, she plucked out the front of her tank top and peered down inside. She shook her head and pursed her lips. "Reckon *they* got some sun. Wanta see?" She met Norman's eyes.

Blushing, he glanced about the diner. It was fairly crowded. He smiled at Boots. "I don't think so. Not right now, anyway."

"Later, then."

"Well . . ."

"We'll get a room, the three of us."

The suggestion stunned him, excited him, frightened him. *The three of us in a motel room. My God!*

Privacy. Beds.

"What?" he asked her. Maybe he'd misunderstood what she was getting at.

"We'll get us a room."

"What kind of a room?"

"A lecture room in a flicking museum. *Duh!* A motel room, dummy." Smiling, she shook her head. "What'd you think we was gonna do, spend the whole night in your car?"

"I don't know. I guess I hadn't really thought about it."

"Thought about what?" Duke asked, coming back from the diner's restroom and pulling out his chair.

"Everything come out all right?" Boots asked him.

Duke smirked. "Can't complain." He sat down. He studied his cheese dog and French fries, then picked up the squeeze bottle of catsup and covered the fries with a mat of thick red sauce. "So," he said, "what'd I miss? What's going on?"

"I was just saying to Norm how we oughta get us a room at that motel right across the street there."

"Hey. Yeah."

"I don't know," Norman said. "I don't have a whole lot of money."

"You got plastic," Duke reminded him.

"I know, but . . . I can't use a credit card for something like that. My father'll get the bill."

"You gotta sleep."

"But I've only made about a hundred and fifty miles today. I should've gone twice that far. When he sees—"

"Hey, use your head. All you gotta do is say you got a flat."

"No," Boots said. "We don't wanta go and use no credit cards. It's like telling who we are. Anyhow, we don't need one. I can get us a room, and it won't cost us nothing."

They both stared at her.

"I just bet you can," Duke said.

"You better believe it."

"You mean like . . . use your charm on the desk clerk?" Norman asked.

"Whatever," Boots said.

"That'll only work if it's a guy," he pointed out.

She grinned. "Oh, don't be too sure."

"Anyway, it wouldn't be legal. Not if he doesn't *charge* us anything."

"So?" Boots said.

"I don't want us getting into trouble."

"Don't be such a wuss all your life," Duke told him. "Boots, here, she's offering to get us a free room. You *really* got a problem with that? Just take a second and think about what's gonna *happen* in that room, know what I mean?"

"I just don't think we should do something that might be against the law. I don't want to end up in jail."

Duke suddenly looked dead serious. "Nobody's gonna end up in jail. I don't do jail. That's for losers. So, long as you stick with me, you got nothing to worry about."

"You guys wait here," Boots said. "I'll come back and get you when it's all set."

"No big rush," Duke told her. "Finish your burger."

"I'll take it with." Holding the hamburger in one hand, she stood up. She shoved her chair away with the backs of her legs. "You guys can fight over the end of my Pepsi. It'll be watered down, anyhow, by the time I get back."

"I don't know about this," Norman said.

"Face it," Duke said, "you don't know about much."

"I know, but—"

"Don't you worry about anything," Boots told him. She squeezed his shoulder. "I'm gonna show you boys the best time you ever had."

She released his shoulder.

On her way toward the door, she sashayed past several crowded tables. Conversations stopped. Customers turned their heads. Gazes latched onto her from every direction.

"Look at 'em," Duke said. "The gals, they all hate her, figure her for a tramp. The guys, they're thinking how they'd give their left nut to shack up with her for a night. They hate us just as much as the gals hate Boots. We're the guys that *have* her, know what I mean?"

"I guess so."

"We're gonna have her all to ourselves, and those poor bastards know it. They can't stand it. They're ready to blow their pants right now."

"I really don't know if we should do this."

"The room?"

"Everything."

"Man, you're a case." Shaking his head, Duke fixed Norman with an exaggerated look of disgust and pity. "You don't watch out, you're gonna go *through* your whole life and get to the end of it and find out you never done nothing. You gotta go for it, man. That's what life's all about."

"If you're living a beer commercial."

"Ha! Good one."

"Maybe I should just go ahead and *pay* for a room," Norman suggested. "I mean, I don't like this idea of trying to get a freebie."

"Take what you can get," Duke said. "Somebody wants to hand us a room for the night . . ."

"But—"

"Look, you're just scared of getting caught. But the thing is, so what if we do get caught? Say Boots finds herself a horny clerk at the front desk—she gives him some head or whatever—he lets her have a room for the night, and the boss shows up and finds out all about it. The *clerk's* the guy that gets his ass reamed. We walk. The worst that happens, maybe we have to fork over whatever it would've cost us to get the room legitimate. See?"

"I guess so. But it still seems like a bad idea."

"That's 'cause you're also scared to fuck her."

Norman's face flooded with heat. "I am not."

"Sure you are. Shit, she's a scary bitch any way you slice it, but it's gotta be *real* scary for a guy like you."

"What do you mean, like me?"

"A guy that's never done it before."

"Who says I've never done it?"

"You told me."

"No, I didn't." He frowned. Had he admitted such a thing to Duke? No! No way! He'd never told that to anyone, much less to Duke.

"You want a piece of advice?" Duke asked.

"I don't need any advice."

"Sure you do."

"Yeah, sure." He rolled his eyes upward. "Okay. Let's hear it."

"First thing you gotta know, dames aren't the same down there as guys."

"Very funny."

Duke tried to look offended. "No! I mean it! Seriously. They haven't got tools."

"Ha-ha."

"You think I'm joking? I mean it!"

Norman started to laugh for real.

Leaning forward, Duke whispered, "It's like their tools got cut off, and all they've got left is just this gash. Now, what you've gotta do is put your tool in *her* gash. Get it?"

"I get it. Jeez!"

"And you gotta make sure you get it in the front. You don't wanta get it in the back by mistake, you know what I mean? That's a good place to stay away from."

Norman, shaking his head, tried to stop laughing.

"Stick it in the right spot, and you got nothing to worry about."

"Except maybe for the clap and a few other things."

"No *problemo*, good buddy. They got a vending machine in the john."

"You mean, like, for condoms?"

"Right on. They got three varieties. We'll go in and stock up soon as we get done eating."

Norman nodded, but wrinkled his nose. "Those things aren't all that safe, you know."

"Sure they are. Ain't you never heard of safe sex?"

"I heard the things don't work too well. Like they break when you're inside her, or sometimes come off . . . that sort of stuff. A *lot* of the time. Like one out of six. I mean, that's not very good odds. That's the same sort of odds as playing Russian roulette with a six-shooter."

Duke frowned. "So what? Just fuck her five times, you're okay."

Duke looked quite pleased with himself.

Norman laughed a bit, then said, "Good one."

"Yeah, I know. I'm a card. Fact is, though, you gotta lighten up. Who's to say she's even infected? It might be as sweet as a rose garden down there."

"Can we ask her?"

"Like anyone's gonna admit it."

"Do *you* have it?"

"You mean AIDS?"

"Yeah."

"Like I'd admit it?"

"Do you?"

"Don't know, don't care."

"How can you not care?"

"I don't worry about shit like that. I live how I wanta live. And I know one thing for sure—I ain't ever gonna let no disease nail my ass. When I go out, I go out quick in a blaze of glory."

"Not with a whimper, but a bang."

"Right on."

"I think I'd rather live to a ripe old age and die in bed," Norman said.

"Yeah? Gee whiz! How come that doesn't just surprise the everlasting shit outta me?"

"Make fun all you want. I don't intend to go around risking my life for a few minutes of . . . screwing Boots, or whatever."

"So you're telling me you ain't gonna fuck her?"

"It just isn't worth it."

"What're you aiming to do, stand around and watch us?"

Another blush scorched Norman's face. "I don't know," he muttered. "I figured I'd . . . just sort of go along to the room and see what happens."

"I *know* what'll happen. We better load up on rubbers."

By the time they were done eating, Boots still hadn't returned. They asked for coffee. Then Norman gave Duke a five-dollar bill.

"What's this for?"

"Why don't you go up to the cashier and get some change? Whatever you need for the vending machine."

"Quarters."

"Yeah. Then, you know—go in the john and buy whatever we need."

"We? Changed your mind already?"

"Okay, whatever *you* need."

"Sure you don't wanta come along?"

"No, that's all right."

"Aren't gonna run out on us, are you?"

He hadn't thought of that.

I could!

Yeah, right, he thought. *I couldn't even make myself drive away from the beach, so I'm sure I'm gonna take off when I've got a chance to end up in a motel room with her.*

Duke stood up from the table, his chair scooting back, its legs squawking against the floor. Bread crumbs speckled his pants. Norman watched him walk toward the cashier's counter. The five was in Duke's left hand. His right hand was shoved partway down the seat pocket of his jeans. He walked with a swagger. Norman couldn't see his face, but he knew there had to be a smirk on it. *Guy acts like he owns the world.*

Norman tried to picture himself walking like Duke, dressing like him, smirking like him.

I'd look like a total dork, he decided. *I just haven't got what it takes.*

What does it take? he wondered. *Does it have to be in the genes to be able to wear jeans like that? Like you're James Dean. Better yet, would I really want to be like him? Let's face it, the guy's a macho jerk, and not all that bright.*

But he sure is cool. What does it take to be that cool? Plenty of time attending the school of hard knocks, he supposed. *More balls than brains. I wouldn't want to be that way,* he told himself.

And a voice in a shadowy corner of his mind whispered, *What good are brains if you're a gutless wonder who hasn't got any balls at all? You've gotta take chances sometimes, or what's the point? Carpe diem! Seize the day! Seize the babe! If you chicken out with Boots tonight, you'll regret it the rest of your life.*

CHAPTER FOURTEEN

Flushed and a little breathless, Boots dropped into her chair. She smiled from Duke to Norman.

"We was starting to take you for 'missing in action,'" Duke said.

"Not me."

"How'd it go?"

She shifted onto her left buttock, reached behind the right, and pulled something out of the rear pocket of her jeans. A big green plastic tab with a key that dangled from its end.

A smile spread across Duke's face. "All *right!*"

"Jeez," Norman gasped. "You did it?"

"Told you I was gonna, didn't I?" She glanced around the diner as if worried about spies, then quickly returned the motel key to her seat pocket. "It was a cinch."

"Really?" Norman asked. He found himself leaning toward her and whispering, "You really got it for free?"

She beamed at him.

Duke grinned. "I think Normy here wants all the juicy details."

"That so, Normy?"

"Well . . ."

"You wanta sit here and listen to how I got the room for us, or you wanta go over and go in it?"

"You betcha," Duke said.

Norman felt as if he face might burst into flame. "Well . . ."

"I think Normy's got the jitters." Duke winked.

"Would you quit calling me Normy? Please?"

Eyes on Boots, Duke said, "Normy's got such a bad case of the jitters, he's about ready to shit."

Boots reached out and took hold of Norman's hand. "What're you scared of?"

Norman shrugged.

"He's scared of getting in trouble with the law," Duke explained. "And he's scared of you. He's a virgin."

"Good deal!" She squeezed Norman's hand. "I'll break you in."

"That's what scares him."

"Well, it ain't like I'm gonna *hurt* him." To Norman, she said, "You got nothing to be scared of, honey. This is gonna be the night of your life. Now, come on. Let's get the show on the road." She took her hand away and stood up.

"Are you sure you don't want anything else before we go?" Norman asked her. "Did you get enough to eat? Do you need a Pepsi or something?" To Duke, he said, "How about you? Don't you want another hot dog or something?"

"Only one thing I'm hankering to eat, good buddy, and it ain't a doggie."

Boots laughed. She leaned over the table and slapped Duke's shoulder. Giving her a smirky grin, Duke got to his feet.

"Just a minute," Norman said. He took out his wallet and removed a few dollars for the tip. His hands trembled as he folded the bills. He tucked them under a corner of his coffee mug. When he stood up, his legs were shaking. *My God, I can't believe I'm really gonna go through with this.*

I'm not going through with anything, he told himself. *Not yet, anyhow. Just gonna pay the tab and go outside. Which I'd be doing anyway. Then maybe I'll go over to the motel with them, or maybe not. I can do whatever I want. Nobody's holding a gun to my dick . . . Dick? I mean head. I wonder if she gives head. . . . Oh, Christ, I'm rambling. . . .*

Duke and Boots waited by the cashier's counter while he paid. Then they walked ahead of him to the door.

As he followed them, he gazed at Boots. She wore her tank top and cutoff jeans and white boots. In the beach parking lot, by the side of the Cherokee, Norman and Duke had watched her put them on. Still in her black knit bikini, she'd stepped into the shorts and pulled them up. Then she'd slipped the tank top down over her head. After getting into her boots, she had untied the yarn at the nape of her neck, then reached up under the back of the tank top, fiddled around in there, and finally plucked out the upper part of her bikini.

It had gone into her big denim bag. But her bikini pants had stayed on.

He wondered if she still wore them, just as he still wore his swimming trunks underneath his shorts. He stared at the seat of her cutoffs. The blue denim, faded almost white, was packed tight with her buttocks. No telltale lines to indicate she was wearing the bikini pants underneath.

Maybe they're in her bag by now.

Maybe she took them off for the benefit of the motel's desk clerk.

She's such a slut, he thought. *Not to mention ugly. I'd have to be nuts to mess around with her. She doesn't even seem like a real human being. Maybe she's the result of a laboratory experiment. A fusion of human and pig DNA. Now she's broken free. She's making men pay for the result of the obscene experiment. The Revenge of the Pig Woman . . . Oh, Christ, I really am rambling . . .*

But it excited him, knowing her breasts were loose inside her tank top and that she was probably naked underneath the ragged cutoff jeans. *Wow, gonna make bacon tonight . . . with the Pig Woman. Gonna make a hog of myself, too. . . .* The excitement made Norman dizzy.

Duke stepped outside the diner and held the door open. Boots walked out. Norman followed her.

The sun must've just gone down. When they'd entered the diner, the town had been aglare with sunlight flashing off glass and chrome. Now all the harsh brightness was gone. The white rocks of the parking lot had a mild blue tint. Boots rubbed her arms.

She started to turn around, so Norman glanced at the slit side of her cutoffs. Bare skin was all he saw.

Nothing under there but Boots, he thought. *I'd bet on it. Pure pork belly . . . Stop it,* he told himself. *You're making crappy jokes because you're nervous.*

Stick around and find out what's under those tight clothes of hers.

"Wait'll you get a look at the room," she said. "It's a real peach."

"You're the peach," Duke told her.

Lame, Norman thought.

Duke stood there in a slouch, a smirk on his face, both arms up as he ran a comb through his greased waves of hair.

If he doesn't watch out, Norman thought, *he'll get mobbed by autograph hounds.*

Except there seemed to be no one nearby.

And the stars he seemed to be copying were long dead: Elvis, Dean, Starkweather. Brando hadn't gone toes-up yet, but the smirking punk Brando of the fifties was as dead as James Dean.

"You gonna stick?" Duke asked.

Norman looked across the road at the Golden Anchor Inn, and felt himself go squirmy inside.

A nice place. A long, two-story complex, with stairways going up to the second level. Freshly painted. Lights aglow in some of the big picture windows of the guest rooms. The parking lot was about half-full, and the red neon VACANCY sign seemed shockingly bright in the mellow dusk.

"Well . . ."

"Come on," Boots said. Turning away, she sashayed toward the Cherokee. The blue-white stones of the parking lot made crunching sounds under her boots.

"How about it, Norm?" Duke asked. "Ready to turn the boy into a man? "We'll see. I don't know yet."

Boots smiled over her shoulder. "If you don't, you're gonna be sorry."

Either way, he thought, *I'm gonna be sorry.* They climbed into his car.

Boots, in the backseat, leaned forward as Norman started the engine. He saw her face beside his shoulder. "We even got cable TV and a thingy . . . a channel changer."

Norman started to back up. "What should we do about parking?" he asked.

"Just do it."

"Maybe we shouldn't use the motel parking lot. Since we aren't registered?"

Duke snorted. "You worry too much. Or have I already mentioned that?"

Norman shifted, and steered toward an opening near the far end of the lot. "Maybe *you'd* worry," he said, "if it was your car."

"Your old man's car, you mean?"

"Which is even worse," Norman pointed out. "I'm just saying maybe we should leave it on the next block or something. Just in case something *does* go wrong."

Boots's fingers slid gently up the back of Norman's head. "Nothing's gonna go wrong, honey." The fingers felt awfully good. They made him squirm. But then she took them away.

"Let's put it smack in front of the room so we don't have to walk so far."

"I don't know."

Maybe that isn't such a bad idea, he thought. *If we're right at the door, we can hurry into the room really fast. Less chance of being spotted. Not to mention how convenient it'll be if we need to make a quick getaway. What if somebody takes down the license plate?*

Big deal, he told himself. *I do worry too much. My God, it's not like we're committing a federal offense or something. We're getting a free room for the night, that's all. It's no big deal, so lighten up.*

No traffic was coming, so he steered onto the road and drove slowly back toward the Golden Anchor.

"Don't take the first entrance," Boots told him.

Norman saw that it led directly to the portico in front of the motel office.

"There's another way in," she added. "Down at the other end of the lot."

"Scared your clerk might wanta join the party?" Duke asked.

"He ain't on duty now. His boss was coming on."

Norman groaned.

"Don't worry, hon. What he don't know ain't gonna hurt him."

"What if he checks somebody into our room?"

Duke laughed.

"I don't see what's so funny. It could happen."

"It ain't gonna happen," Boots said. "My guy took care of it."

"Oh. You mean we *are* checked in?"

"Not as us. But the room's signed up for."

That was certainly good news.

Maybe I'll stay, after all, he thought. *I've gotta spend the night somewhere. Now, at least, there won't be much danger of getting into trouble about the room.*

Just have to stay away from Boots. And keep her away from me.

He drove slowly alongside the motel's parking lot, keeping watch for the second entrance. When he spotted it, he flipped his turn signal on. He swung in.

"It's one forty," Boots said. "That's the last room on this end. See it?" Her arm stretched past the side of his face, her finger pointing. "That one right there. Where that car is."

Norman drove straight toward it. But he asked, "Are you sure? I mean, somebody's parked there."

"Those guys, they went upstairs."

"Oh. Okay. Are you sure?"

"Yeah, I'm sure. Good golly, Norman."

"Just pull in next to it," Duke said.

"Okay." Slowing, he eased his Cherokee into the space to the right of the other car.

"Brand-new Caddy," Duke muttered. "Wonder how much these rooms go for."

"Plenty, I'll bet," Boots said. "It's a real dandy place. Just wait; you'll see."

Norman shut off the engine. "Let's get in fast before someone spots us," he hissed.

Boots put her hand against the back of his head and gave it a gentle shove. Then she climbed out.

Norman cringed when she slammed her door. It sounded like an explosion. He expected faces to suddenly appear at room windows. He grimaced at Duke. "Shouldn't we try and be *quiet*?"

"Got a lesson for you, bud. When you're up to sneaky shit, the last thing you wanta do is *act* sneaky. If you're going in a place, you go in acting like you own it."

Boots strode past the front of the Cadillac and stopped at the door of room 140. She slid her key into the lock.

"Let's go," Duke said.

They climbed out of the Cherokee, and Duke flung his door shut. Norman shut his door gently. In spite of Duke's lesson on sneakiness, he just couldn't bring himself to slam it.

Boots was stepping into the room by the time they reached her. They hurried inside, and Duke shut the door. The room was dark except for a slice of gray dusk light coming in through a gap between the edges of the curtains.

Duke flicked a switch. A lamp came on. It stood atop a round table in front of the closed curtains. The room looked fine to Norman. It had a queen-size bed and a single bed, covers and a carpet that didn't appear dirty, and a nice set of dressers, counters, and mirrors. The TV was elevated in the middle of the unit, where it could probably be seen well from either bed. He glimpsed a counter and sink in the nook at the other end of the room. The door to the bathroom was probably over to the right, hidden by the wall that ran out past the end of the far bed.

Not a luxury room, but not a dump, either. It would be a good place to spend the night. *My God, am I really gonna do it?* His heart hammered. *I can just stay,* he told himself, *and mind my own business and keep away from Boots.*

"Ain't it a peach?" Boots asked. Grinning, she raised her arms and twirled around like an awkward, stocky ballerina. *From "Dance of the Sugarplum Hog."* As she completed her twirl, she flopped backward onto the queen-size bed. She lay sprawled there, her arms out, her legs dangling off the end with the corner of the mattress between her open knees. Her thick thighs filled the leg holes of her cutoffs, so Norman couldn't see in. Her tank top had drifted up, baring her midriff.

She squirmed slowly and moaned. Raising her head, she looked from Duke to Norman. "I'm ready when you are. What say we get the show on the road?"

Norman faced Duke, his mouth dry. "You go first."

Duke lifted his eyebrows.

"I'll . . . I can watch television. Or . . . I know, I can take a shower while you're . . . you know, busy. Unless you'd rather have me leave. I could go for a walk, I guess. Come back in, what, an hour?"

"Up to you, honcho," Duke said. "All the same to me. You can stay and join in, if it don't matter to Boots."

She pushed herself up on her elbows and gave Norman a lazy smile. "Don't you *dare* go running off."

"But . . ."

Sitting up, she crossed her arms over her belly, clutched the tank top, pulled it up and over her head and off. She tossed it aside. It fell to the floor between the beds. Flopping onto her back again, she flung out her arms. "Somebody wanta finish the job?" she asked, and raised one of her booted feet.

"Happy to oblige you, ma'am," Duke said. He stepped forward. When he tugged the boot off, her whole body jerked. Her breasts hopped, wobbled, jiggled.

I've gotta get out of here, Norman told himself. *Before it's too late.* He took a step closer for a better view. In the lamplight, he could see the pink of her sunburn. The color was solid and even except on her breasts. Her breasts were pale, but had pink speckles where the sun had entered through the webbing of yarn. Her nipples were standing up straight. Both the tips looked ruddy, and Norman recalled how they'd been sticking out through her bikini's loopholes.

Her breasts lurched and swayed when Duke tugged off the other boot.

But after the boot was off, they didn't stop. They bobbed, swung, and jumped, and Norman realized that Boots was wiggling slightly to make them do it. She grinned up at him.

"Take these jeans off me, Norman."

"Uh . . ."

"You been wanting to all day."

"Go for it, Normy," Duke said. "Peel her nice and slow, huh?"

"I don't know. I really . . . I'm not sure we should be . . . you know, doing any of this."

Pushing her heels against the floor, she raised her pelvis. "Come on, Norman."

Don't, he told himself. *Excuse yourself. Go out to the Jeep. Get in and drive away.*

Last call. Scram now, or forever hold your peace. He stared at the brass button at the waistband of her cutoffs. A couple of inches below her belly button.

And what's a couple of inches below this button? Oh, man, oh, man, oh, man!

"Come on, Norman." Smiling up at him, she squirmed. "Don't be yellow all your life."

Duke told him. "Come on; do what the lady asks."

Heart slamming, mouth dry, Norman stepped between her knees. His own knees trembled. So did both his hands as he reached down to the brass button.

He unfastened it. *Oh, my God.*

The denim edges spread, showing sun-pink skin.

With the thumb and forefinger of his right hand, he pinched the zipper tab. He lost his grip on it twice, but finally got a good hold and slid it down.

Exposing a deep V of bare skin and tight, wispy golden curls.

When did she get rid of the bikini pants? He curled his hands under the slit sides of her cutoffs, then took hold of the denim and pulled. The tight shorts hardly budged. He stepped backward until he was clear of her knees. She swung them together. Then he pulled again. This time the shorts leaped free. He backed away quickly, racing them down her legs, past her ankles, and off her feet.

Boots smiled up at him. "That was easy, wasn't it?"

He nodded. He swallowed hard.

With that lazy smile on her face, she raised her arms and folded her hands underneath her head. Then she opened her legs wide and squirmed.

"What're you aiming to do, boys?" she asked. "Just stand there and gawp at me all night? Come and get it."

CHAPTER FIFTEEN

Norman thought: *My first time ever!*

His mind whirled. *And it's an orgy. Maybe something like this doesn't count as an orgy—just a threesome—but it sure seems like it ought to count.*

He supposed they'd been at it for an hour. Maybe longer. All three of them naked and sweaty and breathless on the bed, grappling, caressing, humping.

It seemed unreal.

Like some sort of exotic, erotic dream.

The way Boots had done him with her mouth right at the start of things.

Later, the funny stuff with the condom. How he'd unrolled the damn thing, then tried to pull it on like a sock—hilarious for Boots and Duke, embarrassing for him.

Then Boots showing him how it was done. Demonstrating. Taking a fresh one and ripping its wrapper open, then rolling it onto him with slow, gliding fingers, and finally pulling him down onto her and guiding him inside for his very first actual time. *I'm fucking her!* he'd thought, astonished. *I'm really doing it! I shouldn't be doing it, but I am. Anyway, it's all right, using a condom just like you're supposed to . . . hope it doesn't come off or break . . . Sure wish it wasn't so tight. Gotta be tight. But shit, it hurts.* He'd used up three of the damn things so far—including the one he'd ruined by unrolling—and now he was on his knees at the end of the bed, ripping open a fourth. His hands shook badly. Not from nerves—from exhaustion.

He plucked the condom out of its wrapper. It was prelubricated, slippery as a snail.

He started to put it on.

He could hardly believe that he was ready to go again. *My God, look at me.*

Though his penis stood up stout, it was shiny and red, and ringed with marks left by the other condoms. Just as if rubber bands had been wrapped tightly around it.

Why the hell do they make 'em so tight?

So they don't fall off, asshole.

Like Duke's fell off. His second one had come off while he was in her. They'd both laughed as if they thought it was hysterical. Norman hadn't thought it was funny—until he watched them struggle to fish it out. "So much for safe sex," Duke had said.

"I ain't got nothing you can catch," Boots had said. After that, Duke hadn't bothered with any more condoms. He was on his back now, moaning and writhing. Boots, on her hands and knees between his open legs, was using her mouth on him.

Norman fumbled and dropped the condom. It fell onto the sheet. When he tried to pick it up, it slipped out of his fingers.

Duke isn't even using one.

The hell with it, he thought.

He kneed his way forward, running his hands along Boots's calves. They were thick, slippery, prickly with whiskers, but the backs of her thighs felt smooth. So did her rump. The crack felt clammy. Lower, though, she was wet and slick. He fingered her there to be sure he had the right place—the front one, as Duke had called it—then moved forward and in.

In her for real for the first time, skin-to-skin, and she was all heat and slickness.

He couldn't believe the feel of it.

I'm probably gonna die now, but who cares?

It's so wonderful.

So great. Better than anything. So what if it kills me?

What if I get AIDS from this? Or the clap? What if I wake up tomorrow and I'm whizzing blood and pus? My God, I must be out of my mind.

But it probably wouldn't happen, anyway, and it was too late now to stop. He was on his knees, thrusting in as she took her weight on her hands and knees, his lap making slapping sounds against her buttocks, his arms underneath her, hands on her breasts—squeezing them as he slid in and out, smacking against her rump as she sucked on Duke, and Duke gasped and groaned . . .

. . . and a movement where there shouldn't be movement caught Norman's eye. He turned his head. Peered over the edge of the mattress. Saw a man squirming out from under the bed, belly-crawling, facedown. Something wrong with the back of his head. Hair pasted down with blood.

Shoulders furry. *Shit! Got a werewolf under the bed.*

Only dimly aware that he was still embedded in Boots and clutching her breasts, Norman gazed over the side of the bed and watched.

Not a werewolf. A desk clerk?

The guy kept squirming out from under the bed, apparently unaware that he was being observed.

Neither Boots nor Duke had seen him. Not yet. They weren't likely to spot him, either. Not unless Duke sat up on the bed, or Boots slid her mouth off him and looked over her shoulder.

The guy wore black, knitted bikini pants.

"Boots?" Norman asked.

"Mmm?"

"Who's the guy under the bed?"

Her mouth made a quick, slurpy, smacking sound. Then she said, "What?" She sounded alarmed.

"What's going on?" Duke asked.

The man suddenly scurried.

Boots pushed herself up, turned her head. "Shit! Get him!"

"Quick!"

Not me!

But he was on Boots, and Boots was on Duke. *Me or nobody!*

"Get him!" Boots cried out.

Norman let go of her breasts. He backed up, pulled out. The man was clear of the bed and crawling across the carpet toward the door.

He looked stupid in the bikini pants.

Stupid and disgusting, Norman thought, *like a pervert in some sort of crummy porno movie.*

How come he doesn't get up and run?

"Stop him!"

Norman leaped off the bed. He hit the floor and rushed forward.

He knew he ought to jump on the guy. A great, flying leap. But this fellow really *was* repulsive to look at—all hairy and pale, shiny with sweat, his ass showing through the web of the knitted pants.

Don't want to touch him!

Besides, Norman told himself, *it might be a crime to jump on him. Assault and battery, something like that. Dressed like that it might come down as a sex crime.* What would Norman's family say if they read about it in the newspapers?

So he dashed past the man.

Got to the door just ahead of him.

Whirled around and planted his back against it.

The man raised his head. Blinking sweat out of his eyes, he gazed up at Norman. He looked confused and about ready to cry.

Like a disappointed kid. A skinny, forty-year-old kid in bikini pants who'd just had Santa take away his only Christmas gift.

Boots made a running dive. Her body slapped down on the man's back. He made a grunt. His elbows folded, and his face thudded the carpet. Boots hugged him around the waist. She twisted and writhed as if trying to throw him over. "Help!" she gasped. "Come on!"

Norman stood and watched.

So did Duke. He'd hurled himself off the bed a moment after Boots, and now he stood behind her, hands on hips, staring down at the struggle, an odd look on his face, as if he couldn't make up his mind whether to scowl or grin.

"Guys!"

"You're doing fine," Duke told her.

"Gimme a hand!"

"Who is he?"

"He's s'posed to be dead, the dirty fucker."

"This guy your desk clerk?" Duke asked.

"Ain't no clerk."

Duke's scowl lost the struggle. Smirking, he chuckled a few times.

"Don't tell me," he said. "You just came over and knocked on this guy's door, right? Picked yourself some poor sucker, came in, put your moves on him, then bonked him on the head."

"Yeah, sure." She sounded annoyed. "So sue me. Why the fuck ain't he dead?"

"Didn't hit him hard enough."

"I *strangled* him, too."

"Didn't strangle him hard enough."

"Don't hurt me," the guy pleaded from underneath her. "Please?"

"This is *his* room?" Norman asked.

"Help me out," Boots said.

Duke grinned. "Seeing you wrestle the guy naked's turning me on."

"We . . . we'd better let him go," Norman stammered. "You'd better get off him, Boots."

"No way."

"Come on. This is crazy. We don't need his room. We can go some-place else. God almighty. Tell her, Duke."

"Tell her, Duke," said the guy underneath Boots. "Please. You . . . you can *have* my room. Just let me go. Please? I won't tell. I promise."

"He sounds like a friendly sort of guy to me," Duke said. "What do you aim to do with him, darling?"

"Kill his ass."

"Oh, God. No, please. Help . . ." His voice stopped as Boots finally got her leverage right and flipped him over sideways. Keeping hold around his waist, she rolled onto her back.

The man had a bloody nose. Whimpering, he tried to unlock her hands. He twisted and squirmed and kicked at the air. Norman could see through the loopholes of the bikini pants.

He's the only guy around here without a hard-on, Norman thought. *Seeing him and Boots grapple is kinda a turn on.*

Course, he's the one she's trying to kill.

Boots swung her legs up on both sides of the man. She brought them inward and down, bending her knees, driving her feet down between his legs, trapping him.

"Good going," Duke said. "Now what? Gonna squeeze him to death?"

"If you'd just help . . ."

The man yelled, "*Help!*" at the top of his lungs. "*Somebody helll—*"

Norman dropped to his knees and clamped both hands over the man's mouth. "Shut up!"

He snapped his teeth at Norman's palm.

Norman jerked his hand away.

The man yelled, *"Hellll—"*

Norman pounded his fist down like a hammer on the man's nose. The nose squished. Blood squirted from its nostrils. "Now shut up!"

Clutching his face, the man whimpered and gasped for air.

"Thanks," Boots gasped. "Wanta get him off me?"

Norman pulled while Boots rolled. As the man started to fall sideways, she let go of him.

He flopped facedown.

"Gimme back," Boots said. Kneeling, she untied the yarn sides of the bikini pants. She tugged the garment out from under him and flung it out of the way. Then she sat on his rump, dropped forward, and shoved her right arm underneath his neck. She caught his throat in the crook of her arm. With her left hand, she clutched the man's forehead.

"What're you doing?" Norman asked.

"Gonna choke his ass."

"You're at the wrong end," Duke pointed out.

"Ha-ha. Lotsa help *you* been." Her body started to shudder as she strained.

"You don't wanta do that," Norman told her.

She grunted.

"Hey, come on."

The man began twitching and flopping.

She is trying to kill him, Norman realized. He wondered if he should step in and stop things.

Better, he thought. *Can't just stand here and watch her murder the—*

Somebody pounded on the door. Norman jumped and gasped. The heavy blows felt as if they were striking him in the chest.

"Yeah?" Duke called. His voice sounded very calm. He winked at Norman.

"This is the manager." A man's voice. "What's going on in there?"

"Everything's fine," Duke told him.

"Like fun. Open up the door and let me see, or I'll have to call the police."

"No *problemo*," Duke said. "Hang on a second; I haven't got nothing on." His jeans were a heap on the floor. He stepped over to them, crouched, and picked them up.

Boots acted as if she didn't even care that the manager had come to the door. She was still clamped to the man's back, shaking as she applied pressure to his throat.

The guy no longer thrashed. He lay still.

Norman suddenly felt as if an icicle had been shoved into his guts.

Dead? The guy's dead and somebody's at the door and she isn't even trying to hide the body or anything, and Duke's just walking toward the door as if he actually plans to open it, and he hasn't even got his jeans on, must've just dropped them. . . .

Backing away, Norman stumbled against the edge of the bed. It collapsed his shaky legs. He sat down hard on the mattress. Duke swung the door open wide, then held up both his empty hands and shook his head.

"Sorry about the noise," he said.

"Thought you was gonna put clothes on."

"Sorry," Duke said.

The manager looked him up and down, sneering and shaking his head. "The weirdos are taking over the world."

"Yep," Duke said.

He had an open pocketknife behind him, clamped tight between his buttocks.

Must've gotten it from his jeans.

"I never rented this room to you," the manager said.

"My brother took care of it," Duke said.

"Stand out of my way. I want to see him." The guy looked tough. Old, but tough. Maybe sixty. Thick in the chest, thick in the neck, with a broad red face. Bushy gray eyebrows. Hair the color of steel, short and brushed up. As he entered the room, he shoved Duke aside. "Put some pants on."

Stumbling out of the way, Duke reached behind his rump just in time to catch the falling knife. The manager glanced at Norman, then noticed Boots on the floor on top of the dead man.

"What kinda goddamn *orgy* we got goin' on in here!"

Guess it does count as an orgy, Norman thought.

"All of you, get your clothes on and get the hell out of my motel before I call the—"

Duke made his move.

Look out! Norman yelled. But only in his mind. He didn't say a word. Just watched.

Duke got the manager in the back so hard that the blow knocked him forward a couple of steps. Mouth wide open, eyes bulging, the old guy stood very stiff and reached over his shoulder. Apparently he wanted to find the knife and pull it out.

Duke beat him to the punch.

Pulled it out and stuck it in again. The big old guy dropped to his knees.

He started to cry out, so Norman hurried forward and kicked him in the stomach. That quieted him. And doubled him over. Duke, knife in hand, ambled over to the door.

He stepped outside. Looked slowly to the left and right.

Then he turned around, entered the room again, and closed the door. He flipped his knife into the air. It twirled. He caught it by the handle.

"The night's sure gotten off to an interesting start," he said. "What's anyone fancy doing next?"

CHAPTER SIXTEEN

"Mosby's trailer," Lauren announced, then opened the door.

It's not locked, Pamela thought. *But then who in their right mind would drive all the way out into the desert to Pits, pop. six, to steal a TV?*

If they even get TV broadcasts out here. There's no TV aerials I can see. Before entering the big old aluminum trailer, she glanced back. *No telephone lines, come to that.*

Grimacing at the pain in her injured feet, she followed Lauren inside. The cuts and abrasions on her soles when she'd run barefoot from Rodney weren't serious, but they were sore.

"Home sweet home," Lauren announced with a twirl, arms outstretched. "Stay as long as you want. You're among friends now."

A tear burned in Pamela's eye. "Thank you." She whistled. "Gee, this is a big, big trailer."

"A monster, isn't it?"

"A veritable behemoth." Pamela gave a tired smile.

"You've got a shower. Three bedrooms. Lounge. Kitchen through there. Oh, Sharpe put some beers and cold cuts in the refrigerator."

"Sharpe's a hero."

Lauren's eyes went misty and far away. "Isn't he just?"

"I don't know how I can ever repay you."

"Don't think of it. Sharpe believes in helping people who are down on their luck. We all do." She took a breath. "Now the trailer's hardly this year's model. But it's clean."

"And it belongs to . . ." She recalled the name. "Moby?"

"Mosby."

"Won't he mind?"

"No . . . as a matter of fact he won't be requiring it anymore."

"Oh."

"Now, that's my trailer next to this one. If you need anything, just holler. Right?"

"Right."

"Way to go, girl. Okay, I'll leave you to yourself." Lauren paused. "If you need some 'me' time, that is; otherwise I'll be happy to stay."

"No. I'm fine." Pamela appraised the comfortable furnishings. A huge, puffy sofa looked as if it could swallow her whole. *Maybe that's where I'll find Mosby. Twenty fathoms deep behind the cushions.* "It'd be kinda nice just to lie still in the quiet."

"You've got it. There's no air-con but there's a couple of fans. Besides, now the sun's gone down it soon drops cool in the desert."

Lauren made small talk for a while before she left. Pamela figured that the woman in her flowing hippie clothes had a warm hippie heart. She was concerned for Pamela.

Didn't want to leave her dwelling on what happened just twenty hours ago.

Husband murdered.

House burned.

Abducted by disgusting Rodney Pinkham.

He'd threatened to abuse her in such a vile, degrading way.

Twenty hours. Seems a lifetime ago.

On sore feet she made a tour of the trailer. It was spotlessly clean. She drank cold water from a pitcher in the refrigerator. A row of Bud bottles faced her on the top shelf, left there by her bus-driver savior. Sharpe was the kindest man she knew. No wonder Lauren wanted to marry him. Course, he was weird, though, driving around in the bus with the dummy passengers.

But what's best in this world? Rational and mean, or eccentric and kind? Give me the benevolent oddball any day.

The lounge had the lovely soft sofa, comfortable chairs, plastic apples and bananas in a bowl; on a wall, a framed photograph of an old man standing beside a marlin that had been strung up by its tail. The fish was as long as the man. Both seemed to be smiling. Mosby?

Where are you now, Mosby?

In the pit . . . in the pit!

She closed off the sinister thought. *Old Mosby might simply have retired to Palm Springs. Or the Florida Keys, where even now he's sharpening a fishhook to catch his biggest marlin yet. The old man and the sea.*

Apart from the photo there was no personal stuff, like clothes or photos or car keys, or letters addressed, *Dear Mr. Mosby. . . .* This was an old trailer. Clean. Comfortable. An ideal retreat from the world for those hurt in body and spirit.

A tap sounded on the door.

They've come for you, Pamela. The pit awaits. . . .

"Aw, shut up," she told her runaway imagination. She opened the trailer door to find Nicki standing there with a basket under one arm—the kind that might contain complimentary fruit. She still wore the white pullover and red shorts, but the apron must be on the hook until the café opened its doors tomorrow.

"I just thought I'd drop by."

Pamela smiled. "Come on in."

"Not if you're doing anything?"

"No, I figured on turning in early."

"Oh, I thought I heard voices."

"Voices." Pamela gave a soft laugh despite her exhaustion. "No. That was me."

"Uh?"

"Talking to myself. I guess what happened today has sent me . . . you know . . ." She gave a hop of her shoulder. "Nuts." For a moment she thought she'd start crying again. Fighting it back, she made a wider smile. "Come right on in."

Nicki slipped in through the doorway. Her slim body must be the envy of every woman for miles. And the source of hot thoughts for every man. The blond hair turned her head into a golden glow in the electric light. A Nordic goddess, complete with a ponytail. She could braid that into a long Rapunzel-like plait.

"I've been thinking about your feet," Nicki said.

"Me, too. Every time I stand on them. Ouch." She grimaced. "I guess fear and all that shit made for a natural anesthetic. Now that I'm safe my feet are reminding me what they've been through, too."

"Hurts bad?"

"It's starting to kick in."

"Go through into the lounge and lie on the sofa."

"Well, I—"

"Please. Let me do this for you, Pamela. I've brought things to make you feel good." She moved the basket from under her arm.

Instead of fruit it contained jars of silvery powder and bottles of amber oil.

"I don't have any money. I'm sorry that—"

"No. I don't want you to pay." A pink color flamed under Nicki's dark skin. "Please, never mention money again. We're like sisters. We help each other."

"Sorry, I'm so tired. I'm not thinking properly."

"Of course you're not. You went through hell today. Here, lie down. Let me take care of you. I'll just slip this towel under your feet. There. Good girl. First I'll apply an embrocating oil with healing properties."

Nicki smoothed out the fluffy white towel under Pamela's throbbing feet. Pamela relaxed back on to the sofa with a sigh, lying flat out.

Uh. This sofa's as soft as it looks.

"You just relax," Nicki told Pamela. "Close your eyes while I work some of this in for you. It'll feel good. It contains a natural antiseptic, too." She smiled. "Don't worry; I'll be gentle."

"Thank you. I don't know how I'll—"

"Ah, ah." Nicki held up her finger. "Lie back, close your eyes. Nicki's taking care of business now."

Pamela smiled, then eased her head back onto the cushion. Lying on her back on the sofa she looked up at the trailer ceiling that had been covered with paper that bore a wood pattern in imitation pine. Very 1970s; it reminded her of her grandmother's house. There was something reassuring about the old-fashioned feel. It took her back to her childhood. Nicki knelt on the floor at the other end of the sofa so she could work on Pamela's feet.

Pamela heard a bottle being unstoppered.

Then felt the run of liquid along the top of her feet.

Cold.

"I keep it in the refrigerator," Nicki said. "Not too cold, is it?"

"No . . . wonderful." Drowsy now, she still gazed at the ceiling. "It's putting the fires out."

"Good. You just wait till I'm done. You'll feel as if you're walking on air."

"Ohhh."

"Feel good?"

"Outta this world."

And it did. Using gentle circular strokes Nicki massaged the cold oil into the top of Pamela's foot, then worked the embrocating fluid around the injured soles.

"Hmm," Pamela whispered. "Peppermint. I can smell peppermint."

"Oil of peppermint's good for skin as well as for the digestion. There . . . let me know if it stings."

"No . . . perfect . . ."

This is heaven, Pamela thought. *After the hell of last night I'm in heaven today. This foot massage is truly out of this world.* The oil cooled her burning feet. The sting left the grazes. That feeling of well-being spread through her body, releasing tension in the muscles in her back and face. She felt she'd been like a rubber band twisted so tightly it had bunched into hard knots. Now she was unwinding, muscles softening.

And all the time Nicki's gentle fingers flowed from her Achilles' tendon, along her heel, to the arch of her sole, to the ball of her foot, then smoothed away the hurt in her toes.

Her eyes closed. A sliding motion moved through her that told her she was falling asleep. Her arms twitched a couple of times, but Nicki breathed gentle reassurances that she was safe, that she was going to be okay. And all the time that cool, slippery caress of fingers against her feet. Peppermint scented the air, a tingling freshness that flowed through her nostrils into her bloodstream.

A flurry of dream images drifted through her mind. Home. Jim sitting on the porch swing. Rodney tumbling into the pit. Sharpe driving the bus. The dummies sitting in their seats. The old-timer, Hank. Walking into the café. This time she looked more closely at the diners in their booths. They were all shop mannequins. Even so, their plastic heads turned on stiff necks to stare at her. She looked at where Nicki and Lauren stood. They'd turned into mannequins, too. The Lauren effigy wore her hippie dress, while the Nicki figure wore the white pullover and red shorts. In the dream Sharpe loomed over her. She saw herself reflected in his sunglasses.

"They all came as regular people. But they all turned plastic, too." He grinned. "Same's happening to you. How's those stiff little feet of yours?"

She looked down and saw that her feet had turned into the creamy plastic of a mannequin with fused toes.

Her eyes snapped open. The trailer was in near darkness. Peppermint scented the air. Her feet were still being massaged, only . . .

Only differently now. Raising her head a little, she looked down the length of her body. Nicki still knelt by the sofa. She'd removed her sweater. Holding Pamela's feet by the ankles, she rubbed her big, soft breasts against the soles of her feet. The nipples felt like fingertips.

Nicki had freed her hair. It tumbled loose in blond waves down her naked back. Her face was raised to the ceiling, eyes closed. She moaned with pleasure.

I must be dreaming this, Pamela told herself. *Nicki couldn't be rubbing her bare breasts against my feet. It doesn't make sense. I am dreaming. Have to be.*

She forced herself to close her eyes while repeating to herself. *It's a dream. I'm dreaming. I'm dreaming. . . .*

CHAPTER SEVENTEEN

Norman drove. He didn't know where he drove. . . . *Shoot! Where the fuck he drove.*

Only needed to drive. *Gotta drive. Gotta get away.*

"Norman?"

"Shaddup!"

"Hey." Duke sounded hurt. "I only wanted—"

"Shaddup!"

"Normy, Normy," Boots cooed. "Gotta put your lights on, Normy. It's too dark to drive like this."

Lights! Yeah, lights are good, but—

But all of a sudden Norman was shouting. "What did you have to kill those two guys for? Jesus H. Christ! Boots, you just . . . just strangled a guy."

"Yeah, strangled him bare-assed." Duke chuckled. "S'pose there are worse ways to depart the world."

"And you, Duke!"

"Normy, slow down. Pleezy-weezy."

Not gonna slow down. Never gonna slow down. But what the fuck am I doing with these two murderers in the car? Should have left them at the motel to meet and greet the cops. Not driving with the gruesome twosome that are going to end up broiling in Old Sparky.

Aw, shit.

Get them outta the car, Norman. Get 'em out!

"Now that's hardly fair, Norman." Duke unwrapped a stick of gum. "Sure, Boots strangled the pervert. Sure, I stabbed the old guy, but you, Norman, old buddy, kicked him in the nut nest."

"Nut nest? Nut nest!"

"Switch on your lights." Boots sat in the back, rubbing Norman's shoulder as he drove.

Norman didn't see dark streets at midnight; he saw only the world streaked with bright-red blood. "Nut nest! I didn't kick him in the balls. I kicked him in the . . . ugh."

Oh, no.

Did kick him.

But that's not murder.

"Sure, you kicked him." Duke sounded calm. "But you were helping your buddies. Here, let me get those lights for you. Don't want to run into a tree, do we, now?"

Boots cooed. "Where you taking us, Norman?"

To the cops! Those were the words he wanted to yell. But he'd have to be canny. Find a police precinct. Make some excuse. Dash inside. Tell the first cop he saw, "Hey, I've got two murderers in my car." That'd make sense, wouldn't it? Got rid of these two bozos. Hey, he might even get a citation for heroism. He could see the headlines in his hometown newspaper now.

First, find the precinct.

"Drive nice and legal," Duke told him. "If you don't ease offa that gas you're gonna draw attention to ourselves."

Boots rubbed Norman's shoulder. "Don't wanna get stopped by the cops, do we, Normy?"

Wanna bet?

Won't be me getting all gelled up in Old Sparky. Won't be me biting my tongue in two when they unleash fifty thousand volts through my bod.

"Normy, please. Slow down. We've still got some loving to finish up, haven't we?"

"Yeah," Duke said. "Sure can't pleasure the gal if we wind up in jail."

"Remember what it felt like, Norman?"

Jesus. He remembered. The way her titties jiggled as he thrust his cock up inside her. The way she'd sucked him; the way she'd run her tongue around the big old purple bell while moaning with pleasure.

Made him moan, too.

His first time.

Fucking this fleshy woman . . . fleshy pig woman. Then watching in horror as she wrestled naked with a guy he thought she'd already killed. *Dear God. Dear God in heaven.*

Shaking his head, he eased off the gas pedal. The needle dropped to thirty-five.

"Attaboy, Norman?" Duke slapped his thigh. "I like to burn rubber like the next guy, but we need to lie low until this blows over."

"Blows over? You two killed people tonight. Human beings."

"Human beings. Huh."

Boots confessed, "You shoulda seen what the pervert did to me, Norman. He didn't get no stiffy. So he put things inside of me. Lightbulbs. Shampoo bottles. Then he got a soda bottle. I thought I was gonna cry when he shoved the—"

"Okay, okay!" Norman took a right at random. "But you still shouldn't have strangled him."

"Nice way to go, though, eh, Norman?" Duke's teeth gleamed like a vampire's in the dashboard lights. "Boots's wet pussy in the small of your back, titties tickling you as she puts the squeeze on your neck."

"And you stabbed an old man," Norman protested. "He didn't do nothing to you."

"Would've called in the cops."

"You stabbed him in the back. Twice!"

"You kicked him in the birdcage, Norman, old buddy."

"That makes you"—Boots rooted for the phrase before whispering it in his ear—"an accessory to murder."

"I'm no murderer." Norman knew what he was going to do now. Find a police precinct. Stop the car. Dash inside. These two would be in jail within the hour. Then he'd be free to drive home. Her repeated the words with conviction: "I'm no murderer."

"The cops won't see it like that," Duke told him.

Boots whined, "Yeah, you've got blood on your hands, too. Besides, you still like me, don't you, Norman? You're not gonna go all cold and law-abiding on me? After the nice things I did for you? I even sucked your—"

"Shit!"

"Nice and cool, Norman."

"What's wrong?" Boots asked.

"Cops," Duke said. "Two of them. One cruiser. See the lights?"

"Oooh, yeah. Bright, aren't they?"

Norman stared ahead at the road lit by streetlights. He saw the police cruiser. A cop stood on the sidewalk talking into his radio. The second cop stepped out, holding up his hand.

Oh, shit.

Suddenly meeting a cop wasn't such a good idea. And another big "suddenly": he realized that the bodies had been found in the motel. Duke had wanted to leave them one piled on top of the other. "That way it'll look as if they died fucking each other. Heart failure." *Heart failure! Dear Christ.* One had been strangled while wearing Boots's black knit bikini bottoms. The manager of the motel had been stabbed in the back. Twice. *That ain't natural causes. Not even to a cop with his eyes poked out and his ears filled with fucking candle wax.*

Now the APB had been made. The police must have been given a description of his car. Probably another motel guest had seen the license plate, too.

The trooper took another step out into the road, hand raised.

I'll be in the frame for murder too. I'll wind up in the electric chair. Oh, God, I don't believe this is happening to me. Please, if I can only turn back time. Just five hours. I'll be good. I'll go to church every week. I'll learn to love Jesus. . . .

The cop stood facing him, feet apart, hand raised, palm out.

Stop.

The trooper wants me to stop.

Then the cuffs will go on.

I'm on my way to jail.

Norman screamed, "*No way!*"

Stomped on the gas pedal. The car surged forward.

Duke shouted, "Norman! No. Don't—"

The car slammed into the cop. Norman saw the man's false teeth fly out of his mouth due to the force of the impact. Then the big guy folded over the hood, his face smashing against the steel frame of the windshield. Like a balloon bursting, the man's head burst, splashing blood across the glass.

Norman accelerated. The body lay pasted against the windshield. Norman looked into the man's exploded head with brain matter oozing on the glass. Then the body rolled sideways as Norman hauled a left. When it fell onto the road Norman didn't look back.

Duke was amazed. "You just killed a cop. You just drove into him and *pow!* Wasted him. Did you see his brain coming out of the hole in his head? It was like his skull was taking a shit."

Norman couldn't speak. He could only drive.

"Norman?" Boots was dumbfounded. "Open season on perverts. But I don't know about killing the police. Whatcha think, Duke?"

"Whoa, don't matter what I think." Duke looked back. "Norman. The other cop's following."

"*Shit!*"

Norman glanced in the rearview mirror. The cruiser pounded up the road behind, lights whirling. He pushed the Jeep hard as he could through the quiet—normally quiet—residential neighborhood. Its headlights flashed against trees, parked cars.

"Hey, dude," Duke said, "you're a real Viking, aren't you?"

Norman spat out the words: "The police would have arrested us. They know what you two did to the guys in the motel."

"Didn't look like that to me. Didn't you see potatoes in the road? They'd spilled from the back of a truck."

Boots picked up the thread. "So the police were only stopping us from running over the potatoes?"

"Looks that way."

"Shoot."

"But Norman here had got the killing fever on him."

Norman groaned. The police didn't even know about the motel killings. He'd splattered the guy all over his car for no reason. Automatically, he flicked the wiper stalk to scrape away blood and brain matter from the windshield. It smeared real bad.

"Makes a pretty mess, huh, old buddy?"

Norman glanced at Duke. "The other cop? Is he gaining?"

"Sure, he is. You really think you can outrun a cruiser in this peewee?"

"I've gotta! I'm not going to jail."

"I don't want to go to jail." Boots sounded whiny again. "I was born for lovin' and good times."

Duke asked, "What's the plan, Norman, old buddy?"

"Shut up and lemme drive!"

Norman powered the car out of the residential neighborhood into open countryside. Now the road was surrounded by fields. And flanking the road, a pair of deep, deep culverts.

"Getting closer," Duke warned. "Soon the cruiser's gonna be bumping your ass."

"Oh, God. This can't be happening to me!" Norman hunched over the wheel, teeth clenched, eyes locked on a road lit by the blaze of headlights.

Duke thought for a while, then made an observation. "Shouldn't be surprised if the cop doesn't try and shoot our tires out."

"They'll bring in helicopters, too," Boots said. "I've seen it on TV."

"Out here, Boots? They won't have no copters out here. No." Duke nodded with the conviction of experience. "They'll shoot our tires out. That or try and get a shot at the driver's head."

"Oh, Christ." Norman wanted to go the lavatory badly. Very badly. He was panting. Sweat rolled down his face.

Now I'm going to take a bullet in the brain.

It's just not fair.

He glanced in the mirror. The cruiser was just a dozen yards behind his car. He saw the whirl of its lights. He could even see the grim face of the man whose buddy now lay smashed to crud in the road. The man leaned sideways through the open driver's window.

Norman thought, *Gun!*

That was when he brought both feet stomping down on the brake. The car screamed. Slid sideways. The driver in pursuit wrestled with the wheel to stop from slamming into the back of Norman's car.

Norman watched as the police car roared past. The driver swung out to avoid Norman's vehicle that still kidded sideways along the pavement.

Norman watched.

The police car flipped out, turning over into the culvert in a flurry of sparks, exhaust smoke. He even heard its engine scream as the vehicle became a ball of flame that raced along the water channel. The cruiser eventually slid to a stop, a burning ruin. Containing one dead police officer.

Norman's car came to a halt. Its engine idled. The sudden near silence made Norman dizzy.

"Hey, man." Duke was impressed. "You're a cop killing machine. I never knew you had it in you."

From behind, Boots put her arms around him and kissed his cheek. A wet kiss that felt cold as reptile spit against his burning skin. "Norman. You're my hero."

For a moment Norman watched the burning police cruiser send balls of oily black smoke into the night sky.

Then he said, "We've gotta go where they'll never find us."

Light on the gas pedal now, he drove away from the burning car.

CHAPTER EIGHTEEN

Norman moaned.

Moaned as he drove.

Moaned as his sore eyes stared at what was revealed by the car's lights. Passing trees, road signs, roadkill, diners, gas stations, a lonesome truck hauling timber at two in the morning.

"Ohh . . . what have I done? Jesus, what have I done?"

"You've done two cops, that's what you've done," Duke told him as he combed back his Elvis coif.

"Did you see how the first guy's head burst—pop!—on the windshield?" Boots sounded excited rather than appalled.

I'm in a car with two crazies, he thought. *Two crazed killers. Gotta get out. But . . .*

I'm a crazed killer, too. I just killed a pair of cops. I'm pro cop! I'm pro law and order.

"Oh, my God," he groaned. "What have I done?"

"I can drive, old Buddy." Duke sounded concerned. "You need to relax."

"Yeah," Boots cooed. "Come and rest up in the back here with me."

"No. I've gotta get away from here. The cops will be looking for us."

"Yeah," Boots breathed. "You cracked one like a nut, then toasted the other."

"Wicked." Duke nodded.

"Oh . . . oh . . ." Boots suddenly pounded Norman's shoulder. She was breathless. She was on a high over the violence. "Norman. Pull over. Pull over!"

"What?"

"Pull over just here. Oh . . ."

"What's wrong?"

"Nothing."

"But we've gotta get away from here. Cops will be crawling over the roads. They'll shoot to kill."

"Ain't that always the way?" Duke observed.

"But please, Norman. You've got to pull over. I've gotta do something, otherwise my panties will go pop."

"You need to pee?"

"No."

"The other thing?"

"No."

Norman's mind swam as streetlights flicked past the car. *What has gotten into Boots? Crazy woman. Crazy Pig Woman. With bulging thighs and heaving breasts. Christ, I think I'm going to faint . . .*

"Norman, pull over. *Please.*"

Duke said, "Aren't you going to oblige the lady?"

Norman hardly knew what he was doing anymore. Guilt rolled over him in tidal waves. He could only think of the officers he'd killed. *Their families? Oh, Christ, their families . . .*

The moment he stopped the car Boots almost threw herself out of the vehicle. The road was deserted. Here was countryside. No houses.

Maybe she needs to puke?

Wish I could puke. Get all this guilt out of me . . .

Duke said, "Best kill the lights until she's done."

Done what?

Norman turned as Boots dragged the driver's door open.

What on earth is she doing?

Norman stared at her as she stood panting, her breasts jiggling as she inhaled mightily. "Boots?" he asked.

"Duke?"

"Boots?"

"Duke. You watch or not. I don't care."

"What ya planning, girl?"

Boots gasped like she'd run a marathon. "Sweet Mary. I've never been so turned on. Watching Norman kill those cops and all. I got fire in my veins."

Norman watched her in a daze. What was that woman on?

"Norman. You've gotta let me do this for you. You've gotta. I'll die if you don't."

"Boots?"

Like she was ravenous and couldn't stop herself, she pounced. Hands fumbling like crazy she unbuckled his belt, unzipped him; then her hot hands gripped his penis and tugged it like she was strangling a snake.

"Not now," Norman protested. "Jesus. The cops will be . . . ah . . . ah!"

To his horror, despite the wholesale bloody mania of the last few hours, despite the craziness of her doing this at such a god-awful inappropriate time, he felt himself stiffen beneath her stubby fingers as she worked at him.

"Oh, Norman," Duke said appreciatively. "Reckon your birthday just came early."

"Duke." Boots panted. "Be a gentleman. Shut ya' eyes."

"What? And miss the show? No way."

"Suit yourself." Then she went to work on Norman.

Norman drove. The night was starless. The surrounding countryside was just a blackness.

Empty.

Something strange happened to him inside. He could feel it working up through his stomach into his chest. Then it shot out from his mouth; he clenched his fists around the steering wheel.

"Norman?" Duke looked at him from the passenger seat.

"You okay?" Boots asked from the backseat. She sounded anxious.

The noise coming out from his mouth was getting louder . . . *louder. . . .*

The noise was terrible. Electrifying. Some part of him recoiled in horror.

Then he knew what it was. He was whooping. A real cowboy yodel. Sheer exhilaration.

Exultation.

"*Ya-hoo!*" he hollered. "We did it! We really did it!"

"Yeah," Duke sounded puzzled. "We did it, Norm."

He whooped again, and it turned into a laugh he'd never laughed before. A full-blooded, *manly* laugh. A laugh that belonged to football stars, lumberjacks, burly marines, pro wrestlers . . . you name it. Macho, macho, macho.

"I am a *man!*"

Boots and Duke must have been staring at him, wondering if he'd lost his mind.

"*I'm a man!*"

"Never doubted it," Duke said.

"Tonight, for the first time, I've fucked a woman. I've killed two men." Norman whooped again through the open driver's window. He felt stronger than Superman. Cooler than James Dean. Meaner than Satan. Cuter than Johnny Depp. "*I'm the king of the world!*"

He floored the gas pedal. The car roared into the night. And toward whatever waited tomorrow.

CHAPTER NINETEEN

Pamela woke the next morning feeling full of life. The clock radio told her it was ten thirty-four.

Slept late.

Then sleep heals.

Not only had her feet quit hurting; she felt renewed emotionally. She knew her husband was dead; she was a widow at twenty-three, but she no longer believed she'd go insane with grief. She wasn't immune to that grief, but this was the time to start dealing with it.

Mosby's trailer looked good in the bright California sunlight pouring through the windows. Clean, comfortably furnished, it radiated a homey charm. She went to the closet. Instead of old-man clothes (surely Mosby was the old man pictured with the marlin), there were T-shirts in bright colors—red, blue, green, lemon. Also, there were clean pairs of shorts neatly folded on the shelf. New underwear, too.

Lauren or Nicki must have put them there . . . Nicki! Pamela suddenly remembered last night, when Nicki had massaged the oil into her feet. She remembered the woman's slick fingers soothing her damaged skin. Then she'd fallen asleep.

And woken to see Nicki rubbing her naked breasts against Pamela's feet.

What do I say when I see Nicki? How do I look her in the eye?

Say nothing.

You dreamed it.

Had to have done.

Face it. You were exhausted. You'd nearly been killed. Jim had been murdered by the psycho, Rodney. You were mixed-up. You couldn't differentiate between dreams and reality. Face it, girl, in those circumstances who could?

Quickly she showered, using a fruit shampoo that smelled wonderfully of strawberries. Then she dressed in a lemon T-shirt and white shorts. Whoever had thoughtfully provided the clothes also left pairs of sandals in the bottom of the closet. They were different sizes, but at last she chose some delicate brown leather sandals that had crisscross strapwork across her feet. These fit just perfectly.

It's like "Goldilocks and the Three Bears," Pamela thought. *Now all I need to find are three bowls of porridge—one too salty, one too sweet, and one just right.* She spent some time in front of a mirror running a brush through her hair. A solid silver one, hallmarked, and with the initials CJ elegantly etched into the back. The brush felt so good that she lavished more strokes on herself than she would normally. The light coming through the window made her hair shine like gold.

I shouldn't look this good.

Shouldn't feel this good.

Not with Jim lying zippered in a body bag in a morgue. If there was a body after the fire. If it wasn't reduced to—

Before the wave of tears came, Pamela left the trailer at a run.

Immediately, she saw Hank.

He hailed her and lifted his richly stained hat. "Mornin', ma'am. I figure you might be rushing to see my Dillinger Death Car, but I've been told to point you in yonder direction." He nodded toward the café. "They've a nice plate of vittels waiting for ya."

She blinked back the tears and smiled. "Thank you. And good morning to you. But I don't know if I'm hungry."

"Good eating, my young lovely."

"I never bother with much. Just toast and juice."

"*Haw!* Breakfast's most important meal of the day." He rubbed his whiskery old-timer jaw. The red nose quivered like it had a life of its own. "Then lunch, dinner, and supper come a close second."

"I might rest up in the trailer for a while."

"You got the Mosby place. Mighty fine trailer."

"I like it."

"He always took pride in the thing. He brought the sofa all the way from Tucson."

"I slept on it last night."

"Work of art it is."

"Don't let me keep you from you work."

"Nothing that'll spoil for keepin'." He settled the hat back on his head again. "Don't forget that breakfast."

"I'm not hungry."

"If it's not food you're after, then there's good company."

She looked across at the café. A couple of trucks had been parked outside. She thought about Lauren and Nicki. She smiled.

"Yes, company would be fine right now. Thanks."

"Don't mention it."

As she started to walk through the hot desert sun to the café, Hank called after her: "Now, don't you go forgettin' the tour. See all of Pits with yours truly. There's plenty more to the place than meets the eye."

Pamela walked into the café. Straightaway the aromas of bacon and coffee hit her.

Oh, boy, that does smell good. She realized she did have an appetite after all. The booths were empty, but three guys in denim sat at the counter tucking into plates piled high with food. These must be the truckers that belonged to the two vehicles outside. Well, two drivers plus mate. They were too busy eating for talking.

For a moment Pamela stood by a table, wondering if she'd blush when she saw Nicki. Instead Lauren breezed in from the back. She wore a gypsy-style white blouse with embroidered lapels. To that she'd added a flowing skirt in cool cotton covered with a flower pattern. Definitely the fashion spirit of '69. Lauren smiled warmly when she saw Pamela.

"Good morning, Pamela. Sleep well?"

"Incredibly well. You must have something in this desert air."

"Well, whatever it is, it's free."

"Is Nicki here?"

"Sure. She's out back. Shall I call her for you?"

"Oh, no, don't bother her if she's busy."

"Right, first things first. What can I get you to eat?"

"Normally for me it's toast and—"

"Not on my watch, buster." Lauren smiled. "Grab a table. Let me surprise you."

"Thank you."

"Coffee?"

"That'd be lovely."

"I'll bring orange juice and water, too. You soon get a thirst in Pits."

"Lauren?"

"Yes?"

"I have to tell the police what happened. About Rodney. And what he did to Jim."

"Course you must, honey."

"There's a telephone I can use?"

"Not in Pits, I'm afraid. We lost the cable in a rockfall a couple of months ago."

"The phone company's not repaired it?"

"Low priority. We don't make enough calls to make it profitable."

"But what happens when you need to make a call?"

Lauren paused as if the question surprised her. "Really, I don't know. I guess none of us needs to call anyone in the outside world. Funny, I just never thought about it."

"The police must drop in here from time to time."

"Oh, yes. We recharge them on coffee and doughnuts." Lauren looked at her seriously. "But I know you need to report what happened to you. There's a town a couple of hours' drive from here. You can telephone from there. Now make yourself comfortable. I'll get that breakfast."

Pamela sat at the same table she sat at yesterday. The one with the green Formica top. Through a window she could see Sharpe using a broom to sweep the dust from the side of the bus. He wore shades, and despite the heat he looked as cool and as relaxed as the moment she met him. Just seconds after he'd shot Rodney.

The guy must have ice cream in his veins. I'd melt in that heat out there.

Lauren brought the coffee and ice-cold juice. The juice was heaven to her dry throat. *On a hot day like this God lives in a cold drink*, she thought. She watched the truckers finish up, pay their check, then amble out to their waiting vehicles.

I could hitch a ride with them, she thought. *But then what would they expect in return for transport out of here? A ride for a ride, as the old saying goes.*

No, I feel at peace here. Pits is restful.

Pits is a place where I don't have to confront the burned ruin of my home. Or Jim's grieving family. Or the funeral. Or starting all over in a tiny apartment where I'd sit alone at night after a day's teaching in some bad neighborhood where the next kid you scold for chewing gum in class could pull a blade on you.

"Hi, there, sweet pea."

Pamela looked up. "Hi." It was Nicki, with her Nordic blond hair gleaming in the morning light. The hair was neatly braided. Once more she wore the knit pullover shirt and the bright red shorts. Over those she wore the blue apron with its pockets for the order pad. Her beautifully curved figure was the image of health and vitality.

Nicki engaged her in small talk. Pamela didn't blush. The memory of seeing Nicki rub her full breasts against Pamela's bare feet did have a dreamlike quality to it now. In the brilliance of a Mojave Desert morning, such a thing seemed absurd.

Impossible.

Yeah—just a dream.

They engaged in small talk. With no customers to serve, Nicki slid into one of the seats opposite. Nicki chatted about the massage oils she hoped to sell to the diner's customers. "It's important that Pits grows. We've got the beginnings of a real community here. It needs to start trading with the outside world. Then, as Sharpe brings in more people, we'll have a school one day. It would be lovely to hear children's voices again."

"Sharpe's going to do that?"

"Sure."

"But what makes people want to move to Pits?"

Nicki smiled. "Look around you. There's space. It's clean. There's no crime."

"But . . ." Pamela gave a little shrug, not wanting to dis Nicki's town. "But it's kinda light on facilities—movie theaters, stores, and the like."

"True. But once you get used to it you love it."

"And Sharpe just goes out and picks up people to come live here?"

"Not just like that. He saves people. Men and women who don't have a future in the outside world."

Pamela took another swallow of juice. "I do have a future. A career."

Nicki smiled again. But this time it seemed disappointed, as if she were sad at the idea of Pamela leaving so soon. "That's down to you, of course. You've got to make your own mind up about the future."

Lauren appeared at that moment with a plate of bacon, scrambled eggs, steak, plus fried potatoes.

"Wow." Pamela's mouth watered.

"Figured you could use the protein."

"Figure I'll need to be moved around on wheels after all this. It's a feast!"

"Enjoy."

When Pamela had finished Lauren went back to the counter, then returned with a folded newspaper. "I thought I'd let you finish up before I showed you this."

Lauren sat down beside Nicki opposite Pamela. She unfolded the newspaper and laid it flat on the table.

The moment Pamela saw the photograph on the front page, her eyes blurred with tears. It showed a row of houses with a gap between a pair of them. She recognized the street. In the gap was a charred frame.

Gently Lauren said. "This isn't pretty, but you might want to read it."

"No."

"It might help clarify your plans for the future."

"No. Please . . ."

Lauren leaned forward and rested her hand on Pamela's forearm.

"There's something you should know, Pamela."

Pamela used a napkin to dab her eyes. "I know all there is to know. That bastard, Rodney, murdered my husband and burned my home."

"There is more. You don't have to read it now, but it might be best if—"

"Okay." Pamela took a deep breath. "Get it over with."

"We're here for you, Pamela," Nicki said softly. "We're going to help you any way we can."

Pamela looked at the newspaper, but her teary eyes blurred her vision so the newsprint became black streaks.

"It's no good. I can't read it. My eyes are . . . uh . . ." She sniffed. "You'd think I wouldn't have a tear left in me."

"Don't worry. I'll give you the gist," Lauren said. "It says the firefighters found two skeletons in the debris. One male. One female."

"Female?"

"Yes. Pamela, they believe the remains are yours."

Pamela made a hiccuping sound, partway between a laugh and a cry. "So in the eyes of the world I don't even exist anymore." She took a deep breath. "Of course. It must have been Rodney. He killed another woman and brought her into the house before he kidnapped me. That way . . ." She found her voice breaking. "Th-that way, no one would come looking for me, because . . . because the police would think husband and wife died together."

Pamela looked from Lauren to Nicki. Both regarded her with deep sympathy. They were willing her to be strong.

"'S easy," Pamela said. "I go to the police. Once they see me they'll know I'm alive and . . . and—"

"It's not as simple as that." Lauren chose her words carefully. "You see, Jim's wife flew in from New York."

"No. You're mistaken. I'm his wife . . . *widow.*"

Lauren shook her head. "Jim was already married."

"Impossible. I married him. We honeymooned in Maui."

Lauren reached out to squeeze Pamela's hand. "It looks as if Jim had married before. Only he . . ."

"Neglected to mention it." Pamela's voice hardened. She sat up straight. Stared out of the window. The rocky hills rose into the sky. Now they looked like teeth ready to chew a piece out of it. "And never divorced. So it was a bigamous wedding." She shook her head. "My God. The day before yesterday I was a wife. Yesterday I was a widow." A bitter laugh escaped her lips. "Today I'm neither."

CHAPTER TWENTY

Norman woke up and thought: My God. *The nightmare I've just had. Sex with a piglike woman called Boots. Murder. Me, slaying two cops. A bad, bad dream . . .*

He opened his eyes. "Oh, shit!"

A large face looked down at him, framed by short bleached hair. Hell of a lot of makeup, too. He was lying in the backseat of his car with his head on her lap.

Heart pounding, he sat up.

Looked around.

Duke driving.

Boots smiling at him.

"You slept like a baby," she was saying.

Duke glanced back. "Sweet dreams, big feller?"

"Oh, God . . . oh, my God." Norman shuffled his butt across the seat, away from Boots, trying to cower in the corner with his hand over his mouth.

Repeating: "Oh, my God. Oh, my God . . ."

Should've stayed asleep.

"Oh, my God," he said for the zillionth time. "I thought I'd dreamed it all."

Boots looked hurt. "You thought you only dreamed making out with me?"

"Some wet dream, huh, Norm?" Duke drove one-handed, the other arm straight out across the back of the passenger seat.

"Oh, you mean you thought you dreamed all the other stuff? Zapping those cops. That turned me *soooo* on."

"Yeah, you were awesome, man." Duke gave the horn a couple of toots to celebrate his appreciation.

"You shouldn't do that, Duke," Norman warned. "Draws attention to us."

"You mean cops? Shit, Norm, everything's dandy."

"Yeah." Boots waved her hands to point out of every window at once. "No one about."

Blinking against the bright sun, Norman looked out. The road ran through wooded hills. There were no buildings he could see.

"Bear-shit country," Duke observed.

"I like cartoon bears. Don't think I'd like to meet the real thing."

"No bear would dare tangle with you, Bootsy girl." Duke laughed.

Boots laughed along, then: "Anyone hungry?"

"We've got soda and some leftovers from the beach picnic." Duke sounded matter-of-fact.

Matter-of-fact, like—Jesus H. Christ—we never killed four people yesterday. Norman was stunned.

Couldn't speak.

Kept thinking what his father would say.

"Mr. Wiscoff. Your son, Norman, is a cop killer. He'll get fifty thousand volts for the crime." Norman could hear the lawyer's words right now. *What's worse? The murders? Or the shame I'll bring on my family?*

He didn't know.

What was that Oliver Hardy said when his and Stan's plans went awry and they were up shit creek sans paddle? *"Oh, Gabriel, blow your horn."*

Ollie was inviting the archangel to bring the world to an end so he wouldn't have to suffer the consequences of whatever mess the twosome had gotten into.

"Oh, Gabriel, blow your horn."

"What you say back there, bud?"

Norman sighed. "Nothing."

"Sure am hungry," Boots said. "Anyone else hungry?"

"I just told you, girl, we've got leftovers."

"I don't want no picnic leftovers. I want real food. On a plate. With steam coming off of it."

Norman sat up straight. "If you think you can pull up to a diner, think again. The police will be looking for this car."

"The man's right," Duke said. "A red Jeep Cherokee with cop brain stuck to the windshield. Dead giveaway." Then he said something that appalled Norman. "We're going to ditch the car."

"Ditch it?" Norman gasped. "It's my dad's car. He'll be livid."

"Livid? Maybe the fact his loving son's a cop slayer will take his mind off losing the car."

"Besides." Boots patted her hair in place. "If it's your daddy's car then you won't have had the sweat of paying for it."

"We can't just *leave* it."

"Dead straight, Norm. Don't want to walk everywhere, do we?"

"Not me," Boots said. "Makes the skin on my heels hard."

Norman glanced down at thick, sunburned thighs. Those feet had to ship some heavy-duty meat for a living.

"So this is the plan." Duke glanced back. "We find another car. Dump this one where the cops don't find it in a hurry. Then—"

"Then get some chow," Boots stressed.

"Get some chow," Duke agreed.

"I'm never gonna eat ever again," Norman announced with feeling.

"Then we drive due south."

"South?" Norman would have preferred exit to another galaxy. Cops had a long reach.

"South," Duke repeated. "Get out into wilderness country, where we can lie low."

Norman glanced back through the window at the receding road. He expected to see police cruisers appear with lights flashing at any second.

"Don't sweat it," Duke said. "We're three hundred miles from the motel. You know the one?"

"Yeah, I know the one."

"The one where Norman stopped being a virgin."

Boots smirked. "Maybe they'll put up a plaque one day. 'Norman popped his cherry here.'"

"Or rename the motel," Duke speculated. "Norman's First Hump . . . or how about this? The Cockwell Inn."

Duke and Boots laughed.

Norman groaned, "Oh, my God."

Then Duke nodded at a dirt track that led from the road. "This is where we pick up our brand-new conveyance."

Norman began to understand the implications of the plan. "Jesus. We're going to steal one?"

"No." Duke snorted. "We're going to stop the car. Get out. Get down on our knees then pray to the Almighty that he deliver a hot BMW straight from heaven."

Boots and Duke laughed again while Norman's heart sank into the dark pit of his stomach.

The house. Two stories. Shingle roof. Barn. Workshop. Despite the heat of the sun-filled day, blue smoke rose from the chimney.

"They got a car," Boots whispered as Duke stopped the Jeep in the shade of a tree.

"Check out the pickup truck." Duke pointed to where the white pickup was partly hidden by the barn. "That's gonna have more poke than the old rice boiler."

Though it was close on a hundred yards away, Norman could make out that the car parked outside the front door of the house was an aged Datsun.

"What ya gonna do, Duke?" Boots asked.

"I'm going backward, that's what I'm gonna do, Bootsy girl."

"Careful," Norman said. "There's a lake behind us."

"Perfect. Once we have the pickup, Norman, you roll the car into the lake."

"Into the lake? My dad's car?"

"Yeah. Gonna be no use to us now."

"More use to the cops," Boots added. "Fingerprints and stuff."

Norman took a deep breath. "Okay, let's do it."

Duke switched off the motor.

Turned back, a surprised expression beneath his Elvis coif.

"Aren't you forgettin' something, Norman?"

"Forgetting what?"

"Forgettin' to say shit like, 'Are you sure about this? Aren't we break-ing the law? Won't we get into trouble? What if we get found out? What if we get our asses busted?'"

"That's what you say normally Norm." Boots snickered. "Hey, did you hear what I said? Normally Norm? That's kinda—"

"We heard." Duke opened the door, then said to Norman, "That guilt thing ain't eating you no more."

Boots leaned sideways on the backseat to squeeze Norman's knee. "He's becoming one of us."

They approached the house under the cover of bushes at the side. From the porch roof, eaves, house walls, tree branches hung around a hundred wind chimes. Under the hot sun there wasn't much wind, but there was enough.

The chimes turned.

Tinkled.

Chinked.

Sang.

A robot chorus of tinny voices.

I'm going through with this, Norman told himself. *And I don't feel bad. I'm not wanting to wretch with guilt.*

That's because you've done worse than steal a car.

Cop killer.

"Oh, Papa," he breathed. "If you could see me now."

Duke had led the way through the bushes to the house. Now he held his finger to his lips. "You two stay put. Come forward to the porch when I whistle."

Norman whispered, "You going to hot-wire the truck?"

"I figured using an ignition key would make life easier."

"Where you gonna find the key?"

"Where do you think?"

"Leave him to it," Boots whispered. "Duke knows what he's doin'."

Duke winked. "Duke does, baby."

With that he stood up; then, in plain view, not skulking, not looking shifty, he strolled up to the house, giving the Datsun just the barest side-long glance.

"Norman?"

"Huh."

"Kind of sexy here under the bushes."

"Don't start that now, Boots."

"Normy, Normy, Normy."

"Quit touching."

"Betcha I can get you hard."

"Not now."

Norman tried to watch Duke's progress. Especially as he walked with the knife in his hand that stayed behind the back of his thigh, so it wouldn't be seen from the house.

"Norman . . ."

"What?" He turned to Boots, who tried to look coy, one of her thick fingers resting against her fleshy lips. Even in the dappling of shadow and sunlight under the bushes she looked broad. A heavy blend of muscle and fat. Her bare arms were thick, and a patchy red with sunburn from yesterday, while her elbows had scabbed from carpet burn.

Must be from when we made love yesterday.

Made love?

Sheesh. We screwed her, plain and simple.

But there was something about her smile and her take-me-I'm-yours eye contact that sent a shivery tingle up his spine.

"Remember what I did for you in the car yesterday, Norman?"

"Uh-huh."

"Wanna do it again?"

"Now?"

She nodded. "Here."

For a heavy girl she moves fast. She pushed him so he sat on his butt, taking his weight on straight arms, his hands planted just behind him. She got down on her knees, unzipped him.

"Boots . . . ah, ah, you pick your times. . . ."

" 'S good, 's nice . . ." She slurped.

The girl had to be crazy.

Getting horny at a time like this.

Stealing a truck.

Duke knocking on the door.

Oh . . . but it feels so good.

Her bleached hair bobbed up and down in the shadow. His heart thudded. Blood roared through his neck.

His head swiveled from watching Boots . . .

. . . to watching Duke. His body masked the knife. He looked cool as James Dean standing there, oiled blond coif shining in the sunlight. He tapped on the screen frame with his free hand.

Cooing, whispering, Boots did incredible things with her mouth.

Holy shit.

That's good.

That's the best.

Boots is good at this.

Must have had practice aplenty.

Dizzy with the erotic thrill of it all, he watched a thin guy in dungarees step into the doorway while holding the screen open.

Couldn't hear much. But Duke was talking to the guy. A guy of around sixty in a red cap.

Duke pointed at something away in the trees. The guy stepped out onto the porch to look, shielding his eyes against the glare of the sun. Duke smiled pleasantly. Came across as chatty. The bony guy in the cap appeared relaxed. The young stranger turning up at his door didn't make him suspicious.

Boots moaned. She was aroused too. With one hand she opened her blouse, flipped her bra to expose a jiggling white boob.

He moaned. "Uh . . ." This was too much.

Pleasure overload.

But he had to see what Duke did next.

Duke still talked to the guy, circling around to stand beside him, still pointing.

Saying what?

"Hey, mister, you don't know me, but I've just seen a truck come off of the road, yonder. Driver's hurt bad."

Or:

"Is that a helicopter that's crashed in the trees?"

Or:

"*Just seen the mayor buck naked in the lake. He's swimming there with the chief of police and the high school principal.*"

Whatever.

It worked.

The old guy stared good and hard toward a line of trees.

Duke moved.

Raised his knife hand.

Blade catching the sun, a hard quicksilver glitter.

Boots sucked harder.

The old guy shouted.

Norman shouted.

Boots had worked her crazy, erotic magic on him all over again.

CHAPTER TWENTY-ONE

"You've really got to educate yourself not to shout out when I'm taking care of business."

Duke finished rolling the body under the crawl space of the house, then let down the trellis flap to hide it.

Boots wiped her mouth, smearing her lipstick a little. "My fault. I got Norman all carried away."

"Gotta get smart; otherwise the cops will be snapping on the cuffs in no time at all." Duke plucked his knife from a porch timber, where he'd planted it for safekeeping. He wiped the blood off on the grass. "Like I say, I don't do jail."

Boots fluttered her eyelids and in her breathy way cooed, "Sorry, Mr. Duke."

"Aw, shit. Who could stay mad at you?"

Norman looked up at the house. Close up it wasn't looking too healthy, with its paint cracking and peeling, and missing shingles.

"Say. Anyone else at home?"

"Nah. Only old Mr. Brundle." Checking that the blade was clean, Duke slid the knife into his motorcycle boot. "And his wife."

"His wife?"

"Don't have a cow, Norman. She's not going to beat us up."

Boots growled. "I'd like to see any woman *try* and beat me up."

"Ain't our Bootsy girl formidable?"

"Yeah," Norman agreed.

Half woman; half sow.

Only . . .

She is kinda exciting.

He remembered the look of joy on her face as he squirted his twin-pack into her sucking mouth.

Maybe I'm becoming more like Duke, he thought. *I'm seeing the world differently. Seeing babes differently.*

"Anyone hungry?" Duke asked.

"You betcha. Could eat a hairy-assed goat." She licked her lips.

"What we gonna do with the guy's wife?"

Duke shrugged. He didn't care. "Mister said she couldn't move around by herself these days."

"Probably tucked up in bed," Boots observed. Then a thought occurred that pleased her. "Hey, guys. There might be a spare bedroom. We could grab some shut-eye."

"And anything else that comes our way." Duke winked. "What say you, Norm?"

"I've gotta eat first." Boots crossed the porch to the door.

"An army marches on its stomach." Duke gave a little bow to Norman. "After you, bud."

"The guy's wife must be upstairs," Norman said as they helped themselves to beers from the refrigerator in the kitchen.

"Go tuck her in if you like." Duke took a slug of beer.

"Probably an invalid. My grandma was an invalid," Boots said. "Welfare paid us money to keep her, but you know, after a while she got—"

This is a story I don't want to hear, Norman told himself. "Hey, there's bunch of steaks in the refrigerator."

"Great choice, Norman." Duke checked out a shelf. "Got a skillet. Bound to be some grease for frying hereabouts. Ah, tomatoes in the basket."

"I got the bread." Boots held up a loaf.

"I thought I heard something."

"Probably the old lady turning over in bed."

"Or coming downstairs." Norman wondered what the tough guy would do to the dead man's wife.

Duke bit into a bright-red tomato. "Say, Norm, check out the freezer for french fries. I'm as hungry as a horse."

Norman went to the big chest freezer in the corner. Flipped the lid.

"Holy shit!"

"No french fries?"

Norman backed off, staring into the cavernous interior as freezer mist rolled out into the warm air.

"What's wrong, babe?" Boots sauntered across, her white footwear clicking on the boards.

"We gotta get out of here," Norman spluttered.

"Oooh-wee. The old guy was right about his wife being not much of a walker."

"Hey." Duke smirked. "He put the old lady on ice."

Norman stared at the frozen body of an old woman with blue-rinsed hair. The eyes were open.

One peered left.

The other stared right.

Her lips were as gray as her skin. She looked as if she'd sneaked into the freezer for a nap.

"Wonder why he froze her up like that?" Boots poked the old woman in the eye with her finger. It looked as hard as glass.

Duke pursed his lips, considering. "Sentimental attachment."

"Or necro-fuller," Boots suggested, giving the nose an experimental prod.

"Phrase is necro-filler," Duke corrected.

Necrophilia! Norman would have shouted the word, but seeing Boots prodding the rock-solid woman made his insides feel strange.

"Close the lid." Norman swallowed. "Now."

"Guy's right. There's no french fries I can see. Boots, peel some potatoes."

"Like fun I will."

"I'll peel the potatoes," Norman said. Gratefully he released a lungful of air when Boots closed the lid.

"Ain't he a gent?" Duke patted Boots's rump. "He doesn't want to see the lady spoil her nails."

Boots looked around at the kitchen. "We should check the house over. Might be money. We're gonna need cash."

"Smart as well as sexy," Duke said appreciatively. "Ain't she a catch?"

"You betcha, Duke." Norman turned his eyes away from the freezer-cum-casket with an effort.

Went to the sink. Ran water. Started peeling potatoes. He did it mechanically.

Wonder what it's like to kiss a frozen corpse on the lips?

Shit. His imagination supplied the sensations. *Like pressing ice to your lips.*

"We're gonna take a look around," Duke said. Then to Boots: "Coming?"

"Only in ya' dreams, buster."

Then, giggling girlishly—punctuated by swinish snorts—she ran from the kitchen with Duke slapping her heavy rump. Norman heard their footsteps go clumping upstairs. Presently he heard Boots giggling in a breathy kind of way. That was pretty muffled.

But not the *squeak-squeak* of bedsprings coming through the ceiling.

Norman forced himself to concentrate on peeling the potatoes. But every so often thoughts intruded.

Old boy dead under the crawl space.

Wife frozen like a pea in the freezer.

Dear Lord.

What kind of nightmare have I fallen into?

As he carved the skins from the potatoes, nicked out eyes with the point of the blade, he heard the creak of the bed.

Sometimes it sounded like the creak of the deep-freeze lid.

Then his head would twist around so fast his neck muscles would hurt.

She's climbing out the deep freeze.

Gonna get you, Normy boy.

Each time he looked he was convinced he'd see the old girl's gray face, with gray lips, with eyes that looked out to the sides like those of a fish. He'd see her peeping out at him with the appliance lid resting on her blue-rinsed hair.

"*Come join me in the deep freeze, sweetheart.*" He could almost hear the whispered invitation. "Come cuddle up with old Mother Brundle. It's safe and dark in here."

Shut up!

The *creak-creak* of bedsprings sang down through the ceiling at him.

Duke and Boots would be naked up there. He'd be boring into her like he planned to come out clean on the other side.

Then there was the old ice maiden. He was sure he could hear movement in the deep freeze.

Maybe he should check on her? Make sure she was dead.

Maybe he should go upstairs. Make up a threesome.

Maybe he should grab the Datsun's keys. Make dust.

The thought caught him by surprise. He looked across the kitchen where a wooden board had been fixed to the wall. Beneath a picture of a German shepherd were the words: LET ME GUARD YOUR KEYS.

Beneath that ditty were little metal hooks where bunches of keys hung. Some were car keys.

In five seconds he'd have the keys in his hands.

He would need to go close to the deep freeze, though, with its ice maiden.

Worth the risk.

Because in twenty seconds he could be driving away from here.

Alone.

Duke would still be humping Boots.

Never know he'd gone.

Until it was too late.

Sweet.

Where would I go?

Who cares, as long as I've dumped the crazy duo?

He put the knife and partly peeled potato in the sink, dried his hands on a towel, then moved slowly toward the keys that glinted in the light bouncing through the windows. Outside, it was still in the isolated valley. The sun shone down on the trees. In the distance the open road beckoned.

Gonna be free of Duke and Boots. No more madness. No more killing.

Be away from the deep-freeze lady, too. I'm sure I can hear her running her fingernails across the metal sides in there.

He reached the key keep. Yeah, there were the car keys. One had the word DATSUN impressed on its plastic fob. He could be driving away from here within the next few moments.

Norman reached out. Touched the keys.

"Hey."

The shock nearly blew his heart clean out of his chest. He spun, expecting to see the old lady standing up in the deep freeze, hands on hips, demanding to know what the game was.

Instead, he turned to see Duke standing in the doorway with a rifle in his hands. He was buck naked.

"What you got there, Norm?"

"Uh?"

"Those the keys?"

"Uh . . . sure. Just checking them out."

"Good move," Duke said brightly. "You never know when we might have to shoot out of here. Grab this."

He threw the rifle to Norman.

Norman caught it. Its weight nearly dislocated his fingers.

"Found this upstairs. Thought it might come in useful if you get any surprise visitors."

"Thanks."

"How soon until chow time?"

"Not long."

"Just give us a yell when you serve up. That Boots is insatiable, you know?"

"I know."

With his legs shaking, his belly full of watery sensations, Norman went back to peeling the potatoes.

Upstairs the bed began its *creak . . . creak . . . creak. . . .*

Okay, okay, I could go just right now.

Grab the keys.

Race the Datsun down the track to the road.

But he couldn't do it. He realized when he went to get the keys just before Duke showed up in the kitchen doorway that his heart just wasn't in it.

Have they gotten some kind of hold over me? he wondered.

Maybe it's Boots. A sexual magnetism.

Or maybe I need Duke's instinct for survival to protect me.

I'm a cop killer. If I'm busted then it's the end of everything for me.

No future.

Not even a heartbeat.

He thought about the dead woman lying in her ice tomb. *No. Not me. I don't do death.*

CHAPTER TWENTY-TWO

Duke said, "That was great steak, Normy. Just how I like it."

Boots patted his knee. "Yeah, so rare a good doctor could get it breathin' again."

"Thanks."

Norman had been driving two hours. The house was a long way back in the isolated valley.

Along with . . .

The old guy stabbed by Duke.

The old gal in the deep freeze.

And . . .

Ouch!

His red Jeep Cherokee.

Duke'd released the brake so it'd coasted down the slope into the lake, where it disappeared with a gurgle. In minutes all that remained were a few bubbles and spreading blooms of oil on the water, painting iridescent rainbow colors.

Shit.

Loved that car, man. Really loved it.

Only they had to ditch it, and replace it with the pickup truck that had belonged to the old guy, who now lay in the crawl space with only spiders for company.

The Ford pickup was a dull blue. Ten years old. But it ran well.

The old-timer must have lavished attention on it. Loved it, just like I loved my little red Jeep.

Norman imagined the old guy checking the oil, or inflating the tires with an old hand pump, while his wife baked apple pie in the kitchen. Then one day the guy had gone indoors to find his wife dead.

Couldn't bear to say good-bye.

So he'd emptied the deep freeze. Plonked her inside.

Norman shivered despite the heat.

Ahead the road was clear of traffic and sunlit.

Now all three amigos sat in the single row of seats in the front of the truck, Duke nonchalantly resting his elbow on the door frame with the window rolled down inside the shell. He chewed gum, wore shades, looked cool.

Boots sat beside him, legs apart, dirty white footwear gleaming under the dash. She hummed. There was no tune. Could have been a crappy old refrigerator motor sound for all Norman knew, or cared.

"Hmmm . . . hmmm . . . hmmm . . ."

Duke grinned. "Hey, that's one of my favorite songs."

Favorite song? Christ. That noise is flat and as tuneless as you can get!

Duke started to sing the Elvis classic, "Are You Lonesome Tonight?"

Boots could change the words to sing, "Are You *Loathsome* Tonight?"

Yeah, that's the woman's own personal anthem, for sure.

Duke sang most of the song. He was pretty good. Maybe he could have made it as a bar singer, with his cool, bad-boy looks. He'd never be an Elvis impersonator, though. Norman was sure Duke would figure that as being too cheesy, too uncool. Duke probably worshiped Elvis as a god. Though he probably wouldn't admit that either.

"What we get?" The breeze zithered Duke's hair.

Boots paused her hum. "Back at the old boy's house?"

"Yeah."

"Got some homemade jerky, cookies, soda—"

"No, Bootsy babe. The gold that folds."

"Uh . . . oh . . . six hundred . . . and eight dollars."

"Not bad."

Yeah, so we robbed the house, too.

Add it to the charge sheet, why don't you?

In the light of me killing two cops that's kid stuff. Bring it on, Joe Blow. . . .

Norman drove one-handed. His window was down. He could smell the grasses in the fields as well as the asphalt of one hot road that rolled due south. Here the countryside was flatter. There were cows. Farms. Small, drowsy towns with diners, barbershops, convenience stores.

I'm turning into Duke, he thought. *Here I am driving with my elbow out the window, wearing shades, chewing gum. For the first time in my life a girl might look at me and think, "Hey, that guy's cool."*

Norman smiled.

Yeah, what I've done in the last twenty-four hours has buried Normal Norman. Meet the new guy, Norm, prince of cool.

"I got something else, too," Boots said. She was rooting something from a brown paper grocery bag. "Normy, you think you could get these off for me?"

Norman glanced down.

The prince of cool saw a pale hand with slender fingers.

Boots had short, stubby fingers. Like thick pegs. Chewed nails.

This hand had a speckled back. Thin fingers. Gold wedding band. A diamond ring on the middle finger.

A fingertip touched his bare forearm.

"*Holy shit!*"

He braked so hard the pickup screamed three-sixty. The smell of burning rubber polluted an otherwise finely scented day.

"Shit, shit, shit!" He threw open the truck door. Jumped out.

Danced.

Shouted, "Shit, shit, shit!" while wiping at that cold sensation on his arm where the finger had made contact.

"I didn't mean to startle you, Normy," Boots said, looking out through the door. Her eyes were all innocent-looking.

"You broke off the old woman's hand? You broke it off? You brought it with you!" He was shouting the words. "I don't believe you'd do such a—"

He held his breath. *Jesus Christ. That's just it. I do believe she'd do such a thing. Boots is capable of anything. She'd choke the pope if she took a fancy to his robes.*

"Jesus, Mary, and Joseph." He had to remove his sunglasses as a fear sweat ran down his face. "You could have waited until I'd stopped the car."

Duke laughed. "Just a little Boots joke. Ain't that right, Boots?"

"Yeah, I thought you'd see the funny side." She held up the hand so she could see how the diamonds caught the light. "I like these sparklers, though."

"You keep it, Boots," Duke told her. "You're worth a tubful of diamonds. Isn't that right, Norman?"

Norman managed to grunt, "You betcha."

"Here's your present, Boots."

"Oh! Thank you, Duke."

Norman watched the pair in the truck. She kissed Duke's cheek. She was overjoyed. Tearful.

"No one's never given me a diamond ring before. I'm just so happy to hang out with you two. You're the best."

"Don't mention it, girl." Duke broke off the frozen finger. Threw the snapped digit out of the cab. Norman danced to avoid the white stick-like thing as it bounced on the road near his feet.

"There you go, beautiful." The ring wouldn't even make it over the first joint of Boots's stubby middle finger. With some spit and shoving he got it onto her pinkie.

Boots gushed with a mixture of tears and smiles. "Oh, thank you, guys. I'm never gonna take it off. Never, ever."

"You deserve it. Ain't that so, Norm?"

"You sure, do." Norman backed away as Duke broke off the third finger. *Know what's coming next.*

Duke slid off the wedding band. Then he threw the finger out of the truck, where it bounced onto the road tar near Norman's feet. In the hot sun the fluid content of the digit began to melt. Liquid blood began to ooze from arteries that trailed like soggy noodles from the raw end of the finger. Duke now hurled the hand. It sailed close by Norman's ear.

Thumped down into the long grass at the side of the road.

"Something for the coyotes to snack on," Duke said, then, "Hey, Norman, you gonna start driving?"

An eighteen-wheeler swept by. The driver laid into the horn, as their pickup still blocked half the road sidelong.

Boots complained, "You don't want to see us get killed out here, do you, Norman, honey?"

Hold that beautiful thought.

As he returned to the pickup a police cruiser glided up.

The cop rolled down his window. "You guys in trouble?"

Norman thought he'd crap his pants. But to his surprise his reply was cool as milk. "We just spun out there, Officer."

"Yeah?"

"My fault," Norman said. "A bee flew into the cab. Tried to sting me."

"You don't say."

"Guess I just panicked."

"Sorry, Officer," Duke called from the pickup. "Our friend's a bit of a wuss."

"Looks like that to me, too," the officer observed. "Y'know bees don't bother you, unless you bother them."

"I'll remember that, Officer," Norman said. "Sorry to trouble you."

"No trouble for me, son. You'd best be on your way before another big rig comes this way; otherwise your vehicle's gonna end up tinfoil."

"Yes, sir."

Norman smiled. Waved. Climbed into the driver's seat.

Just hope that the cop doesn't glance down on the road and see those deep-frozen fingers melting there on the road tar.

Norman keyed the ignition. The engine clunked, rolled, whirred.

Didn't start.

"Sure you're not having any trouble?" the cop called from his car.

"No, sir. We're fine."

Fine, fine, fine. Oh, God, please don't let him recognize us. We've ditched the red Jeep, but surely every cop in the state has been radioed our descriptions.

"Come on, truck," Norman muttered. "Start. In the name of God, please start."

He turned the key again.

Click. Whirr. No go.

"Take it easy," Duke said coolly. "Just try a little more gas."

Norman tried again. The engine fired.

He waved at the cop to say everything was okay.

Yeah, as if . . .

The cop nodded, his face impassive.

Oh, God, maybe he's remembering the APB. Two guys and a girl in white boots. Cop killers.

The cop pulled a wad of gum from his mouth, rolled it between thumb and forefinger. Then he flicked it through the open window.

Norman watched the gob of gray drop beside the old woman's wedding finger sans gold band.

Oh, Christ on an ass.

The cop stared impassively at Norman in the truck.

Norman's artificial smile took on huge proportions.

Stop grinning, you ape, he told himself. *That kind of grimace screams guilt.*

Any second the cop was going to pull his revolver. Maybe loose off a couple of caps into Norman's chest for good measure.

Then the cop gave a nod, eased the cruiser past the pickup. Norman pressed the gas pedal. Not hard, so he pulled away in a smooth, law-abiding way.

No wheel spin.

No fugitive dash.

"That's it," Duke purred. "Drive away nice and slow. Don't give Mr. Police Officer any cause for suspicion."

"Norman's turning into one cool customer." Boots rubbed his inner thigh. "I like Normy more every hour that passes. I'm gonna treat him to something nice tonight."

Norman gently accelerated along the road. He glanced back in the mirror.

The police cruiser was pulling away, too, in the opposite direction. Norman expected at any second that its lights would start whirling and the cop would pull a tight U in the road and chase them.

But the cop had other things on his mind.

He eased his big black-and-white along the highway, receding all the time.

Norman let out a sigh and a half. "Phew-wee. I did okay, didn't I?"

"You did just fine, Norman, old bud. Just fine."

As the sun started to set Norman was figuring they'd done six hundred miles in the pickup.

Still aiming the Ford's nose due south.

Duke said. "We need to eat. We need to sleep."

"I'm thirsty, too," said a drowsy Boots.

"We've plenty of cash. We'll stop at the next motel."

"Ooh-wee." Boots sighed. "My skin's itchy. Could use a shower, then a big, big, soft bed."

"You've got it, babe."

Boots ran her fingers up Norman's thigh. "Could you use a nice, clean motel room?"

In a laid-back way, Norman shrugged. "Yeah, cool."

Inside his heart lurched.

Oh, my God. A motel room. Here we go all over again.

CHAPTER TWENTY-THREE

Pamela's life had been exploded.

Demolished.

Torn asunder, as the old phrase goes, she thought. *Marriage was the foundation I'd built my life on. Rodney was a murderer who killed my husband and made me a widow. Now I've learned that Jim was still married when he went through the wedding ceremony with me. He's a bigamist.*

A dead bigamist.

Rodney killed him. Burned him.

But who's the biggest rat? Rodney or Jim?

Pamela had walked out into the desert to be alone. She'd climbed into the rocky hills that seemed to glow like fire beneath the afternoon sun. Now she stood on the edge of a rock that ended in a fifty-foot drop. Below her, and quarter of a mile away, was Pits. She could see the diner, the old house, the line of trailers, vehicles. Even Sharpe as he crossed the road to climb into his bus full of mannequins.

Sharpe saves, she told herself. *Saves people who are so down on their luck that even the bottom of a well would be a long way up for them. And then some . . .*

I could end it here. Just requires one step forward. Then a fall of a few seconds through hot, dry air to even hotter rocks at the bottom of this cliff.

No more hurt. No more misery.

Just the perfect forgetfulness of oblivion.

Takes one step, Pamela . . . that's all. . . .

Pamela's head spun. Heat rising up from the white rock bore the intensity of a furnace. In the desert stood saguaro cacti. Like a whole army of people watching her. Waiting for her fall.

Waiting for the crunch of her meat and bone on rocks. The hiss of her blood leaking onto stones that were thirsty after a hundred years of drought. Above, clear blue sky. Vultures whirled.

Yup, they knew what she was gonna do.

Seen suicide before. Knew the signs.

Knew the sweet taste of self-killed flesh.

Pamela's knees turned watery. She leaned forward. When she looked down now it was all the waaaayyy down. . . .

"There's a better way than this, miss."

"Sharpe?"

Pamela squinted into the brilliant sunlight. There was Sharpe in silhouette. Easy to make out his flattop haircut, the glint of his shades reflecting two perfect images of her face with the cluster of buildings that was Pits behind her.

"This is only a fifty-foot drop," he said. "If you go across yonder you can drop into the mine pits themselves. Don't know how deep they are."

"How'd you know I was gonna—"

"Kill yourself? Know the signs. When someone has that defeated look in their eye that's so deeply rooted it goes all the ways through into the soul. That's when I know."

"You know what my husband did?"

"Bigamy. Sure."

"I could face being a widow. Not this."

"Ashamed?"

"Wouldn't you be?"

"It's your fault?"

"I was gullible. I should have—"

"Gullible don't make you guilty. Anyways, I don't see how you could have known. Married men don't come with the word tattooed on their chests."

She looked up at his face but could see no expression, because the dazzling presence of the sun was directly behind him. "This is just *so* not fair."

"Not fair isn't a self-execution offense, is it?"

A tear squeezed onto her cheek, where the fierce sun stole the moisture in a second. "I just want to stop thinking about what Jim did . . . hell, what Rodney did, too. It hurts, Sharpe."

"Sure, it does. And if you want to stop the hurt, there's the pit."

"Where is it?"

"Back that way. It's a long drop, but it'll do the job."

"Show me, will you?"

"So long, you might fall all the way to China."

Despite her misery, she laughed. "China. Yeah, China's just about far enough away." A smile had found its way to her face. She raised her head to show Sharpe that maybe she wasn't as deeply depressed as she had first seemed.

There was no Sharpe.

She looked down at Pits again. Sharpe was stowing cartons into the hold of the bus.

Hey, Sharpe . . . how come you got back down there so quick?

That's impossible.

Can't be two places at once. Not even Sharpe.

But then, he found me just as Rodney was going to shoot me. Right time, right place.

"Gee, Sharpe, you've gotta be an angel in disguise."

Just for a moment, the shadows falling on Sharpe from the bus's luggage compartment doors fell across his shoulders. Dizzy, eyes blurred, Pamela saw the shadows as wings unfurling from Sharpe's back. He straightened after stowing a box.

Even from this distance he seemed to be looking at her.

Looking directly at her through those shades of his.

Impossible.

Can't see me way up here. Not properly anyway.

But Sharpe is special. "Sharpe, you are an angel," she whispered.

Light-headed from the heat, she tottered forward. Below, the rocks at the bottom of the cliff seemed to leap at her. Quickly, she stumbled back to safer ground.

She shouted, "No!"

I'm not going to kill myself. Rodney was a murdering rat. Jim was a lying rat. Both rats are now dead.

And there's no reason you, Pamela, need join them.

"I'm going to live," she told herself, her head held high. "I'm going to make my home in Pits. And I'm not going to let Rodney or Jim, and what they did to me, ruin my life." She called out to the sky: "This is Pamela Wright. This is my declaration of independence. From this moment on I am a free woman. And I am going to live my life exactly how I please. And do exactly what I want! Whenever I want!"

The echoes died away. At that moment Sharpe looked in her direction again.

She fancied she saw him nod in agreement to her statement, even though he couldn't possibly have heard from this distance.

Angel Sharpe.

Then he climbed on the bus, started the motor, and drove away along the desert road.

CHAPTER TWENTY-FOUR

"Motel Ha-Ha." Boots read the sign as Norman stopped the truck fifty yards from the motel's reception office.

From the truck's cab Norman scanned the place. It consisted of individual pine cabins standing on a gravel track that ran out into a field before looping back to the lot. Beyond the motel the landscape consisted of cornfields.

Not much else.

Seems like a quiet place. No cops . . .

Duke said, "You planning on us walking everywhere, Norm?"

"Uh?"

Boots slid her fingers inside the top of her tank top to pluck it away from her breasts. "It's too warm to walk."

The duo sat beside him. Their faces were flushed with heat. That and too many miles on the road.

Norman was doubtful. "Yeah, but . . ."

"But what?"

"The cops are going to be looking for two guys and a girl with short bl—" He was going to say, "bleached hair," but you didn't mess with Boots; he neatly morphed the word into: "Blond hair."

Duke shrugged. "We're not in a red Cherokee Jeep. All the clerk will see is three honchos in a truck."

"Yeah, going to visit our white-haired grandmother." Boots snickered.

"Drive us in, Norm." Duke slid him a tough-guy look. "Don't make me ask twice."

"I just thought—"

"Just thought shit, Norm. It's been a long day. The lady needs to bathe her beautiful bod. Okay?"

"Okay."

Norm clunked the gears. The truck lurched forward into the Motel Ha-Ha driveway.

Boots leaned forward, fanning her fat throat with her hand.

Trotter hands, Norman thought. *How can anyone be attracted to the pig-faced woman?*

But you are, aren't you, Norm?

Shit, damn straight. That's it with sexual lust. Sometimes—most times!—you just can't control it.

And out the window goes your better judgment.

"Motel Ha-Ha," she repeated again, seeing the sign standing proud on the reception office roof. "Funny name."

Duke nodded. "You mean, funny ha-ha?"

Good joke. Norman laughed.

"What's so funny, Norm boy?" Duke sounded irritated for some reason.

"The joke."

"What joke?"

"Motel Ha-Ha. Funny ha-ha."

"Are you pulling my rod, Norm?"

"No."

"Better toe the line, Normy boy. You gotta show some respect."

"Okay, guys. Argue when we're in the room. I'm so close to that shower now I can almost feel it on my boobies. Norman, check in."

"Me, check in?"

Duke reached over Boots to flick Norman's shoulder with the back of his hand. It was aggressive, ill-tempered rather than friendly.

What's eating Duke?

"Okay, okay," Norman said. He wanted to avoid a confrontation.

"Oooh, you're a hero," Boots said, stretching luxuriously. "Sooner I get out of these dirty clothes the better. My feet feel like two oven-baked chickens. My fanny's just cooked, too."

Duke said to Norman, "Step on it, bud."

"I'll need cash. The cops will be able to trace us through MasterCard."

Boots pushed back her sweat-damp hair before handing him a wad of notes that they'd taken from the old guy, who was now sleeping the sleep of the eternal in his dusty crawl space. Relieved to get out of the cab and away from the gruesome twosome, Norman trotted across the dusty driveway to the timber office. An accommodation tariff sat on a table just inside the window alongside a vase of purple flowers. The place was far from modern, but it looked clean.

The prices were reasonable, too.

Norman pushed open the door. A guy of around forty sat at the desk. More of the purple flowers stood in vases on the desk. The room smelled of pine and flowers.

A good place, Norman thought, and wished he were here by himself. *Or with a girl.*

Any girl but Boots.

The clerk looked up with a bright, welcoming smile. "Hello, there. Cabin for one?"

"Three."

"No problem, sir." The guy was smartly dressed in black pants and a black roll-necked sweater. Even the hair was an intense black that matched the clothes. Could have been a dance instructor, with that slim build and air of poise.

"If I could ask you to complete the registration card. Vehicle license. Home address. Names of occupants. Et cetera, et cetera."

"Sure." Norman was getting his cool back now that he was away from grumpy ol' Duke. He wrote fictitious details in the boxes on the form, though he glanced back and wrote the license plate number—the actual plate number. That was one detail that the registration clerk could check out there and then.

The clerk said, "My name is Darren. If you need anything just call. Would you prefer a two-bedroom cabin or a three?"

"A three-bedroom's great," Norman said.

Jeez, he thought. *A room of my own. I could use some private time right now. Killing two cops takes a while to digest.*

The rest of the registration procedure went smoothly. Norman paid cash for one night. As he finished up counting the notes he glanced at the timber wall behind the desk. There were five picture frames. Each one contained the cover of a *TV Guide*. A couple featured single-person portrait photographs of a handsome Hispanic-looking guy. The others were of a posed group of men and women in white coats.

Norman looked from the photograph of the dark-haired guy to Darren the clerk as he counted the cash out into a drawer. Darren glanced up. He smiled when he saw where Norman was looking.

"Yeah, this office also doubles as the altar to my ego." He smiled again. "Or alter ego, as it were."

Norman blinked. "You're Dr. Sanchez Guido?"

"In another life." He tapped the printed card standing upright in a holder on the desk. "Now Darren Klein, dispensing rooms in the Motel Ha-Ha."

"Shit! Uh, excuse my language."

"No problem. I love the word. Must do, the times I use it."

"But shit, man. *Intensive Care*? I used to love that show."

"No shitting?" The clerk studied him with those handsome brown eyes. "I guess you caught the reruns. You'd have been too young to see it first time out."

"You played the doctor who all the nurses fell in love with. Hey, even my sister had the *Intensive Care* cast poster on her bedroom wall."

"We looked good back then. A long time ago, though."

"Just wait until I tell her."

Then his stomach dropped. *If I ever see sis again. Cop killers don't just go home whenever they feel like it. I'm on the run now.*

"*Intensive Care* was good to us," the guy said as he lifted a key from a board that held a bunch of others. It had a bright-yellow fob the size of a flattened table-tennis ball. "My first pro acting job, and it ran for six seasons. But . . . let me think . . . the last episode aired ten years ago to the month." He shrugged as he handed Norman the key. "Time moves on. Different places. Different roles."

"You quit TV?"

"I prefer live work." He winked. "I'm playing a motel clerk now."

"It's . . . different."

"Yeah, different is a good word. Not too judgmental. There you go, sir. Cabin twenty-one. It's at the far end of the plot. Have a nice stay."

"Thanks."

"Say." Darren had an idea. "We're having a barbecue tonight. A few beers, that kind of thing. Why don't you join us?"

"Us?"

"Yeah, I'm in partnership with some of the guys from the show. Nurses Lowe and Petri. Guti the paramedic. And Doctors Rennin, Brown, and Pearman."

"Dr. Pearman? But he was the guy who gave your fiancée the insulin overdose, then tried to embezzle the children's charity."

"It was just a show, sir."

"Ah, of course."

"They're really nice people."

"I'm staying here with a couple of friends."

"Bring them. More the merrier."

"Sure. Thanks."

But Norman thought, *No way. Not those two lowlifes. I'll slip out myself. Just think. To meet the cast of* Intensive Care. *These people were household names!*

Then why did they vanish from the show-business radar?

"There's a patio area around the back," Darren said. "Amble up between eight and nine. We're as informal as you can get around here."

"Great, thanks." Norman was pleased. "I'll see you later."

"*Ciao.*"

"Took your own sweet time," Duke said.

"We were baking in here. It's like an oven."

Boots sat sideways in the driver's seat of the truck so her plump legs dangled out. The heels of her dirty white boots thumped against the vehicle's metalwork as she swung her feet from side to side.

Norman was more than ready to fire back an irritated, *Why didn't you get outta the truck and sit in the shade?* But Duke had been antsy. He wasn't the kind of guy you get angry.

Remember the knife he keeps in his boots?

Norman remembered. Wasn't in a hurry to feel that blade part his ribs.

Instead: "I got us registered. We've gotta be discreet so I didn't want to rush it and make the clerk suspicious."

"Yeah, like we walk in terror of the big, bad motel clerk. He'll be a wuss faggot boy like you, Norm, old buddy."

What's eating you? Norman wondered.

Boots swung her legs into the cab as Norman climbed in behind her.

"I got the key," he said, holding it up by the bright yellow fob.

"Whoop-de-do, wuss. Now if it ain't too much trouble, boy, drive us to the room."

The pine cabin was roomy, with three bedrooms, a lounge area boasting a kitchen in the corner, and a good-sized bathroom. The sun was low in the sky as Norman closed the door behind him, locked it.

"Afraid someone's gonna steal you from us, Normy?" Duke lit a cigarette, then lay back on the sofa, gazing up at the ceiling.

Boots closed the blinds. "Don't want anyone lookin' for free." She peeled off her tank top to expose her jiggling breasts. They looked too small for that wide-shouldered body of hers. "Norman?"

"Yeah?"

"Wanna soap my back in the shower?"

Jeez, not at this moment. I want to lie down in my own room, just be alone and still, and not have to think or talk or listen to the gruesome twosome articulate their same old shit.

"I might grab some sleep."

"You sure you ain't no faggot?" Duke blew smoke toward the ceiling.

"Please, Normy. Come and cover me in bubbles."

"That's an offer no red-blooded man can refuse, bud."

Norman forced a smile. "Sure. I'll be right in."

Boots said, "I'll just drop my bag in my room." She smiled. "I'm getting naked in there, so no peeking when I come out." She laughed.

Duke didn't laugh. His face was grim.

Norman thought, *Best grin and bear it. Duke's acting so weird. He's got a dangerous look about him.*

Boots slipped through one of the pine doors. He heard her "oooh" and "aaah" over clean sheets and a soft bed. More purple flowers adorned every room in pink vases. Norman thought of saying something to Duke to placate him.

Can't think of anything.

Come to that, anything might enrage the man. He's unpredictable.

Dangerous.

Crazy dangerous.

Norman left Duke smoking. He went into his bedroom, where he peeled himself out of his dusty threads. Ah, that did feel good to be out of the clothes. To feel that cool, air-con atmosphere taking the heat out of his skin. The bed looked so clean he longed to lie down on it right now. Then—

"Normy . . . oh, Normy . . . you ready to shower?"

He sighed when he heard the voice. Then he took a breath, puffed out his chest.

Showtime. Here goes. . . .

Keeping his voice pleasant, he sang out, "Coming."

There were clean, folded towels on the bed, so he wrapped one around his hips. Then he left the bedroom, walking by the supine Duke. Still smoking. Still staring ceilingward.

As he passed Duke the man stretched out his arm and gripped Norman by the wrist. The grip was the fiercest Norman had ever felt.

"Don't ever shit me, Norman. If you ever get me angry, I'm gonna . . ." He grunted, then let go of Norman's arm, breaking eye contact at the same time to resume his ceiling stare.

Norman shuddered.

Yeah, he was reading the warning signs. A volcanic anger was brewing in the guy. Making Duke's eyes meaner than ever.

"Oh, Normy . . ." Boots's voice wailed from the bathroom. "Normy, Normy, Normy."

Norman walked into the bathroom. He was wary now. He expected to feel the point of Duke's blade between his shoulder blades at any moment. Thankfully, he closed the door behind him.

Already the room filled with steam. Water hissed into the shower stall.

Through an opaque plastic curtain a figure moved.

She's rubbing shower gel into her breasts, he told himself. *Then she's working down over the swell of her stomach.*

Down, down . . .

Into that enticing area between her legs.

Norman groaned.

Ten seconds ago he was worried about what Duke was building himself up to do.

Now . . .

He groaned again. Boots—ugly, unlovable Boots. She worked the voodoo on him.

He looked down as his body betrayed him.

The front of his towel had formed a pyramid.

"Hmm, Norman. You come right in here and let me bathe you, honey." She moaned with pleasure as the silhouette soaped itself.

God, he was so aroused.

So aroused it hurt. He let the towel fall from him; then he slid aside the shower curtain and stepped into the stall with Boots.

CHAPTER TWENTY-FIVE

Norman finished making whoopee to Boots in the Shower by seven o'clock that evening. She swathed herself in towels, not to mention dreamy smiles, then disappeared into her room.

Norman dried himself. Shaved.

His knees still shook after what he did to her.

She loved it. Begged for more.

When he left the bathroom he found Duke asleep on the sofa. The cigarette had burned itself out. Now the dead butt poked from his lips.

Norman didn't wake him.

Didn't relish arousing the tough guy's wrath.

He went to his own room, slipped on a pair of clean undershorts. Then he lay down on the bed. The clock radio scrolled over to seven eighteen. Outside it was still bright, but there was an orange tint to the sunlight now.

When he closed his eyes he thought, *I'll just rest here for five minutes.*

When Norman opened his eyes again the clock radio told him it was eight fifty-three.

"Shoot," he murmured. "Barbecue time."

Darren had told him to turn up to the barbecue between eight and nine. Sweet Jesus, despite everything—all the crud, the sex with Boots, the slayings—he wanted to meet up with the cast of *Intensive Care.*

There had to be a pretty cool story about how half a dozen actors from one of the most popular TV shows of its decade had wound up out in the middle of Nowheresville. And running a motel, to boot.

What about Duke and Boots? They'll want to come.

Boots will wet herself when she hears that there are famous actors having a barbecue just a minute's walk from the cabin. This will be paradise for a backwoods girl like her.

Shit. Make something up.

Tell them you're just going for a walk.

But that's the kind of thing that Duke doesn't want to hear. Might piss the big guy off. The notion of Norman just walking for the pleasure of it could be a source of major irritation.

"Oh, well, nothing ventured." Norman grunted.

In ten seconds flat he'd pulled on a clean white T-shirt, stone-hued chinos, and sandals. No doubt Duke would have something smart to say about Norman's choice in clothes, too.

Norman popped his head around the bedroom door to the living room. It was gloomy now. But to his relief—major, *major* relief—Duke still slept on the sofa. The butt of the unlit cigarette looked to have taken root in his surly mouth. When he realized there was no sound coming from Boots's room either, he checked in on her.

She lay bare-ass up.

Dead to the world, too.

Yeah, come to that she looked like a freshly killed porker. Now her muscles had gone slack as she softly snored, her face looked as if it were in the process of melting. The features drooped, then slid sideways as gravity pulled them down to the pillow, where part of her face pooled.

He looked at her wide rear. The crack of her ass had become a deep gully that you could lose a moose in. And deep down in the center was the intimate place that one of his friends called "the old Jap's eye."

Norman grinned. Wow, if he had a firecracker right now he didn't think he could stop himself.

The gruesome twosome were both sleeping royally. He could slip out without having to answer any questions.

Stealthily, he exited Boots's room, crossing the living room to the cabin door. He glanced back.

Hell.

Those two didn't even seem like regular sleepers. There was something of the corpse about them. They slept like they were rehearsing for the biggest sleep of all.

The sun was low over the cornfields when Norman headed up toward the motel office. From here he could see the reverse of the name sign that was lit already as dusk fell. Motel Ha-Ha.

A friendly kind of name, Norman figured. *In a funny kinda way.*

Behind the motel office a tall, thick hedge enclosed an area of land. He saw that an archway had been cut into the vegetation to form a narrow gateway. He heard conversation, the sound of a cork being pulled.

This's gotta be it, Normy.

Now he caught the aroma of flame-seared meat. His mouth watered.

He stepped through over the threshold into an enclosed lawn area.

And there they were. The cast of *Intensive Care.*

Norman goggled.

They weren't in the uniforms he'd gotten to know so well after watching close to a hundred episodes. The nurses had worn surgical green tops and pants. *Sex-eee!* The doctors had worn pristine white coats. He saw nurses Lowe and Petri. Petri was the male nurse. Guti the Native American paramedic. There was Dr. Sanchez Guido (a.k.a. Darren, motel clerk) flipping burgers at the barbecue grill. Then Dr. Rennin, a glamorous redheaded woman of around forty-five, sipping a cocktail. Nearby, were Doctors Brown and Pearman, their hair now graying as they jugged through life into their fifties.

Holy shit.

The cast of *Intensive Care.* Despite the years their glamour still shone brightly.

Dr. Sanchez (a.k.a. Darren) noticed Norman.

"Hey, sir. Good of you to show."

"This I wouldn't miss," Norman said with feeling.

Darren waved him closer. "Come and meet our troop of players." He laid a steak on the barbecue. Instantly it began to sizzle with the heat. Puffs of flame jumped up from the coals. "Everyone . . . Hey, guys. This is one of our customers. Mr.—"

Norman jumped in. "Norman. Call me Norman."

"Welcome aboard, Norman." The guy who played the evil Dr. Pearman smiled. He looked like such a warm and friendly guy. Nothing like his screen persona.

Norman smiled back and hello'd and hi'd his way around the group. Shook hands. The redheaded woman held his hand longer than the rest and fixed him with her green-eyed gaze as she greeted him.

Darren said, "Norman, give me a hand with these burgers, won't you? They're just about done."

"Sure."

"Plates are there on the shelf under the table."

"Got them."

"If I pile the burgers onto the plate, hand them to Gillian over there, although you'll know her better as Nurse Petri. She's been slicing tomato and cheese for the buns."

"Great." Norman was in awe.

Here I am, mingling with the famous beneath open skies. It's like a Hollywood party.

Evil Dr. Pearman handed him a bottle of beer. *Gee, he really is a nice guy.*

Not like his on-screen character that blocked IV tubes or deliberately withheld anesthetic during surgery, so the patient woke up screaming with his guts spilling out his stomach.

In real life this guy wouldn't tread on an ant, never mind sew up the lips of the kid in series three. Norman could even recall the dialogue word for word.

"Now, you can't tell the police what you've just seen," the doctor had intoned as he pushed the suture needle through the kid's top lip. "What's that you say, child? You wish for anesthetic? Let me tell you, young sir, there'll be no pain relief on my watch."

Oh, boy, oh, boy. What an episode. What a series!

"You happy with your cabin?" Dr. Sanchez—oops, Darren—asked.

"Fine," Norman enthused. "Really comfortable."

"And your friends?"

"Oh, they couldn't come. They're catching up on some sleep."

"No, I mean do they like their accommodation."

"Oh, sure. Say, Darren?"

"Yes?"

"What was the real reason for canceling the series?"

"The real reason?" Darren raised his dark eyebrows.

"Man, that show could still be running. That's how a medic drama should be."

"It was a good show. But the real reason it was canceled is it got too expensive."

"But it had millions of viewers."

Darren shrugged. "If a show stops being profitable, even if it's watched by everyone plus the president's mother, they'll pull the plug."

"That's not fair."

"Tell me about it. Here, the steak's done if you like it rare. Grab a plate. The cutlery's on the tray."

Norman gratefully received the sizzling steak onto his plate. It looked so inviting, but he didn't want to stop talking to Darren. "Surely they could have trimmed the budget and kept the series running."

"They did."

"Uh?"

"*LAICU.*"

"*LAICU?*" Norman shook his head, puzzled.

"Exactly. No one remembers it. They sacked the cast of *Intensive Care*, then applied the format to a new show with new actors—low-cost actors—and set it in an intensive-care unit in L.A."

"Hence the name."

Dr. Pearman joined them. "And, dear boy, did you hear of such a diabolical title for a show? *LAICU?* I ask you: who knew what it even meant?"

"So here we are ten years later. Hey, Norman, sit at the table there so you can eat your steak. We'll join you."

Norman sat at a picnic table with Darren and Dr. Pearman sitting opposite.

So I know it's not really Dr. Pearman. But then, I don't know his real name. Don't like to ask.

Hell, it's cool to think of him as Dr. Pearman. The baby butcher of Ward Thirteen. Heh-heh-heh . . .

Norman grinned. "Sorry. I can't stop smiling."

Dr. Pearman smiled back. "No problem, my boy. We like happy people around here, don't we, Darren?"

"Sure do."

Norman cut into his steak. Luscious red blood flowed from its nearly raw center. "It's just I remember the episode from the last season when the college student was admitted onto the ward."

"How I hated college students." The white-haired man grinned. "At least, my character did."

"Then you insisted on performing an emergency circumcision on the guy." Norman sliced another piece of bloody beef from the filet. "And as you picked up your scalpel, ready to slice off the foreskin, the student cries out, 'Anesthetic. Give me anesthetic,' and you say, cool as ice . . ." Norman paused, giving the actor an opportunity to speak his catchphrase line.

"'Let me tell you, young sir, there'll be no pain relief on my watch. Ah . . . circumcision, where is thy sting? As the immortal Bard might have penned.'" Dr. Pearman smiled. "Of course, every episode required me to utter the notorious phrase at least once: 'There'll be no pain relief on my watch.'"

"It's a great line."

"I wish I had a dollar for every time I've declaimed it since that final season."

Norman swallowed a mouthful of the delicious steak. Refreshing himself with a chug of beer, he asked, "But why did you guys quit acting, and . . ." He didn't finish the sentence, merely gestured in the direction of the motel office with his beer bottle.

"Buy a motel?" Darren shrugged.

"You were still famous."

"Yeah, but ask even famous actors how secure their career really is."

Dr. Pearman nodded his agreement. "Parts come and go. Shows open and close. But motels are here to stay. A poet might wax lyrical on their constancy in the American way of life."

"So we pooled what was left of our paychecks, and the Motel Ha-Ha was ours."

Norman swallowed a piece of steak. "Motel Ha-Ha. It's an unusual name."

Darren answered, "Some people come here thinking there's a Native American connection."

Dr. Pearman gave a theatrical wave of his hand. "But the truth is a little more prosaic, my dear boy."

"When I floated the idea with the cast that we pool our resources and invest in the motel business, their response was . . ." Darren nodded a cue to Dr. Pearman.

"Ha-ha."

"They all scoffed. At first. But I ran the numbers for them."

"And here we are this beautiful evening." Dr. Pearman sipped his wine. "Prosperous businessmen and -women. In the appropriately named Motel Ha-Ha, a reminder of our initial doubts."

"And . . ." Darren worked his way through his hamburger. "It's working out so well we're planning on expanding, buying a couple of motels nearer to town."

"And expanding the units we have here," Dr. Pearman added.

Norman thought back to his arrival at Motel Ha-Ha. "But it doesn't seem that busy. There weren't many cars parked at the cabins. In fact, I can't remember seeing—"

"No, dear boy, there weren't. That's because passing trade isn't our main business. Conventions are the thing."

"Conventions?"

"Yes." Dr. Pearman warmed to his theme. "We take mass bookings for the entire motel. Last week we had a hundred Baptists on a scripture-interpretation course.

"Next week we have a bunch of horror writers coming from all over the world. That'll be one whole week, fully catered, and prepaid bar. Those horror writers drink like fish. Just their beer bill's gonna pay for the upkeep of this place for six months.

"Motel business is a great business to be in, my boy." Dr. Pearman stroked back his silver hair. "Many people prefer our homely environment to the big hotels." He gave a theatrical shudder. "Soulless things, my dear boy. Soulless."

Darren looked at Norman thoughtfully for a moment.

"You know . . . I shouldn't be saying this, Norman. But you seem to me to be a decent and honest young man."

"I am, sir," Norman said brightly. Then he thought, *If you disregard killing a pair of cops.*

Darren appeared to be wrestling with some dilemma. "But I wondered if—"

"Darren, Darren." Dr. Pearman shook his head. "This young man wouldn't be interested in what we have to offer."

Norman's curiosity was tickled. "Interested in what?"

"Well, Norman. You see, we're looking for . . . Actively looking for, but . . ." He quickly shook his head. "No, my partner's right. It's not for you."

"It might be," Norman said eagerly, not having an inkling what the two former actors were talking about but passionately craving to be part of whatever it was they were discussing.

"Investors, Norman."

"Investors?"

Dr. Pearman nodded wisely. "We're inviting people we can trust to invest in our motels."

"But we have to be careful," Darren added. "Our investors must be discreet. They mustn't talk about the business."

"Why?"

"The return is so great we fear a gold rush. You see, Norman, we're breaking new ground by catering for conventions at motels. If our competitors learn what kind of profits—huge, huge profits—we're reaping they'd rush to copy us."

Norman breathed out, seeing dollar signs float in front of his eyes. "I understand."

"So you appreciate, dear boy, we have to be selective? We choose only individuals who we know are discreet."

"Absolutely."

"So . . ." Darren rested the cold beer bottle down on the table. "Are you interested?"

"Very, but—uh, how much?"

"As much as you care to invest, dear boy. Speaking for Darren, I think we know a man of integrity and vision when we see one."

"Thank you, sir," Norman gushed.

"We've pegged the minimum investment at five."

"Five hundred dollars?" Norman ran calculations through his mind. "I might be able to manage that, if you give me a few days."

"Norman." Dr. Pearman looked pained. It was the same flinch he'd perfected in his days in the medic drama when his professional integrity was questioned. "Norman. Norman. Dear boy, we are talking in thousands here."

"Five thousand dollars?"

"A trifling sum, when all's said and done, but it is symbolic of your faith in our business acumen."

"Oh, sure, sure," Norman nodded, trying to appear wise. "Five thousand dollars."

"Does that sound reasonable?"

"Oh, yes. Completely reasonable."

Maybe I can raise the five thou on MasterCard? Or maybe I can rob a bank? After all, after killing a couple of cops, armed robbery is no great shakes.

Dr. Pearman raised his glass. "Then may I propose a toast to our new business partner. And I have never seen such a wise head on such young shoulders. If I—"

"You rogues! You damn rogues!"

Startled by the sound of a female voice in an outburst of sheer fury, Norman turned to see a young woman in a white nurse's uniform come striding through the entrance to the enclosed lawn.

Norman goggled. The woman was curvaceous in the nurse's outfit. Her dark hair was cut short. Somehow angular, too. The effect, combined with flashing eyes, was formidable.

She advanced on the table where Norman was sitting with the two men.

"So," she said looking at Norman, "who's this pathetic bastard?" She gave a contemptuous toss of her head. "The next poor lamb to slaughter?"

CHAPTER TWENTY-SIX

The moment the woman began advancing across the grass, that was the moment that everyone stopped talking.

Stared.

Bubble burst.

Party pooped.

Norman had been starstruck in the company of these still-glamorous actors and actresses. Now—

Bingo!

What was I doing agreeing to invest money in a motel?

The guy who played Dr. Pearman gave a charming smile. "Dee-Dee."

"Don't Dee-Dee me."

Jesus. This nurse . . . was it a real nurse? . . . was formidable.

Norman thought, *I'm in love.*

His eyes swept over the figure in the tight-fitting nurse's uniform. How old was she? Twenty-three? Twenty-five?

Her short-cut hair was immaculate.

Dark.

Glossy.

Uh, not like Boots. Not bleached. Not spiky.

This was beautiful hair.

The nurse strode up, her eyes sweeping over the food and drink on the tables.

"Dee-Dee, honey," Dr. Pearman purred. "Sit down; have a glass of wine."

"Oh, Dad, you promised you wouldn't do this," the woman called Dee-Dee groaned.

Darren tried a disarming smile.

It looked on the thin side.

"We're only entertaining one of our guests," Darren said.

"Of course," Dr. Pearman agreed. "We thought a little barbecue. A pleasant interlude."

"Interlude my eye," Dee-Dee stormed. When she spoke it was directed at everyone on the lawn. "You've all decided to put on one of your shows again, so you can fleece the first no-brained sap that comes your way."

"Hey," Norman said, stung by her insult.

She turned to Dr. Pearman again. "Dad. We can't save all this by defrauding our guests."

Norman stared at the woman in the nurse's uniform.

She stared back.

"You oughta go," she told him.

"You were in the show?" Norman asked, puzzled. "I don't remember—"

"No, I wasn't in *Intensive Care*." She sounded as if she'd explained this so many times it bored her to repeat it again. "I'm too young for that pile of crap. Besides, I'm not an actor. I'm the only one here with medical qualifications. I'm a nurse at St. Jude's Hospital downtown. A *real* nurse."

She looked real enough.

Looked good through and through.

He noticed that the zipper on the uniform that was all glacial whiteness in the light of the setting sun ran from her throat all the way down to the pit of her stomach.

Now that's a zipper worth unzipping, he thought as he watched the angry rise and fall of her breasts.

"Sir," she said in a softer voice. "You won't report this to the police, will you?"

"Uh, no, of course not, but—"

"But you're wondering what's going on?"

He nodded.

Dee-Dee walked around the assembled cast of ex-actors and former actresses who had that glassy-eyed expression of people who know they're in the wrong. As she walked she explained.

"They've probably told you . . . uhm?"

"Norman."

"They'll have explained, Norman, that after the show was canceled because they'd all demanded huge hikes in salary that they bought the motel?"

Norman made with the nod again.

"They didn't explain that they were so inept, and so lacking in business acumen, that they bought a motel that wasn't on a major highway?"

"No, they said it was thriving."

"Thriving, huh. We're lucky to have a dozen paying guests a week. Isn't that right, Dad?"

Dr. Pearman nodded.

"Isn't that so, Darren?"

Uncomfortable, Darren nodded, too.

"So this bunch of retired thespians lives in the motel, taking it in turns to play the role of chalet cleaners, motel clerk, groundskeepers."

Dr. Pearman looked pained. "This young man doesn't want to hear all this . . . this *fact*. Facts are the weighted boots of reality. Facts, my dear, make the world miserably trudge when it should be dancing."

"Dad, you can't charm people out of their money. That's a painful fact of reality you've got to learn." She shook her head sadly.

Norman got up to speed. "You mean there are no conventions? No horror writers turning up next week?"

"Alas, no, dear boy."

"And we couldn't even give the place away," Dee-Dee told Norman. "So it's my nurse's paycheck that feeds these scoundrels. It meets the loan payments, too . . . *just* . . . and this is how the damned ingrates repay me."

"Are you sure you wouldn't like a nice glass of chilled white wine?" Darren asked.

"Maybe I should, seeing as I've paid for all this." She glared at Darren. "What happened to the list I gave you for the groceries?"

"Well, eh, we—"

"I don't recall putting wine and T-bone steaks on the list."

"No. Dee-Dee, we're sorry; we thought—"

"Thought? That's it, you never do think. Dad, you could go to jail for trying to pull a stunt like this."

Norman watched Dr. Pearman swallow. This was getting to be too much for him.

"I don't think they really meant any harm by it," Norman told her.

"That's just it." She sounded weary. "They are harmless. They're ineffectual, too. They cook up grand schemes over martinis, and they're all just daydreams. I gave Darren a hundred dollars to buy the groceries on my list. A list budgeted so tightly because we don't have any money in the bank. And look, they've spent it all on beer, wine, fancy steaks. Shit . . . I don't think I can carry on anymore."

"Darling, darling," Dr. Pearman cooed. "We can work something out."

"No, you can't," she said. "None of you can."

Norman winced at the expressions on the faces around him.

Sorrow. Guilt. Remorse.

Dee-Dee continued, "When it comes to remembering your lines and pretending to be someone else, you're great. When you try to live in the real world you're . . ." She shrugged. "Oh, what's the point?"

There was a pause when no one spoke. No one moved.

Insects hovered on the air as day turned into night. Somewhere a sensor activated floodlights that lit the lawn a garish green. A hamburger that had been forgotten on the barbecue gave a pop. It started to burn with a greasy, yellow flame.

Phew, what a night.

Sure is cool to hang out with the cast of Intensive Care, *though. Even if they are a bunch of con men.*

Not very good con men.

Now the girl called Dee-Dee shows up, the daughter of Dr. Pearman.

Probably just in time before he, Norman, went out to rob a liquor store for the five thou.

It was the kind of pause that could be filled by anything.

More remonstrations from the formidable, though sexy Dee-Dee?

A tearful breakdown of Dr. Pearman? Leastways the guy who played him.

But:

Three figures stepped through the gateway in the hedge.

Two burly guys and a rugged woman of around thirty.

They wore police uniforms.

Dared he hope these were actors, too? Three tired players from a cop drama wanting a room for the night.

Dee-Dee groaned. "See, Dad? One of your victims has reported you."

"Oh, my," he breathed. "I don't think jail is my preferred venue."

Darren paled.

The rest of the has-been actors and actresses looked as if they'd faint.

"The game's up," Dr. Pearman muttered.

Dee-Dee took a step toward the three officers. "Please. I can explain. My father is an actor. He tends to live in a fantasy world."

"Dee-Dee?" Dr. Pearman looked pained.

"Whatever my father and his friends have done I'm sure we can resolve it."

The three cops slipped revolvers from the holsters and aimed across the table laden with wine bottles and potato salad.

"My dear sirs, madam." Dr. Pearman rose to his feet. "There is no need for weaponry. I shall not resist arrest."

The oldest cop spoke. "Wiscoff. Norman Wiscoff. I have a warrant for your arrest."

Now all eyes swept toward Norman as the three police officers closed in, aiming their handguns at his chest.

Norman swallowed a lump the size of Tennessee in his throat.

Tried to.

Failed.

His heart thudded against his chest.

The female officer reached down to pull out a pair of handcuffs from her utility belt.

She still kept her eyes and the gun bead on him, though.

Norman raised his hands.

"Okay, okay." His voice came as a rasp. "You've caught me."

That was when it all became too much for Darren.

"Oh, my God."

He fainted. His head hit the tabletop with a forceful clunk.

All three officers glanced at him.

This is your one and only chance, Normy, old buddy. Uncannily, it could have been Duke's voice in his ear.

Gotta take it.

Don't wanna shake and bake in the chair.

Norman stood with his back to the hedge. Its branches were densely woven. It was taller than him.

If he could only . . .

He turned and ran hard at the hedge.

"Stop!"

Those were the cops' commands.

Don'tcha know what's gonna come next?

He was right.

Gunfire.

Bullets smacked into branches at either side of him, tearing holes through the greenery as he ran into the hedge. His weight and speed carried him through.

He busted out the other side, then ran in zigzags to spoil their aim. In the darkness he saw the bullets fly by him like spits of red fire.

Am I hit? I don't know. Can't feel anything.

But then, they say that if you're shot you don't feel anything.

At least, not at first.

Natural anesthetic.

In his mind he heard Dr. Pearman's chilling TV persona: *"What's that you say, child? You wish for anesthetic? Let me tell you, young sir, there'll be no pain relief on my watch."*

He ran like crazy across the motel site. He weaved around cabins. He didn't know where he was going; he only knew he had to get away from the cops.

A figure glided toward him from his right. In this near-darkness it looked like a ghost.

"Run straight down to the bottom of the plot."

"Dee-Dee?"

"Keep running. They're right behind you!"

He glanced back.

No shit.

Flashlights.

Gotta run faster.

Beside him the slender nurse ran.

"Dee-Dee. What are you doing here?" he panted.

She flashed him a wild grin. "Figured it was time I ran, too."

They climbed over the fence. Dee-Dee hauled him by the arm, guiding him to a narrow track that ran between cornfields. A vehicle approached from behind.

"We can't outrun them," he gasped.

"I don't wanna go back. I don't wanna keep working to keep those old has-beens in booze."

Now wasn't the time to stop and discuss her folly. Norman sprinted.

The vehicle drew closer along the dirt track. Norman expected cruiser lights to whirl any moment. Maybe the report of a twelve-gauge before the buckshot chewed his back to mincemeat.

The car swished alongside of them. From an open window came a voice:

"You two gonna jog all the way to Mexico?"

"Duke!"

He glanced sideways through the open driver's window.

Sure enough. Duke. Beside him in the passenger seat, Boots.

"Get in," Duke told them. He stopped the car.

Norman dragged open the rear door of the car. Dee-Dee bundled herself across the seat, her skirt rising up over her thighs.

Norman followed her into the backseat, slammed the door shut behind him.

"Nice uniform," Duke said to Dee-Dee.

Then he floored the gas pedal. The car roared away along the dirt track.

CHAPTER TWENTY-SEVEN

"I'm enjoying this," Pamela told Lauren as she collected dirty dishes from the café table.

"Really?" Lauren smiled.

"First time I've waited tables in a restaurant."

Lauren's smile broadened. "You might find the glamour wears off after a while."

"It's good, honest labor."

"It is that. Filling an empty stomach is God's work."

Pamela glanced askance.

Lauren shook her head. "No, I'm not particularly religious. But it is satisfying to put full plates of hot, tasty food in front of hungry customers. Oh, table seven needs more coffee; I'll just—"

"No, no," Pamela insisted. "I'll get it."

"Who'd have thought it? Nine o'clock in the evening and we get a busful of pool players."

"They're good tippers, too." Pamela smiled. "I'll keep that coffee flowing."

"You're a hero. I don't know what I'd have done without you."

"No worries. Like I said, I'm loving it."

"Say"—Lauren touched Pamela's arm as she turned to grab the coffeepot from the counter—"you know you could make this a permanent arrangement?"

"Lauren? You're offering me a job here?"

"You like the work. I like how you handle customers. Kind of go together, don't they?"

"Jeez . . . I don't really know. . . ."

"I'm not rushing you. Sleep on it tonight. Okay, looks as if those guys are ready for my apple pie and whipped cream."

Man, the café was buzzing tonight. Pamela didn't have a uniform but she wore a dinky white cotton apron with pockets for her order pad and pen. Quickly she sashayed across the café to refill the coffee cups of four guys in white shirts. They were appreciative of the attention and made friendly comments. She'd expected some bawdy comments, but then she noticed the badge on the team shirts: *Shearvill Pentecostal Chapel Pool Team.*

The booths and tables were all full to capacity. There must have been forty people on the team bus. But there'd be no rabble-rousing from these guys. They had plenty of appetite for steaks, lasagne, meatballs, pizza, even a Pits Burger or two, but no appetite for cussing or slapping the waitresses' butts.

The love of the good Lord was intoxicating enough for them. They were happy with their sodas and coffee.

Pamela moved from table to table. Her offers of refills were accepted with polite thanks.

She glanced back to see Lauren serving massive wedges of apple pie, topped with a gleaming mountain of whipped cream. Terry worked the griddle. He'd probably cooked more steaks tonight than he had in a week.

When she returned to the counter with the coffeepots, Terry glanced back at her. He was a slim, good-looking guy in his twenties, with a red-brown fringe that hung down to his eyebrows. Young-looking for his age. He could have passed for a high school student, with a wisp of dark hair on his chin.

Probably had to shave only once a week.

He was perspiring hard. The griddle was hot work.

Above the buzz of diners' conversation she heard the sizzle of beef turning a succulent brown before the lick of flame.

"Pamela?"

"Yes, Terry?"

"A car full of people has just turned up. I'm running low on steak; would you bring more from the refrigerator, please?"

"Sure."

"Refrigerator ain't in the kitchen. It's farther out back in the utility."

"Okay, Terry." Lightly she made her way around the back of the counter. This was the first time she'd actually been into the back of the café. It was all new to her.

Hope I don't walk into a closet by mistake.

Or the john.

Sight of the grizzled old-timer, Hank, sitting on the lavatory bowl chewing a plug of 'baccy while dumping a fresh load wouldn't be the prettiest sight of the evening.

The kitchen was clean. It smelled of fresh herbs. There were gleaming stainless-steel fixtures complemented by white tiled walls. On shelves were catering-size cans of cooking oil, vegetables, coffee. Tubs of flour, sugar, salt, spices. Racks of cutlery, copper pans, tableware—a real working café kitchen. With Terry cooking behind the counter and Lauren serving apple pie to customers, Pamela was alone.

Humming to herself, happy to be busy, she breezed through the kitchen.

Ahead lay a door.

She read a sign: UTILITY.

This's got to be it.

She pushed open the door. It was gloomy inside but she entered nonetheless. Terry needed to start grilling those steaks. The door swung back behind her. With it being night outside suddenly it was absolutely dark in the utility room.

Come to that, there might be no windows anyway.

She reached out to one side where the light switch should be. Groping for a switch in an unfamiliar room wasn't easy.

Should have held open the door to the kitchen before switching on the light.

Goofball.

Might wind up tripping over a pail.

After all you've been through, to fall and kill your fool self in a culinary-related accident would be stupid beyond belief.

Not able to see anything but a glimmer of light in the crack of the kitchen door, she set to work searching with both hands. Her fingers found the wall. They ranged over it like a pair of five-legged spiders.

Though she still couldn't see squat.

A shelf. Maybe the switch was above that.

She ran her hands across it.

Something sharp. Angular.

A plastic tub?

Something soft?

Cloths?

More objects. Cylindrical. Aerosols?

Just don't touch anything warm and furry.

Fondling mice in the dark isn't my thing.

She wasn't frightened. She even chuckled at the thought of it.

Yeah, mice. Right. Like I'd be scared of a little rodent after Rodney nearly killed me.

"Shit."

She'd run her fingers around the obstacles in search of the elusive light switch when she knocked a flat surface with her knuckle. Whatever it was slipped off the shelf to make a light clattering sound on the floor.

Oops. Hope that wasn't an antique clock.

After all, it's good here in Pits. I don't want to do anything that sours my relationship with a bunch of nice people.

"Oh, light switch," she breathed, "where are you?"

Got it.

No.

A nail in the wall. Probably where Terry hangs his apron.

Ah!

Bingo!

Found switch . . . and—

Click.

The light burst from the darkness with a brilliant intensity.

Pamela blinked, then looked down in the hope that a precious Swiss clock didn't lie on the concrete floor in a mass of cogs.

Nope.

Just a shoe box and a bunch of . . .

"Uh, that's odd."

She stared at what had spilled from the box in surprise.

"False teeth. Spectacles. Wristwatches."

She bent down. There must have been five or six of each. Those sets of false teeth didn't look too tasty.

Some stained. Nicotine. Coffee. Red wine.

One bottom set of dentures still had a little green fleck of broccoli stuck between incisors.

The watches.

Mostly cheap everyday watches with plastic casings. A couple worked. Then a bunch of spectacles that could have been worn by a mix of young and old.

Pamela grimaced as she put the spilled contents back into their box.

"Ooo-weee."

Handling a stranger's eyeglasses was a little on the icky side. Handling a stranger's false teeth was a supper raiser. She gulped down the taste of chilli she'd eaten earlier as she quickly picked up the pink-and-white dentures. When she'd scooped them all up she quickly rose to her feet.

Returned the box to the shelf that was at her shoulder height.

The things you find.

What was worse—stranger's dentures or a used condom?

She pushed the box back onto the shelf. The shelf was a deep one with kitchen cleaning products lining the front. Concealed behind the regular domestic stuff were another two shoe boxes without lids. One contained sets of car keys. They'd been there long enough to have a spider's web spun across them to create a dusty membrane over the box.

She saw the keys clearly enough.

Some with personalized key rings.

DAD'S KEYS . . . SOUVENIR OF MIAMI . . . I GOT OUT OF ALCATRAZ . . . As well as those with messages. There was a novelty skull fob, a mini plastic hamburger, a red plastic heart.

"House keys, too."

Strange.

The next box contained a dusty array of pens, asthma puffers, cigarette lighters, button badges (JESUS SAVES. MILWAUKEE CANINE LEAGUE. I BELIEVE. PEACE), penknives, a pencil sharpener, one of those little pocket diaries that was smaller than a carton of cigarettes. It was three years old, from the gold numerals embossed on a black leather cover.

Curious.

Must be lost property. But can customers misplace so many sets of dentures? Surely it's the kind of thing you notice is missing?

Can't be easy to gum through a pork chop, can it?

Car keys, too. Soon as you got back in your car after leaving the café you'd realize they'd gone.

She plucked the diary from the box.

Opened it.

Benny Loscoff, age ten (and last will and testy mint).

She turned over the dinky little page; the next one was crammed with a child's handwriting in pencil.

My name is Benny. This is what happened to me and my bud, Gyp, when we ran away from—

Feet on tiled floor.

Pamela heard the noise. Suddenly she was flustered, not wanting to be discovered here in the utility room. Not found to be reading this child's diary from the box full of lost possessions.

She stared at the door to the kitchen.

Heard approaching feet.

Any second the door would fly open and—

Shit.

Hands moving lightning fast, she plucked her order book from the pocket of her apron and threw it on the floor; then she slipped the tiny diary into the pocket just as—

Just as the door swung open.

"Lauren, hi."

I'm blushing. I know I'm blushing.

"Pamela? Is there a problem?"

"No . . . no." She grinned in an attempt to look relaxed.

"Terry said you'd come to collect the steak."

"Oh, I was just about to get it, and . . . and I dropped my order book."

"Pamela. It's there on the floor."

"Oh."

"Behind you."

"Right. Great. Thanks. Can't see for looking, can I?" She picked it up. Stuffed it into the apron pocket. Felt the hard oblong of the diary beneath it.

Hope its shape doesn't show through the cotton apron.

"I'll get the steak for Terry," Pamela told Lauren, backing across the utility room to three large refrigerators. One was marked DAIRY. The second MEAT. The third OTHER.

"No, don't, Pamela." Lauren's eyes were suddenly hard.

"Pardon me?"

"I'll bring the steak."

"But I was just—"

"No, don't worry. The refrigerator door sticks." Lauren smiled. It looked forced. "Got a mind of its own, that door has."

"Oh, right."

"Will you attend table three? They're ready for ice cream."

"Yeah, sure. Uh . . ." Pamela was going to add something inconsequential so as not to appear to be acting suspiciously, but decided that to say any more *would* look suspicious. Smiling, she turned to walk away. She noticed that Lauren didn't make a move to open the refrigerator door while she was in the room.

Pamela went to serve the ice cream.

The pool players were cheerful. Delighted with a great meal.

Terry flipped burgers for another bunch of diners who'd just taken a booth.

Pits Burgers for three: two middle-aged women and an older man with red pimples on his baldhead. He wore purple spectacles that reminded her of diver's goggles.

Pamela was troubled.

Why those keys and personal effects in the shoe boxes?

What made her take the boy's diary?

A little voice in the back of her head said, *There's a story in that diary. It's got facts about Pits. About Lauren, Sharpe, and the rest.*

Facts you don't know.

She couldn't wait until the café closed up for the night.

Then she could return to her trailer.

Read the diary.

A gut feeling told her it was important.

CHAPTER TWENTY-EIGHT

"Where'd you get the car?" Norman asked as Duke drove along the dirt track between cornfields. Duke and Boots rode up front. Dee-Dee and Norman sat—bounced, rather—in the backseat.

"It's Darren's car." Dee-Dee leaned forward in her tight nurse's uniform. Even in the near darkness Norman saw the curve of her back.

Sexy curve.

Sexy white uniform in cool, crisp cotton. She smelled good, too. Soap scents, maybe.

"Darren who?" Boots asked. She sat in the front passenger seat with her feet resting casually on the dash, like she was ready to take a nap.

Not being pursued by cops.

Norman remembered the way the bullets had flashed like shooting stars by his head.

Man, close call.

"Fuck cares who," Duke growled. "We got a car. That's the main thing." As he drove he looked back. "We saved your ass, bud."

"Thanks." Norman meant it, too. *God knows what might have happened if the cops had arrested me.*

I'm a cop killer. If they hadn't shot me they'd have pistol-whipped me.

Maced me.

Maybe kicked my jonglies black and blue.

The same jonglies that Boots kissed and ahhed over . . .

Now they were in a sedan tearing through country fields.

"Are we being followed?" Norman asked, keeping his head down.

"Take a look, wuss boy. Do you see any lights?"

Norman glanced back through the rear window. Saw nothing but darkness.

"Speaking of lights," Dee-Dee asked. "You do know you're driving at night without headlights."

"Who's the stripper?" Duke asked.

"Hey, I'm not a stripper." Dee-Dee sounded stung.

Boots looked back at Dee-Dee as she sat in the backseat. "Looks like a stripper. That ain't a real nurse's uniform."

"It is. I am a qualified nurse."

"That qualifies you to query my driving methods, miss?" Duke asked in a sarcastic-respectful voice.

"If you don't switch on the headlights we'll wind up smeared over a tree trunk."

"Get her," Boots said.

"Preferred mode of driving," Duke added.

"At least the cops won't be able to see us in the dark without lights." Norman risked another peek back.

"Give the kid a doughnut." Duke casually teased a cigarette from a pack with his teeth. "Hey, miss?"

"The name's Dee-Dee."

"Miss Dee-Dee. Do you know where these tracks are headed?"

"They run for miles. Only people use them are farmers."

"You don't say."

"I'm trying to help, you lummox."

"Lummox." Duke grinned back at Norman—an alarming action, as he wasn't looking where he was driving. "You've picked up a live one there, boy."

Dee-Dee fumed. "He didn't pick me up!"

"Say, he's not boned you yet?"

"No!"

Boots turned around to smirk. "He will soon enough. Normy can't get enough. The guy's a fucking love machine."

Duke laughed. "That's 'cause he's been saving it up for years."

"Hey." Norman didn't like this kind of talk in front of Dee-Dee.

Too personal. Too revealing.

Too damn embarrassing.

She's beautiful. Sexy. Best girl I've ever seen.

No, no, no! Don't want Boots and Duke, the gruesome twosome, ruining any chance of romance.

But . . .

Boots turned around so she could look at Dee-Dee properly; then she whispered, "Did you know that until two nights ago Norman here was a virgin?"

"That's none of my business."

"None of my business." Duke guffawed. "What's your business hitching a ride with us?"

"Yeah," Boots said. "We don't know you. You might be a weirdo or something."

"Dear God, that's rich." Norman couldn't stop the words coming out.

"Hey what's that supposed to mean?" Boots was hurt.

Duke snarled, "You gotta show respect to your girlfriend, man."

"Boots isn't my girlfriend."

"Coulda fooled me. The way you were stickin' it in her the other night I thought you two were on your honeymoon."

"Shut the fuck up, Duke," Norman snapped.

He stared at the big guy's silhouette as he drove. Then Duke did something that made both Dee-Dee and Norman shout out.

Duke floored the gas pedal. The car roared along the track in total darkness. Norman couldn't see anything but flitting shapes in the starlight at either side.

Then Duke took his hands of the wheel. Placed them behind his head. Gazed forward just like *he* was the passenger, not the driver of a budget sedan hurtling along a dirt road.

That was when Dee-Dee and Norman shouted.

"Hey, what do you think you're doing!"

"You'll kill us all!"

"Duke, get your hands back on the wheel!"

"You crazy fuck!"

Boots turned back to laugh at the pair in the backseat. "Serves you right for being rude to me."

"Boots, make him steer!"

Both Duke and Boots laughed and whooped. They slapped the car roof with their hands. Duke switched on the car radio.

A country-and-western song jangled out.

Shit, Norman thought. *That's the song I'm gonna hear as I die.*

I hate country and western.

Boots and Duke sang along, adding cowboy yodels.

The mad fucks.

Dee-Dee moaned.

Fainted.

Leaned sideways against Norman.

"Duke! You mad son of a bitch."

Duke swiveled back so both of his hands rested on his seat back. "Norman, your lack of faith disappoints. Ain't that right, Boots?"

"Right, Duke."

"Ya think you've got me down as this cretin." The car sped on. Sixty? Seventy miles an hour?

And here was Duke, acting like the car was on autopilot or something.

"You underestimate me, Normy, old buddy. That makes me sad. 'Cause I've done so much to educate you in the ways of the world. To change the boy to a man."

"Duke, steer the fucking car. Please, Duke."

Norman felt like fainting, too. Dee-Dee was a deadweight against him.

"Now here's another fact," Duke told him. "Dirt tracks like this always have deep ruts from where tractors and combine harvesters have gone backward, forward, backward, forward for years—"

"Duke. In the name of God, please put your hands on the steering wheel."

"—so they act like rails on a railroad. The car's wheels lock into the ruts. The ruts steer the car. *Comprende, amigo?*"

Norman could only stare at Duke's grinning face there in the gloom.

Any second the car's gonna flip over.

Then we'll be dead.

Norman sweated.

Sweated rivers of perspiration down his chest.

And all he could see was Duke grinning at him like a demon.

"I trust, Duke, Normy. He won't crash us into nothing. See? The car's running like God's steerin' it."

After what seemed a long, long time, Duke shook his head, then, still smiling, turned back to the steering wheel. He slowed the car. Put his hands on the wheel.

Norman sagged back in the backseat with a massive sigh. His muscles were locked hard with tension.

It would take a while to relax.

A long while.

Duke said matter-of-factly, "I've lost the cops. It's time we found a highway."

CHAPTER TWENTY-NINE

"Midnight," Lauren said as she looked the café door.

"The witching hour." Pamela stood with her hands in her apron pockets, making sure that no one saw the oblong bulge of the diary.

"Couldn't have put it better," Lauren said. "Oooh, look at the sky. You know, you don't appreciate how bright the stars are until you see them out in the desert."

Pamela looked up at the display of shining stars. "Awesome," she agreed. "And it's so wonderfully cool after being in the diner."

"It was sizzling today. And you did marvelously."

"My pleasure." Pamela smiled.

"Remember, if you want that waitressing job, it's yours."

Pamela opened her mouth to speak.

"No, don't decide now. Let me know in the morning."

"Thanks."

"We did real good business today. I'll see you get your share of the tips come Saturday."

"Oh, there's no—"

"Hush. You've earned it. The place was a furnace tonight." Lauren walked alongside Pamela as they strolled across the parking lot. The chill desert air was as refreshing as a glass of cold champagne. "And if you decide to join us we'll agree on a fair wage. You get accommodation, too."

"That's a generous package. I really do mean it."

"What we're short of is glamorous nightlife. What we're not short of is peace and plenty of quiet." She paused, looking down the road that appeared as a gray strip in the starlight. In this eerie ghost light her face, which was bony and hollow-cheeked at the best of times, could have been the face of an ancient Indian warrior.

"Lauren, what's wrong?"

"Oh, I was just wondering about Sharpe."

"He drove out in his bus today, didn't he?"

"Hmm, looking for more people to save."

"How long will he be gone?"

"You never know with Sharpe. Days. A week."

"You miss him, don't you?"

She signed. "Sure do. But that's the nature of Walter Sharpe."

"His mission?"

"Yeah . . ." Lauren's forest green eyes were far away, then: "Come on, it's getting late."

They walked across the lot by the assortment of cars, trucks, vans, and a motorcycle or two.

Never struck me as being so odd, she thought. *That parade of abandoned vehicles.*

But in the light of those shoe boxes in the utility room, crammed with pens, spectacles, false teeth, car keys . . .

Where did all those cars come from?

In the meager light they looked like sleeping beasts.

How easy is it to lose car keys and your eyeglasses?

Sure a darn sight easier than losing your truck?

You don't simply forget to climb in and drive away after eating a Pits Burger, do you, now? You don't walk off along that desert road thinking, I'm sure I've forgotten something important.

At Pamela's trailer she and Lauren said, "Good night; sleep well." Then they went their separate ways. Pamela let herself into the trailer. It still held the heat of the day. She was grateful to bathe in the warm air. Outside it had seemed suddenly too cold.

Too chilling.

Rodney's just walked over my grave.

Not funny.

She closed the door behind her. Drew the bolt. Then pulled the diary from her apron pocket. She had a feeling the contents of the diary wouldn't be funny either.

Pamela showered, relishing the pummeling jets of warm water. After the fried meat smells of the diner, the scent of the green-tea shampoo was pretty good, too. After drying herself she slipped on a long T-shirt that she was using as a nightshirt.

Then she went into the trailer's kitchen, where she poured herself a glass of cold milk. She took that into the lounge, where she'd left the boy's diary on the coffee table.

She remembered the words in a child's hand on the first page: *Benny Loscoff, age ten (and last will and testy mint).*

Testy mint.

Clearly he meant "testament." But why would a child write his will in a diary?

Did this form part of the equation, when she added in the boxes of personal effects in the utility room, plus the row of vehicles—new as well as old—abandoned in the café's lot?

She took a sip of milk. Cold and creamy, just how she liked it.

Settling down into the sofa, she opened up the diary and began to read.

My name is Benny. This is what happened to me and my bud, Gyp, when we ran away from summer camp.

As she took another sip of milk she heard the gasp of air brakes. Just opening the drape a fraction of an inch, she took a peek out. Sharpe's bus had pulled into the lot. The door opened. Out stepped a figure of what appeared to be a young guy with a mass of curly hair.

Too dark to see properly. But he seemed hunched forward.

Tired? Hurt?

She didn't know.

Sharpe left the bus next. He always walked upright. Almost like a marine, proud of his uniform and his flag, ready for a parade. He closed the bus's door behind him, said something to the curly-haired guy, who nodded. Then both went around the far side of the diner.

She watched for a moment; they didn't come back.

Pamela let the drape fall. Took a moment to make sure there were no chinks where anyone on the outside could peer in.

I'm getting paranoid.

No one cares if they see me reading a kid's diary.

Or am I developing a heightened sense of self-preservation?

Shoot.

She shivered. Opened the diary.

Began to read.

My name is Benny. This is what happened to me and my bud, Gyp, when we ran away from summer camp. Mabley and his gang was going to pound us because we told Mr. Taylor about what they did with the snake. We snuck out before sunup and took the bus to Vegas. Only the bus broke down, so me and Gyp ran into the desert, because the driver said we didn't look old enough to be traveling by ourselves to Vegas, which he called Sin City. And that there were women downtown that kiss guys for money.

Anyway me and Gyp ducked off into the desert so we couldn't be taken back to summer camp.

Pamela took a swallow of milk. It stroked a cold pathway down her throat. She glanced at the next pages of the diary. Benny Loscoff talked a lot about trying to catch birds to eat—with no success. And getting thirstier and thirstier until they couldn't walk any farther.

That was when the bus had pulled up on the desert road.

A bus full of mannequins.

A bus driven by Sharpe.

The diary continued with an account of the two boys staying in a trailer in Pits. How they helped out at the diner and played in the abandoned cars in the lot. And that an old guy who looked like a prospector was going to show them the old mine workings. They were looking forward to that.

Then the diary came to an abrupt end.

Pamela read the words scrawled across the page. Words scrawled in a hurry.

THEY MADE GYP BURGERS! AND THE OLD GUY SAID THEY'RE GO-ING TO MAKE SAUSAGE OUT OF ME!

CHAPTER THIRTY

Duke was still driving at sunup.

Driving south. *"When you need to flee,"* he'd told them, *"flee south."* So he pushed the sedan hard along Oregon's roads in the direction of California.

"California?" Dee-Dee had said as she woke up in the backseat to the sight of a passing road sign. "L.A. or San Francisco?"

"Neither," Duke said. "When you lie low you take yourself off to wilderness country."

"I thought you said you should drive south?" Norman asked from the backseat of the car.

"Yup. South into wilderness country."

Boots awoke with a stretch and a yawn in the front passenger seat. "Gee, I'm hungry and thirsty."

"We're gonna refuel soon," Duke said. "Us and the car."

"The cops will be looking for a gray sedan," Dee-Dee pointed out. "They'll have the license plate."

"No sweat." Duke drove one-handed, scratching his stubbled chin. "We ditch the car, pick up a new one."

"Oh, shit," Norman said, remembering the last time.

He saw Boots was looking back at Dee-Dee. Probably getting a good look at the nurse's uniform for the first time in the daylight.

That uniform.

Oh, boy. It still looked cool, crisp, and very sexy to Norman.

Maybe Boots is finding it sexy, too.

She's hinted that she's seduced women, hasn't she?

Dee-Dee is very beautiful in a dark, pixie way. Come to think of it, that sharply defined hairstyle is short as a boy's, so maybe—

"Quit staring at Dee-Dee's boobs, Normy."

Norman flushed. "I wasn't."

"You were, too," Duke said. "Saw you in the mirror."

"And we can all guess what you were thinkin', too," Boots said with a smirk.

"Aha. Busted, Normy boy."

"Norman won't be the first man to stare at a woman in a nurse's uniform," Dee-Dee said with a smile that was somehow prim and sexy all at the same time.

What happens if we stop at a motel again?

Dee-Dee and Boots lying side by side in a big motel bed. Giggling. Inviting Norman to join them.

Something stirred in his underpants.

"You look uncomfortable there, bud."

Norman noticed Duke watching him in the rearview.

"I'm fine." Norman grunted.

"Don't look that way to me. Looks like you're sitting on something hard."

"Just keep watching the road, huh?"

"Ohhh, Normy boy, that's no way to speak to your best bud."

Norman folded his arms and looked out at the passing scenery. There were hills. Forests. A lake beneath a perfect blue sky.

It felt hotter. Maybe they weren't far from California now?

The air smelled of pine.

Boots shuffled her butt until she sat almost looking back at Dee-Dee. Her piggy eyes kept sweeping up and down Dee-Dee's slender bod.

"Had enough of nursing?" Boots asked.

"Not really."

"Why come with us, then?"

"Heat of the moment."

"Must have been a hot moment."

"I was sick of the motel. It was my salary that kept it going."

"Sounds like a major responsibility," Duke observed.

"It was."

"So you decided to skip?"

"Yes."

Duke glanced back at her. "How do you propose to pay for the ride?"

"Pay?"

"Gas don't come free, y'know?"

"You stole the car in the first place."

"'S mine now."

"There's a kind of logic there," Dee-Dee said.

"So how you gonna pay your fare?"

"You've got something in mind?"

"Sure do."

"Okay, then. Let's get it over with." She sighed and rolled her eyes. "Here will do."

"Hey . . ." Norman protested. "She can ride with us if she wants."

"Course she can," Boots said. "Gotta pay the driver, though. It's only right."

Duke pulled over to the side of the road, then ran the car onto the dirt and under some bushes.

"Shit," Norman said. "I don't believe this."

"Jealous, Norm?"

"No, but—"

Dee-Dee hissed, "Deal with it. I've been screwed over at the motel for years." Norman saw impatience in her eyes at his slowness when she added with a weary, "Figuratively."

"Oh."

"So taking a porking in return for my freedom from a whole heap of debt isn't going to hurt, is it, now?"

"Oh, I . . . ah . . ." Norman didn't know what to say.

They were out of sight from passing traffic here. Duke opened the driver's door.

"My apologies, ma'am, for there not bein' a bed or nothing."

"It's okay by me."

Norman felt his face burning as he opened the back door.

"Where ya goin', Normy?"

"I thought you . . . well . . . thought you might want to make use of the backseat."

"Very considerate of you, Norman," Duke said politely. "But we haven't got time for that."

"Your call," Dee-Dee said. "You're doing me a favor, taking me to a new life, so name your pleasure."

Dear God, Norman thought. *Dee-Dee's beautiful. It should have been me.*

Duke unbuckled his belt. "You just pop yourself around here. No time for a regular screwin', so I thought you could practice your microphone technique."

Norman frowned. *Microphone technique? Oh, my dear Lord. Does Duke mean what I think he means?*

Norman watched Dee-Dee get out of the car. She smoothed the crisp uniform down over the swell of her breasts and her hips.

Jeez, that dress is short.

He looked at her slender bare legs. *Wow . . .* Her delicate fingers. The swanlike neck.

She pushed her dark hair behind her ears as if not wanting it to get in the way.

Boots leaned forward. Her piggy face was a picture of excitement.

She was gonna watch?

Duke was gonna let her watch?

Norman gave a polite cough. "Uh, Boots. Maybe we should step out of the car and give these two some privacy."

"Shit, man." Duke shook his head. "No time for that. If the pair of you wanna watch, then watch. Don't bother me."

Boots's eyes flashed as an erotic burn flamed through her. "Hey, Norman, lean forward next to me. You can see better."

"I don't want to see better." His voice rose in a protesting squeal.

Norman closed his eyes and clamped the palms of his hands over his ears. *See nothing. Hear nothing.*

Norman felt sick.

Am I revolted that Duke's demanded sex for driving Dee-Dee to California? Or am I sick with jealousy?

He loosened his hands a little . . . just enough to hear Boots breathe, "Normy. You gotta watch this. You won't believe your eyes."

Norman couldn't bear it. He pressed his hands so hard against his ears all he could hear was the sound of his own blood pumping through the arteries to his brain.

He tried not to picture what Dee-Dee might be doing to Duke. Even so . . .

Norman had to adjust himself. His shorts were binding. His heart beat faster.

Then moments later . . .

The whole car shuddered.

"Sweet Lord on high!" Duke's sudden shout made it through Norman's hands clamped against his ears. Dear God, what had happened there in the front seat?

It was a while before Norman could bring himself to uncover his ears, open his eyes.

Dazed, Norman saw that Dee-Dee now stood by the car. Her normally pristine hair was mussed. Her skin was flushed.

"Thank you, ma'am." Duke zipped up.

"Pleasure's all mine." She licked her lips. "I could use a drink of soda."

"Sure didn't look like thirsty work," Boots said, grinning.

Dee-Dee ran her tongue around inside her mouth as if checking that her teeth were all still in place. Then she said, "All the same, a drink would be nice."

Duke pulled his door shut, then nodded back through the open window. "There's some sodas in the trunk. Grab one before we go."

He pulled the trunk release lever. Watched her in the rearview mirror as she pulled out a can of orangeade. She slammed down the trunk lid.

That was when Duke started the motor. Floored the pedal.

Left Dee-Dee staring at a cloud of dust preceded by a departing sedan.

"Hey!" Norman shouted. "Wait! What're you leaving her behind for?"

Boots laughed a wet, gurgling laugh.

Duke made one shoulder hop. "Didn't she look wacky to you?"

"No!"

Boots still laughed as she looked back through the window at the diminishing Dee-Dee. "Aw, no fair. I thought she'd try and run after us."

Norman glanced back to catch one last look at Dee-Dee as she stood there with a can of orange soda in her hand.

"Cooee! Bye-bye, Dee-Dee!" Boots waved.

Duke said, "Good mouth."

Norman groaned, "Oh, God."

An hour later they traded the sedan for a yellow SUV. Driving along a twisty backwoods road, they had come across a solitary guy fishing by a lake. The SUV sat a few yards behind him on a swath of dry earth.

No other traffic.

No people.

Duke pulled up. Sauntered across to the fisherman, who didn't even look up as he dozed in the hot sun.

Duke slipped the blade into the back of the guy's neck. Norman climbed out of the sedan with Boots, who ran forward to throw the guy's rods and tackle into the lake. Duke rolled the guy across the ground with his foot until gravity took hold and the corpse tumbled down the bank into the lake.

Ripples spread across calm water.

A red stain started spreading, too.

Norman heard Boots say, "As the guy rolled into the lake he farted."

Duke was disgusted. "In front of a lady, too. Some people've got no manners."

Norman said, "You did remember to take the car keys out of the guy's pocket?"

"Shoot."

"Duke, what a dumb-fuck thing to do."

"Best get them before he drifts too far out, Normy."

"No *fucking* way!"

Norman watched the bloody corpse. It farted again, popping up bloody bubbles between the guy's legs.

"Norman. We need the keys. Go fetch."

"No way! I'm fucking sick of you giving me orders!"

Boots stuck out her bottom lip. She looked as if she'd cry. "Don't get mad at Duke. He's been drivin' all night. He's wore out."

"Wore out? Pumped out, more like. I mean, what the hell did you leave Dee-Dee behind for, Duke? What dumb-fuck trick was that?"

"I told you. She was a flake."

"Jesus H. Christ."

"Best get the keys, Normy. If the guy keeps blowin' gas like that he's gonna lose buoyancy."

"I'm not going in there, Duke. It's your fucking idiot mistake. You get the keys!"

"Are you disrespectin' me, bud?"

"Disrespecting you! Of course I am, you dumb fuck."

"Please, Norman." Boots's eyes watered. "Don't fight with Duke."

"If he used that brain of his for once, he—"

Duke struck.

And, boy, did he know how to strike.

The blow landed under Norman's chin. This was pain the likes of which he'd never felt before. He went spinning to land on his butt.

Duke, there's no need to fight. We can resolve our differences by discussing them.

The words he planned to say drowned in the blood that filled his mouth. He climbed to his feet, but stayed bent over at the waist. He marveled at the pretty patterns the spots of red were making on the dry earth.

"Oh, poor Norman," Boots cooed.

Duke walked smartly forward. Then he rained more punches into Norman's face. This time Norman crashed backward like falling timber. Once more he started to climb to his feet.

Only made it as far as his knees.

Boots wiped away a tear. "Poor Normy. What a pickle you've gotten yourself into."

Pickle!

Duke stepped up to the line again. This time he gave a savage kick that sent Norman rolling like a soccer ball as far as the road.

Norman was past speaking.

Nevertheless, he held up his hand.

Enough already.

I've had enough.

Norman figured the hand gesture would be clear enough to anyone. Groggy with pain, he looked up.

Duke looked down.

Face impassive. Stonelike. Eyes hard.

Then Duke swung back his motorcycle boot.

Norman groaned.

This time the full-blooded kick slammed into the side of Norman's head. That was the mother of all hurt.

The sky turned black.

Then the whole world.

Dimly, far away, he heard his mother's voice. *"Norman? Didn't I always tell you not to give lifts to strangers?"*

No shit.

Was this his moment of dying?

What he'd done over the last forty-eight hours would take some explaining to God. But then, He'd have already seen everything, wouldn't he?

The sex with Boots.

The cop slaying.

The old guy at the house with the wife in the deep freeze.

Shit. Those dead cops would be waiting for him in heaven. Even being dead wouldn't save him from having the shit kicked out of him. He could imagine them smiling as they pulled out their batons. They were gonna kick his sorry ass all over heaven.

Heaven?

Hell!

Satan wants me for a moonbeam.

His thoughts disintegrated as his mind sank deeper into unconsciousness.

Maybe gonna sink so deep I'm never coming back up. . . .

CHAPTER THIRTY-ONE

When Norman woke he was being hit all over again.

No fists.

Brilliant sunlight that felt like steel spikes was being driven into each eye.

Uh . . .

Least I'm not dead.

Yet.

But that light alone was punchy enough to hurt.

"Lay still."

That was Boots.

"Lay still, will you? I'm putting a sticking plaster on your eye."

"Uh. I'm sore." Norman winced. "All over."

"You should see yourself. Your face is a mess."

"Thanks. I feel better for knowing that."

"Duke broke you up real bad."

He squinted up at her as she leaned over him. Couldn't see much more than her porky silhouette. The sun blazed behind her head.

"Where is Duke?"

Norman was suddenly aware of unpleasant possibilities.

Duke's digging a shallow grave?

Boots shrugged, then spoke in that vague (and more than a little stupid) voice of hers. "Oh. Around."

"The fisherman. We need to get away from the lake."

"We are away from the lake."

"Uh?"

"Sit up, Normy; take a look-see."

Sitting was hurting. Royal hurting.

"If you see a lake I'll somersault bare-assed for you."

Norman realized he lay in the back of a pickup truck on bales of newspaper that formed a mattress. A tarp had been pulled to one side.

Something tells me I've been riding in the back all covered up like a baby.

Maybe Duke doesn't want to kill me after all? Or maybe he's just saving me to hurt for fun later?

Duke's the kind of guy who'd really know how to inflict pain.

Boots knelt beside him on the bales. As she leaned forward he saw the sway of her breasts inside her top.

She saw he was looking.

"From the way you're looking at my boobies it shows that Duke hasn't busted your eyeballs."

"Sorry."

"I'm the one who's gonna be sorry when men stop admiring my goodies. Well?"

"Well, what?"

"Are you gonna sit up or just lie there?"

"I'm trying. It hurts like hell."

With a sigh, as if she were being inconvenienced like you wouldn't believe, Boots helped him to sit.

"Ah, my fucking back!"

"A twinge?"

Norman grunted. "No, I just like screaming out names of body parts for the hell of it."

"Who's woken up in a grumpy mood, then?"

"I took a wee bit of damage, you know?"

Boots fluffed her spiky bleached hair. "None of it's lasting. And before you ask, I checked your John Thomas and his two sons. They're all fine."

"Thanks." He grimaced.

The idea of Boots fiddling with his genitals while he was unconscious . . .

Dear God.

At last Norman managed to sit upright in the back of the truck.

"What happened to the SUV?"

"We've traded in a couple of times since then. The cops are hunting hard for us, you know. We heard it on the radio."

"Oh, Christ."

"Duke telephoned them to tell them they're wasting their time. He says the only time a cop will lay a finger on him is when he's breathed his last."

"Oh, Jesus Christ." He managed to focus on his surroundings. "Holy shit."

"Yeah," Boots looked around. "Looks kinda funny, don't it?"

"Where in the hell are we?"

For the first time since he woke he forgot about the orchestra of pain playing the "Agony Overture" all over his body.

"This is desert . . . fucking desert!"

He blinked. A blazing sun lit sand dunes. A straight desert road.

No vehicles.

Heat haze rippled Joshua trees so they looked like drunken men dancing. Beyond sand, desert shrubs, mesquite trees lay a ridge of strangely red mountains.

And the heat, this fucking heat . . .

"The motherfucker's brought us to Death Valley."

"Don't be silly, Normy. This ain't Death Valley."

"Damn well looks like it."

"We've driven *through* Death Valley. This is Furnace Creek."

"We're in California?"

Boots nodded, smiling. "After your disagreement with Duke you slept all the way."

"Slept? Beaten unconscious. Half fucking dead."

"Norman, that's all in the past now. Besides, Duke got all upset about what happened."

"I wasn't in a fit of giggles over it, either."

"Duke's, you know . . . sensitive."

"Just hides it well, huh?"

Norman stood up in the back of the truck. The newspaper bales shifted under his feet. Worse was the sudden wave of nausea.

Then vertigo.

He took a deep breath.

He must have slept days as Duke drove them south through Oregon, northern California, then probably through the High Sierras; its wilderness country, not too many cops, then picking up Highway 190 into the Death Valley National Park before winding up here in the sand dunes of Furnace Creek in the Mojave Desert.

Was there ever such an unforgiving place?

Snakes, coyotes, kangaroo rats, ghost towns.

But at least no cops.

"I sure could use a meal and a cool shower." Boots fanned her face with a chubby hand.

"Hell, I could use some shade." Norman shielded his eyes.

No houses. Certainly no welcoming diner.

Nothing.

Nothing but god-awful wilderness. Arid wilderness. Snake-filled wilderness.

"So? Where's Duke gone again?"

"He just took himself for a walk."

"A walk?"

Crazy guy. "Boots, you don't stroll aimlessly through the Mojave Desert. This is the kind of place you carry a snakebite kit."

"You'll allow it looks kinda peaceful, Norman."

"Peaceful, right? There's also the Edwards Air Force Base out here, along with the China Lake weapons center, where they test the biggest, baddest bombs known to humanity."

"Gee, I ain't seen no soldiers."

Norman sighed. "We should sit in the shade of the truck."

"I'm working on my tan."

"Your tan? In this heat you'll fry."

Norman climbed off of the truck. His legs didn't work too well.

Stiff from lying on newspapers for days.

He caught sight of his reflection in a side window.

"Uh, I don't look too pretty." Bruises, contusions. A cut through his right eyebrow that Boots had taped shut with a Band-Aid.

"I've had worse," she said lightly. "You'll soon heal up nice."

"I hope—"

"Norman, catch me."

She jumped off the back of the truck. Norman did his best.

"Shit!"

Like catching a sow.

My arms! My back!

Grunting, he fell back with her in his arms. They landed sprawling in desert sand.

"Norman. You were supposed to catch me."

"I think you've snapped my spinal column."

"Don't joke. Just 'cause I carry an extra couple of pounds."

"Couple of pounds. Jeez."

As Norman disentangled himself from the chunky Boots, a shadow fell across the pair of them.

Norman looked up.

Duke.

Oh, shit.

Norman climbed to his feet while beating clouds of dust from his clothes. Damn desert grit was in his mouth too.

He looked up at Duke. His blond, greasy hair was still swept high. His blue eyes were hidden by a pair of mirror shades that reflected the black and green bruises on Norman's face.

Bruises that Duke had made with those rock-hard fists of his.

The face was impassive. He was staring at Norman.

Maybe figuring to finish the job with his knife. In minutes I could be lying in the desert with blood squirting from my throat.

Norman waited for Duke to speak. It was like waiting for the outbreak of war.

Tension built in Norman's stomach.

I feel sick.

Boots watched without talking, waiting for Duke's first move.

Duke raised his arms at either side of his head. His biceps bulged.

Norman flinched.

Duke stepped forward to inflict a massive bear hug. It reminded Norman how sore his ribs were.

This is it. The monster's gonna crush me to death.

Duke kept squeezing.

"Norman?"

"Uh . . . Duke?" he managed to say with his face pressed into the hard muscle of Duke's chest.

"That was a bad thing that happened between us, Norman. We've got to stand together like brothers. Never let it happen again. D'ya hear? Never again."

"Gnnaa . . . sure. Never again."

Duke released his grip.

Norman breathed.

That was a good feeling.

"But you made mistakes, Norman, old bud. I had to correct them. It broke me up inside, but I had to show you what you mean to me."

Boots chipped in. "All friends now. That's the main thing."

"Sure, we're all friends now." Duke beamed, then slapped Norman on the back. It was a friendly slap; the force of it nearly made Norman swallow his tongue.

"What you say, bud?"

Norman forced a weak smile. "Sure. Best friends."

"More than friends," Duke told him. "We're family now. We stick together to the end."

Now, that part of the reconciliation didn't thrill Norman. *Together to the end?*

No way.

For a few minutes Duke and Boots chatted with Norman. They checked his face. They reassured him that he'd be fine.

After that, Duke opened a can of Pepsi, took a swallow, handed it to Boots. Boots took a slug, then handed it to Norman.

Uckk.

Warm.

"We've got three of those left," Duke said, nodding at the can in Norman's hand.

"I'd give a hundred bucks for a cold beer right now."

Duke guffawed. "You and me both, big fella."

Norman shielded his eyes against the raging sun. Beneath a clear sky the dunes wobbled in the heat haze. Farther away hot air on the road surface created phantom pools of blue water.

"Not much of a road," Norman ventured.

"No, sir."

Boots added. "At least it's quiet."

"Sure doesn't look like a regular desert highway."

"Yup," Duke agreed. "The pavement's all broke up."

Norman had learned that disagreeing with Duke, or even questioning his decisions, could have pretty bad side effects, so cautiously he said, "Boots said we were close to Furnace Creek. Is this Highway 190?"

"Hell, no, bud. Where you find highways you find cops."

"So this is an offshoot from the highway?"

"Yup."

"I see." He took a breath as he judged the risk of suggesting the obvious to Duke. "It's just that when I was down here in the Mojave last, we were warned to stick to the main highways." Norman shrugged as if what he said next was someone else's observation. Not his. "Some people say it's dangerous to leave the main desert routes."

Boots held her hands above her head to create a little shade for her face. "Wusses always say things like that; ain't that so, Duke?"

"No shortage of wusses, babe. The shortage is in real men like me and Norm here."

"Damn straight," Norman agreed.

There was a pause. Duke stared at the dunes at nothing in particular. Boots stood with her hands over her head, smiling at Norman.

Norman knew he'd another obvious question to ask, especially as he'd just seen a rattlesnake poke its head out of a burrow at the side of the road.

Not a good sign when the local wildlife started to get interested. He glanced up.

Black specks circled in the sky. The local bird population was taking a gander, too.

All we need now is a pack of coyotes along with a few of their bobcat friends and everything will be dandy.

When moments passed with no movement from Boots and Duke, Norman posed the question.

I just hope that Duke doesn't take offense. The last thing I need right now is another beating.

"Duke?"

"Huh?"

"How about that cold beer?"

"I don't think you're gonna find any out here, bud."

"No. I thought we could drive farther. . . . Maybe find a store?"

"Can't do that."

"Oh?"

Duke nodded at the truck. "Motor's busted."

"You mean we're stranded here? *In the desert?*"

Boots said, "Darn thing just went boom under the hood."

Duke looked at Boots. "Didn't you mention to Norm that we'd broken down?"

"Ooops. Must've slipped my mind. Sorry, Normy."

Norman said, "Shit happens."

But he would've liked to yell at the pair. Another beating wouldn't help, though.

"Yeah, shit happens," Boots agreed.

Norman looked up at the circling birds.

Vultures. Now I know why they're so interested in us. Forget beef jerky. In this heat we'll dehydrate so fast we'll soon be human jerky.

Those desert critters are gonna have themselves some tasty snacks.

Again, Norman had to voice the fact. "I guess you could say, technically, we're stranded in the desert."

Duke nodded. "Technically, I guess you could say exactly that."

"We've got some soda left," Boots said optimistically.

"Three cans." Norman nodded, digesting the situation that faced them. "I just wondered . . . has anyone any idea what we do next?"

CHAPTER THIRTY-TWO

Pamela crossed the dessert with only a glass of water and a little bread; the glass wouldn't even last her an hour. Maybe the bread would last longer than Pamela. . . .

She half dozed on the couch with the fan streaming air over her. In the heat of the afternoon it felt so good to lie here in the trailer. She let thoughts drift through her head.

Thoughts of escaping across the desert. But she was right about the bread lasting longer than her. This time of year the heat was a killer.

Walk out of here?

Might as well put a gun to my head.

Then do I want to escape?

My liar husband is dead.

Got no home.

No future.

Pits is a good place.

Only a weird place. There are the shoe boxes full of people's personal possessions. Dentures. Asthma puffers. Spectacles. And why are there so many new cars left to gather dust in the cafe's parking lot?

Only too well she remembered the last entry in the kid's diary she found in the cafe's utility room. It ran: *They made Gyp burgers. And the old guy said they were going to make sausage out of me!*

"So, you're concluding," she murmured to herself, feeling the rush of cooling air on her face, "you're concluding that two young boys came to Pits as runaways after being rescued by Sharpe. And that the boy called Gyp was murdered by Lauren, or by someone who lives in Pits, and they fed the boy into the meat grinder and turned him into hamburger meat. And then the 'old guy' . . . Hank? Told the kid who wrote the diary that they were going to make him into sausage?" She rubbed her forehead as troubling thoughts circled behind her eyes. "Does that sound genuine? Maybe the kid wrote that stuff in the diary as a joke?"

She cast back to last night, when Sharpe arrived with a curly-headed guy on the bus.

Had they killed him, too?

Last night Lauren didn't want me opening the refrigerator door. Maybe I'd find heads on the shelves with open staring eyes. Maybe a tag stapled to an ear that read, Best Before May 23.

"Shit," she breathed. She liked Pits and everyone in it.

Sharpe had saved her life.

An overactive imagination was poisoning her enjoyment of the place. "Here be cannibals?" she mused. "As if."

Even so, she must get the ridiculous notion out of her head. The one that suggested that Pits was turning passersby into Pits Burgers, then leaving their cars in the lot.

Pamela started work at the café in an hour.

Gonna lay this ghost to rest.

I'll open the refrigerator door. Take a good long look inside.

All there'll be are burgers, chops, steaks—just regular food you find in any diner.

There won't be human heads waiting to become soup. There won't be butt-filet steak. There'll be no truck-driver oven-cooked ribs, or schoolteacher burritos, or student dim sum.

Pamela headed to the shower, peeling her clothes off as she went.

Time to freshen up.

Change into the uniform of a knit pullover shirt in white with *Pamela* stitched in red thread above the left breast. Bottom half: red shorts—bright red! Last on was the blue apron with pockets for order pad and tips.

Cute as a squirrel's nut, as the old saying goes.

Then take a little walk to the café's utility room and open that refrigerator door.

Prove that Pits is no cannibal town.

Pamela left the trailer. She saw the old-timer, Hank, with a shovel over his shoulder. He seemed to be walking back from the cemetery. He was too far away to hail her.

He gave her a casual salute nonetheless.

The sun was sinking toward the rocky hills now. Beyond the town of Pits the desert burned.

Arid. Implacable. Snake infested.

Not your average walking country.

God take pity on any poor soul stranded out there.

She gazed across the sandy ground to the road. It was empty tonight. Feeling the heat from the desert earth, she headed across the parking lot, passed the parked cars in front of the café.

She noticed a motorcycle parked near the front door. It was a big purple Honda with silvery tassels hanging down from the ends of the handlebars. Painted on the gas tank was a howling wolf in profile.

My what big teeth you've got. . . .

She moved toward the front door.

Then she remembered her mission.

I've got to do it, she thought. *I've got to prove to myself that Lauren, Sharpe, and the rest aren't cannibals.*

What the kid wrote in the diary was probably just a joke.

Hell, I remember a kid at school who always wrote the "what I did on my vacation" essay about flying around the solar system.

The schoolteacher always told him he'd wind up in jail.

Kid proved them wrong.

Went into politics instead.

So the diary she'd read about the couple of child runaways . . . it was probably just fantasy.

But gotta be sure.

I need to know that they aren't turning customers into bologna back there.

Round the back, girl.

Be brave.

So instead of entering through the café's door, she turned and followed the line of the wall. It took her to the back of the café. It was awful quiet. No sign of Sharpe's bus with its mannequin riders.

Nor Wes's old pickup.

The only people in the diner were probably Nicki, Lauren, and Terry. Oh, and a customer. The biker, possibly a pillion rider, too.

But won't they have seen me when I headed for the front door? They'll wonder why I'm skulking around the back.

A suspicion tickler or what?

No.

When she'd approached the café, the window blinds were closed to shield the interior from the full force of the sun. It was low in the sky.

Still sizzling-hot though.

So, no one would have seen Pamela.

So far so good.

She headed for the rear of the café. Here were trash cans.

And flies . . .

Man, oh, man, the flies.

Millions of desert flies had flown in to enjoy the café cuisine, too.

They've found the curly-headed man in the Dumpster. Or what's left of him.

"Gee," she whispered to herself. "Sure does smell raunchy."

The trash can that played host to the flies stood some distance from the back door. That was the one that contained discarded food.

Maybe even the offal of a passerby.

Suddenly, gritting her teeth, she strode forward, gripped the lid of the trash can. Held her breath.

Boy, the stink and the flies.

Then she lifted the lid.

Gonna see a curly head with a bloody face staring out at me.

Chicken carcasses. Maybe six of them.

That was all.

No young guy's giblets.

Unless they have uses for all parts of the body. Maybe Lauren uses his butt-hole as a penholder?

Relief at not seeing human remains there in the trash made Pamela so giddy she laughed to herself.

But you're not done yet, she told herself. *Gotta check those refrigerators.*

As she moved toward the rear door of the café, the setting sun now cast a red light on the walls. A bloodred.

It looked as if someone had thrown a pail of gore against the stonework.

Ominous, Pamela thought.

Then, steeling herself, she eased open the door and stepped into the utility room.

Well . . . just like it was before. A windowless room lit by fluorescent strips in a hard, white light. On the walls were shelf after shelf of stores. Big catering cans of vegetables, cooking oil. Bottles of ketchup. Jars of creamy white mayonnaise. There were boxes of crockery. Spare cruet sets. Hefty bales of napkins. Spare kitchenware.

She spied the shoe boxes full of stuff customers had left behind.

Whatever happened to them?

These were pushed to the back of the shelves, partly concealed by packs of dried foodstuffs. She could even see a pair of dentures grinning at her from the gloom.

What happened to the owner of those?

Sliced.

Diced.

Stir-fried in peanut oil. Served with grilled polenta and zucchini.

Black beans are fine. Baked beans are dandy. But nothing compares to human beings.

Now that's sweet eating, for sure.

"Shush," she scolded her runaway imagination in a whisper. "Just take a look around. Reassure yourself that nothing weird's happening. Then walk in through the front door with a friendly 'hi' as if nothing's happened."

Goddamn it. I like Pits.

Pamela realized she was seriously thinking about staying on.

So check the refrigerators. If it's regular food, fine.

If not . . .

Then she couldn't stick around.

No, sir.

Hell, I might be coated in bread crumbs to be served up as dish of the day.

Before checking the contents of the refrigerators she listened at the closed door that led into the café's kitchen.

I don't want anyone to walk in on me, do I, now?

Then I really would have had my chips.

Holding her breath, she listened. Nothing but the thud of her own heartbeat. With only a couple of diners at the most, Lauren, Nicki, and Terry might be taking a break themselves.

No smells of cooking either. Just a faint aroma of coffee. Perhaps the biker and his chum had just called in for caffeine fix.

Now, speed up the investigation, girl. You're due to start work in seven minutes. Don't want to be late.

She moved quickly along the narrow room toward the two refrigerators and massive deep freeze set against the end wall.

Clang!

Her elbow caught a roasting tray that had been hung on a hook from a shelf. The big metal tray flipped up from the hook, turned over; then gravity took hold. It fell toward the concrete floor.

Where it would make a hell of a crash.

That would bring people running in here, asking awkward questions. As a waitress she had no reason to be in here.

So why sneak in through the back door? they'd be asking.

As the heavy tray sped downward she knew she couldn't catch it. *Deaden its fall.* Like lightning she kicked her foot under it. *Slam!*

The tray hit edge on into the top of her foot. She was only wearing pumps, so that steel edge felt like a guillotine blade.

No metallic clang.

But the agony . . .

She pushed her knuckle into her mouth to stop herself from screaming out—Something that would have brought the staff running just as surely as the metallic clang of the tray striking concrete. Tears oozed from her eyes. The scream came as a gasp of pure pain. The tray toppled off her foot to hit a carton of paper towels.

Its only sound was a very, very soft thud. With an effort of sheer will to stop her blubbering with pain, she returned the tray to its hook. Then she hobbled to the end of the room. There she checked for damage.

An angry red line ran across the top of her foot just below the ankle. It felt like red-hot pincers crimped the flesh. Lucky it wasn't bleeding. Probably nothing fractured.

But that mother would swell.

"Come on," she hissed. "Finish this."

She opened the refrigerator marked with the word DAIRY. That sign didn't lie. Here she found an impressive stock of butter, cheese, milk, cream, and yogurt, along with a tub of guacamole.

Of course, if there were going to be any butchered people here, they were going to be in the refrigerator labeled MEAT. Its door was as big as a house door. Someone had welded a couple of steel loops where the edge of the door met the appliance's carcass.

The kind of loops that would be home for a hefty padlock.

Lauren liked to keep the refrigerator locked.

Only there was no padlock now. Her eyes roved to the left. On a steel shelf full of pans she spied an open padlock.

Saves having to gnaw the thing off, she thought, her flippancy trying to mask her anxiety.

"Okay, here goes . . ."

Door opens.

Chill mist rolls out.

She stared until it felt the desert heat had sucked the moisture from her eyeballs.

"Okay, inventory," she murmured as she scanned the shelves.

The interior of the appliance was pristine aluminum. On the shelves there was meat galore, from T-bone steaks to burgers to pork chops.

Severed human hands?

Eyeballs in cut-glass bowls?

Face kebabs?

Nope.

Not a sign.

Sheesh. Just paranoia on her part. Stoked a little by some kid who'd been fooling around with an old diary. She checked the deep freeze. A moment's perusal revealed that it contained frozen foods you'd find in any food store.

Still, there was a cut of meat suggestive of a human thigh. Gingerly, she lifted it out.

The cold was biting. She saw the bloody marrow in the sawed-through bone at the end. It was wrapped in clear plastic with a mass-printed label that read, *Pork. Defrost and cooking instructions.*

This definitely wasn't the curly-haired guy's upper leg. This came from a beast with four legs and snout.

Voices. She heard a clamor from the kitchen area. Someone was hurrying this way.

Someone knows I'm here, Pamela thought, panicking.

Any moment they were going to bust through the door from the kitchen. Find her standing here by the open deep freeze with a good fifteen inches of frozen swine leg in her hands.

They'd dismiss her as a nut.

Or a thief.

She shut the appliance door. *Great, you idiot, you were supposed to put the frozen meat back first.*

Voices—louder and louder.

The door to the kitchen banged open. Gasping, Pamela wedged herself into the gap between the deep freeze and the shelves where two walls of the room met.

Fine. The shelves were piled so high with packs of flour and sugar no one could see her.

Unless they'd come to grab something from the freezer.

Explain your way out of this one, Pamela.

Suddenly there seemed to be a lot of movement in the utility room, even though she could see nothing from where she crouched. Voices. Loud ones. Feet scuffing the floor.

Lauren's first: "Just leave her here with us! She's not going to say anything."

Talking about me?

But then: "I'm not coming back with you, Zak."

"The fuck you are!" A man's voice she didn't recognize. Rough-sounding.

Violent-sounding.

The man bellowed again: "Think you can just run out on me, Nicki! Did ya think I wouldn't find ya? Ya dumb bitch."

The sound of a smack. Nicki cried out.

So they're not talking about me.

Pamela raised her head a little to peep out through a crack between two giant packs of dried rice. In the harsh light of the fluorescent strips she saw Nicki and Lauren standing side by side with their backs to the kitchen door. Fear blazed in their eyes.

And standing with his back to Pamela was a youngish guy in leather pants and a jacket that gleamed with metal studs. He wore a red bandanna. The biker. She remembered the Honda she'd seen parked outside the café.

Most of all she saw what was in his hand. A revolver. He was pointing it in Nicki's face.

"You're my bitch; ya don't walk out on me," he snarled. "So ya get two choices. Ride back with me. Or kneel down and start prayin'."

CHAPTER THIRTY-THREE

Pamela watched in horror from behind the shelves. The guy pulled back the hammer of the handgun with his thumb. He pointed the muzzle at the center of Nicki's face.

Both Lauren and Nicki stared transfixed, eyes wide open.

"Nicki was my best whore," the leather-clad guy said. "Earned five hundred bucks a trick."

"I'm not going back to do that again, Zak," she whispered. "It nearly killed me."

"I gave you grade-A smack, ya bitch. Ya could be fucked by a mule on that stuff and not feel squat."

"I'm clean now, Zak."

"You'll never be clean. Not as long as ya live."

"She's not going back, mister." Lauren faced him, defiant. "She lives here now."

"With you bums? Shit . . . Pits? What a dump."

"It's her home. We're her family now. Nicki's not going back with you."

"Okay." The pimp nodded as if this didn't faze him. "Her decision. But I'm just going to deliver her severance pay."

Even from here Pamela could see the guy's posture alter as he tensed as a prelude to shooting Nicki.

"I'm popping you, too, sweetheart," he told Lauren. "Ya've seen too much of my face. Okay, Nicki, say a little prayer. . . ."

Pamela looked down at her hand. It had stopped hurting now. The ten-pound hunk of frozen pork had numbed it.

The hunk of meat. Hard as concrete.

Then she stepped silently from behind the shelf. With all her strength she swung the frozen joint.

Down on the punk's red bandanna. The icebound meat made a low clunking sound as it struck the punk's head bone.

"Uh." He dropped down to his knees.

But he still kept his grip on the pistol. He began to raise it to shoot Nicki.

This time Pamela wielded the frozen pig leg like an executioner's ax. Gripping it with both hands, she swung down.

This time there was no thudding sound.

A sharp snap. Bone had broken. She doubted if it was the pig's leg bone that had just busted.

Nope.

The pimp lay facedown on the concrete floor. Blood seeped out of one his ears. His eyes were open, but they were darting around like he was trying to lock onto a dancing hornet. His breathing sounded funny, too.

Sort of snorting. Irregular.

Pamela let the frozen pork joint slip from her fingers to the floor.

She looked up at Lauren and Nicki.

Pamela swallowed. "I think we ought to get an ambulance."

"Forget that," Lauren said firmly. "Nicki, get me the meat cleaver."

Pamela stared at Lauren, who coolly returned her gaze.

"Pamela. Once I'm through here we need to talk."

Lauren closed the diner early that day. She told Pamela that she had work to do in the kitchen. Probably something centering on the big old butcher's block on the table. Hank, Wes, and Terry helped out, too. She guessed Sharpe would have worked alongside them too, if he hadn't been out on the road in his bus.

Nicki asked Pamela to sit with her in her trailer.

Pamela obliged. She felt a kinship with these people.

As Nicki showered, Pamela fixed her a sandwich and a cold drink.

Nicki emerged, toweling dry her long blond hair. Despite what shit she'd been through today she still looked like a Viking goddess. A Viking goddess in a white cotton nightshirt, that is.

"Oh, tuna and tomato," she said, beaming as she sat on the sofa. "I love that combination. Cool and refreshing. And soda. Thanks."

Pamela set the tray bearing the plate and soda on Nicki's lap. "Don't mention it. After what you've done for me the last few days it's the least I could do." Pamela didn't mention what had happened earlier. About Zak. About the frozen pork knocking the daylights out of him.

Nicki talked freely, though.

"And thanks for what you did earlier." She sipped her drink with a "Hmm." Then she looked Pamela in the eye. "He really would have killed me, you know."

"He looked the type."

"Once I saw him cut the throat of one of his girls because she kept back some money to buy her baby some formula."

"Gee. The guy's a little shit."

"Yeah." Nicki nodded, her eyes misting. "Shittiest guy I've ever met. And I've met a few."

"Was Zak your . . ."

"Pimp. Yeah." She took a bite of her sandwich. There was a look of recollection in her eyes as she chewed. "I was at college, and I went and fell for a bad boy. I thought it was so cool that he'd pick me up on the motorcycle. The leathers were a turn-on too. A real turn-on. Shoot . . . he was my first real love, you know? The first guy who I let . . ." She shrugged. "Well, I thought he loved me for myself; only then he started to spin this line that he owed some gang members money and that they'd kill him if he didn't repay."

"So he asked you to help him out?"

Nicki delicately nibbled a slice of tomato. "Yeah . . . I thought I was helping the guy I loved. And I was convinced Zak loved me. But he spun the same line to lots of different girls. He didn't owe any money; he was just preying on our naïveté to earn him easy money."

"That's horrible."

"He fixed me up with a room. Painted purple it was, with purple drapes and purple sheets on the bed. I'd turn up at nine in the morning and guys would come to the room to fuck me until midnight; then I'd go home."

"Oh, Nicki." Pamela felt a lump in her throat. "That has to be the worst thing."

"Oh, there are worse things. Like you saw today. Anyway, I stuck it out for fifteen months. During that time I learned Zak had other girls doing the same in other rooms in the building. Guys screwed us girls for cash, and Zak collected at the door." She grimaced. "He beat girls up when they didn't perform like they should. And he supplied the heroin. The drugs kept us going." She blinked as if the mental images had gotten too vivid. "Stopped the hurt, too."

"But you got away in the end."

"Sure. One morning Zak gave me the address of a hotel and told me I was going into corporate entertainment. A Peruvian sales team was in town. They wanted to pass around a blonde for the morning before they went to the conference in the afternoon."

"The guy was a monster."

"Anyway, he gave me enough money for a cab to the hotel. Only I walked to the bus station. I didn't have a destination in mind, so I bought a Greyhound ticket that would get me farthest away from Zak."

"And wound up here."

Nicki smoothed back her still-damp blond hair. "Yeah. After another five weeks' worth of adventures."

"Sharpe found you?"

"Yeah. I was renting out old pussy here to a bunch of soldiers who'd gone AWOL down in Victorville. They'd taken some bad acid and were planning to drag me behind their truck on a wire. They said they wanted to see how fast I could run. Even took bets on what speed I'd reach before I lost my balance."

"And *he* showed up just in time."

"That's Sharpe's trademark." Nicki sipped her drink. "It's uncanny, but he's always there just at the right time."

"Like an angel."

"I'll say. Anyway . . . Sharpe took care of the guys."

"And you rode back on his bus full of mannequins."

"Absolutely." She smiled. "That was two years ago this spring. They welcomed me here in Pits like a long-lost daughter. For a spell I did a lot of cold turkey; the heroin addiction took some shifting. But Lauren and the rest were there for me. Night and day."

"Sounds like you went through hell, Nicki."

"And then some." She smiled warmly. "But I'm in heaven right now."

"That explains a lot," Pamela said. "But when I knocked Zak cold Lauren had no plans to turn him over to the cops, had she?"

"You popped a blood vessel in his brain anyway."

Pamela recoiled. "You mean I killed him?"

"He deserved it. The rat."

"But the police will accuse me of homicide."

Nicki shook her head. "Pamela, listen to me. The cops will never know."

"They're gonna get rid of the body? Just like Sharpe did with Rodney, the guy who tried to kill me?"

"Oh, they'll dispose of it properly. He'll even make a valuable contribution to our little town's economy."

"You're going to eat him, aren't you?"

"You'd best wait until you hear what Lauren has to say." Nicki took another bite of her tuna sandwich.

Lauren turned up at the trailer at eleven o'clock. Outside there was a perfect desert darkness. Plus silence absolute. Beautifully cool, too. Lauren looked exhausted.

She looked satisfied as well.

"A job well done," she told them as she eased herself down into one of the trailer's armchairs in the lounge. She gave a huge sigh that came all the way from the straps of her sandals.

Pamela asked, "Could you use a cold beer?"

Lauren nodded. "Oh, yes, please; that'd be wonderful."

When Pamela returned with a bottle white with refrigerator frost, Lauren gave a little moan of pleasure. "Oh, that looks good."

Nicki smiled. "As you always say, on nights such as these God lives in a cold drink."

"Hear, hear." After she'd taken a deep good swallow of amber liquid she nodded to Pamela as she stood by the doorway. "Best rest your bones. I've got a story to tell."

Pamela sat down beside Nicki on the couch.

Okay, she thought. *Lauren has hippie looks, but she does things no hippie ever would. Something tells me that she's going to tell me that Pits is a cannibal town after all.*

Pamela had a sense that her world would change once again as she sat there in the trailer with Lauren and Nicki.

"Well," Lauren began, "the first news is that we're going to have some new specials on the café menu. We'll be featuring the Pits Burger Largesse; that's a double meat patty in a bun. We'll also be offering two pork steaks for the price of one."

"Zak?" Pamela ventured.

"After using Nicki here for so long, we get to use bad-boy Zak for at least the next few days."

Pamela couldn't believe her ears. "You mean we're eating the guy?"

"It's not compulsory for us," Lauren said in a no-nonsense way. "But we're serving him to the cafe's customers."

"Although Hank likes to make his own recipe for blood sausage," Nicki said. "He calls it his vampire bait. Sorry, Pamela. This is all a bit new to you, isn't it?"

Pamela gulped. "Just a tad."

I'm glad it isn't suppertime. And I don't want to even think how the old-timer, Hank, makes blood sausage. . . .

"Okay." Lauren set her beer bottle on the table. "Let's begin at the beginning. Back in the sixties Pits was a ghost town. Years ago they used to mine borax here. It was a rootin'-tootin', son-of-a-gun kind of place." Lauren smiled. "A real Wild West town with shoot-outs at the saloon. There was a population of more than five hundred. Then by 1920 the borax was all mined out; people drifted away. Soon it was deserted. Then in 1970 a man settled here. They called him Priest."

"He was the town's only inhabitant?" Pamela asked. "Sounds more hermit than priest."

"I guess you could say his was a spiritual calling," Lauren continued. "You see, he'd come from a family that was rich in money but poor in love. He believed that building a society where people cared for one another was more important than owning lots of possessions. Priest had drifted around the hippie communes of San Francisco—summer of love and all that. Only he was antidrug, and so the communes weren't for him. Also they—the people who claimed they were dropping out of society—still wanted to live in the big cities. Priest hankered for wilderness country."

"So he found Pits."

"Indeed he did," Lauren said. "He moved into the big house near the cemetery. Of course, it was long abandoned by then. First he fixed it up. Then he went out on the road looking for society's casualties—the men and women who have fallen through the cracks due to drink, drugs, poverty, mental illness. One by one, he started bringing them in. Some left after a while; some stayed on and found healing in this place."

"Hank must have been one of the first," Pamela said. "He told me he came here in 1972."

Lauren nodded. "Hank was the ninth person Priest saved."

"Just like Sharpe saves people now?"

"Sharpe stepped into Priest's shoes when he couldn't continue anymore."

"What's Hank's story?"

"That's for Hank to tell. If he chooses. But it's enough to say that modern life didn't suit Hank. He opted for something that suits his nature."

"I see."

"Here in Pits we're all refugees from the modern world in some shape or form."

Nicki added. "Pamela knows what happened to me. And about Zak."

"And good riddance to him," Lauren said with feeling. "At least he's going to bring some money into the neighborhood. And as for me . . . I suffered anxiety attacks. It got so I couldn't ride a bus or walk down a street, never mind visit a store. I just got it into my head one day four years ago that if I camped out in the desert by myself everything would be fine. Of course, city girls don't come to a place like the Mojave and pitch their tent under a cactus and everything will be hunky-dory. I got sunstroke, drank bad water from a spring, got dehydrated and delirious; then to round off a hell of a month, a snake bit me. I was laid out on a sand dune waiting to die when I saw a bus on the road, way in the distance."

"Sharpe?"

"Yup. Guardian-angel Sharpe. My future husband." Lauren gave a weak smile. "If he'll marry me."

"He will." Nicki leaned forward to squeeze Lauren's knee. "Just give him time."

Lauren blinked away a tear. "How Sharpe saw me from that distance I'll never know. But I remember lying there being burned to cinders by the sun and seeing this giant with a flattop haircut walking right through the heat haze toward me. There were times I'd swear his feet never even touched the ground as he walked." She smiled. "Or maybe I'm being too romantic for my own good. Anyway, he brought me to Pits. Together we fixed up the café. It was just a ruin in those days. Opened it up; we've been doing nice business ever since. And somewhere along the line I stopped being anxious about the world. The panic attacks just vanished."

Pamela had to broach a difficult subject. "I understand what you're going to do with the guy I walloped with the frozen pork. But I don't understand *why* you took to eating people."

"Priest started it before we all came here. He told us that eating human flesh is like a magic rite."

"Magic? Lauren, Nicki, that's cannibalism. Cannibalism is barbaric."

"It's misunderstood." Lauren took a deep breath as she explained. "Rites of eating human flesh have been commonplace in human history. It empowers people. Eating human flesh cured us of our anxiety attacks, our drink and drug addictions. It even cures people of low self-esteem. You see, if you eat a person's flesh you absorb their power."

"So all those abandoned cars out in the lot belong to people you've eaten?"

"Mostly from a long time ago. Priest told us that society chews good people up and spits them out; therefore, we had every right to chew society up."

"Only we didn't spit—we swallowed," Nicki added.

"My God."

"That's how Priest was able to buy the things that Pits needed. He even had the dirt road through here paved on the proceeds of jewelry and cars he could sell."

"But you preyed on innocent travelers," Pamela said in protest. "You murdered people. Stole their belongings. Ate their flesh!"

"I guess we came to that conclusion, too. You have to understand that

Priest was a visionary. He had this charisma. Everything he told us we believed. Then maybe his cure for us worked better than he could have dreamed. We realized we shouldn't murder travelers and devour them. So we stopped. And"—she sighed—"Priest had to go."

"And Zak?"

"Every rule has its exceptions." Lauren picked up her beer. "If someone comes here intending to do us harm, like Zak, then they're gonna end up on the menu."

Nicki said, "And we sell their possessions to add to community funds. Zak'll have enough gold in his fillings and jewelry to buy us another trailer."

"But what about the guy I saw last night?" Lauren asked.

"Ah, Marvin White?"

"I don't know his name. A curly-headed guy. Sharpe brought him in on the bus."

"That was Mr. White."

"Are we eating him, too?"

"No." Lauren laughed as if the idea were ridiculous. "Mr. White is a geologist. He got lost in the hills. Sharpe found him. He figured it best to bring him here to spend the night. Then in the morning he drove him back to find his car."

"So he didn't wind up as dish of the day?"

"No, of course not. Mr. White is a perfect gentleman with a career and a family. So he didn't need saving in the sense that we needed saving when we couldn't live in regular society. He certainly wasn't planning to do us harm. So we offered him hospitality like any civilized human beings would. Now he'll be safely back home in Barstow."

"Hmm."

"You don't believe me?"

"Well, I did see all those shoe boxes in the utility room, full of spectacles and dentures and stuff."

"Oh, they're years old."

"Back from when Priest was in charge," Nicki said.

Pamela remembered what she'd found in one of those boxes of personal belongings.

"But there was a diary. Two boys who'd run away from summer camp.

They wound up here. . . . One claimed that you'd eaten his friend and planned to eat the other one later."

"Oh, that'll be Benny Loscoff."

"Loscoff. That's the one."

"Back then Priest told Benny that's what had happened to his friend, Gyp, and that we planned to munch on Benny, too. In truth, Priest was getting a little soft in the head. Sharp drove the boys home." Nicki smiled. "We've got a letter of thanks from the mothers for saving their sons, if you don't believe us."

"What happened to Priest?"

"Priest's no longer here." Lauren didn't add any more about the mysterious guru, Priest. Instead she said, "In fact, Mr. White said he planned to drive out here with his wife and family on the weekend to have lunch at the café."

"Okay, Lauren, Nicki, I believe you. Eating people is a strange notion, but . . ." She shrugged. "Like they say, it's a dog-eat-dog world."

"Ain't that a fact."

For a second all three stared at each other. Then Pamela gave a snort . . . followed by another snort. A second later she had a fit of giggles.

Lauren looked at Nicki.

They were relieved. Pamela knew what they were thinking.

Pamela's all right. She's one of us now.

They started smiling.

Smiles turned into laugher. Soon all three were rocking too and fro, they laughed so hard.

At last Pamela could catch her breath.

Grinning, she asked, "Is it true? Do people really taste like pork?"

None of them could answer. Laughter had them in fits again.

CHAPTER THIRTY-FOUR

The same moment that Pamela, Lauren, and Nicki laughed until tears rolled down their eyes in the trailer, Boots, Duke, and Norman warmed themselves around the campfire.

"Midnight," Norman told them as he looked at his wristwatch.

"Is that a fact?" Duke was nonchalant. He lay on his side smoking a cigarette. He was at ease with the place.

Boots sat with a jacket around her broad shoulders. "Sure gets cold in the desert at night."

"Sure does," Duke agreed.

"I guess tomorrow we'll have to find some way of getting to the nearest habitation." Norman poked the fire with a stick. Sparks flew into the night sky.

Duke yawned. "Sure. We need to pick up a new set of wheels."

"And something to eat and drink." Norman thought about sizzling steaks, cold beer, ice cream.

And all we've got left is one lousy can of soda.

"Could use a shower," Boots told them. "I'm itchy like I got ants in ma' pants."

"Ain't that a picture to conjure with, Normy?"

Norman grimaced. "Ain't it just."

Hell, the pair irritated the bejesus out of him.

Only it's not wise to criticize Duke. I sure don't want another beating from the guy.

Next time it might not be fists.

Tough guy might decide to use the knife.

"Know what feels good?" Duke asked them.

"Clean sheets?" Norman ventured.

"Nope. Better than that."

Boots said, "Making whoopee in clean sheets."

"Nope." He sat up. "Being with your best buds. Just like now."

"Gee, I don't know what to say." Boots's piggy eyes filled with sentimental tears.

Don't blow it, Norman, he told himself.

"I couldn't agree with you more," he said with a cheesy smile.

"I'm kinda thinking it's like my honeymoon," Boots told them with a gulp. "Only I got two husbands for the price of one."

Oh, Christ, woman . . .

"Maybe the King is up there watching over us." Duke's face was solemn. "You know, I think he brought us together like this for some"—he rooted around inside his brain for the apt word—"for some higher purpose."

Norman bit his lip.

I wanna laugh.

But if I laugh in his face I'm a dead man.

But the idea of it: Elvis Presley looked down from heaven and decided the three of us should meet? For crying out loud.

Norman had to bite his lip harder, then put his head down as he sat in front of the fire, his knees pulled up toward his chest.

"What's the matter, Norman?"

Oh, Jesus. Duke had seen him choking back the laughter.

He kept his eyes closed but knew his shoulders were shaking as a peal of laughter tried to escape his body.

He put one hand over his eyes. Duke would be reaching for knife.

Then something red and wet was going to smear the pristine desert floor.

Then Boots said in a low voice, "Poor Normy. Look at him, Duke."

"I'm looking." An ominous tone.

"The poor pet lamb is crying."

"Crying?" Duke sounded surprised.

"Poor Normy can't have had no close friends like us before, Duke. He's getting all emotional."

A lifeline!

This I gotta grab.

Now it was suddenly easy to change genuine laughter into fake sobs.

Boots shuffled around to him on her backside to hug him in a mothering kind of way. "Don't worry, Normy. We're here for you. We're proper friends—just like that TV show. Here, let me kiss those tears away for you."

She kissed his eyes.

It felt more like the lips of a hog snuffling wetly over his eyelids.

Dear God, I've gotta get outta this place!

When Duke spoke next it was surprisingly caring. "This kind of thing's hard on a college boy. But we'll take care of him. He's one of us now.

Holy shit. I'm stranded in the desert with a pair of crazies. Them telling me I'm one of them isn't what the doctor ordered.

Gotta get away from them somehow. Otherwise they're going to be the death of me.

CHAPTER THIRTY-FIVE

Norman woke with the morning sun on his face.

The first thing he saw: Boots taking a pee behind a cactus.

Oh, no, it's not a pee she's having!

Norman turned over. His bed for the night had been desert sand, surprisingly soft.

Duke stood by the truck, smoking a cigarette. Sleeping rough had left his dirty blond hair even spikier. Even though he'd been staring out across the barren land, with nothing but dunes, rocks, and cactus in sight, he seemed to know that Norman looked at him.

Without turning, Duke intoned, "Gonna have to move out today, bud."

"Sounds good to me."

"We're gonna have to do it on foot."

Norman was going to point out that he knew the truck's motor was busted, thank you very much. But he'd learned to be wary of Duke's mood swings.

Duke said, "We should find a motel before long. We'll check in. Rest awhile."

Motel? Out here? On a Mojave Desert back road? The guy's gotta be out of his frigging mind.

But Norman wasn't going to risk yanking the hard man's cord. "Yeah, we should find one before long."

"All finished," Boots called out brightly. "You boys can look now."

"Uh, sorry." Norman looked too quickly. He saw her hoisting her denim cutoffs up over a creamy expanse of skin interrupted only by a strip of dark hair.

She giggled. "Oh, you boys. Betcha you were peeping at me all along."

"No, ma'am," Duke said. "I wouldn't watch a lady squirting her nuggets."

"Nor me," Norman added with genuine feeling.

"Well, maybe I believe you; maybe I don't." She finished tugging up the zipper. "Only don't go walking near this cactus here or you might step in something."

With that Boots came out walking what she must have imagined her dainty walk, her grubby white boots chugging through the hot sand.

Man, how those boots must be cooking her feet.

"Okay," Duke said. "Grab your belongings from the truck. Time to hit the road."

"I'll show some leg and get us a ride." Boots raised one of her thick legs.

Norman saw white skin through the slit in her cutoffs.

Ugh, what makes her so deluded? Only guy who's gonna give her a ride will either have to be a pervert or desperate for a poke.

Yeah, just like me, Norman thought. *You do crazy things when you're desperate for a woman.*

"What're you scowling at me for, Normy?" Boots asked.

Jeez, he must have pulled a sour face when she'd been talking about how eager a guy would be to stop for her.

"Yeah, what you so unhappy about?" That annoyed tone crept back into Duke's voice.

Norman thought fast. "Boots is wearing a tank top."

"You got a problem with that?"

Boots puckered her lips in a hurt, little-girl expression. "I like it. Don't you like it, Normy?"

Duke grunted. "You weren't complaining when you were aiming to catch a look at her titties."

Norman forced a smile. "No. Course I like her top. It's just that she's got bare shoulders, and that sun's going to get pretty hot today."

Duke nodded. "You got a point, Norman. See, Boots? He just had your interests at heart."

"Oh, Normy, you're always taking care of me." Delighted, she kissed him on the cheek.

"Don't want that bootiful skin to burn," Duke said. "Best cover up your shoulders before we start marching."

"I've got just the thing." Boots delved into her big denim bag. She pulled out a huge white T-shirt. "I bought this for bedtime." Beaming, she gave a hop of her shoulders. "But as I sleep naked as a jay in the summer, it's gonna work fine as a shawl." She draped it around her shoulders.

"Don't forget your bag, Norman." Duke reached into the truck, then hauled out Norman's rucksack.

"Thanks, Duke." Norman hoisted it onto his shoulders.

"Okay." Duke slipped on his shades. "Let's roll."

They started walking. Behind them the useless truck receded into the heat haze. In front of them the road shimmered as it cut a line through the wilderness to a distant horizon.

Nothing but cactus.

Nothing but sand.

Man, I'm thirsty, Norman told himself. *If we don't get fluid soon we're going to die out here. That is, if a rattlesnake doesn't strike first.*

From the clumps of cactus at the roadside he heard the rustle of desert critters. No doubt beady eyes watched the three humans pass by.

Gonna be a tasty snack for all those carrion eaters out there.

Norman glanced up.

Vultures circled.

Great.

Just great.

If only I hadn't stopped at that particular gas station Duke wouldn't have climbed into my car. Would never have met Boots either.

Or killed those two cops.

I'd have been at home with my parents right now.

Not on the run. Holy shit, we're not even on the run now. We're walking through the third circle of hell. We're gonna dehydrate, then die in the dust at the side of the road.

Gonna have some ugly lizard nibbling on my eyeballs by sunset.

"Hear that?" Duke stopped to scan the arid scenery.

"Let me know if you hear a motor," Boots said. "Then I'll start flashing some leg."

There's not going to be any vehicles out here, Norman told himself. *We're way off the highways.*

"Sounds like diesel," Duke said with confidence. He nodded. "Bus or a truck."

Norman could hear squat. Nevertheless he joined the two in scanning the terrain. They held their hands above their eyes to shield them against the unforgiving sun.

"Not a new motor," Duke told them with absolute confidence of someone who knew engines. "But well maintained. New muffler, too."

Norman wasn't going to disagree.

Boots whined, "I don't see shit out there. Only sand and rocks and things."

Norman looked hard. Heat haze made the whole world ripple like it was soft plastic. He saw Joshua trees that resembled men waving at him. Then—

"Hey," Norman crowed. "I see something!"

Boots saw nothing. "Sure it ain't one of those mirror jars?"

"Pardon me?"

"You know—*mirror jars*. When you think you see rivers in the desert that aren't there."

"A mirage? No, it's real."

"I see it," Duke said. "'Way over there to your left."

"I can hear it as well." Norman was pleased.

Salvation!

Norman stared through the distorting effect of hot air at a long vehicle perhaps a mile away from them. Dust billowed high behind it as if it were some old-time locomotive throwing off steam.

"It's a truck," he said.

"Nope," Duke corrected. "A bus."

"Cooee," Boots sang out. She waved both hands over her head.

The bus driver won't see you. It's too far away, you dimwit. Norman would have liked to spit the words at her. Then he figured Duke would disapprove.

He bottled it.

Duke said, "Still heading east."

"The road will bend around," Boots said, hopeful.

Duke shook his head. "These roads are straight."

"You mean it's not headed this way?" Norman was appalled.

"Damn right."

"Oh, shit. We're never gonna be saved."

"Don't give up hope." Boots rubbed his back.

"Never give up hope," Duke said. "Unless you wake up dead in your casket."

Boots laughed at the joke. Norman thought, *Oh, Christ. Gallows humor I don't need.*

I've gotta get a drink.

Gotta rest in some shade.

Duke said, "Come on. Start walking."

They continued along the dirt road. Cactus. Sunlight. Dust. Dunes. Mountains. Plenty of those. But no diners, no houses. No proper freaking road.

Shit. Do I want to die out here?

Not with the gruesome twosome I don't.

Duke must have read the pessimistic expression on Norman's face.

"Don't fret, bud. That bus was running along a regular highway. You can bet your last dollar that this back road plugs right into it."

"A ride would be good."

"I could sure use a little air-conditioning right now," Boots said with a sigh.

Duke grinned, the desert reflecting in his sunglasses. "In a couple of hours from now we'll be in a motel room and Norman will be soaping your mazoomas in the bathtub."

She perked up. "I'll hold Norman to that."

Norman pulled a tight smile. "The pleasure'll be all mine."

Duke tapped his finger against his nose. "But I reckon it's only right Boots sucks my cream pump dry first. After getting us away from trouble I reckon I've earned it."

"Sure you've earned it, Dukey, honey. I don't mind blowin' you right here."

Duke considered. "Later."

Then all three continued walking.

* * *

An hour later saw them at the junction. Now a paved two-lane road ran east and west. In the heat of the midday sun there was no traffic. Not at first . . .

Then Duke tilted his head. "Here she comes again."

"Uh?" Boots's face was red with sunburn. "Here comes who again?"

"Same vehicle," Duke told them. "Big old diesel motor. Purring sweet as honey."

They peered to the east.

Like a ghost manifesting itself from the ether came a large, shining object. It rippled. Was distorted.

Eerie-looking, Norman thought.

A ghost bus.

Here it comes.

The bus surged by with a blast of hot air and dust.

Kept on rolling.

Boots let out a whistle of surprise. "You see that?"

"Yeah," Norman said mournfully. "It went right on by without stopping."

"It's an old school bus," Duke said.

"But not painted yellow," Boots pointed out. "It was a funny-looking gray. And did you see the drapes covering *all* the windows? They were bright yellow."

Duke nodded. "Boy, that motor was running sweet. Someone loves the old girl."

"It didn't stop," Norman reminded them. "It went on by."

Bastard.

Must've seen us. Two guys and a gal.

Drying out under a murdering sun.

"Bastard saw us and left us out here to die." Norman didn't stint on words now. "He'll have been fucking laughing at us as he drove by."

"You can't be sure of that," Duke said.

Norman's throat felt raw, but he still yelled. "The bastard knew we were here. He's fucking laughing at us. Murdering bastard!"

"You might want to revise your opinion of said bus driver," Duke said.

"Why's that?"

"Check out the bus. It's coming back."

CHAPTER THIRTY-SIX

The bus's door opened with a hiss.

Norman was ready to fall on his knees.

Thank God!

Thank Beelzebub, Stalin, and the IRS man, come to that.

Anyone who brought the bus—the miracle bus!—along the road is all righty by me.

He stood by Boots and Duke, who gazed through the open door at the driver. It was hard to see against the glare of sunlight, but he looked like a young guy in sunglasses and boasting a flattop haircut. A suggestion of being lean and fit.

"Your call," the driver said in a controlled voice after the pause. "Ride with me or walk, either's okay with me."

"Riding's my bag. Thank you, sir," Boots enthused. She dashed up the steps.

Duke nodded an understated thank-you at the driver. Then he climbed the steps.

Norman followed, half stumbling in his eagerness to get on board. The strap of his backpack caught on the door mechanism, yanked him back.

Could be a sign?

Could be a demon driver.

But he struggled free. Three seconds later he stood in the aisle with his two amigos. They blinked.

In the dull yellow light sat rows of passengers.

"Not a lively bunch, are they?" Duke observed.

"Please take a seat," the driver told them. "Company rules. No standing while the bus is in motion. No smoking. No talking to the driver."

"You're the boss," Duke said.

"You're a nice man, too," Boots cooed. "I sure am grateful. Really, really grateful. Know what I mean?"

"Thank you, thank you. Oh, Jesus. I thought we were gonna die out there." Norman was close to babbling. "Thank you."

"Take a seat, sir." The driver was scrupulously polite. "You, too, ma'am."

Norman sat alongside Duke and Boots, who had taken the long bench seat behind the driver that faced the aisle.

"Nice drapes," Boots said, waving her arm to take in the yellow fabric covering the windows. "After blue, yellow's my favorite color."

The driver said nothing. Merely released the air brakes. With a whooshing hiss the bus rumbled away. The well-maintained motor rose smoothly in volume as the bus picked up speed. Duke nodded. He knew a healthy internal combustion engine when he heard one.

Norman leaned forward to try catch a better glimpse of their driver. *There's something steely about him. Something kinda righteous, like a preacher on . . .* Norman gulped at his next thought.

A cop.

All he lacked was an officer's hat. His black hair was cut short close to his head at the back and sides. On top his hair stuck up as stiff as bristles on a brush. Norman looked at the man's reflection in the rearview mirror. The eyes covered by shades revealed nothing.

Maybe nothing, that is, but an aura of steely determination.

The face possessed that aura, too. The features were lean, a little rough-looking. Yet the guy had shaved that strong jaw of his so expertly that the skin had a glossy smoothness to it.

Yeah, something of steel in that, too.

Wonder who would win if bus-driver man and Duke went head-to-head in a battle royal?

An elbow dug into Norman's side. He glanced back at Boots. She was making eyes at him.

Not here, woman.

Norman smiled. Nodded.

Then she dipped her elbow into his ribs again and made little tugging movements with her head.

She was gesturing to Norman to notice what was happening in the main seating area of the bus. Norman looked back into the hazy yellow glow.

Odd.

Scratch odd.

Weird.

The yellow drapes appeared to be rugs that had been fastened with silvery strips of duct tape to the frames of the bus's windows.

Whoa, Mr. Bus Driver Man takes his passengers' eyesight seriously. He's not exposing these suckers to the old retina-searing Mojave sun.

But what kind of passengers are these, anyway?

He frowned. Old people. Middle-aged. A young couple in tennis wear. A kid of around eight in a ball cap, jeans, and a T-shirt. There was a slogan there, half-hidden by the strap of a safety belt.

I've been to Pits, it read. *It is the Pits. Pits—something or other . . .* He couldn't read the rest.

And why did everyone sit so upright and so still? No one tried to peek out the covered windows. No one sneezed.

Coughed.

Not a fidget among them. And you always had at least one fidgeter on a bus.

He was still working out the freaky nature of the passengers when Boots piped up.

"Sir . . . Oh, sir? Did you know that you got yourself a busful of dummies?"

The driver didn't turn back. He kept his attention on the road.

Boots persisted. "Sir, there's dummies sitting on the seats."

"No talking to the driver while the bus is in motion, ma'am. Company policy."

Boots scrunched her shoulders with a smile of apology on her piglike face. "Oh, gee. I'm sorry. Just thought you should know, that's all."

"Boots, the guy's gonna know, isn't he?" Duke growled. "His bus, his business who rides in it."

"I guess." She fanned her face with a thick-fingered hand to cool it. "Looks kinda peculiar, don't it, Normy?"

Agree with Boots, and disagree with Duke?

Norman shrugged. "At least they're not throwing peanuts at us."

Duke nodded as if those were wise words.

Boots chuckled and said, "I guess."

Norman's eyes had all but recovered from the hell-glare of the desert sun. In the murky golden gloom of the old school bus he now began to make out its inanimate passengers a little more clearly. Dummies. All of them. Like the kind you find in clothing stores. Most modeled casual wear. Knit pullovers, Bermuda shorts, T-shirts (including one "girl" mannequin who wore a white T-shirt with the slogan, *I ate a Pits Burger and lived to tell the tale*). There was one mannequin dressed in a pin-striped suit and tie. He even wore gold rims to make him look like a well-heeled executive.

"Make great conversation, don't they?" Norman observed.

The driver said nothing. Neither did Duke. To him this was a ride. That was all that mattered. Could have been chimpanzees back there dressed in Hawaiian shirts and tennis shorts. Wouldn't have bothered him.

A ride is a ride, you dig?

Under her voice Boots said to Norman, "They give me the willies."

Norman couldn't resist saying, in a spooky whisper, "I see plastic people."

"Oooh." Boots elbowed him with a girlish laugh. "You're making me all goosefleshy." She pointed at her breasts. "Just look at that. My nipples have gone all hard."

Her breasts jiggled under the tank top as the bus went over bumps in the road. Then Boots slipped her hand onto the inside of Norman's thigh. She smiled up with him with what experienced people called come-to-bed eyes.

Oh, no . . .

He felt himself getting hard against the confining fabric of his underpants.

Man, she's so ugly. So piglike. Only she's got a certain something that fires me up inside.

A cool, air-conditioned motel room would be pretty damn wonderful right now. Nude Boots. Lying on a bed. Stroking her stomach. Teasing strokes that work down toward that magic zone of crisp hair and moist—

"Ten more minutes," the driver announced. "Then you folks can get yourselves some vittles."

He didn't turn around. Didn't say any more.

Norman turned away from hot, sweaty thoughts of a hot, sweaty (and naked) Boots to the view through the bus's windshield. Still brush, mesquite, and cacti. But more ravines and jagged piles of rocks and mountains. Just as desolate as the desert. In fact, seeming even more remote. The granddaddy of wilderness country.

Then straight up ahead a sign:

MAKE A PIT STOP AT PITS
IT'S REALLY THE PITS
PITS, CA.
Pop. 6

The T-shirt on the kid. Norman looked. The slogan blazed across the chest read, *I've been to Pits.*

Norman thought, *Looks like we're heading to Pits, too.*

Hell of a name. He ran his tongue over his lips.

Hell of a name.

CHAPTER THIRTY-SEVEN

That Friday afternoon was a busy one. Pamela had been waiting tables since noon. The weekend traffic had started early. Now there were plenty of people with appetites to satisfy and thirsts to quench, everyone from truckers to vacationers.

Phew-wee. Hot work.

Yet satisfying, Pamela thought, as she served ice cream to a young couple with a child in a high chair. The two-year-old sat munching on a french fry. Once he'd yelled out loud. The little tyke had bitten into his own finger instead of the golden sliver of fried potato.

He was happy now, though. Already he had a dribble of strawberry ice cream on his chin.

At the counter she met up with Nicki.

"The Pits Burger Largesse is really flying today," Pamela said.

Nicki smiled warmly. "Yeah, and to think I never thought Zak had a tender side."

From the griddle Terry sang out, "Three Pits Burgers for table five."

"This job's going to keep me slim," Pamela murmured. "I must walk five miles a day waiting tables."

"You think you're gonna stay?" Nicki's eyes were hopeful.

"Just try and drag me away." She winked at her, then moved to where Terry had set three massive plates on the counter. Double meat patties turned the hamburgers into miniskyscrapers. Surrounding those were fries, coleslaw, and potato salad.

Even though I know what the dish of the day consists of, I'm starting to feel hungry myself. Pamela lifted the plates onto the tray, then whisked them across to three guys in shirts and ties. They waited with eager anticipation for the delicious feast that glided their way in the hands of a beautiful girl.

There was a great tip coming her way. She could sense it.

As she took their appetizer dishes away, Lauren intercepted her with a serious look in her eye.

"Pamela," she whispered by the counter. "Sharpe's brought some people in."

Pamela experienced a sudden thrill. "He *saved* them?"

Lauren nodded. "Look like teenagers. Two men and a girl."

"They're okay?"

"They were stranded in the desert when the their truck broke down. They're tired. Very dehydrated."

"Looks as if they could use some cold drinks."

"And then some."

"You want me to prepare a table?"

"The empty booth. I'll need to talk to them when they eat. Find out their story, that kind of thing."

Pamela sensed a dizzying swirl of déjà vu. *Just a few days ago it was me being brought to Pits. Saved from psycho Rodney by Sharpe.*

"You okay?" Lauren asked, concerned.

"Oh, me? I'm fine. It's just all so new." She looked up at Lauren. "Do you think they've been in trouble?"

"They look pretty tired. Sharpe figures they're running from something." She shrugged. "All they'll say is they were heading down to Las Vegas when they got lost; then their truck died from under them."

"You think they might be lying?"

"'Judge not, lest ye be judged.'" Lauren gave a little smile. "That's what the Good Book says, doesn't it?"

"Wise words." Pamela nodded.

"We always take people as they are. It's how they act and what they say now that defines their character. Not what they did to people, or what people did to them in the past." She handed a menu to a plump old guy in a ball cap. Clearly he looked like a man ready for dessert, in Lauren's eyes. "We've got a real nice fresh-baked apple pie," she told the man.

"Sounds sweet to me, ma'am."

"Large slice, sir?"

"Absolutely."

"Cream or ice cream?"

"Yes, please."

"Apple pie, cream, *and* ice cream." She wrote the order down on her pad. "Table seven. Be right with you in a moment, sir."

"Thank you, ma'am. And let me tell you I've never eaten a hamburger like I've eaten here. Flavor's out of this world."

"Why, thank you, sir. I appreciate your feedback."

"How'd you make 'em taste so good? Kinda sweet and savory at the same time."

"Oh, our secret recipe, sir."

"Secret, eh?" He chuckled. "Oh, you can tell an old man, my dear."

Lauren leaned over to whisper into the man's ear, "If I told you, I'd have to kill you and serve you to the customers."

The man threw back his head and laughed. "Ah, that's rich," he said, wiping his eyes. "Just you keep griddling up hamburgers like that, sweetheart, and I'll keep coming back."

"And you're welcome anytime, sir." Lauren beamed. "Now, I'll get that apple pie."

"And cream and ice cream."

"Shan't forget those, sir."

Lauren and Pamela left the man chuckling to himself.

"Another happy Pits visitor," Pamela observed.

"And speaking of which." Lauren nodded toward the café door. "Here comes Sharpe with his three lost lambs."

Pamela turned to look at the three as they walked through the doors. *Lost lambs?*

Sharpe held the door open for the trio as they sauntered in, covered in desert dust, plus radiating a certain aura that Pamela found somehow disturbing.

She looked at each in turn.

First in: a girl of around eighteen, but she looked a lot older. She had a wide face. Blunt features. Shoulders and hips were broad. Short bleached hair. Clothes consisted of cutoff jeans with slits up the sides that exposed dimpled white skin that contrasted with sunburned legs. Her bare shoulders were exposed by a tight—overly tight—tank top. Her makeup needed refreshing. Looked on the heavy side, too. She carried a heavy denim bag.

What was most striking about her were the boots she wore. Dirty white cowgirl boots with high heels and pointy toes from which a pair of stocky legs emerged.

Second in: a college boy for sure. Late teens. Looked unkempt, as if a nice, tidy kid had been sleeping in a field for a week. He'd gotten nasty-looking bruises on his face. *Sheesh, what was his story?*

Third in: a swaggering tough guy. Could have passed for a young Elvis. Beneath his blond, greasy hair that was swept high, a pair of shades rested on the bridge of his nose. Age? Might be a teen; certainly no more than twenty-one, she guessed. He wore a muscle-hugging T-shirt that would have brought appreciative gasps from girls and jealous glances from guys. On his bottom half, oh-so-tight blue jeans that had faded in a kind of interesting way around the crotch and buttocks. Below the cuffs of the jeans she saw a pair of black motorcycle boots. Metal side buckles winked at her in the late-afternoon light.

Sweet Jesus, this was the template for a bad boy. The kind that good girls fell for.

The kind that girls' dads hated.

That their moms secretly fancied.

But three lambs?

Hardly.

This threesome looked like trouble to her.

But Pits policy, Lauren had said, was to treat everyone as if they were as innocent as newborn babes. Until they did something bad, that is.

Sharpe followed them in, then directed them to one of the booths along the wall. Nicki had gotten pitchers of ice water ready, waiting on the counter. Pamela picked up a couple and weaved through the tables of customers to where "three lost lambs" had taken their seats. The girl and the college boy looked around at their surroundings.

The bad boy didn't give a damn. He stared at his fingernails. He was used to people coming to him with respect writ large on their faces.

Sharpe remained standing by the table.

As she walked up Sharpe extended his hand to the three people. "Pamela," he said. "Allow me to introduce you to three new guests of ours." He nodded at each in turn as he recited their names. "Boots, Norman, Duke."

Pamela didn't get much of an opportunity to talk to them. They downed pitcher after pitcher of ice-cold water. Lauren took a seat beside the college boy. He was called Norman. Duke and the funnily named Boots sat opposite them at the booth. Lauren chatted with them, then signaled to Pamela to take the order.

"You must be hungry," Pamela said. "What can I get you guys?"

"What's good to eat here?" the bad boy called Duke asked, nonchalant as James Dean.

"We've got a special today. Pits Burger Largesse. It comes with all the trimmings."

"Oooh," the girl with the boots—called Boots—cooed. "Sounds scrummy diddly to me. What say you boys?"

"I'll have the Pits Burger Largesse, please. Thank you." Norman was the polite, well-spoken one.

"Got any beer?" Duke asked.

"Bud."

"Bud's cool. Three Buds for me and my buds."

Pamela gave a polite laugh to indicate she noticed the guy's play on words.

But he doesn't laugh. Did he even realize his pun?

This one needs watching. He might be bad news for Pits.

Norman downed another glass of water, then said, "I'm afraid we don't have much cash on us. And I lost my MasterCard when I—"

Lauren waved her hand as if to waft away his words. "Don't worry about money. You've obviously been through an ordeal. This is our treat."

"You don't want us to pay?" Boots sounded dumbfounded.

"No."

"But you'll want something in return?"

"Nothing. It's the least we can do."

"Mighty Christian of you," Duke said.

"Yeah," Boots said. "Last so-called free meal I got left me with a bloody butt and pube lice."

Pamela saw even Lauren gape at the coarse admission.

"Just shows," Boots said, then sipped her water. "Not all preachers are gentlemen."

"You can rest assured," Lauren said firmly, "there'll be nothing like that happening to you in Pits."

Boots shrugged. "I wouldn't have minded, but the preacher promised me that God would—"

"Boots," Duke interrupted. "Let the lady take the orders. She's too busy to hear the life story of your fanny."

Boots clammed up, looking hurt. Her face had the look of a sow badly wronged.

Pamela noticed that Norman looked uncomfortable, as if these two weren't his companions of choice.

Talk about an odd couple—this was an odd trio.

Pamela smiled her professional waitress smile. "So that's three Pits Burgers Largesse and three beers."

Duke touched his eyebrow by way of salute. "Thank you, ma'am."

Pamela went to pass the order on to Terry. Then Nicki joined her at the counter.

Nicki whispered, "Three more Pits Burgers?"

"Yup."

"Looks as if Zak finally did something useful in life. Well . . ." She smiled. "You know what I mean."

"Yeah, for everyone else it's the grave that's inevitable. Zak wound up in the gravy." Then she became serious. "Nicki?"

"Uh-huh?"

"Those three that Sharpe brought in . . ."

"Oh, yeah, I haven't had chance to say hello yet."

"I don't want to put three strangers down, but . . ." Pamela shrugged. "There's something kinda unsettling about them."

"Believe me, Pamela, there was something *unsettling* about all of us when we first arrived here. I screamed for a fix for three weeks solid."

"Yeah, but, these guys are—"

"Shh, honey. Don't fret. They'll be fine."

Nicki hurried away to refill a diner's coffee cup.

Under her breath Pamela breathed, "Gee, I hope they'll be fine. Something tells me there ain't a cop for miles around."

Moments later Terry was flipping some of those pink Pits Burgers on the skillet.

Human flesh sizzles just like a cow's, she told herself. *If only the three strangers knew what—or whom—they were eating.*

From deep down came the additional thought: *Somehow, looking at those three, I don't think they'd give a damn.*

CHAPTER THIRTY-EIGHT

"Who'd they say this trailer belonged to?" Boots asked as she walked into the lounge area with a huge, fluffy white towel around her body and another swathing her head.

Duke shrugged. "Who cares?" He lit a cigarette and sprawled back on the sofa.

Blew smoke at the ceiling.

Thinking.

I get uneasy when Duke starts thinking, Norman told himself. *The guy's planning something.*

Illegal.

Lethal?

Boots took her ease in a black leather armchair. It was old. Worn. Still comfortable, though. Norman sat in its twin by a picture window that looked out toward a cemetery. A real Boot Hill.

Probably a few outlaws sleeping with their boots on up there.

And speaking of boots . . .

Boots frowned. "Didn't Lauren say this trailer belonged to someone by the name of Valeria?"

"Valdemar," Norman corrected. "Lauren said it belonged to a Gregor Valdemar, but he moved on two years ago."

"Shoot. Leave a lovely place like this? I could make my home here, couldn't you, Duke?"

"I don't take root in any one spot. I move around."

"I've moved around too much," Boots said.

"Well, I guess we need to keep moving," Norman said. He watched as Boots bent forward from where she sat on the sofa. She examined a small blister on her little toe where her beloved footwear had rubbed.

Bending had loosened the towel.

He saw soft white cleavage.

Hmmm . . .

Those old thoughts were coming back.

"I'm all for moving on," Duke said, then blew a smoke ring at the ceiling. "Eventually."

"Oh, Dukey, that sounds good to me. We can rest here awhile."

"But the cops—" Norman began.

"You worry too much, bud."

"Besides, I see no cops coming to a little place like this." Boots examined her other foot. One of her boobs flopped out. "Oops, 'scuse me, fellas."

Duke grinned. "Our pleasure."

"You guys ready to shower? That water's awful nice after days on the road."

"Sounds good to me." Duke stood up with a yawn. "Might hit the sack soon, too."

Boots pulled on the towel to make sure she was covered. "Wasn't it nice of these folks to give us the trailer home? It's so big. And there's a refrigerator and a stove and everything."

"They seem like good folks," Duke said. "We should stick around and make sure we show our appreciation."

Duke made that seem ominous.

"Okay, shower time." He left the lounge area.

Boots removed the towel from her head, then rubbed her jaw with it, moaning a little with pleasure at its softness.

Norman looked out the window.

He didn't want to make it seem like he was looking at her bare legs. That towel only just covered her broad rump.

Some rump, too.

His heart beat faster.

Those moaning sounds. She made those when I reamed her.

Oh, boy.

Duke's in the shower.

Now we're alone again. She's making those sounds. Oh, no.

I'm getting a hardy.

Any second she's going to notice. How come part of me finds her repulsive, piglike? But then another part, a part getting bigger by the second, finds her soooo sexy . . . soooo desirable . . .

He was suspicious at the way his emotions adopted these crazy swings from lust to disgust.

Norman stared out the window as if he were enjoying the sunset. His eyes focused on the cemetery on the rise of land. At the top was a freaky-looking house. Just like the Bates house that overlooked the psycho's hotel. The kind of place that had ghosts in the attic.

Vampires in the cellar.

Zombies in between.

Then, behind the house, glowing a deep and bloody red, were rocky hills.

Gee, funny little place. Pits. Population six. Lauren looked like a hippie. Sharpe, the guy who drove them in on the freak bus full of store dummies, could have passed for a cop on his day off, or even a marine on leave. Then there were the waitresses at the café. Pamela and Nicki. They were a toothsome twosome.

Sexy.

Briefly he imagined himself in bed with the pair of them.

Oh, yes . . .

He shifted in the leather armchair as the blood ran hot in his veins.

How about a nice sandwich with those two?

With Norman as the salami filling.

More meat than you can eat, girls.

Blood pounded through his veins. His groin ached.

"Normy?"

"Yes?"

Boots's eyes sparkled. "I know whatcha thinking about."

"You do?"

"You're thinking hot, sexy thoughts."

"I am?"

"And you're thinking 'em about me."

He looked at her. After the shower she did look good; he had to admit that. Her short hair was fluffed. Her skin was clean. A fresh smell filled the lounge from her recently showered body.

"Duke's gonna be some time in the shower yet."

"I guess."

"Norman, you've been really sweet to me. You've taken care of me."

"I do my best."

"You're not like other guys."

Well, you could take that two ways, but Norman took it as a compliment.

"Thank you. Just doing my job, ma'am."

"Now you sound like a cop."

"That's me, ma'am. Officer Norman Wiscoff, reporting for duty."

"Is that a fact?" She scrunched her shoulders.

Yup, no doubting it: her smile was sexy.

He let his eyes roam over her bare legs to where they vanished beneath the fluffy towel.

Hmm . . . She did look good.

"I think the sofa looks more comfortable." She went to it and lay back flat. Her head was raised on cushions.

He stood up. Walked toward her. Some little bit of him found her sexually exciting. And that little bit was growing all the time.

Norman stood over her as she made a pretend sad face. "You're not here to arrest me are you, Officer?"

"I think you might be carrying a concealed weapon, ma'am."

"Then you oughta do your duty, Officer."

Reaching down, he whipped open her towel. Exposed a milky expanse of body. Her breasts had firmed. Nipples hard, pointing.

He groaned under his breath. He was so aroused it hurt.

So he unzipped.

Unbelted.

Undressed.

Oh, God, here I am again. Naked with Boots. I think mean thoughts about her, but when we're naked together . . . I can't stop myself. This is lust. I've gotta have her.

He knelt down on the floor beside the sofa. He buried his face in her breasts. Began kissing her nipples. Tonguing them.

Then he made love to her.

Five minutes later Duke walked into the lounge area. Shower-wet hair. Wearing nothing but blue jeans.

Duke gazed down at the pair of them locked together. His face was expressionless.

Norman looked up at him. Boots looked up at him.

Norman knew it seemed kinda absurd to be still pumping away at Boots.

But both were on the cusp of orgasm. He couldn't stop himself. So he went for the finishing line, thrusting harder and harder, faster and faster into Boots's warm, cummy slickness. Her body convulsed.

Then both climaxed in a rucking, bumping, grinding chorus of squeals from Boots and a panted "Yes!" from Norman.

Duke still stared down at them as they stopped moving and their cries subsided to postclimactic panting sounds.

"I've gotta plan," Duke told them, just as if he'd found the pair doing nothing more than reading magazines. "This place Pits . . . we're gonna make it ours."

CHAPTER THIRTY-NINE

Lauren showed the three newcomers around. Pamela went along, too, at Lauren's request.

"It'll be dark soon," Lauren told them. "So it's gonna be a short tour, I'm afraid."

"That's just fine," Boots said. "I'm about all done walking."

"Thank you for showing us strangers your hometown." This was the bad boy, Duke. He spoke respectfully.

A little too respectfully for Pamela's liking.

Or am I just naturally suspicious now?

Hardly surprising after a guy marries you—and he's already married. Then a creep you know from school kills your pseudo-husband, burns down your home, then tries to kill you.

Those life experiences make a girl sorta wary.

Lauren walked a little ahead, while Pamela walked with the three strangers by the sprawl of trailer homes. Boots had an odd quality: naive yet worldly at the same time. She wore lots of makeup, but took a child-like delight in the things she saw.

Norman had a hunted look in his eye. He had education. Probably came from a wealthy family, too. His casual clothes and footwear looked expensive.

Duke swaggered like the young Elvis. He was cool, confident. Possessed an air of danger. She guessed nothing fazed him.

Seen all, done all. Still had a taste for more.

He lit a cigarette with panache.

Guy acts like he owns the world.

Lauren pointed. "This is Pits's cemetery."

"Looks like something out of a Wild West show," Boots commented.

"This was a frontier town in its heyday. Folks moved out when the mines closed." She nodded at two acres of dust where old wooden crosses leaned this way and that with tumbleweeds and cacti for company. "No one's been buried in there for years. Except dogs and monkeys, that is."

"Monkeys?" Norman echoed.

"Owner of the house up there used to own a whole menagerie of monkeys."

Duke gazed through the gathering dusk at the old house with its decaying shutters. "Who lives there now?"

"Oh, no one."

"Big house. Looks as if it could be valuable."

"I guess," Lauren said. "If you were prepared to sink a whole hill of cash into restoring it."

"So, no monkeys there now?" Boots sounded disappointed.

"Not one. Well, no live ones, that is. Hank tells me there's still a couple of stuffed ones up there in the attic."

"Cool," Norman said.

"Who's Hank?" Duke asked.

"The mayor of Pits," Pamela answered. "He's around somewhere."

Duke's eyes narrowed. "And you say there's only seven people who live in Pits?"

"Yup," Lauren said with a smile. "That is, if we include Pamela, and she might just be passing through. But we're optimistic about our population growing."

"I hope it does, ma'am." Duke nodded. "Looks like a nice town."

"We like it."

They continued to the cemetery but stopped short of the old house on the hill. Then they backtracked to the café.

Lauren opened the door for them. "While we've no customers at the moment we might as well grab the opportunity of meeting Pits people under one roof."

They filed in.

"Looks like the whole town turned out to meet us, guys," Boots said. She was beaming at the younger guys—Terry and Wes—and especially Sharpe. Sharpe was as smartly dressed as ever in a crisp white shirt and chinos. He was clean-shaven.

Then there was the old-timer, Hank. He didn't get a second glance from Boots in his weather-beaten clothes and stained hat.

Boots stroked her hair.

Fiddled with the strap of her tank top.

Drawing attention to unfettered breasts beneath the fabric.

Got an eye for the men, haven't you, girl?

All of Pits was there—all seven of them. The guys sat on stools with their backs to the counter, so they faced the new folk in town. They drank bottles of Bud, with the exception of Sharpe.

He hefted a glass of water.

Sharpe had his mission. There was no place for liquor in his life.

Nicki sat at the table nearest the counter.

Lauren introduced the three. "Ladies and gentlemen of Pits, I'd like to introduce you to Boots."

Boots gave a little curtsy.

Elegant it wasn't.

"And these are Duke and Norman."

Pits said, "Hi," "Pleased to meet you." They were friendly, smiling. They were genuinely pleased to have visitors, Pamela realized.

Lauren indicated Hank, in his prospector's clothes with a face shriveled like a sun-dried plum. "And this is Hank. Mayor of Pits."

"Pleased to meetcha. You look like real fine people." He winked at Boots. "Especially you, *mademoiselle*. A real peach, if I might say so?"

Boots fluttered her hand over her face as if it were a fan and she were a Southern belle being courted by an old-money gentleman. "Why, thank you."

Lauren said, "Seeing as it's near to closing time anyway, what say you we have ourselves a little reception party for our new guests. Nicki? Will you get the drinks? I'll set out some snacks. Oh, Pamela?"

"Yes?"

"Would you turn off the café sign and lock the door?"

"I'm right on it."

Soon everyone was chugging down bottles of beer.

Except Sharpe. He still favored water.

If anything, he was the only one who retained his cool reserve. Everyone else was smiling. Lauren stood close to Sharpe several times, showing Boots that they were a couple.

So hands off. He's mine.

Norman looked a little tipsy on the beer. He smiled a lot at Nicki. Her blond Nordic beauty had caught his eye. She politely smiled back.

But I see Terry, who has got the hots for Nicki, starting to show signs of jealousy.

Then, Nicki's never shown any interest in boys.

And Duke's standing almost toe-to-toe with Sharpe as he talks to him.

No aggression whatsoever.

But I get the feeling that Duke is sizing Sharpe up, as if assessing the guy's physique and demeanor just in case he needs to fight him one day.

As Pamela helped Lauren hand out plates of cold cuts, potato chips, dips, nachos, sourdough bread, she felt that unsettling tug of paranoia again.

Is it really paranoia, she thought, or am I reading a whole heap of sinister body language here in the guy who calls himself Duke?

Then there's the hunted expression that haunts Norman's face.

Then Boots? Strange, strange Boots.

It's cruel to label another human being dysfunctional without really knowing her. But then Boots is odd. Sort of not connecting with the rest of the human race.

But then, Pamela was a minority of one.

What happens if I go to Lauren and Sharpe and say, "Hey, those three strangers . . . I don't trust them. They're up to something"? Maybe they'll think I'm the weird one.

Maybe ask me to leave.

And that's what I don't want to do. I like Pits. I like the people here (except the gang of three). I want to stay here. I really do.

CHAPTER FORTY

Norman explored. Though he'd not shared his emotions with anybody, just like Pamela he was uneasy, too.

Duke's got plans for Pits.

He hadn't explained anything in detail. His line had been, *"We're gonna make this place our own."* Duke'd repeated the line often. But he still hadn't described how this would work.

Now, at eight o'clock in the morning Norman decided on a stroll to clear his mind before the heat of the day took the desert and everyone in it prisoner.

But, jeez, he had slept well. No wonder. They'd been on the run for days; he'd been knocked unconscious by Duke; then they'd hiked through the desert and damn near died of thirst.

Would have, too.

If it hadn't been for Sharpe.

Now there's a man who's a mystery wrapped in an enigma. Why does he cruise the desert roads in that old bus full of mannequins?

Some religious conviction?

Some psychotic impulse?

But Sharpe had brought them to a quiet cop-free place. A place with good food. A place with a mobile home that had soft beds.

So he'd slept the sleep of the dead. Never heard a thing.

Even so, he'd been disappointed that Boots had elected to share Duke's bed rather than his. Boots was peculiar. Irritating. Had weird piggy looks.

But Norman couldn't get enough of boning her. He loved it when she sucked his cock. Or when she hunkered down onto all fours with a smiling invitation to screw her dog-oh.

Loved to see her skin blotch as sexual excitement kicked in when he reamed her. The way her titties jiggled with the force of his groin pounding against hers.

His heart began to beat harder. A tingle started in his penis.

Ohhh . . . Just the thought of Boots naked set him on the path of hot, erotic thoughts.

Instead, last night in his bedroom as he undressed for bed, he heard the pair moan with pleasure. The thin walls of the trailer held nothing back. He could even hear the squelch as Duke pumped his rock-hard cock into her wet 'n' happy valley.

Lucky bastard.

He clicked his tongue. "Leave it, Norman. Do some sightseeing."

And at least the noise didn't stop him from falling asleep the second he closed his eyes.

Norman sauntered across the café's parking lot. On one side was the straggling line of trailer homes. On the other was a bunch of cars that seemed abandoned.

Some were real wrecks, so old that Henry Ford himself could have personally pumped the tires before they rolled out of the workshop. Then—and this piqued Norman's curiosity a lot—there were newer cars, several in good shape, despite the dust.

He could see someone stepping into one, starting it up, then driving off in a swirl of dust.

But they clearly hadn't been driven anywhere in a couple of years—tires partly deflated. Windshields thick with dust. One silver Pontiac boasted a big green lizard sunning itself. Who'd leave cars like this at a desert café?

"Someone who couldn't pay the tab," Norman mused. "But would you exchange a new Toyota Land Cruiser for a couple of pizzas?"

No dice.

Not buying that, Tonto.

There was even luggage in the cargo space. Windborne sand had seeped in through the door seals to leave a yellow film on the baggage. He walked along the line of vehicles. Cars, trucks, vans, a pair of motorcycles. A couple of cars were rusted shells. One even had bullet holes in it.

Someone tries to run without paying for the Pits Burger. Lauren, or the sexy Pamela, rakes the car with machine-gun fire. The silly train of thought amused him. He chuckled.

Then the chuckle dried.

This line of abandoned cars is weird, though.

Hey! Who's that strolling up through the cemetery?

Shielding his eyes against the sun rising over barren hills, he stared hard. *Looks like Boots and the blond girl. The Swedish-looking girl. Nicki? Yeah, Nicki. Man, is she a sexy piece of work. Cool as glacial runoff, but, boy, would I like to scale her snowy peaks.*

They were over a hundred yards away. Both seemed to be talking to each other in an earnest kind of way.

"Sharing secrets, girls?" he murmured to himself. Only there was one secret Norman didn't want spilling about himself. And no, not the one about his being a virgin until a few days ago.

Killed two cops, didn't I?

Word of that gets out, I'm gonna fry in the chair.

The Mojave heat had been climbing steadily since sunup. Only now Norman felt a distinct chill creep up his backbone.

He whispered to himself, "I've got to hear what you're telling her, Boots. Don't want you revealing any confidences about me."

Glancing around to make sure no one was watching him, Norman strolled back through the line of trailers to the cemetery gates. Behind him the desert road was deserted. He could see no one. A little blue haze rose from the café flue, Terry must have been frying bacon and eggs. *Hmm, breakfast . . .*

'S gonna have to wait. I need to find out what these two are talking about.

So here goes . . . walking through the cemetery gates . . . following the path up the center.

Brush, dry grasses, cacti; they'd infiltrated the cemetery to grow around old tombstones, wooden crosses. Iron plaques spelled out names, dates, and invitations to RIP. Sometimes an epitaph: *Long was his race, longer will be his rest; Little Jimmy tried his best, only his best weren't good enough. Died weeping for his mama.* Then there were some real old stones that had been almost weathered out.

Norman paused to read one out loud to himself. "'Eli Crabber. Shot by Sheriff Dunbar, Christmas Day, 1878.' Holy shit. A real-life shoot-out."

He looked back at Pits. It still had the look of a frontier town. It was an island standing in a whole ocean of sand. Across the road from the café he could make out rectangular depressions in the earth where buildings once stood. Probably the town's jail alongside the saloon and maybe a brothel or two. All rotted, then blown away by the Mojave winds.

He peered against the hot sun.

Boots and Nicki still walked uphill. They'd left the cemetery now—heading up toward the abandoned house on the hill.

Probably this was the only original house from Pits's glory days as a working mining town. Must have belonged to the richest guy in town. The guy who owned the bank, maybe.

Or, more likely, the owner of the mine. Back then a guy like that would have had the power of life and death over the people of Pits.

His mine.

His town.

In Norman's mind he could see a big man of around fifty dressed in a suit and stovepipe hat. He'd have had big, bushy side-whiskers and would stoop up there on his porch with one of those old-time pocket watches in his hand.

Gotta make sure that the miners aren't late for work.

And when they were all down in the pits, hacking rock faces with their picks, Mr. Big would stroll down through *his* town until one of the miners' women caught his eye. Then he'd order her up to his house to wash. Once she was freshened up he'd exercise his rights as employer to the max.

Oh, boy, oh, boy. Norman sure wished he were that mine owner.

The fantasy was so pleasurable he nearly had an accident in his underpants.

Pausing, he took a few steadying breaths. Up ahead the two women had almost reached the house. Boots could have asked Nicki to show her the stuffed monkeys.

Yeah, whatever floats your canoe.

Just hope she doesn't bring one back to the trailer as a souvenir. Don't want to share the place alongside a fusty chimpanzee with glass eyes staring at you all the time. Give anyone the creeps.

Even as he walked the last few yards through the cemetery, he saw rows of newer headstones that were in a different style to the rest. These had just a single name painted on them: *Jango. M'pallar. Mansize. Rebo.*

Never ever owned a monkey, he thought, *but these sure look as if they could be names for baboons and shit.*

He headed for the cemetery exit. The path continued to wind up the hillside. Here it was pretty much barren, although off to his right he could see a thicket of cottonwood trees where there might be some moisture oozing up from the rocks below ground.

Beyond that the land rose to more arid territories. All he could see were greenish swatches of cholla cacti. From here their "fingers" looked fluffy and soft, but he knew they bristled with sharp spines.

From dry plants near a tombstone with *Stoker* written on it came the ominous rattle of one of the desert's bad guys.

Norman hastened.

Soon he was through the rickety fence—just in time to see the pair of women disappear into the house.

If Boots blabs about the way I killed the police officers, Nicki's gonna race out of the house and come running down through the cemetery to the café, where she's gonna dial 911.

You can bet your bottom dollar that's not gonna happen. 'Cause I can't let it happen.

Wild thoughts rose in his mind. Of him beating down on Nicki's head with one of the broken tombstones. Then burying her.

Best place to bury the person you murdered is in a cemetery. Place is full of stiffs anyway.

He licked his suddenly dry lips.

Course, Normy, before you murder the beautiful blond woman you must make use of her facilities first.

Oh, my God. He stopped. His own thoughts startled him. *Am I really starting to think like Duke now? That people are like gum? Chew 'em up, then when the flavor's gone, spit 'em out?*

Even though it was hot, his bones got even colder.

Still, it was his survival he was thinking about now.

Gotta put numero uno first. Me, myself, I is the important one.

Even if that means the delicious Nicki winds up lying in the ground with monkeys.

Norman walked faster to the house now that the pair had gone inside. Upon reaching it, he immediately tiptoed around the side, rather than up to the front door through which Boots and friend had entered.

His heart beat faster.

His palms sweated.

Afraid?

Yes.

Excited?

Definitely.

Norman wondered if one way or another he'd wind up leaving a mess in his pants after all.

He circled around the back of the house. Shutters sagged from hinges. Sandstorms had long ago taken the paint off the woodwork. They'd even begun to sculpt the window and door frames into weird shapes. All the glass in the windows was in place.

Maybe a modicum of care had been exercised on the building. Perhaps by that old-timer who looked like a mule skinner. Hank probably came up here to keep the building secure.

So does that mean there's something of value in there?

Norman reached the far side of the house. There was no yard to speak of. It looked as if the whole house had been picked up from someplace else, then plonked down here onto the hilltop. Surrounding the house was nothing but loose, dry earth and stones. A tumbleweed had rolled up to sit against a basement window. At the back of the house were craggy yellow hills. The place was an advertisement for wilderness. It was as barren as the dark side of the moon.

For a moment he stood eyeballing the two-story house with its spooky crooked roof from which poked an even more crooked chimney.

No sounds from inside.

Boots was chuckling over the stuffed monkeys, no doubt.

Better that than telling Nicki about their adventures on the drive south from Oregon.

No one from the café or the trailers could see him on this side of the house, so he didn't have to be furtive anymore. He strolled forward to take a gander through the window. Through the dusty glass he saw red-checked drapes that were part open. Between the gap he saw an old-fashioned kitchen with a big iron stove. A kitchen table and chairs, too. On the table were a couple of china plates.

Not quite the wreck Norman expected.

Not quite home away from home, either.

Probably a snake or two curled up under the john in the bathroom, just waiting for the unwary to slip down their pants as a prelude to a dump, then—

Wham!

A pair of poison fangs right in the butt.

Hell, who in this place would suck out the poison? He thought about the full lips of Pamela. *She'd be first on my list.* But as so often happened with imagination, it shot images into his head that were just plain unwelcome.

As he smiled to himself, picturing Pamela walking toward him saying, *"Best get out of those clothes, Norman. I've got to suck out every last drop of that venom,"* the unwholesome image sneaked in. This time of old Hank in the prospector's hat that looked as if a mule and his best friend had shit in it for luck.

Norman couldn't stop the imaginary episode from kicking in.

Poor Norman running back into Pits yelling that a snake had bitten his right buttock. Then Hank licking his scabbed lips that in turn revealed gums that were barely interrupted by a few brown, twisted teeth. And surrounding the mouth from hell was the thick mustache and beard.

The man's bloodshot eyes would gleam in anticipation. *"Looks like ya got yerself an ass full of venom there, feller."*

Norman would say he'd be just fine.

Only old Hank would hitch up his belt, all the time shaking his head. *"Nope. Nothing fer it; I'm gonna have to suck out the poison meself."* Pause to spit out a plug of tobacco in a stream of yellow saliva. *"Yup, you drop them college-boy panties; then I'll suck out that rattler juice before it rots your tricky dicky right off of you."*

"No, I'll be fine, thank you."

"Don't want to go through life whizzing like a dame, do you?"

Then the indignity. Dropping his pants in front of Hank. Then bending over waiting for the wet mouth to batten on his buttock. Then the slurping, sucking—followed by spitting—as Hank drew out snake venom.

Of course, as Norman bent over bare-assed, Hank would say something like, *"Now young, feller, I'll be saving your life, so you don't go doin' a number two in my face, all right?"*

A cry.

Norman jerked himself out of his imagined scenario. Jeez, he'd have to learn to stop his imagination from running away with him. Thoughts of Hank sucking on his butt like a baby sucking on its mother's breast weren't a pretty sight. Not even plug-fuck imagined ones.

Norman looked up at the storm-scarred walls of the house. *Shit.* Where did the cry come from?

And who cried out?

Nicki?

Boots?

Could be Nicki. Boots killed the guy in the motel. Murder was no stranger to her. Maybe the stuffed monkeys weren't to Boots's taste. Now she was extracting suffering from the beautiful blond waitress.

Shit. No fair.

Norman wanted a peek at Nicki's goodies first. He ran to the next window.

Peered in.

Some kind of office. A typewriter on a desk. Racks of files.

He hurried to the next window just as another cry sounded. This one higher. What the hell was Boots doing to hurt that blond goddess? Probably hammering a nail into her forehead.

The cry had that kind of quality. Made Norman's hair stand up on his neck.

Next window.

Norman thrust his face to the grimy pane. Stared in. And saw . . .

And saw . . .

Holy moly!

He couldn't believe his eyes.

Boots had done all kind of things, but he couldn't believe she'd do that.

What's French for sixty-nine?

Norman's mouth dried. His heart hammered. Blood whooshed

through his neck to swirl around his brain so forcefully vertigo nearly tipped him backward onto the ground. His eyes bugged. He couldn't stop watching.

Hell! He didn't want to stop watching!

Couldn't stop watching if I tried. Nicki and Boots. Both naked. They were in a room empty of everything but a large rug that covered half the floor. Boots's short, stocky body was a hell of a contrast to Nicki's long, slim bod with firm breasts that were in perfect proportion to the rest of her frame.

Unlike Boots's small, soft breasts that were set on a broad-shouldered torso.

Man, oh, man. Norman looked at the women, trying to work out who was doing what to whom. Nicki was on all fours with Boots lying underneath her. It was the classic sixty-nine position.

Right now Nicki wasn't doing anything with her tongue. She held her head up. Her blond hair cascaded softly about her shoulders. Her eyes were closed, her lips partly open. She was smiling.

And she was the one crying out.

Cries of pleasure.

Norman turned his attention to Boots. She lay with her head under Nicki's groin, with Nicki's knees planted on either side of Boots's head on the rug.

But what was Boots doing to Nicki? He could see the blond spiky hair bob as Boots moved her head up and down. Only he hadn't bargained on—

Damn!

His breath had gotten so hot it steamed up the windowpane. Now all he saw were misted blobs. He raised his hand to wipe the glass. Decided against it.

The *squeak-squeak* of his sweating fingers on glass would betray him.

And, jeez, this I gotta see, he told himself, panting, groin aching.

Instead, he had to move his head to a different pane of glass in the window, then find part of that that wasn't too obscured by dust.

"C'mon, c'mon, you're missing all the action," he hissed to himself.

Then he found another area of the glass that possessed a heaven-blessed clarity.

Thank God!

Oh, now he could see. Could see real well.

So this was how it went: Boots lay flat on her back with her head raised by a pillow.

Great!

Only this was unusual: what was Boots doing with her hand?

Nicki cried out in pleasure. Almost howling. Boots grunted, too—a snuffling sound that Norman could hear through the window glass.

Norman was gasping as well. His knees shook.

His breath misted the window.

Oh, no . . . missing the action, missing the action!

He found another clear area of pane.

Looked in. Saw that both women moved faster with excitement.

Both were sweating.

Both were flushed with exertion.

Both were panting.

And Norman was panting, too.

And his breath went and misted the window all over again. He found another pane. Only this one was obscured by a spider's web. All he could see were two pale shapes jiggling around in there. It looked good. It looked real fine . . . but he couldn't make out detail.

Boy, he realized he did need detail. And plenty of it. He found a clean corner of glass. All he could see were Nicki's bare feet. The way she scrunched her toes in ecstasy excited him more than words could say.

Uh . . . Norman didn't know if he could take any more of this.

"Oh, yes, oh, yes!" That was Nicki!

Norman darted his face to another corner of the window. Now he could see Nicki from the shoulders up. Damn, he couldn't make out the rest of her bod, nor Boots's. Nicki cried out the words again while twisting her head from side to side so wildly her long blond hair flew. Norman marveled at it. He'd never seen hair as beautiful as this. Like summer cornfields and gold dust all rolled into one.

But Norman had to see *all* the action. Had to witness what those two sex-crazed women were doing to each other.

He risked wiping away a misted section of glass with the tip of his finger. It squeaked a little, but he figured those two were making enough noise to drown out a mule braying, never mind the faint *squeak-squeak* of his sweaty fingertip.

He saw naked bodies . . . but . . . *Oh, God, no.* The glass was still blurred with grime. All he could discern were two indistinct shapes. Even so, he knew they were feminine. They were Boots and Nicki going for broke.

Faster . . . faster, faster, faster . . .

The pair cried as they climaxed in body-shaking judders.

Moments later they lay side by side on the rug, panting, sucking in air so their chests rose and fell.

At last Norman found he could move back from the window.

Oh, no, I don't believe it.

Norman realized that the clean underwear he'd slipped on just an hour ago was no longer in a condition he could be proud of.

He decided to go back to the trailer. To swab away the "night custard," as one of his high school buddies used to call it. Change into a fresh pair of boxers.

Norman had just turned the corner of the house when he noticed something else. At the bottom of the slope at the far end of the cemetery was a shallow gully.

There was Duke.

He was engaged in strange behavior as well.

CHAPTER FORTY-ONE

Norman stared.

Duke walked backward in the dusty gully. He walked backward because he was hauling a sausage-shaped object wrapped in a tarpaulin.

In dry grass by the cemetery fence a creature Norman couldn't see chattered to itself. It could have been chattering over and over, *Oh, no, here we go again.*

Because Norman saw what the shape in the tarp was suggestive of. Other than sausage, that is. Because it would have to be a big sausage. A big, guy-sized sausage. And Duke was having to dig his heels into the dirt so hard to find purchase that he was kicking up a whole fog of yellow dust.

Norman glanced down toward the café. No one could see Duke from there, but they might see the dust cloud, then start wondering what was happening near the cemetery.

Maybe some kind of resurrection action. That had to tug their curiosity string. Or maybe they'd picture a funky zombie-monkey scenario. *Long-dead baboon's coming back to life, clawing its way to the surface. . . .*

Oh, shit. Norman would have to do something about his maverick imagination.

He turned back to the big old house. Boots and Nicki would still be busy exploring each other's bods. Too busy for Nicki to see what Duke was doing.

At that moment Duke looked back over his shoulder. "Hey," he called. "Come here and give me a hand."

Shit, I'm involved again. Another of Duke's adventures.

This's all gonna end in tears one day soon.

Norman shot glances down at the café as he picked his way across the stone-covered ground. He still hadn't forgotten that rattlesnake/Hank scenario that his imagination had treated him to. So he trod carefully toward Duke.

Can't give those snakes a free shot at my rear.

Luckily, it was still early. No one seemed of a mind to stroll around Pits at this hour. Sharpe's bus with the yellow drapes still sat in the lot alongside the abandoned vehicles.

Norman descended into the gully. It was a small one, little more than a slit in the earth between the rise of the hill and the boundary of the cemetery. Its sides rose only as high as Norman's ears.

"Wanta take a peek at sleeping beauty here?" Duke asked. Then he whipped back a flap of the tarp.

"Terry?"

"Yeah, he kept staring at me, so I figured I had to teach the kid a lesson."

I remember the lesson Duke taught me.

Norman looked down at Terry's blood-covered face. More blood matted his red-brown fringe.

"Kid put up a fight?" Norman asked.

"None that you'd notice."

"I guess Pits is gonna have to find another cook for it's café."

"You guess right, Normy."

"Uh . . . where you plan on taking him, Duke?"

"Back there into the scrub. They'll bury him later."

"They?"

"Sharpe and the rest."

"You don't think they might be . . . uh, upset that you've killed one of their townsfolk?"

"They'll learn to get over it."

"I know, but they might have been fond of the guy, Duke. He could have been a—"

"Norman, are you going to stand there chinnin' me to death? Grab a corner of the tarp—start pulling."

Norman grabbed a corner. Arguing with Duke wasn't healthy.

Hell, looking at Duke wrong wasn't a healthy option either.

"Jesus. This is harder than it looks," Norman panted.

"You need to work on those muscles, bud. Girls like 'em; guys respect 'em."

"Some guys like 'em, too."

"You faggin' out on me, Norman?"

"No . . . uh . . . just making an observation."

"You make with pulling Sleeping Beauty here; leave the observing to me."

"Sure, Duke."

Pulling a corpse over uneven ground was tough. Norman's back ached. His arms hurt. He thought his shoulder might dislocate pretty damn soon.

Sweat came. Not a moistening of the temples, but a salty river running down the inside of his shirt.

And that sun . . .

Damn hot. Damn, damn hot.

The both tugged what could have been an oversize dim sum. Only this roll wasn't stuffed with fish or meat; it contained 160 pounds of the thing that the Good Book reckoned was made in God's image.

Namely, Terry, late of Pits.

Duke hardly broke a bead. Still cool under pressure.

Norman boiled like he was in a pressure cooker.

Glanced back. Saw the roll of tarp with its heavy cargo sliding through the dust, rolling stones under it, flattening a cactus here, a tuft of grass there. At one point Terry's bare arm flopped out. Duke told him to ignore it. Keep hauling.

Norman kept hauling.

Ached like crazy, though. Sweated like a pig that'd learned the truth about bacon.

Oh, Lord. And he still hadn't gotten to change his underwear after his accident watching Boots and Nicki make out.

"Don't worry, Norman. I've got it planned out."

After a series of grunts as they hauled Terry over a rocky outcrop, Norman managed to echo, "Planned?"

"Yeah," Duke said. "This place. We're taking it over."

"Oh . . . right."

"I'm gonna be mayor instead of the old guy."

"Sounds like a good move." Norman decided to humor the big guy. For obvious reasons.

"You and Boots will be my deputies."

Isn't there a fundamental flaw? What about Sharpe—a tough guy in his own right—and the rest?

"Once we've taught them a lesson they won't forget, they'll do as we say." Duke was as confident as ever.

"Sure," Norman agreed. "Like dogs need discipline, we can discipline them."

"See, Norman, that's the value of a college education. You grasp the concept. That's why I like you. You think like me."

Norman had to pause for a minute to catch his breath. Also to wipe his sweating palms on the legs of his pants.

Duke put his hands on his hips, then looked around like he already owned the place. "We'll share out the town between us. Cars and trailers and stuff."

"That'll be great."

"And . . ." He shot Norman a look in the eye. "And we'll share the women out, too."

Norman almost doubled up as if winded. Now Duke's plan did appeal. *The women!*

"I'm gonna have Lauren and Pamela," Duke told him. "You can have Nicki."

"Oh, right!" Norman couldn't stop himself from letting out a howl of excitement.

"I've got eyes." Duke allowed himself one of his coolest smiles. "I saw you got the hots for the dame."

"Oh, thanks, Duke. You're the best!"

"You earned it, Normy. You're my number two."

"Um, but what about Boots?"

"Aw, Boots is special, ain't she?"

"She sure is."

"A real peach."

"Top-drawer, Duke."

"Right. So I decided we share her between ourselves. You take her weekends; I'll have her weekdays."

"Thanks, Duke. That's a great idea."

"See, Norman. You gotta plan ahead." He spit on his hands. "Okay, time to lose stiff boy."

Norman shielded his eyes against the rising sun. If he lifted his head he could see down through the haphazard mass of tombstones to the café. A truck carrying lumber was just pulling into the lot in a swirl of dust. First customer of the day.

"Wonder who's gonna cook the trucker's breakfast now?" Norman wondered.

"Guy ain't gonna pull himself, Normy."

Norman and Duke started to haul the body again along the dry-as-bones gully.

Norman felt he was in as poor a shape as Terry by the time Duke said, "This'll do."

They'd dragged the body into a concentration of cholla cacti.

"No paths nearby," Duke said, "No one will see any dead bastard in here."

"Coyotes'll probably start to work on him soon enough."

Duke chuckled. "Well, that ain't no skin off of *my* nose."

Norman dropped the corner of the tarp, then stretched his arms up, arching his back. *Dragging the corpse this far has nearly been the death of me, too,* he thought sourly.

Duke bent down to grip the edge of the tarp where the corpse's head would be. "You wanta give him a good-night kiss, Normy?"

"I'll pass."

"Wuss."

"Duke?" Norman swallowed as an unpleasant taste came into his mouth. "You're not gonna—"

"You prejudiced against a different sorta love?"

"Holy shit." Norman looked down in horror as Duke began to lift the tarpaulin from the dead face. "Duke . . . I-I don't know. . . ." *Oh, God, the guy's out of his mind; is he really gonna—*

Duke grinned. "Relax, buddy. Ain't you ever been on the receiving end of a windup before?"

"You mean you don't want to . . . to . . ."

"Boy, oh, boy, Norman."

"It's just, when you asked if I wanted to give Terry a good-night kiss, I-I—"

"Joke, Norman. Just a laugh, okay?"

"But what're you doing with—"

"Don't worry; I'm not gonna make you touch him." Duke opened up the tarpaulin to expose Terry's body. He was wearing a chef's apron over his clothes.

Bloody clothes.

Man, Duke knows how to use those fists of his with killing effect.

Duke explained. "You don't just dump a body without checking it for stuff. Might be gold rings. Cash in pockets. A nice Rolex."

"Anything?"

"Plastic watch. Not worth taking it off. Thirty bucks in the shirt pocket. Lousy cheap shitter."

Even being dead didn't thwart the wrath of a guy like Duke. He punched the corpse in the family jewels.

The corpse screamed. Norman screamed louder.

"So the guy's not dead," Duke remarked. "What do you think I am, a brain surgeon?"

Terry sat bolt upright. He was gasping, blinking weirdly in the bright sunlight.

Duke pulled the knife from his boot.

"Norman, pull his head back so I can take a piece of his throat."

"Oh, shit." Norman's knees felt about as stiff as ice cream on a summer's day.

"Don't take all day about it. We've got work to do."

Norman pounced on Terry. Terry fought like a crazed puma, slashing with his hands, snarling.

Suddenly he was on top of Norman, pushing him against a cactus. Sharp spines stabbed Norman's arm. He cried out.

And all the time Terry's wild-eyed face was jammed up close to his. Eyeball-to-eyeball.

Blood from the guy's bleeding lips sprayed against Norman's face.

Duke remained patient. "Norman. You were supposed to be holding *him*."

Norman managed to put the heel of his palm against Terry's forehead. He pushed hard. Shoving the head back.

"Way to go, Norman."

With the guy's throat exposed, Duke reached around with the knife. Then he drew it slow and deep across the throat, just below the bobbing Adam's apple.

Immediately Terry lost interest in wrestling Norman. Instead he became preoccupied with holding the gash closed with both his hands. Even so, blood streamed through the fingers.

Norman watched in horror. The guy made like a goldfish, with his mouth opening and shutting. He was trying to gulp in air, but none was going down into his lungs. Blood covered his hands, so he looked as if he'd been mashing raw strawberries with his fists.

Fingers, hands, wrists—all a slick crimson.

Terry stared at Norman. Eyes pleading with him.

Norman stared back.

Then Terry began to make a strange mulelike screaming.

"Blunt knife," Duke explained. "Didn't cut all the way through."

"Duke, do something."

"He'll quieten down soon enough."

Only he didn't. He kept that weird braying sound going—louder and louder, too.

Christ, I can't take this anymore. He's going to bring everyone running.

Norman dropped down into a squat, found a hunk of stone the size of a football. Then he stood up, heaving it up high over his head until his arms were straight, elbows locked.

Terry still hee-hawed. Still stared at him.

Duke stood, coolly watching what Norman did next.

I've gotta do this, Norman thought. *I've got no choice. Gotta stop him from yelling out like that.*

Gotta stop him from staring at me.

Freaking me out.

The huge hunk of stone lifted straight above his head in his two hands must've weighed twenty pounds. His elbows quivered. *Can't hold it much longer.*

Gritting his teeth, Norman brought it down onto Terry's head. The top of the guy's skull caved in.

One eye popped clear of the socket.

Terry went down.

Lay twitching.

Feet kicking up a swirl of dust.

The mindless hee-hawing stopped. Norman thought the silence was beautiful.

Duke was impressed. "Nice work, Norman." He gave the body a casual kick with the toe of his motorcycle boot. "He won't wake from that one."

"I killed him." Norman wasn't sure if that was a statement or a question.

"Yeah, and how. You know, you're getting some bloodlust on you." He grinned. "You've become a killing machine. A real Term-in-ay-tuh."

"I'd like to go back to the trailer now."

"Sure. You need to clean up. That damp patch in your crotch is unsightly, you know? You're supposed to leave that in a woman's cunny, not in your shorts."

Norman could only nod. Half staggering, he turned, then walked back toward the trailer.

Duke called after him, "I'll be there in half an hour. It's time we started work."

CHAPTER FORTY-TWO

"Anyone seen Terry?" Pamela asked this of Hank, who was dragging a plastic sack full of trash from the kitchen toward the utility room.

One of the old-timer's chores. Part-time mayor, part-time tour guide, part-time trash man.

"I ain't seen Terry, but I got an eyeful of you." He winked the old-lecher wink of his. His scabbed lips stretched into a wide grin. The grin put his gums on display again, with their half a dozen yellow teeth. "Ye're a beauty; that's God's honest truth."

"Thank you, Hank." Pamela smiled. She was used to Hank's ways now. "There's customers waiting for food, and I can't find Terry. Do you know where he might be?"

"I don't rightly know." He scratched his white whiskers. "He's always here by nine."

Pamela colored a little as she said, "You don't think he might be with Nicki? In her trailer?"

"I know he's taken with Nicki, but that ain't reciprocated."

"Terry's nice; she might have . . . you know . . . warmed to him."

"Oh, don't get me wrong, ma'am. Nicki likes Terry, but not in that kinda way."

"What makes you say that?"

"I've been round God's earth long enough to know a thing or two. If you ask me, Nicki plays for the other bowling team, if you see what I mean?" He winked his bloodshot eye again.

"Hank, that's not nice; you shouldn't speculate about things like that."

"It's not just specu-latin'." Again the crusty wink. "I've got two eyes in m' head. I seen Nicki enter-tainin' ladies in her trailer 'fore now."

"Oh, Hank, you shouldn't spy on people."

"So I seen Nicki on the old beaver hunt, if ya catch my drift."

"I catch it, all right."

"Seen her do the scissor-sister thing. Watched her drink from the hairy cup. Saw her plow a fresh furrow. Took a gander as she—"

"Okay, okay, Hank, I get the picture."

"Me, too." His purple tongue licked his lips. "A nice, clear picture." He patted his chest. "Makes the old ticker step up a beat, too."

From the café behind her came the sound of someone pounding a fist on the counter.

"Hello! We gonna get any service in this dump?"

Hank resumed dragging the sack of trash in the direction of the rear door. "If you could use some advice, ma'am, it's not smart to keep a hungry feller from his vittles."

"Oh, great." Pamela simmered.

I can't find Terry. I'm alone in the café. And there's a trucker and his buddy grumping for food.

"Catch ya later, sugar pie."

She glowered at Hank. "Thanks a bunch. If you see—"

"Terry. Sure, sure. I'll tell him ya can't live without him. Tee-hee." He cackled with laughter.

"Hey! Anyone home!" The trucker calling out again.

Pamela made sure her best professional waitress smile was on her face, then walked back into the café.

The trucker and his friend sat at the counter. They rested their muscular bare arms on the countertop and glared at her. They both wore white T-shirts with a brown log running across the nipple zone. Beneath that were the words *We Love Lumber, Too.* Then a telephone number.

Company uniform.

Came with regulation sweat circles in the armpits, too.

The two guys were in their forties. One wore a baseball cap. The other had a mass of curly hair that must have added three inches to his height.

"Ain't our money any good here?" said the one in the cap.

The other added, "Yeah, or do you only take Iraqi pesos here?"

"I think you'll find it's Iraqi dinar."

"Uh?"

"The currency of Iraq," she said, smiling. "It's dinar, not peso. Coffee?"

"Oh, a smart waitress, eh?" The one with the curly hair said this with a sneer. "You got a university degree or just in love with an Iraqi guy?"

"I know what she has got. . . ." This was the trucker in the cap. "She's got long legs that go way up to her fanny."

"Yeah, and what a fanny." The curly-haired one smirked. "Nice titties, too. Make a nice, soft pillow for a workin' man."

"You're dead right. Won't you pass me my X-ray glasses, Frank?"

The one called Frank slipped a pair of Elvis-style shades with large aluminum frames from his pocket and held them out to his buddy.

The trucker slipped them on, then looked Pamela up and down with an appreciative whistle. "Best thing we ever bought, Frank, these X-ray spectacles."

"Oh, very droll," Pamela said. She plucked her order book from her apron.

"Lovely breasts. The right one has a freckle. Nice flat stomach. And man, oh, man you should see her—"

"Okay." Pamela plucked the cap from his head. "Either you quit the commentary or I'll fry your hat alongside your eggs."

"At least you'll be fryin' something," the curly one said with feeling.

"Yeah, and you can give me my bitchin' hat back."

Pamela's patience was running low. "What're ya going to do if I don't give it back? Sir."

"I'll come around there and give your sweet fanny the slappin' it deserves." He nudged his buddy.

Both laughed.

Maybe they're thinking I'm all alone here.

They're getting ideas that dessert might not come in a bowl.

Oh, where are you, Terry? Where's anyone? Lauren? Nicki?

"Okay, you're both hungry. I'm a waitress. What can I get you?" She stood with the pen poised over the pad, ready to write.

The one called Frank had a look in his eye now that needed no explanation. "Oh, I know exactly what I want. How about you, Joe?"

"Sure. Something hot and spicy." Both laughed.

Pamela sighed. "Are you two going to keep up this dazzling repartee all day or are you going to give me your order *for food*, so I can fix you something?"

"Give me some tasty rump, followed by—"

Pamela's schoolteaching experience kicked in. "Okay, you two. I've had just about enough of this." Her voice was a perfect balance of ice and steel. "Either you order your food now or you can go hungry for the rest of the day."

"Hey, listen, we—"

"No, you listen to me, buster." Pamela slammed her hand down on the counter. "The next diner is four hours' drive from here. So it's your choice. Eat here or hit the road."

"I—"

"And if you eat here I expect a modicum of civilized behavior."

The two men looked at each other. One handed the sunglasses back to the other.

"Now, do either of you wish to say anything?" Pamela shot them her best steely-eyed look. The kind she reserved for the hoodlum kids in class.

"Yes, ma'am." The trucker visibly sagged under the weight of her formidable stare.

"Yes, I'm waiting."

"May I have my cap back, ma'am?"

She handed it back to him.

"Now," she said briskly. "Coffee?"

The two guys nodded and were quick to say their pleases and thank-yous.

"That's better. So, gentlemen. What would you like to eat?"

Respectful now, they gave their order.

With a no-show Terry I'm going to have to cook, she thought. *But no big deal. I can fix bacon, fried eggs, and the usual breakfast extras.*

As she turned away she heard one of the men whisper to the other, "Time of the month."

She smiled to herself. They couldn't resist reassuring themselves that they'd lost the battle to the superior biological force of menstruation, not that a waitress had stood up to them. When confronted with the period thing, most men yielded like a vampire cringing back from a crucifix.

Without turning to them as she laid rashers of bacon on the hot skillet, she couldn't resist saying, "Bathroom's over there. You might want to wash your hands before you eat."

She turned to smile at them as they looked at their grubby fingers in surprise. As if washing their hands before eating were alien to them.

Which it probably was.

They nodded. The one in the cap touched the peak. A respectful gesture.

"Good idea, ma'am."

The pair scuttled toward the bathroom.

Game, set, and match.

"Nice work." She spun to her right.

Duke stood in the kitchen doorway.

"Oh," she said, "I didn't see you there."

"You soon got the upper hand with those two," he said. "I'm impressed."

"Just a little firmness."

"Worked, too. You're some gal."

"Thank you." She cracked eggs onto the hot metal. The clear liquid turned a sizzling white around the yellow yolk.

Duke slipped a stick of gum into his mouth. He gave her an appraising look as he chewed.

"You're not a waitress."

"I'm both waitress and cook now."

"I mean you've not done this line of work long."

"No, I used to be a schoolteacher."

"How come you wound up in Pits?"

"Long story."

"Sharpe bring you in?"

"Uh-huh." She flipped the bacon rashers over. Bubbles of oil seemed to dance on the cooking meat. Even though she kept her eyes on the food she was aware of the guy studying her.

Yeah, he's good-looking in a bad-boy way. Blue eyes, blond hair. Tattoo. Narrow waist. Broad shoulders.

Course, a guy like that's gotta be trouble.

"You could set two plates out here for me." She guessed Duke didn't take orders from anyone.

But he gave a little nod, as if what he saw in Pamela he approved of. So he was prepared to give a little help.

Oh, God, I hope he doesn't have any romantic intentions. I'm not ready for that yet.

And especially not a guy like Duke. He looks as if he's running away from a whole heap of trouble.

Could have broken out of jail.

Or poisoned his grandmother for her life savings.

The two guys returned from the bathroom. They looked cheerful and relaxed now that she'd laid down some ground rules.

They both held their hands up, palms facing Pamela.

"Nice and clean, miss," said the one in the hat.

"You'll pass muster. Grab a seat; breakfast's ready."

Pamela glanced over to see how Duke had reacted to her handling of the customers.

Duke had already vanished.

Like he's got somewhere important to go.

The shiver that ran down her spine wasn't lost on her.

A goose just walked over my grave.

And as she served up the bacon and eggs, wishing that Terry wouldn't be long in returning from wherever he'd taken himself to, she didn't know that the café's cook lay under a cactus with ants busily crawling across the unholy mess of his crushed skull.

CHAPTER FORTY-THREE

Norman sat drinking cold, sweet water from a glass. He was back in the trailer.

He'd changed his underpants before they formed a crust. His mind was full of all kinds of shit.

Boots and Nicki making naked whoopee in the old house.

Duke hauling Terry in the tarp.

Norman killing Terry with a rock.

Oh, Christ, I'm a killing machine.

Three men in less than a week.

Norman shook his head, then let it rest against the back of the sofa. The fan blew air to cool his face. But that desert heat was seeping into the living room of the trailer.

Gonna be hot today.

Have a feeling it's gonna get hotter than hell yet. In more ways than one.

Norman swallowed another mouthful of water.

The cold liquid sliding down his throat felt good.

I wish I could stay like this for the next zillion days. Do nothing but feel the fan on my face. Drink cold water.

'Cause every time I move from one place to another I wind up killing someone.

Or nearly getting killed.

Dangerous times, Norman. So stay in the trailer. Hey, stay on the fucking couch. That way no one gets hurt. Least of all me.

A tap sounded on the door.

"Now you've got a dilemma," he told himself. "Either answer the door, or stay here. If you answer the door it'll be someone trying to kill you. Or you'll trip on the mat and head-butt them to death by accident."

Oh, shit.

The tap came again, this time followed by a croaker of a voice. "Young 'un. You in there?"

Holy cow. The old-timer. What's-his-name?

Hank. Yeah, Hank.

Only old Hank. Should be no danger.

To the old mule skinner or to Norman.

Norman headed to the door. Then suddenly he paused.

Maybe Hank had heard that Norman had been bitten by a venomous snake.

I haven't, of course, but that might not stop the guy from wanting to suck out the poison. Norman couldn't stop himself from remembering the mind movie his imagination had made for him. Of Norman being struck by a rattlesnake that had planted its fangs in his fanny. Then lurid mental images of toothless old Hank with the cracked lips and bushy whiskers taking his own sweet time in sucking out the poison.

Shit.

What an imagination. Why did it have to torture him twenty-four/seven?

"Huloooo!" More tapping.

Norman went to the door.

He opened it. The sunlight hit him in the eyes like a couple of pistol rounds. He recoiled, blinking at its brilliance.

"Had a mind you were in there, young feller. An' I wuz right."

"Good morning," Norman said politely, wondering why the hell the guy'd shown up at his door.

Hank stood in the dust at the bottom of the trailer steps. He looked up at Norman. His eyes were puckered into folds of skin to stop the sunlight from dazzling him. His nose showed through the foliage of bristles. It was as red as a strawberry—an overripe, stood-upon strawberry. The coot could have been an old-time prospector in those clothes. Even in this heat he wore a plaid flannel shirt that had long sleeves. Below that were blue jeans. On his feet were dusty black cowboy boots. Good scorpion-stomping footwear, those.

Norman saw the man was grinning. He held that filthy hat of his that was probably held together by nothing more than dust and the old coot's sweat.

"Figured you might want to take a look-see in my hat."

"Look in your hat?"

"Yessirree."

My God, why do I want to stand here admiring the inside of the old shit shoveler's hat? What's the man thinking of?

"See what I got fer ya and yer two buddies."

Norman peered into the shadowy interior of the hat. Were those poop stains on the brim?

Come to think of it, toilet tissue could be in short supply when you're walking out in the desert.

And the brim of a hat's got to be softer than a cactus.

Norman began, "I don't quite see—"

"Right there in the bottom."

"Oh? Eggs."

"Damn straight. Fresh today."

"Thanks, but we've got some in the refrigerator."

Hank's lopsided grin broadened. "No, these ain't come from no hen's tush."

"They're not hen's eggs." *Duck, goose, quail?*

"These eggs are the best ye'll ever taste." Hank smacked his lips. "Rattler eggs."

Norman's jaw sagged. "Snake eggs!"

"Sure, they're snake eggs. You never tasted 'em afore?"

"Never."

Never likely to either.

"Fresh rattlesnake eggs are good fer whatever ails yer."

"I don't think that—"

"Just pick it up, like so." Hank took a round white egg from his hat. "See, they're soft. Ya can squish 'em." Hank squeezed gently. "Ya can pickle 'em, or boil 'em in milk." He winked at Norman. "But ya can't beat 'em just as God made 'em. Just like this . . . Now you watch, young feller." He chewed on one with the remains of his yellow teeth. "Got a tough outa membrane. But you stick with it, you'll bite a hole clean through. Now tilt ya head back, open ya mouth, and squeeze."

Hank followed his own instructions. Norman watched in a kind of horrified fascination as the old coot squirted the contents of the rattlesnake's egg into his mouth. It shot from the hole in the membrane like a ball of green mucus streaked red with blood.

"Ah . . ." Hank crowed with relish at such a delicious morsel. "Betcha ye'll have tasted nothing like it!"

"I bet you're right." Norman swallowed. His mouth tasted of bile. His palms were sweating.

Dear God, that looked just awful.

Hank held out the hat so Norman could see the cluster of glistening white eggs nestled in there. "Want me to get one started fer ya?"

"No, thanks. I'm a . . . I'm a . . ." His stomach twitched. "I'm a vegetarian."

"Shit, is that so? I'm a Libra."

Norman muttered something about leaving the shower running, then closed the door on the grinning man standing there with his hatful of snake eggs.

Norman went back to lie on the sofa. Air played on his face from the fan.

He had to work hard not to recall the image of Hank gulping down the slimy green contents of the snake egg with gusto.

Had to work very hard.

Ten minutes later he realized he wasn't going to puke after all.

But it was a close thing.

And just when he began to think that life was looking better, the trailer door opened. In stepped Boots and Duke.

They had guns in their hands.

"Norman. Time to start the show." Duke sat down in the armchair opposite him.

Boots chose to park her butt on the arm of the sofa.

Norman remembered how a naked Boots made love to a willowy, naked Nicki. The thought made him warm.

Made it hard to look Boots in the eye as well.

But then, the guns they carried had their own magnetic attraction for his attention. Boots carried a revolver. It looked like a .38 home-protection model. Duke carried a .357 Magnum in his right hand, and in his left, a Glock automatic. It was gold-plated, too. A rich man's toy.

Norman had to ask an obvious question: "Where'd you get the guns?"

Boots said, "While you were sleepin' on the ride down here we got them from a guy driving a motor home."

"Guess he didn't complain." Norman wore his fixed smile, so as not to rile Duke.

"Boots worked the ol' Boots magic," Duke said. "While he was on top of Boots pluggin' her water hole like lives depended on it, I . . ." He made a clicking sound as he ran his thumb across his throat, miming a knife slicing a trachea. "I relieved him of these beauties that he'd got stowed in the motor home."

"Nice work," Norman said, nodding.

"Boots is the gal who gets all the praise."

"Oh, I did nothing," she simpered. "Just smiled and opened my legs."

"Like I said," Duke told him. "The old Boots magic."

"They look like formidable pieces." Norman eyed the guns. "Know your way around them?"

"Sure, we do." Boots spun the ammo cylinder. It made a clicking sound. "While you were sleeping we got some practice in, too."

While I was sleeping? While I was unconscious, more like. After the beating Duke gave me it's a miracle I woke up at all.

"Here's your piece, Normy." Duke handed him the Glock automatic.

"But I don't know anything about—"

"Nothing to it, Normy. It's an auto. Just point and pull the trigger. It's a ten-millimeter. A fucking cannon. Course, you gotta remember to take the safety off first. It's this little doohickey here." Duke showed him how to slide the safety catch across.

"But we're not actually gonna shoot anybody."

"I guess not." Boots sounded disappointed.

"These are to back up our suggestion that we take over the running of the town," Duke said.

"They'll be a powerful persuader," Norman allowed, as he felt the weight of the gun in his hand. And when he remembered what Duke told him, about Nicki being his when the plan was complete, he began to smile.

Duke asked, "What're you smiling about, bud?"

"I'm just thinking about the future. About how much we're going to enjoy ourselves."

"Damn straight." Duke smiled. "Okay, if you guys are ready"—he smile became a leer—"let's do this crazy thing."

CHAPTER FORTY-FOUR

"Café first," Duke told them.

Holy shit. This is like a Wild West showdown.

And we're the Jesse James gang.

Mean, dangerous, armed.

The time was nearing high noon. Norman walked to the right of Duke, Boots to the left. They walked purposefully across the parking lot, their feet raising puffs of dust with every step. Boots wore her white cowgirl boots. Duke strode manfully in his motorcycle boots. Norman wore sneakers. The sun burned down from directly above, hardly casting a shadow.

Deserted.

Not a sound.

No vehicles on the road.

No people.

No birdsong.

Only a death silence. Like the grim reaper had put his bony finger to fleshless lips and breathed, "Shhhh . . ."

Old Mr. Death knew what was going down.

He'd seen it happen before in Pits. This was frontier country. A hundred years ago there were plenty of shoot-outs. Some gambler, maybe, who'd slipped an ace from his cuff once too often. Or two guys arguing over the burlesque dancer.

The story was the same.

Out would come the guns.

Blam! Blam! Blam!

Then came the solemn procession up to the desert cemetery behind the long pine box.

Norman felt terrified.

Felt excited.

Now this was a hunk of history repeating itself.

The three of them walking in a line with guns in their hands. Three desperados.

Gonna make this town of Pits our own.

They'd chosen their time. Waiting for a lull in customers.

Duke squinted against the sun. "Sharpe's gone," he said.

"One less to worry about," Boots added.

"Yup."

They crossed the furrows in the dust left by Sharpe's bus. He'd gone out "saving people" again. Ahead lay the line of abandoned trucks and cars, then the café itself.

"In through the back way?" Norman asked.

"Nope. The front door. We own this place now." Duke spit into the dust.

Above them vultures glided in circles.

Norman nodded. "Okay."

They circled around the front. There were customers after all. Two big Harleys stood by the front door.

"I never saw those arrive," Boots said.

"It's not a problem. Come on."

Duke shoved open the café door. They followed him in.

Inside were two bikers, chunky guys in black leather. They were a couple of hard nuts. They sat at the counter.

Waiting tables was Pamela. Cooking the food was Lauren.

Norman ran the mental file. That meant Wes, Hank, and Nicki were absent.

"Café's closed," Duke announced.

"Hey," one of the bikers snarled. "We ain't eaten yet."

Duke raised the hand that held the Magnum. It's six-inch barrel in blue steel looked wicked beyond belief.

"Take that fucking gun out of my face," the biker warned. "Like I said, we ain't eaten yet."

"Steak's off, but here's your chips." Duke fired. The big round smacked into the biker's forehead. He flopped back like a dead seal. Rubbery. Heavy. His head made a loud smacking sound as it hit the floor.

"It's cool," the other biker said. "I don't want no—"

Boots fired. A cock shot. The biker squealed and clamped both hands between his legs.

Duke nodded at Norman. "Finish him."

Norman fired the automatic. The big cartridge filled the café with blue smoke. A glass shattered on the table beside him, the report was so loud.

The 10mm round struck the guy dead center in the chest. He went down, pumping blood.

Duke shook his head. "You should have listened to me first time around. I said the café is closed."

Norman saw Pamela and Lauren staring at the three in horror.

Duke touched his eyebrow in salute. "Let it be known that . . ." He rooted for the phrase.

Norman supplied it. "From henceforth."

"Thank you, Norman. Let it be known from henceforth that I am the master of Pits. Boots and Norman here are my deputies. My word is law. Okay?"

Lauren opened her mouth, ready to protest.

Norman stepped in. "Just relax; take it easy. Everything's going to be fine."

Boots sang out, "We're gonna have a great time. This is the start of a real good friendship."

Norman glanced at her. She smiled. But there was an emptiness to her brown eyes. As if a whole chunk of her vision were directed inward to some dark recess of her mind, not outward to the people in the café.

"That's right," Duke agreed. "A real close friendship. And we're gonna make this town a cool place to be. More girls. More fun."

"All right," Norman enthused. He stared at Pamela in the figure-hugging sweater and shorts. He liked the dinky waitress outfit. Kinda sexy. Shame that Duke had laid claim to her.

Duke still pointed the handgun, but he used his free hand to reach into his shirt pocket, pull out a pack cigarettes, and slip one long, cool cylinder from the pack with his lips. After returning the pack to his pocket he lit a match one-handed, too, then inhaled deeply.

"We regret the mess the two guys made." He nodded at the dead bikers.

Hot shit. Duke's blaming the two guys for bleeding out all over the frigging floor. It's as if his shooting them had nothing to do with it.

Norman went along with Duke's line. "We'll get it cleaned up in no time."

"Don't worry," Lauren said. "We've handled plenty of dead meat before."

Norman noticed the little glance Pamela shot her friend. As if there were more meaning loaded into those few words than was first apparent.

"Question is"—Boots wiggled her finger against the trigger as if her skin were getting itchy—"what are we going to do with you two?"

"Lock them up," Norman said quickly, before Boots decided to dispatch the two babes.

"Here?" Boots wrinkled her snoutlike nose. "They'd escape easy."

"No," Norman said.

"Trailers are no good either," Duke observed.

"The house on the hill. Bound to be a cellar or something," Norman said.

"Sounds good to me, Norman, old buddy."

Boots moved so she could look through the door into the kitchen. "Where are the others?"

Probably wondering where beautiful blond Nicki is, Norman thought. After I saw Boots making love to Nicki this morning she might be wanting to stake her claim.

No fair.

Duke promised Nicki to me.

Norman began to wonder if there was a way of getting rid of Boots down the line. Those brown, dead eyes gave him the creeps. Watching that girl-on-girl action had been fun, but he didn't want Boots hogging all the good times with Nicki.

Lauren looked at Pamela, then said, "I don't know where they are."

"You sure you ain't seen Nicki?"

See! Norman's face flushed. *Boots wants a second helping.*

Boy, oh, boy, does Boots have to go.

"And when you expectin' Sharpe back?" Duke asked.

"He can be gone for days," Lauren answered.

"Where are the others likely to be? Wes and the old-timer?"

"Around." Pamela shrugged.

Lauren added, "They've all got their chores."

"Okay." Duke slipped the gun into the belt of his pants. "You ladies are gonna give us no trouble, are you?"

"What do you think?" Pamela's shock was being replaced by anger. "You three have got the guns."

"Feisty. I like it." Duke was pleased.

"I'll give you feisty," she snarled.

Boots raised the gun again. "And we can give you a tit full of lead, so don't get antsy."

Norman played the diplomacy bit. "Remember? Nice and easy; then no one's gonna get hurt."

Duke nodded. "Norman's got brains. Take his advice, okay?" His eyes hardened. "*Okay?*"

Both Lauren and Pamela nodded. Norman noticed the fire still burning in Pamela's eye. She wanted to take a swing at Boots.

Norman wondered if she ever would.

Catfight.

Could be fun.

Could be a way of getting Boots out of the picture.

"Now we're all being sweet with one another, let's take that walk up to the house. Norman, lock the door to the café. Put up the closed sign."

"I'm on it."

"Ladies." Duke nodded toward the kitchen door. "Promenade time. We'll head out back, then up to the house. If we see any of the others don't do anything bitchin' stupid, like shouting out warnings or shit like that. You follow?"

They both nodded.

"Sweet. Lead the way, ladies."

* * *

They worked their way up through the cemetery. By the tombs of guys who lost gunfights a hundred years ago. Then by the tombs of the monkeys. The house shimmered in heat haze in front of them.

Lauren and Pamela led the way, their bare legs looking captivating to Norman.

Boots complained about the heat.

Complained that Nicki was nowhere to be seen.

Duke walked in silence. Cool as ever.

They didn't see any of the remaining four inhabitants of Pits.

As they climbed onto the porch of the house Nicki was just stepping out of the front door.

"Makes three," Boots said brightly.

"Now to locate Wes, Sharpe, and Hank," Duke said.

"What's happening?" Nicki asked. The sight of the guns startled her.

"Nothing to worry about, ma'am. We're taking charge of Pits for your own protection."

"Our protection?" Nicki echoed. "We don't need—"

"Nicki," Lauren said calmly. "Do as they say."

Nicki looked at Boots with pained eyes. Norman figured she was recalling that sweet, sweet tongue loving by Boots this morning and was hurt by the betrayal.

"Boots, why are you doing this to me? I thought we—"

"It's getting mighty hot out here," Boots said. "If I don't get cool soon I won't be able to stop myself from pulling this trigger."

"Okay, okay," Pamela placated. "Don't worry. We're doing as you say. Nicki, go back into the house, please."

"But—"

"They've promised they're not going to hurt us, Nicki."

Nicki nodded. Her blue eyes were watchful as she pushed her long blond hair back behind her shoulder.

Clearly doesn't trust us an inch, Norman thought.

The interior of the house was dark as a cave. Norman hoped it would be cool as one, too.

But no.

He followed everyone into the gloomy hallway. It was hot, with a musty atmosphere. At least they were out of the fierce sunlight.

Duke said, "We need to find somewhere comfortable for the ladies." He opened a door at random.

Norman nearly told him not to bother with that one. That was the big empty room with no furniture where Boots and Nicki had got throbbing-well naked with each other.

Norman decided against saying anything.

Don't want to give myself away that I was watching them. I don't want them thinking I'm some kind of pervmeister, do I?

"Empty room," Duke told them.

Boots said, "Has it got windows? It's no good if it's got windows."

Instead of that simpleminded character Norman had first encountered, Boots'd become edgy of late. Instead of being easygoing, she now had a brittle quality.

Wish she'd put the fucking gun away.

He began to sweat.

Anxiety sweat. Nothing to do with the heat.

Duke checked the downstairs rooms. "All got windows," he announced. "Too easy to break out of."

"There's gotta be a basement," Boots said, hopeful.

"I don't doubt," Duke replied. "But a basement's no place for a lady."

"They'll live," Boots said. Then she added, "Or we could tie 'em up."

"These are our friends. You don't tie people up who're your friends."

Norman decided a contribution was needed from him. "An upstairs room. They're not gonna jump out of a bedroom window and risk busting a leg."

"Good thinking, Normy." Duke glanced up at the grand stairway that ran in a long curve to the next floor.

Norman looked up, too. It was a huge void of shadows. Spooky.

Duke put his boot on the first step.

The step creaked.

That creak went echoing up the staircase like the footsteps of a ghost.

At last Nicki blurted out, "You can't go up there."

"Can't?"

"No."

"Why?"

"You just can't." Nicki was gasping with fear.

"Oh, can't I?" Duke pulled the Magnum handgun from his belt. "Wes up there?"

"No."

"The old-timer?"

"He's away dumping trash."

"What's so important up there you don't want your bud Duke to see?"

Nicki blurted again, "You can't go up there."

"Oh? See anyone trying to stop me?"

"No." This was Lauren speaking. "You mustn't."

Pamela joined in. "You see, it's not safe. The timbers are rotted."

"Looks sound."

"Too much weight could bring the whole house down on top of us." Pamela nodded at the walls. "See the state it's in?"

"Just looks like peeling wallpaper to me."

"They're shitting you, Duke," Boots told him. "Slap the bitches up. Teach 'em respect."

Duke raised his eyebrows. "I might just do that. If they give me just cause." He stood back and raised the gun. "After you, ladies."

Lauren repeated, "It's really not safe up there."

A slow smile spread across Duke's face. "Now you've really got my curiosity in gear."

In the near dark of the old house they climbed the stairs. He glanced at the three women. Both Nicki and Lauren looked wired with anxiety. Pamela appeared puzzled.

She genuinely doesn't know why the two women are so nervous about us going upstairs.

But there must be something up there.

Any minute now we're going to find out what it is.

CHAPTER FORTY-FIVE

They reached the landing. Light filtered through a corn-flour sack that had been nailed over the landing window. Little needle-sharp rays scattered points of light on the floor.

Clean floor, Norman noted.

Someone's maintaining the property upstairs.

From the landing led six doors. All but one had been boarded up. The single functional door lay at the end of the passageway in near darkness.

"Okay, Normy," Duke said in a low voice. "Go ahead and check the status of the room."

"Status?"

"Yeah, check whether there's anyone in there. Of course, if you're too much of a wuss . . ."

"No. I'll check." Norman smiled to show he wasn't afraid. "Probably only old Hank in the bathtub or something."

"Or Hank and Wes in bed playing bury the salami."

"Boots." Duke disapproved. "Guys don't do that to other guys. They do it to girls."

Norman noticed that Pamela shot a glance at Lauren as if to ask, *"Is this guy for real?"*

Oh, Duke's for real, all right. Something tells me you're gonna get to know all his little quirks real well.

"What're you waiting for, Norm?"

"It's cool, Duke. I'm going. I was, uh, just checking that the safety was off."

Norman advanced slowly along the passageway. He held the Glock automatic out at arm's length. Its gold plating was the brightest thing there. Norman licked his lips. They were dry. Dusty. He didn't like the look of the sealed doors. They made him think of the entrances to tombs.

God alone knew what lay behind them.

Open one of those doors, Norman, you're gonna die screaming.

"Shut up." Norman addressed this to his rebel imagination that was forever skimming troubling scenarios across his mind.

"You say anything, Norman?"

"No, nothing, Duke. Just clearing my throat."

"You don't want to take all afternoon opening a bitchin' door; we've got work to do."

Norman reached the door, keeping the gun at arm's length, and pointing at the woodwork.

Just in case Wes steamed out with a knife.

He reached out the other hand. Found the doorknob in the gloom. Turned it.

Creak.

The mechanism was old.

Hinges were old, too. The door opened with a wailing creak.

Inside.

Dark. Very dark.

Holy moly. It smelled funny, too. Like they'd kept a sick dog in here. Kind of an animal smell . . . a shitty smell.

He advanced through the open doorway. He couldn't even see his arm in the near dark, but the gun glittered in what light filtered through heavily draped windows.

What's that sound? Norman asked himself.

The sound of scratching? He brought to mind an image of a sick dog pawing the bars of a cage.

Or is it the sound of breathing?

Breathing!

No sooner had he thought the word than a wet *something* folded around the hand that carried the gun.

"Jesus," he gasped. The gasp became a yell.

Pain flashed through his hand. He cried out again.

Duke dashed through the door. In the gloom Norman only saw his silhouette. He raced to the window, grabbed the drapes in his two hands, dragged them down.

Sunlight blasted in. Its brilliance made Norman close his eyes even though some monster was chewing on his hand.

Hell—must be an alligator, or a puma, or a wolf, or—

He opened his eyes.

Or a man! Norman stood blinking in the bright light and watched as an old coot in a wheelchair gnawed at the back of his hand.

"Get him fucking offa me!" Norman yelled.

Suddenly everyone seemed to be in the room.

Nicki cried, "Please don't hurt him!"

Pamela gaped. "Who the hell is that?"

Duke aimed the gun.

The old guy in the wheelchair looked around ninety. He had no hair on the top of his skull, but he had plenty around the back of his head and around his jaw, so it formed a snowy white collar. The eyes were glistening slits surrounded by red skin. Arching over them were fuzzy eyebrows of white hair.

"He's biting my fucking hand!" Norman wailed.

"Stand back," Duke told him. "I'll blow his face off."

"No way, Duke! My hand's in his mouth!"

Nicki and Lauren pleaded with them not to hurt the guy.

"He's breaking skin; he's breaking skin!" Norman wailed louder.

Boots angled the gun to shoot the guy in the stomach.

"Don't you dare; you'll wind up hitting me," Norman warned, then "Here!" He handed her his gun.

Now with his hand free he could do something about the biter. He jammed his thumb into one of the slitty eyes. Warm, soft. Norman pushed harder. At last with a yell the old guy quit biting.

Duke scolded Nicki: "Hey, you got a grandpa, you gotta feed him now and again."

Nicki rushed forward to the old man. "You'd better not have hurt him."

"What about me?" Norman asked, pained. "The bastard drew blood. Look!"

He showed her his hand with puncture wounds in the skin. Wincing, he clamped his handkerchief to it. "And see his teeth? The old coot's got fangs."

"Hey, Norm's right," Duke said, impressed. "Just look at those pointy teeth."

Pamela stared, too. "They've been filed down to points." She glanced at Lauren. "Did he do this to his own teeth?"

Norman was maybe the only one not impressed by the old guy's mouthful of canine teeth. Despite the guy's being a physical wreck, his teeth were perfectly white and healthy. Perfectly sharp, too. Red splotches soaked through Norman's handkerchief.

"I should get a tetanus shot," Norman told them. "And rabies."

Duke nodded at Lauren. "So who's Father Time?"

"They call him Priest."

"Priest. Hey, Priest, meet Duke." Duke held out his hand.

Priest looked at it with interest through the slitted eyes. They seeped with a syrupy stickiness. Especially the one to which Norman had delivered a damn good thumbing. Then the old dude spoke.

A dry, cracking voice. Like desert brush being disturbed. "You want me to eat all of them? Now?"

"No, Priest." That was Nicki. She stroked the old guy's forearm while crouching beside the wheelchair.

Priest didn't seem to hear her. "Ya know you gotta kill 'em and cook 'em before I eat 'em. That's why I wrote out all those recipes for ya."

"This is Priest?" Pamela said in disbelief. "I thought you said he was dead?"

"Not dead. I didn't say that," Lauren explained. "I meant no longer in charge."

"Ya can fry these guys' balls," Priest was saying. "Grind fresh pepper on 'em, then serve 'em on a bed of lettuce."

Duke said to Lauren, "Mebbe you need to do some explaining. Who's the old guy?"

"Like I said. His name is Priest." Lauren made a gesture that seemed to encompass the town. "He rediscovered Pits more than forty years ago. He brought it back to life."

"But what's this about eating us?"

"He's old, Duke. He's getting confused."

"Confused, hell!" Priest disagreed. "Got the appetite of a young man, I have. See the girl there?" He pointed a wrinkled finger at Boots. "I'd wager I could down four pounds of her flesh in ten minutes and still have room for her tongue." He smacked his lips. "Stir-fried with garlic."

"Hey . . ." Boots was unhappy at the man's discussing her culinary possibilities. "No one's eating any of me."

Duke chuckled. "You weren't complainin' when old Normy boy, here, was munchin' on ya glory hole."

Boots turned sullen. If anything the brown eyes looked more dead somehow. There wasn't even a spark of anger there.

To Norman that seemed even more dangerous.

Norman took the opportunity during the conversation to look over the room. This one was furnished. Heavy velvet drapes covered the windows. There was a bed in the corner of the room, neatly made. Nicki, he guessed, had been doing the housekeeping. There was also a table, a windup gramophone. Cases with old books.

Cookbooks stuffed with recipes.

Then Norman took a gander at the man who'd taken a snap at his hand.

The white whiskers and strip of hair around the back of his head formed a hairy collar. The top of the head was bald and pretty much ruinous-looking, with cracked skin, pimples, and scabs that resembled around fifty Rice Krispies that had been stuck to his bare scalp.

He wore a dark pullover and dark pants. He may have been confined to the wheelchair for many reasons, but a good one was that he'd only one leg.

The vacant leg of his pants had been doubled over so the turnup could be pinned to where the knee should be. On his remaining foot he wore a white sock. Oddly, it was a dazzling white.

But then, he never walked on it.

Figures.

"You're not going to hurt Priest, are you?" Nicki asked. She was so anxious Norman wanted to take her in his arms.

Comfort her.

Take her mind off the here and now.

He remembered Duke's promise. His groin began to ache.

"What do you take us for?" Duke appeared mildly shocked by the implication. "Course we're not going to hurt him."

"You already have," Priest said with feeling. He shimmied the wheels with his hands to spin the chair around. "College boy there tried to poke out my frickin' eye with his thumb."

"You were biting me."

"I thought you were lunch."

"Lunch!"

"Don't worry," Priest said, wrinkling his nose. "Don't care for rare meat anyway. I'd have sent you back."

"Old-timer's certainly got a thing about eating folk," Duke observed.

"He's confused," Lauren said.

"Stop saying that," Priest snapped. "My mind's gin clear. Why, I remember—"

"Priest. Shush now, please." Lauren looked uncomfortable.

"I remember when we all sat down around the table. You and Sharpe and Wes and Hank. Course, you weren't there, Nicki." He smiled fondly as he remembered.

"Please don't say anything, Priest. These people are from out of town."

"And we all sat at that table at Thanksgiving," Priest said proudly. "And"—he slapped the leg stump in his pants—"And you ate a whole quarter of me."

Lauren groaned, realizing she couldn't stop the flow of words.

"Foot, calf muscles, thigh. We ate the damn lot. Been simmering for a whole day in red wine and herbs." A smile illuminated his face. "Man meat. Once tasted, never forgotten. Food of the gods." He made a gesture that could be described as priestly. Priestlike. "My gift to my friends. My people of Pits. I gave them a piece of me."

Norman glanced across at Pamela. She was surprised. But there was an expression of understanding, too. As if what the old man told them filled in gaps in her knowledge of Pits.

Boots said, "No offense, but I think the guy might be loopy."

Duke was impressed. "Hell of a story."

Priest held up his finger again, his eyes fixed on Duke's. "A true story, young man."

Norman began to make sense of random clues. "All those abandoned cars outside the café . . ."

"Manna from heaven," Priest said. "You know, there's an almighty prejudice against eating our fellow human beings."

"Oh, shit." Lauren shook her head.

The cat's out of the bag?

Priest continued pontificating. "Our ancestors knew it made good sense to eat not just their enemies but their own parents—when they died of natural causes, of course. It don't make no sense to waste valuable protein. Also, human flesh has a special, *special* quality. It's like a magic potion. Once you've eaten it, you'll know what I mean."

"It does what to you exactly?" Norman said. "Eating human flesh?"

"Ah, young friend. I'm not going to spoil your first time. You'll find out the effect—the *extraordinary* effect—for yourself."

Norman thought hard. *Is this really the rambling of a senile old coot? The guy seems lucid enough to me.*

But eating people? Can we really have found a community of cannibals?

Holy shit.

Boots wasn't impressed. "We gonna stand and listen to his stories all day? We've gotta find Wes and Hank."

"Sure thing, babe." Duke motioned to Norman to follow him and Boots out of the room. "I'm gonna lock you folks in here. Norman's gonna be right outside. So no shouting out the windows, do you hear?"

"Who is that young feller?" Priest asked. "Reminds me of my first *real* meal."

Norman followed the pair out onto the landing. Duke had plucked the key from the lock on the other side. Now he closed the door. Locked it.

He handed Norman the key.

"Keep it safe. We'll be right back."

"Sure," Norman said.

Pits, he thought. *A hell of a town.*

Even with all that talk of cannibalism his mind strayed to Nicki. Slender, blond Nicki with the soft blue eyes.

He'd seen her naked.

Now he leaned back against the wall with his arms folded, his eyes closed, and pictured himself doing the same kind of things Boots had done to the Nordic beauty this morning.

* * *

Norman didn't have a long wait. In fact, his daydream of lounging back, watching Nicki straddle him bare-assed was just starting to warm up real nice when Boots and Duke came stomping back up the stairs.

They had Wes and Hank.

Hank, the old-timer, wheezed, "I'm not used to steps. You'll have to let me take 'em slow."

Boots jabbed the muzzle of her pistol in his spine to move him on.

"Ya can shoot me, miss," Hank panted. "But it ain't gonna make me move any faster."

Wes said, "All you had to do was *want* to stay. We'd have been happy to invite you folks in."

Norman heard Duke say, "We're stayin', but from here on in we'll be in charge."

They reached the top of the stairs. Norman unlocked the door, opened it. Then he stood back to allow the two new captives through.

"Once we've got Sharpe, we've got everybody," Boots said.

Old Hank went through the door first. Then Wes.

Boots followed.

When they were all in the room Duke demanded, "So where will we find Sharpe?"

Lauren shrugged. "He's out on the road."

"Saving people," Nicki added.

"He's sure got a thing about that, ain't he?" Duke rubbed his jaw, thinking.

Lauren said, "We don't know how long he'll be gone."

"Well, how I see it, if he brings back more people that's a good thing, especially dames. Norm and me have keen appetites in the whoopee department, don't we, Norm?"

Norman felt uncomfortable answering the question in front of Pamela, who even now was shooting him an accusing stare. Instead he changed the subject a little. "What is it with Sharpe?"

"How do you mean?" Lauren asked.

"Why the mannequins? Why does he drive around with a bus full of them like they're real passengers?"

"They're kinda souvenirs," Lauren said. "They represent all the people he's saved out on the road."

"Then you ate their asses." Boots grinned.

"No, we did not eat those people." Nicki sounded insulted. "Sharpe rescued them. They were stranded in the desert when their vehicles broke down."

Hank piped up. "They woulda died of thirst if it weren't for Sharpe."

Lauren added, "Sharpe made sure they got safely home." She took a deep breath, as if explaining some quality of Sharpe's she didn't fully understand. "But it's important to Sharpe to keep the image of the people he saves."

"Might be easier to take a photograph," Duke pointed out.

"Sharpe is special. His ideas are unique. When he found an abandoned truck full of store mannequins out in the hills he dressed them in the same kind of clothes of the people he saved, then put them on the bus. Of course, he gave them the names of the people he rescued as well."

"Crazy." Boots whistled.

"Makes sense to me," Priest chipped in. "I always kept a tooth from every single person I ate. Made a mighty fine necklace, I can tell you."

Lauren strained to make her explanation of Sharpe's habit sound logical. "What Sharpe does with the dummies is an art form, as well as creating a remembrance."

"Art?" Boots made a weird puffing noise to highlight her disdain. "Who's gonna put a bunch of dummies in an art gallery? Sharpe's as crazy as a—"

That was the moment Wes attacked. He spun around and pushed Boots hard. She crashed back into Duke.

Suddenly there was pandemonium. Folks shouting. Wes and Duke fighting.

Norman ran into the center of the room, where he could get a clear shot of Wes. Priest kicked out with his one remaining leg. Norman stumbled over it. His hand spasmed. He fired a bullet down into the floor. Hank lunged at him. Norman sidestepped; the old-timer fell flat on his belly. The impact was enough to make Hank fart with a loudness and a violence Norman wouldn't have believed humanly possible.

Shit. Smells worse than a reptile house at the zoo.

Boots was picking herself up from her fall. She grunted, "That's no way to treat a lady." Her thick legs had been grazed during the rough-and-tumble.

Wes was brave.

It wasn't enough.

Three swift punches from Duke knocked the guy cold.

Barely ruffled, Duke stood back in the doorway. He leveled the gun to cover the milling people in the room.

"Okay," he called out. "Everyone stand still."

They saw the gun.

They stood still.

Lauren and Nicki were next to Priest. He shook his head and spat, "Pah!"

Boots's piglike eyes roamed around the room. "Hey, where's Pamela?"

Duke turned to look back at the empty landing. "She must have slipped out."

"I'll go get her." Boots cocked the pistol.

"No, you stay here with me," Duke ordered. "Norman, what're you waiting for? Go bring Pamela back before she calls the cops."

The cops!

Norman had forgotten all about those guys.

"What're you waiting for, Normy?" Then he said something that electrified Norman. "You find her, bud, you've got my authority to be the first to take her."

"Don't worry; I'll find her."

Norman jumped over the unconscious Wes, then ran along the landing to the stairs. He took those two at a time.

Pamela?

I get to take her first!

Oh, boy, oh, boy.

CHAPTER FORTY-SIX

Pamela thought, *I've traveled back in time. It's happening to me again.*

Is it really Norman chasing me?

Or is it Rodney?

Back from the dead.

Zombie Rodney Pinkham. He'll do the bad things to me in death that he couldn't do in life.

Her mind chatter went into overdrive as she ran from the old house on the hill. When Wes attacked Duke in the bedroom she saw Boots had landed on her fanny. She was in no position to fire her gun. The scary old guy, Priest, had tripped Norman.

So she took her chance.

She'd fled.

Down the stairs. Through the door. Out into brilliant sunshine. Dazzled, she could barely see.

Didn't stop her from running, though.

Unlike last time, when Rodney pursued her, firing his pistol at her as he went, she wasn't barefoot as she ran across the arid, stony earth of the Mojave. She wore new trainers that Lauren had given her for her waitress work. Clean white ones with a soft rubber sole.

Even so, those sharp stones made themselves felt as she ran.

But where am I going? she thought, dazed. *I'm running away from the café. I should be running toward it. Might be some would-be customers. One might have a cell phone, or they can drive me to the nearest town so I can tell the cops.*

Tell the cops what?

When they come to investigate Duke's gang's armed takeover of Pits they'll also find that we've been killing and eating people.

Go figure.

Pamela's eyes were somewhat accustomed to the sun's midday glare. Even so the yellow rocks reflected a hell of a lot of rays. She had to almost close her eyes to see.

Above her was the burning blue of the desert sky. In front of her the ground rose up into rocky hills. These were sliced by brutal ravines. She saw the ruins of mine buildings. Rusty hunks of machines littered this side of the hill. There were the remains of iron rails complete with a corroded ore hopper or two.

She also could see that she was being chased.

Norman had raced after her. She discerned the golden gleam of the automatic in his hand.

Chasing her. Just like Rodney.

Only he'd not fired yet, thank God.

As she climbed the boulder-strewn hillside she glanced back. Norman must have been nearly quarter of a mile away. He weaved between clumps of cacti. She'd gotten a good start. Was he gaining on her? She couldn't tell.

Could she hide?

No tree cover. No intact buildings.

Only rocks, sand, skeletal ruins. Not many options when it came to concealment.

Press on, she told herself. *You might find somewhere in the hills.*

So she pressed on. She could almost see herself from a vulture's point of view. A young woman with blond hair, dressed in the uniform of a Pits café waitress: knit sweater, bright red shorts, dinky apron, white sneakers. Still had her order book in the apron pocket.

Could do with a Luger. Or a machine gun. Then I could blow Norman away.

She huffed for air. Sweat ran in a salt river between her breasts. The sun burned the back of her head. She dodged a cluster of prickly pear, then pushed for speed again: chin tucked down to her collarbone, back hunched, arms pumping, feet splashing dust.

"Pamela!"

Norman sees me, all right, she told herself. *I must still be out of range; otherwise he'd have tried for a lucky shot. . . .*

She considered a change of direction. Making a run back to the café. Or even the highway in the hope that a passerby would pick her up. Whisk her to safety. Maybe even Sharpe again in his bus.

But to double back would take her too close to Norman.

Gotta keep running away from him. That means running in the opposite direction of the café, too.

"C'mon, Pamela," she panted. "You need a plan. You can't run all the way . . . to Vegas."

She was slowing. She knew it. Heat, exhaustion, running uphill—all conspired against her. Norman would catch up with her soon.

Or close the gap enough for him to fire a round or two at her.

She slowed her pace to a lope. Still she had to dodge cacti and mesquite. But she knew she had to pump oxygen into her brain. *Gotta do some thinking.*

A plan. Need a plan.

What are you doing, Pamela?

Stop here? Fight him? Brain him with a piece of old iron from the mining equipment?

"Iron bar versus automatic pistol? Think harder, Pamela."

Now she was almost walking. A stitch penetrated her side. Ahead, the hill split in two.

Can't keep climbing. Gotta take the easier route.

Pamela entered the V-shaped depression in the hillside. She soon realized she was entering a canyon. The ground beneath her began to run downhill. There was still a lot of loose rubble underfoot. Sun beat at her from the canyon sides. But it was a little easier to make progress.

If she couldn't outrun Norman this might give her more time to consider a plan.

"C'mon, Pamela, think . . . think! What are you going to do to save your life?"

CHAPTER FORTY-SEVEN

Norman was no athlete. The upside? He was young. At college he jogged—but mainly so he could watch the female joggers jiggle pleasingly around the track.

Also, he had incentives.

Duke gave him permission to bone Pamela. His reward for catching her.

Course, there's a downside, too. Duke will beat seven yards of crap outta me if I don't catch her.

And if I don't catch her she'll call the cops.

I'm a cop killer. Therefore the conclusion, then, isn't hard to make.

I fry in the electric chair.

All that was enough to keep Norman running as hard as he could. Which wasn't great when it came to marathon standards. Not terrible either. He reckoned he was gaining on her as he dodged cacti with their sharp spines, or jumped over boulders, and even sidestepped a snake with red bands running along its body.

The gold Glock automatic in his hand grew a mite too heavy from time to time, so he'd pause to change hands.

Ahead was Pamela running up the slope of the barren hill. He saw the flicker of her long, bare legs. Saw the sway of her butt clad in bright red shorts.

He wondered about claiming his prize.

Should he take her there and then on the hot ground? Or escort her down to the trailer, where he could enjoy the comfort of a soft mattress?

Hell, she'll be my mattress.

Norman even began to wonder about afterward. If he pleasured her sweetly enough there might be a bond. Pamela might fall in love with him.

It'd be a shame to hand her over to Duke.

He paused for a second to wipe sweat from his eyes. Glancing back, he saw the lone house on the hill, the cemetery with its long-dead gunslingers and monkeys. Beyond that was the café beside the deserted highway.

Still quiet.

Quiet as a grave.

He pushed himself hard to run across the slabs of rock and by discarded mining machinery. At one point he had to leap over the skeleton of a mule. Perhaps three hundred yards ahead of him he glimpsed Pamela. Again the sight of her slim-waisted figure sent a fire running through his veins.

Man, was she beautiful.

Desirable.

He couldn't wait for that slippery moment of entry.

Squinting against the sun's fierce glare, he saw her hair fly out as she spun her head to look back at him. He couldn't see her face, so he didn't know if she wore an expression of fear.

But being chased by a horny guy with a gun, how would you feel?

Feel shit-ya-pants-full scared, that's how you'd feel, boyo.

Norman grinned. This was a rare feeling of power, of being in control. He realized he was enjoying himself. He even called out her name a couple of times. He never expected her to stop, but that was part of the chase game, wasn't it? Let the victim know that he was hot on her trail.

He upped the pace. Now it was hot perspiration on his face that dried the second it beaded from his skin. Only his shirt became damp and itchy from sweat.

Once he'd tamed Pamela he'd put her to good use soaping his back in the shower. That would feel good.

He circled a patch of prickly bushes. Now he could see that a section of the hill ran into a gully. Pamela was headed along it.

She can't run forever, can she? I'm going to catch her soon. And then . . . ?

CHAPTER FORTY-EIGHT

Questions Pamela asked herself—whether her stamina would hold out, or whether she'd suddenly find she'd happened upon the main route to Las Vegas, crowded with vacation traffic—were suddenly answered for her.

"Damn."

She gazed up at the rock face in front of her. The canyon had ended as suddenly as if someone had built a fifty-foot wall in front of her. Pamela looked left. Looked right. Looked forward. Sheer cliffs.

Only one way out.

That's back.

Back the way you came.

Right into the arms—and firearm—of Norman.

But Norman is no Rodney Pinkham. He looks like a college boy from a good family. He speaks politely. He doesn't act like bad-boy Duke. And he certainly seems no psycho like Rodney.

But who can tell a psychopath from a friendly, well-mannered guy? There's no knowing who's nice and who's a killer.

"Pamela!"

Pamela looked back along the canyon. It was perhaps a hundred feet wide, flat at the bottom and covered with a loose scree. Almost like the dried-out bed of a river.

"Pamela!"

The sun had passed its zenith now. A strip of deep shadow ran along the right-hand side of the canyon floor. She still saw Norman.

He had gained on her.

Now he was a hundred yards away.

"Pamela!" His voice echoed along the canyon walls.

Oh, God. She saw the glint of the gun, too. A gold brilliance.

After being nearly killed by Rodney she couldn't just stand there and wait for Norman to stroll up and shoot her.

"Pamela. There's nowhere to run."

He didn't even seem to shout now. The narrow gap between the horizontal planes of rock amplified his voice. And it channeled it to her as well, lending it an eerie quality.

"So here you are, Pamela," she hissed to herself. "Caught like a rat in a trap. So . . . what ya gonna do? Stand and fight? Or walk toward him? Beg for mercy? Offer anything he wants?" She gulped. A tear came to her eye.

And when she wished for someone to save her it wasn't the man she once believed had loved her—her dead husband, Jim—it was Sharpe. Guardian angel of the freeway. Driver of the gray bus of salvation. The tear rolled down her cheek.

"Pamela."

Norman was now maybe eighty yards away. He stepped over knee-high boulders. Sometimes he'd vanish into shadow, then reemerge closer.

Shockingly closer.

"No," Pamela hissed. "I'm not giving up!"

Eyes scanning the rock face, she searched for something—anything! A cave. A niche to hide herself. A secret passageway.

The sunlit cliffs were featureless. Very nearly as smooth as a man-made wall.

Only now she took a closer look at the cliff that lay beneath a veil of dark shadow. *Aha.* This was different. More exposed to the west wind. She saw that the yellow rock had been weathered. There were fissures, hollows, recesses, and protrusions. Not big ones.

But, God willing, big enough.

"Pamela!"

Closing out the voice, she ran across the stones that shifted beneath her feet. She stumbled. Almost fell. But sheer willpower helped her keep her balance. Seconds later she reached the rock face.

Good-bye fingernails. Hello, gazed knees. But needs must.

Pamela began to climb the vertical rock.

"Pamela. You're wasting your time."

She didn't care. She climbed. A born-again rock monkey driven to scale a vertical wall of stone because her survival depended on it. Her eyes scanned the rock, locating handholds. Some were more like burrows in the cliff.

Pray God that there are no snakes in them.

Her fingers probed hidden voids. She expected the needle-sharp sting of fangs in the back of her hand at any moment. But her luck held. No snakes, no scorpions. Steadily she worked upward. Her back ached. She panted. Her fingertips were sore. One finger bled from the nail. Not a bite, just relentless wear and tear.

"Pamela. Don't risk it. You'll fall."

"No, I won't."

She glanced down. Thirty feet or more to the canyon floor. As she began to climb again she glimpsed Norman. He was perhaps forty yards away now. Close enough to fire on her.

Gritting her teeth against pain, gravity, exertion, she drove herself higher. Still a hell of a long way to the top. She'd never make it before Norman reached the bottom of the cliff.

She glanced to her right. Almost level with her, there was a protruding lip of rock. It formed a ledge a good five feet in width. Ten feet long. It didn't go anywhere. It was covered in boulders and loose stones that had dropped from above due to erosion over the years.

It had one thing she prized, though.

Sanctuary!

Not risking another look to see where her pursuer was (though she could hear his feet clattering over stones—must be close), she shuffled sideways across the cliff face. Her body ached. Her muscles felt as if they were on fire. She'd grazed her chin because she'd hugged the vertical surface so closely. Fifteen seconds of shuffling like a human fly brought her to the lip of rock. Almost recklessly she flipped sideways so she could grip the ledge with her hands, while her feet were still wedged in a crevice on the rock face.

It was awkward. Her torso was twisted. Elbows locked straight, she took her body weight on the palms of her hand that were flat against the horizontal surface of the ledge. Then, like someone climbing out of a swimming pool without using the steps, she hauled her body onto the platform of rock. A moment later she lay panting on a mattress of jagged stones.

As mattresses went it was uncomfortable. But right at that moment an exhausted Pamela thought it the most beautiful place to rest on the planet.

A voice wailed from below: "Pamela. There's no way out of here. Come on down."

"No way."

"I won't hurt you."

"Yeah, like I believe that, Norman."

She realized that her legs from the knees down still hung out over the edge of the ledge. A bullet in her shin wouldn't help matters, so she wriggled forward. The dust she raised made her sneeze. But when she glanced back she saw that her entire body was laid flat on the rock.

Not even a heavy-duty handgun, like the gold one Norman hefted, could punch a slug through three feet of sandstone.

"Pamela," Norman called. "There's nowhere to go from there."

"I'm not coming down."

"Aw, don't be like that. Climb down here. We can talk."

Pamela worked herself into a sitting position with her back to the cliff. She didn't risk glancing over the edge just in case Norman shot her in the head.

"Please, Pamela. I wouldn't hurt you for the world. Believe me."

She called back, "If you don't want to hurt me, prove it. Go back down to the café."

"What? And leave you here?"

"Yes."

"You'll call the cops."

"How? The nearest telephone must be fifty miles away."

"You might have a cell phone?"

"They don't work out here."

"Pamela," he pleaded.

"Go away; then I'll come down."

"You know I can't do that."

"Why not?"

"Orders. You saw what Duke's like. He'll rip me a new corn chute."

"Norman. Go away. I'm not coming down."

"I'll come up and get you then."

A boulder as big as a basketball sat on the brink of the ledge. She pushed it off with the sole of her foot.

A crash. A loud one echoed back as it struck home.

Silence.

Dear God. It hasn't hit him, has it?

Then came an aggrieved tone. "Hey, be careful! That nearly hit me."

"If you try to climb up here I'll make sure the next one cracks your skull."

"You wouldn't do that."

Pamela folded her arms. "Try me."

She heard a more reflective Norman mutter, "Shoot."

For a few moments silence descended on the canyon. It would be too dangerous to expose her head by looking over the side of the rock ledge, but if she knelt up with her back to the cliff she could see the shadow creep across the scree floor. This would become a waiting game now.

Waiting for dark? What would Norman do then? Retreat? Or try to reach her under cover of darkness?

At last she heard Norman say, "Looks as if we've got a dilemma."

"I've no dilemma," she retorted. "I'm staying put."

"You can't stay there forever without water. Not in this heat."

"Neither can you, Norman."

"One of the others will be along in a minute."

"So you're a telepath. You can communicate with them that you're way up here in a hidden canyon?"

"Ugh."

She heard the grunt as he realized the flaw in his thinking.

No one knew they were here. So no one would bring Norman a cool bottle of water to slake his thirst.

To sit it out in this arid channel of rock would be an endurance test. Whoever's craving for liquid got the better of them would lose.

"I don't want you to die of thirst, Pamela."

"Women survive longest without water, Norman. We've got a thicker layer of liquid-filled fat under our skin. Boobs are pretty much all fluid anyway. Y'know? Like camels' humps?"

When he spoke next she realized he was changing his strategy. "Pamela? We're alike, you and me."

"Don't think so, Norm."

"We're educated. I can tell you are from the way you speak."

"How observant, my dear Holmes."

"Well-read, too."

"I saw the old Sherlock Holmes movies."

"Yeah, Basil Rathbone, he was the greatest, wasn't he?"

"Norman, you're patronizing me."

"Listen. We both know it's stupid for us to sit out here in a godforsaken canyon without water. If you come down here we can walk back to the café and talk all this through over a glass of cold white wine. How does that sound?"

"Sounds wonderful. But you'll shoot the fuck out of me the moment I start climbing down."

"Pamela. I'm not a barbarian."

"What about Duke and Boots? They psychotic or what?"

"Um . . . that's one of the subjects I need to discuss with you."

"Say again?"

"You're intelligent. I need your advice. To be honest with you I'm in a bit of trouble. Well . . . more than a bit of trouble. A hell of a lot of trouble."

She realized she needed to see his face. His expression would support whether he was telling the truth. Come to that, the look in his eye would indicate whether or not he'd murder her in cold blood.

She inched toward the edge of the rock ledge. Just one glimpse down. One glimpse at his face would be enough.

That was when the shot rang out.

"Norman, you double-crossing son of a—"

"Pamela. Pamela!"

"You promised you wouldn't try to shoot me."

"I didn't! I've shot a rattlesnake. It just struck out at me."

"Like I'd believe you." She hunkered back against the cliff. Out of sight.

"Pamela, you've got to believe me. I shot a snake. There's another thing. . . ." His voice sounded troubled.

"What's that?"

"Pamela, you've got to help. The rattler bit me!"

CHAPTER FORTY-NINE

"You're shitting me, Norman."

Norman looked up the cliff face. It was in shadow, but he could still make out where the rock ledge bulged out. He couldn't see Pamela, though. She must be hunkered back against the cliff out of sight.

"Please, Pamela," he called, his voice echoing from the canyon walls. "There was a rattler. It really did bite me."

"Yeah, and the second I poke my head out you blow a hole in it."

"No."

"Can't trust you, Norman."

"It's starting to burn. It's the venom. . . ."

"Where'd it bite?"

"My leg."

"Where on your leg?"

"Come down, Pamela. See for yourself."

"As if."

"Please."

"Are you sure it was a rattlesnake?"

"Take a look for yourself."

"Put the gun on a rock; somewhere I can see it, but well away from yourself."

"Yes, yes, anything. As long as you help me."

He still couldn't see her, so he walked twenty paces, then lay the gold-plated handgun on a boulder. Then he returned to the bottom of the cliff.

But he noticed something.

Something bad.

He was limping now. The venom burned up through his veins like hot wax flowed there instead of blood. A moment ago he'd felt overwarm; now cold shivers ran down his spine despite the heat in his veins.

Oh, God. All of this, now I get chewed by a snake . . . a fucking rattler, of all things . . .

His legs had become wobbly by the time he'd gotten himself back to the bottom of the cliff.

When he called out, his voice had taken a turn for the croaky . . . start of the death rattle? "Pamela . . . I got rid of the gun. . . . You're safe. . . . Please . . . you gotta do something. I feel weird. . . . I . . ."

"Okay, Norman. You've gotta stay calm. Breathe nice and slow."

He looked up. The sky was a dazzling blue. This side of the canyon was dipped black in shadow now. But he saw her!

A lithe figure with blond hair. Long, bare legs swinging over the ledge thirty feet above him. She moved fast.

Her hands and feet found handholds so she could descend.

So she could save him!

His heart pounded. An awful taste filled his mouth. The venom? Was it invading every part of his body in a tide of bitter poison? *Oh, God . . .*

Norman closed his eyes. He opened them only when he heard a thump of feet. Pamela had jumped the last five feet to the ground.

"I really think it's kicking in." His voice was weak-sounding. Hoarse.

"Where's the snake?" She sounded suspicious.

She doesn't believe me.

Swaying slightly, he pointed.

His finger had swollen.

Shit. That stuff acts fast. He was inflating like a balloon.

"There."

He pointed to three feet of tube-shaped reptile lying in its own snake blood. His shot had blown most of the head away, leaving strands of skin and gristly bits of snake muscle.

"My God," she breathed. "That's a rattler, all right. Do you see the tail?"

"Saw the tail? Felt its teeth, too. Bery farp."

"Say again?"

He moistened his swollen tongue, then took a run at the two words again. "Very sharp. Rattlesnake bangs. Bery farp."

"Here, sit down on this rock, Norman."

"Bank yar."

"It's affecting your speech, Norman. The venom's entering your bloodstream fast."

"Uh . . ."

He felt like death.

Pamela cupped his face in her two hands. She looked into his eyes. He saw the anxiety there.

"Norman," she said in a calm but firm voice. "I need to get as much of the venom out of the wound as I can."

"Uh-huh." He grunted the affirmative. His hands felt cold as frost.

Circulatory collapse. Toxic shock.

She spoke again. "Norman, listen . . . no, stay awake for me. Norman. Where did the snake bite you?"

"Thigh."

She stepped back to see where he pointed.

"Your inner thigh?"

"Uh."

"Okay, Norman. Help me drop your pants. I'm going to have to suck out the poison."

He'd wondered what Pamela's lips would feel like against his skin. Now he was going to find out.

But he hadn't anticipated these circumstances. Not for one minute.

With her help he slid his pants down. Then he sat on the boulder with his bare legs apart. They were awfully pale-looking. Shaky, too.

"I see the bite mark, Norman." She took a deep breath. "Okay. Here goes."

Norman felt her cool lips on the burning wound. The fangs had punctured the skin on his inner thigh, midway between knee and groin.

Now Pamela'd clamped her lips on the two bleeding holes.

Oh, man, and how she sucked!

When she paused for breath she also spit. Despite Norman's dizziness he saw that her saliva was bright pink with blood.

"Ya gonna apply . . . apply a tourniquet?" he croaked.

"Nope. Never apply a tourniquet to snakebites." She wiped her lips with the back of her hand. "Always make sure the patient is calm; keep the affected limb lower than the heart. With luck, the venom will localize and not spread through the body."

"You really know what you're doing?"

"I should hope so," she told him. "I'm a teacher. I took first-aid courses so I could take the little darlings on field trips. Of course, they never got bitten by snakes, stung by scorpions, or chased by grizzly bears. Instead they got drunk on beer or whacked out of their skulls on E. Here goes again." Again she ducked her head down to suck his naked thigh.

Norman's mind was fuzzy, to say the least. His hands were cold as ice. His leg was swelling. But he realized what this must look like to anyone watching the pair of them.

Here I am sitting on a rock with my pants down. Pamela is crouching in front of me. Her head is below my waistline. She's sucking away like crazy. Her head's twisting from side to side. I'm moaning.

Only not with pleasure.

Snakebites don't suck. They hurt. Fucking hurt!

"Yee-ow!" he cried.

She spit and wiped again. "Hurting?"

"You could say."

"I think I've got some of it."

"I'm gonna die."

"No, you're not."

"If you felt the agony I felt you wouldn't say that."

"Norman." She was panting from the exertion. "In this country more than eight thousand people are bitten by snakes in any one year. Less than one percent die."

He grunted. "One percent still sounds like scary odds to me."

"*Less* than one percent. *Far less.* More people die from wasp and bee stings."

"You've gotta get me some antidote."

She shook her head. "You won't get any antivenom within fifty miles of here."

"Aw, crap."

"Besides, not a lot of doctors administer it for snakebites. Sometimes the side effects of the treatment are worse than the snake venom."

"That doesn't make me feel any better."

"Well, you *sound* better." Pamela looked closely at his face. "Your speech's improved. So has your color."

Norman straightened up. Experimentally he moved his arms, and then turned his head from side to side. "Hey, I don't feel as bad as I did a few minutes ago. The dizzy spells are passing."

She smiled. "You'll live, then."

"Yeah," he said, pleased. "I will, won't I?"

Pamela turned to look at the gun on the boulder twenty paces from them. "You still going to shoot me, Norman?"

"No. I never planned on killing you anyway."

"But you're going to take me back to the house and lock me up with the others?"

He shook his head. "I've decided. This madness has got to end."

"Oh?"

"I'm gonna call the cops." He paused. "At some point."

"Why some point? Why not now?"

He grimaced. "That's why I need to talk to you."

"We'd be more comfortable talking down at the café."

"With the dead guys there"—he shrugged—"it's a bit of a mess, I'm afraid."

"My trailer then."

"Okay."

He stood up.

She looked at his legs. "Norman?"

"Uh?"

"Your pants. Before you walk anywhere, best pull them up."

CHAPTER FIFTY

"So, there it is," Norman said. He took a swallow of ice-cold soda. He'd talked so much his throat burned. "You know everything that happened to me in the last seven days."

"You killed two police officers?" Pamela stared at him.

"Yes . . . but I didn't mean to. You've got to believe me."

"Shoot."

"It's being with Duke and Boots. It's like some kinda dope. You can't think straight. They make crazy stuff seem the most perfectly rational ideas in the world."

"You mean like taking over Pits at gunpoint?"

Norman nodded. Then he glanced across the trailer lounge to a table where the gold handgun gleamed in the afternoon light.

Norman winced as he shifted in the armchair. The snakebite still seared his thigh. Although it was a little easier than before. Pamela had washed the puncture marks with antiseptic, then taped on a dressing. After shuffling to get comfortable he sat brooding.

At last he said to Pamela, "You must think I'm the worst."

"I think maybe you've done some stupid things, but . . ."

He looked up at her. The change in tone when she said "but" suggested something weighed pretty heavily on her mind, too.

"But?" he echoed.

"But Pits isn't what you think." Pamela went to the table where she'd left a pitcher of chilled water. She refilled her glass.

Pamela'd ditched the waitress apron.

Norman noted with some pleasure that its absence revealed more of her slim figure. She wore the café's uniform: bright red shorts, plus a white pullover shirt.

Boy, she looked good.

'S *easy to get distracted when a babe looks that hot*, Norman told himself. He took his mind off the curves of her bod, concentrated on what she was saying.

"Norman, I thought Pits was just a little desert community."

"Doesn't look like much more than a ghost town to me," he added.

"Just what I thought. It's only got the café, gas station, and the trailers. Those and a population of six people."

Five, Norman thought. He realized that Pamela couldn't know that Terry, the cook, was lying dead in a patch of cholla cacti. He let it pass. Such admissions now would complicate the situation with Pamela . . . delicious Pamela.

Pamela, he realized, was trying to explain certain facts. "You remember what the old guy was saying earlier?"

"The one-legged guy?"

"Priest." She nodded.

Norman shrugged. "He's a crazy old coot, isn't he? All that talk of eating people? Has to be certifiable."

"He's not crazy, Norman." She took a steadying breath. "Here in Pits they eat people."

Norman laughed out loud. Then he clammed up. *Pamela ain't laughing*.

"Jeez," he hissed. "You're not kidding me, are you?"

"Nope. That's how they funded the café refit and the trailers. You see, what they couldn't eat they sold. Jewelry, watches, and stuff."

"Holy moly." He had to remember to close his jaw. His chin was nearly resting on his chest in amazement. "And you've . . . ?" He mimed gnawing his hand.

"You have too."

"Me?"

She nodded.

"Oh, no, no." Norman shook his head so hard it made the snakebite sting. "I've killed people these last few days. I've never, *ever* eaten anyone. Shit, as a kid I didn't even eat my own boogers."

"Have to disagree, Norman," she told him matter-of-factly. "When you first arrived you ate the Pits Burger. Lauren's special-recipe burger."

"Christ on a motorcycle." He swallowed as if he could taste human flesh.

Cannibals say humans taste of pork. That's why they call their victim "Long Pig." Did those Pits Burgers taste of pork? They were kinda spicy.

He gulped. "The person I ate . . . anyone you know?"

"Nicki's pimp."

"Holy shit."

"The guy rode out here to kill her for running out on him."

Norman gave a bilious smile. "I guess it couldn't happen to a nicer guy."

"If it helps . . . I killed him."

"Wow."

"I biffed him on the head."

The nausea passed. His smile broadened. "Looks like we've got a regular killing spree here."

"But you're right, Norman. The madness has got to stop."

"Any ideas?"

She stood up. "I'm going to tell the cops."

"The cops?" He shifted uncomfortably. Thoughts of the electric chair crackled into his mind.

"No time like the present, Norman. After all, we don't know what Duke and Boots are doing to my friends up at the house, do we?"

"No," Norman replied. "We don't."

But knowing those two psychos I have a fair idea.

"Stay here," she told him. Her expression was businesslike. "I'll be back as soon as I can."

Norman got cold feet. "Is it wise to telephone the cops? Maybe we should wait awhile? Boots and Duke might just decide to take off."

"There's no working telephone in Pits. We'll have to drive to the nearest pay phone. You sit and rest that leg."

Fifteen minutes later Pamela hurried into the trailer's living room.

She rattled a set of keys. "We'll take Wes's truck. It's parked next to the gas station."

"I don't know. . . ."

"What do ya mean, you don't know, Norman?"

"Where we gonna go?"

"To a pay phone. Or to the nearest town. Find the sheriff's office. Listen, Norman. My friends are in danger up at the house. If we don't bring help they're likely to wind up dead."

Norman realized she saw the doubt on his face. Her nostrils flared with anger.

"Norman. Don't wuss out on me now. I saved your life, remember."

"I know."

"So I'm owed a favor, and I'm calling it in right now."

"Okay, okay." He grimaced as he stood up. The snake venom had swollen his leg. It felt tight.

Hurt like a sliver of red-hot iron had been forced into his skin.

Her anger changed to concern. "You can walk okay?"

"I'll be fine. Let's just get to that truck."

He limped from the dining room into the kitchen. If he kept walking maybe the tightness in his leg would ease. Couldn't do much about the burning sting, though.

Pamela opened the trailer door to the desert sunlight. Even though the day was headed toward evening the light was still fiercely bright. He followed her down the three steps to the dusty earth. She waited for him.

Took his arm.

That feels nice. The gentle pressure of her fingers around my arm. A guy could get used to this.

"Keep walking, Norman. I'll help."

"I'll try."

"Try as hard as you can. We don't want to stop until we're in that truck."

She was right. Norman wanted to be in that truck. He wanted to drive out of here as fast as those big old tires could carry them. It was the bit about the sheriff's office he wasn't too happy about.

They moved away from the trailers, heading toward the parking lot with its line of abandoned cars. Beyond the lot lay the café. Just a few yards beyond that was the gas station. He could see a truck parked beside it. That must be Wes's truck. Just another three minutes, and—

"Norman. What happened to you, bud?"

He stopped dead. Duke's voice.

Oh, shit . . .

"Yeah, Normy." Boots's little-girl tones. "We wuz worried that you might have got hurt."

Norman stopped, turned. Pamela stood beside him, supporting him.

"Guys," he said with a forced smile. "Am I glad to see you."

Duke scowled. Norman saw himself reflected in the tough guy's shades. "You sure you're glad to see us?"

"Sure, I'm sure." Norman made it sound like he'd been having fun.

Boots nodded. "You found Pamela, then?"

"Yup. I found her."

"Why didn't you come back to the house, Norman?" Duke eased the big revolver out of his belt.

Norman saw that Boots's gun was in her hand as her arms hung loosely by her side.

Gun? Oh, fuck!

Realization hit Norman like a deluge of ice water.

I've left my gun on the table in the trailer.

"Norm, buddy." Duke's voice was chilling. "I asked why you didn't return to the house when you found runaway Pammy, here?"

"We couldn't," Pamela told him.

"He wasn't asking you, Miss Smarty-pants," Boots said.

Norman pretended an easygoing shrug, but in reality he was getting anxious. "It's embarrassing to admit this," he said.

"What's embarrassing?"

"In truth, Duke, I got bitten by a snake."

"So?"

"I needed treatment. Pamela helped me."

"She sucked out the poison?"

Norman nodded. "Look, Duke, you can see where the rattler's fangs went through my pants."

Boots was impressed. "See that, Duke? He really did get bit." She looked at him. Her eyes were big and dewy. "Did it hurt, Norman?"

"Nothing I can't handle," he replied.

"Okay, Norm." Duke chewed an idea over. "I buy the snakebite. But where were you headed now?"

"The café," Pamela said. "They've got a first-aid kit there."

"But ain't that square pad in your pants a dressing, Norman? Or is it your time of the month?"

"Uh? Oh, a temporary dressing."

"He needs painkillers, too," Pamela added quickly.

Duke looked from them to the café. "It ain't no direct route. You were heading toward the gas station. And there's a truck parked just there."

"No, Duke. Like I said, we—"

"A truck," he interrupted. "All gassed and good to go. And ain't those the truck keys in Pammy's hand?"

"Oh, Normy." Boots looked as if she'd cry. "You weren't figurin' on running out on us?"

"No."

"We're your bestest friends in the whole wide world, Normy."

Norman tried to change the subject. "Shouldn't we be getting back to the house? The others will be making a run for it, too."

"We locked them in the attic," Boots said.

"Like maybe we should've locked you in, Norman," Duke hissed. "Then you wouldn't have been tempted to double-cross us."

"I didn't." Norman heard his voice rise into a squeal of protest.

Gotta persuade Duke I wasn't deserting him and Boots. If I don't he's gonna use that Magnum handgun on me.

Duke considered.

Norman stood beside Pamela. Boots stood beside Duke. The two pairs faced each other. The sun had taken on a rusty tint now as it sank toward the hills. The highway was deserted. The silence was so intense it almost hurt Norman's ears.

What would Duke decide?

Norman looked at Boots. She stared at Pamela with those dead brown eyes of hers. She lifted one of her dirty white boots an inch, then set it down, then raised the other. As if marching on the spot.

Weird.

Duke slid a cigarette from the carton. He lit it. Then:

"I want to believe you, Norman. But you can see my dilemma."

"God's honest truth, Duke. I wasn't planning on leaving you and Boots here."

"I'm thinkin' I need proof of your loyalty."

"Anything. I'll do anything."

He nodded at Pamela. "You got your test, Norman," he said. Then he handed Norman the Magnum. "Shoot her in the head."

"Pardon?"

"Pardon?" Duke mimicked. "Why doesn't it surprise the everlasting shit outta me that you still speak all polite, like a duchess?"

"But—"

"You heard me, Norman. Prove your loyalty to me and Boots. Blow her bitchin' brains out."

Norman hefted the gun. It was heavier than the automatic. He looked up at Pamela. She was backstepping through the dust. She was shaking her head.

"No, Norman," she whispered. "Please don't do it."

"You *can* do it, Normy," Boots encouraged. "Just pop one of them caps into her face."

"Won't feel a thing, Normy." Duke grinned. "You'll be doin' her a favor. Now she'll never grow old and wrinkled and suffer from arthritis and piles and shit."

Norman raised the revolver. The blue metal barrel glinted.

Pamela was gasping while she backed away. "Please, Norman. Don't kill me. Not after all I've done for you. You won't—"

"Shut up!" Norman snapped.

"Attaboy," Duke praised.

Then Norman turned. Fired.

Fired at Duke. The guy jerked sideways.

Lost his balance. Went down.

Did I hit him?

Norman raised the gun as Duke sat up. He was ready to fire again.

Wanted to fire again! Right plug-fuck center of his chest. But his hand shook so much the gun jumped out of sweat-slippery fingers. It fell into the dust.

Duke looked dazed for a second. Blood streamed from a nick at the edge of his ear where the big-caliber round had brushed it.

So I did hit him. Only just.

Duke's eyes cleared.

Dragging the sunglasses from his face, he snarled at Boots, "Kill them both."

As Boots raised the revolver Pamela flew at her.

If Norman expected a catfight he was mistaken. Pamela swung her fist to deliver a hell of a punch at that piggy face.

Boots squealed.

Dropped down.

But not out. She climbed up onto all fours in two seconds flat. She raised the hand that held the revolver.

Pamela followed through with a full-blooded kick.

The sneaker thudded into Boots's chunky side, right where the kidney was located.

Boots gave a cry that sounded strangely orgasmic. The kick didn't stop her either; slowed her, though.

Panting, she shuddered so hard that Norman saw Boots's small breasts jiggling like Jell-O. Then she started to climb to her feet again. The pistol was in her hand.

Norman glanced at Duke. He moved on all fours to where the hefty Magnum revolver lay in the dirt.

Do I make a run for the pistol? Kill them both? he asked himself, but at that moment Pamela turned to him, hair flaring out, eyes flashing with urgency.

"Norman! *Run!*"

Norman didn't ask *where* they were running. He simply followed Pamela. Her legs covered distance in an easy sprint. Norman limped. His teeth were gritted. He grunted with pain.

That snakebite burned like fury. His leg felt so tight, and heavy, as if it were clad in iron.

Can't run; can hardly walk . . .

A gunshot rang out. The bullet whined past him to smack into the ground with a splash of dust twenty yards in front of him.

Now Norman ran, pain or no pain.

He caught up with Pamela. They ran side by side.

"This way," she panted.

He followed as she hurtled around one of the trailer homes. Now the fifty-foot aluminum box was between them and the two maniacs with guns.

Crack . . . crack-crack!

"They're still firing," he panted. "Morons!"

"Don't bank on them not hitting. Those trailer walls are like foil."

He glanced back. She was right. Boots and Norman must have fired again from the other side. Bullets came busting through flimsy aluminum walls, right through the trailer, to ricochet on the stony ground close by.

"Where now?" he asked, running hard. "To the house?"

"Nope." Her eyes blazed toward the horizon. "To the hills."

Norman's leg hurt. That snake venom must have been fizzing in his leg muscle. He looked up toward the rocky hills turning red in the setting sun.

Panting, he gasped out the words: "Pamela. I don't think I'm gonna make it."

CHAPTER FIFTY-ONE

Norman realized a rock-solid fact: *I'm gonna be dead by tonight.*

Prospects weren't good. Here he was running up through Pits's cemetery with Pamela. The pair was being chased by Boots and Duke. Two crazy people with guns.

Crazy people with a proven track record of killing in cold blood.

Nope. The bottom line is: it doesn't look hopeful at all.

"You've got to run faster, Norman." Pamela panted the words as they exited the cemetery. Ahead was the old house on the hill. Beyond that, a craggy landscape littered with rusting mining gear.

"I am running as fast . . . as I can." Norman struggled to breathe. "Snakebite. Hurts . . . hurts like hell."

Pamela might have intended to offer words of encouragement. But the pair behind, letting loose with the handguns, was all the encouragement Norman needed.

Bullets buzzed through the evening air to ricochet off the rocks around them, or chew flesh out of a cactus.

"That's better," she gasped as he piled on the speed.

Sweat blinded him; a stitch began to dig at his side. He risked a glance back.

Boots had fallen back. She now hobbled through the cemetery clutch-

ing her side. A stitch? Or had that kick of Pamela's finally made itself
felt through her sluggish—*her hoggish*—nervous system?

Duke continued strongly. He was lean. Fit.

Muscular.

That guy wasn't going to tire easily.

So much for the government telling you cigarettes are bad for you,
that they silt up your lungs and clog your arteries. Duke chain-smoked.
Only he ran like an athlete.

"We can't keep running forever," Norman panted.

"We've got to make it into the hills again. Need somewhere to
hide."

"For God's sake . . . keep out of the canyon this time . . . dead end."

"Don't I know it."

He glanced at her. Her clear eyes were locked on the path ahead.
Blond hair flew out around her head. Her breasts moved in motion with
her body. A pleasing motion. Not a loose wobble.

God, was she something?

Something special.

If we make it outta here alive, maybe we could—

Crack!

The sound of Duke's Magnum handgun stopped that particular line of
thought. The round passed so close to Norman's head he felt its slip-
stream snatch at his hair.

The leg where the rattler had planted its fangs ached like nothing on
earth. He was sure it had swollen to twice its normal girth.

"Keep running," Pamela urged him. "Once we're in the hills we can
give him the slip."

"Might be time to say a prayer to your guardian angel," Norman
panted back.

He glanced over his shoulder.

No fair!

Duke was maybe forty yards behind them. And closing.

The guy didn't look tired.

Hadn't lost his cool.

A killing machine in human form.

Norman's legs quivered as if the strength were pouring out of them.

Any second now he knew he'd drop to his knees with exhaustion. Then . . . *blam-blam! It's the big sleep for Norman Wiscoff.* . . .

"Bear left," Pamela told him. "There's a track leading . . . leading into the hills by all that machinery."

"But we're running uphill." His breath whistled in his throat. He could hardly inhale.

Still managing to run, he glanced down at his fingers. They were swollen. He couldn't even see his knuckles, his flesh was so puffed.

Snake venom. This exertion was pushing it through his veins.

His heart seemed to beat uncannily loud. Maybe the toxins were invading cardiac muscle.

He staggered.

"What's wrong?" Pamela asked.

"I can't run any more."

"You've got to, Norman."

"I know . . . but I can't. . . . My leg's seizing. I can't breathe."

She's going to run on and leave me. That realization struck Norman hard. He'd been running for days. Now he couldn't flee anymore.

The moment of reckoning.

Oh, God . . .

But Pamela wasn't quitting on him yet. "In here," she shouted.

Walking ability had almost left him now. Never mind running.

Pamela gripped his arm, then dragged him across a stretch of ground that was covered with fine stones. They were so deep that Norman sank to his ankles. They shifted when he tried to lurch forward on his stiffening leg.

He glanced back. Duke was thirty yards away.

The man paused, aimed.

Squeezed the trigger, and—

Click!

Even from here Norman heard the hammer fall on a spent cartridge.

Duke began to reload. After emptying the dead shell cases from their chambers in a golden rain onto the ground, he took fresh rounds from his shirt pocket and began to reload one by one.

He grinned at them. "No point in running folks. Pammy? You might live if you're real nice to me. Normy? Stop running away like a kid. Come here and take your punishment like a man."

"Don't listen to him," Pamela hissed.

Still, she yanked Norman by the arm. She guided him across the rug of loose stones that were so hard to walk on. Ahead he saw the crumbling structure of a mine building. There was no roof to speak of. Not much in the way of walls either. Just a course of bricks about waist high, with a few weathered boards hanging to a timber frame. Through the holes in the walls Norman could make out hunky lumps of machinery that by turns had been sandblasted, then ravaged by rust, and crusted white with bird droppings.

Probably was a desirable residence for scorpions, too.

Yeah, why not get a scorpion sting on the other leg, Norm? It might even out the snakebite.

"You can't run," Duke called after them as he coolly reloaded the handgun. "Not much of a place to hide." He laughed. "Unless you figure on shrinking yourselves down to the size of a bug."

Toiling up the hill behind Duke came Boots.

Oh, great.

Now Boots is gonna watch me weep and beg for my life. Not that Duke's the kinda guy who favors groveling. I'm still gonna get a bullet in the head.

"Keep moving!"

Pamela kept urging him on as she dragged him through the doorway into the building. The floor was covered with windblown sand. There were a couple of tumbleweeds. The sloughed skin of a snake—a yellow, papery thing. There was even the skeleton of a dog or coyote in the corner.

"Not much of a place to a hide," he panted.

"If we can't hide, we'll fight."

My God, is she feisty! He was impressed.

"We don't have any weapons," he reminded her.

She looked around. Her eyes were razor sharp. She was assessing everything for its assault potential. A length of chain that was orange with rust. A shovel with a broken handle. A couple of perished truck tires.

There were more gaps than wall. Norman could see the desert hills rearing up into the dark blue of the evening sky.

"No helicopter. No machine gun," he observed.

"Sarcasm won't help us, Norman."

A revolver round smacked into the timbers.

"It's your time, Norman." Duke's voice sounded frighteningly close.

"Yeah, come on out." This was Boots. She still sounded winded from her climb up here from the trailers.

Norman limped around an engine that must be the size of an ice-cream truck. It had cogs the size of bicycle wheels. Levers longer than his arm. A conglomeration of valves, tubing, drive belts (long perished), dusty gauges. But nothing to use as a weapon.

Pamela followed him.

Another bullet smacked into the machinery. It rang like a church bell.

"Damn, that was close," Pamela hissed. "What are we going to do, Norman?"

Norman looked up at the remains of the wall that faced the sunset. Through foot-wide gaps in the boards he discerned that tonight's dusk was a dazzling red. Two figures—one tall and lean, one short and squat—stood in dark silhouette.

We're caught like rats in a trap.

"Okay," Duke told them. "You've had your fun. The chase is over, guys."

"We win; you lose," Boots said.

Norman stepped back, his feet drawing furrows in the dust.

"Pammy," Duke said. "Keep your hands up. Now walk forward to the door."

"She's cute." Boots must have been smirking, from the tone of her voice. "Can I have her tonight, Duke? Pleaseer-weezer, just for li'l ol' me."

"Sure. You've earned some fun time."

Pamela knew what was in store for her. She groaned. "Oh, dear Lord in heaven."

Norman took another step back. This time his foot didn't step into dust.

Nothingness.

Fresh air.

Surprised, he glanced back.

There was was a hole, four feet by six feet.

A dark hole. An abyss kind of hole.

The bottomless-pit variety.

Warm air flowed up from it. That air stank so bad he nearly up-chucked there and then.

"Stand perfectly still, Norman, old bud." Duke's voice grew colder. "If I get a good clean shot, it shouldn't hurt you none . . . at least not too much."

"Okay," Norman said. "You've no objection my turning my back to you, so I don't see you fire the gun?"

"No objection at all, Normy. I should be able to plant the round smack between your shoulder blades."

"Poor Normy," Boots sympathized.

Norman figured that from this angle Duke and Boots couldn't see the opening of the mine shaft in the floor.

He turned around, his hands held high.

"Want me to count you down, Duke?" Boots asked.

"Sure."

"Three . . . two . . ."

Before "one," Norman grabbed hold of Pamela by the sweater. He heard the rip of fabric.

Heard her aggrieved, "Hey!"

But when he jumped she toppled with him.

Into the pit.

Madness, he thought as both of them fell.

But when you're faced with death by shooting or death by falling, which one do you pick?

Norman didn't want to give Duke the satisfaction of blowing his brains out.

The fall was a long one. Longer than he thought possible.

Pamela screamed.

Kept screaming.

Until . . .

CHAPTER FIFTY-TWO

Pamela screamed until they hit the bottom of the shaft.

Norman expected hardness. Hardness like he wouldn't believe. Bone-breaking, head-cracking.

Sharp debris. Discarded mining tools. Boulders. Shards of rock.

Instead squelchy. Wet. Soft. Uncannily soft.

Wet?

And when he recovered from the concussion he detected something else, too.

Pamela voiced it first. "Oh! That smell. What is it?"

Norman realized everything he'd eaten in the last twenty-four hours did its darned hardest to hurtle back up his gullet. He gulped.

"What a stink . . . it's suffocating."

Asking her if she was uninjured by the fall was moot now. Both were focused on the appalling smell at the bottom of the pit.

"Welcome to the pit that put the *pit* into Pits," Norman managed to say. "But . . . sheesh . . . what an odor."

"It's so thick you could cut it with a knife."

Norman looked around. Too dark to see anything. Above them he saw the bright hole where they'd fallen though. Parts of the upper walls of the shaft were illuminated by the bright setting sun.

But down here . . .

Darkness.

Darkness and stink . . .

A sweet smell, only nauseating. Decay. Fermentation. On the shitty side as well. Like an almighty crap after gorging on chocolate.

Norman said, "Feel around . . . use your sense of touch. Feel what we've fallen into."

"Oh . . . my . . . God." Pamela knew what they'd fallen into.

Norman knew, too. "Damn . . . this can't be happening."

Pamela's voice whispered from the dark: "We've found where Pits dumps its leftovers."

"I think I've just picked up a hand," Norman said. He felt stiff fingers. The wrist appeared to be sawed through. His own finger felt a stub of cut bone.

"I've just put my hand on a head," Pamela told him. "Ugh . . . I can feel the eyes . . . ick . . . no, I can feel where the eyes *were*."

"Anything else?"

"Feels like body parts. Can you see yet?"

"Not a thing?"

"Probably for the best."

"Ugh, what a stink . . . I don't know how much more of this I can take."

Norman agreed. "And we know who created this." He gulped. "This is where the good people of Pits dumped the bodies. Or what's left of them."

"Jesus. They'll have been dropping human remains down here for decades. There might be hundreds."

"Lucky they did," he told her. "Least the cadavers broke our fall."

"Oooh-weee. I'm covered in corpse juice. Can you feel how sticky your skin is?"

"Don't . . . it's on my lips, too."

"Can you see yet?" Pamela asked. "Anything at all?"

"Down here, not a thing." Then he added, "Which is probably a *good* thing."

He heard scrabbling. Pamela must still be searching the debris in the dark.

"Find anything?" he asked.

"As well as you-know-whats . . . heads and arms and shit . . . there's plastic bags full of stuff."

He felt too, until his hand closed over a crackling membrane. "Seems like a sack of clothes."

"Probably the possessions of these people."

He heard a squelch, followed by a rattling sound.

Pamela said, "I think I've just sat on someone's belly . . . oh, God, postmortem farts . . . they're the worst, aren't they?"

Norman would have agreed, only he was fighting the urge to vomit.

Just when he began to forget a current event that should have been uppermost in his mind he heard a voice quavering down from above. "Oooh, Norman. Cooeee! Are you all right down there, Normy?"

"Oh, shit, *those* two," He whispered.

Neither of them replied to Boots's call.

Then Duke shouted, "Hey, Norman, reply to the lady. Don't make me come down there!"

The gruesome twosome on the surface thought this was funny. They both laughed.

Then a second later Norman heard a noise someplace between a thud and a squish.

Pamela warned, "Norman, they're throwing stuff down at us."

Norman looked up at the circle of light that was the entrance to the shaft. He made out two heads looking down from about thirty feet away. He also saw a truck tire sailing down through the air toward them.

He flung himself to one side.

Thud.

"Pamela, you okay?"

"Fine. I suggest we get out of the line of fire."

Just for emphasis one of the pair above fired the revolver down the shaft.

Crack . . . splat.

One of the body parts got that one.

"Norman," Pamela hissed. "Over here."

"Where the hell is over here?"

"Here. Follow the sound of my voice."

"What's wrong?"

"I'm in the entrance of a tunnel . . . I think I am anyway . . . if you follow me in they won't be able to hit you."

"It's so dark they're firing blind anyway."

Crack . . . A ricochet whine, then another splat.

"But then again," he added, "if you shoot into the dark you still might hit something . . . and I don't want to be that *something*."

"Then quit gabbing and follow the sound of my voice."

He didn't have a clue where her voice came from. Instead he reached out groping hands until he found the rock side of the shaft. Then he followed it. The snakebite stung his thigh. The air stank. His body was sticky with sweat and ichor leaking from body parts. But he kept going.

Until he reached the tunnel mouth. Then he fell forward onto another piece of anatomy.

"Ouch. Norman, you've just landed on me."

"Sorry, Pamela. I can't see squat."

"Shuffle back here . . . away from the shaft."

"What now?"

"Wait. They'll get bored."

They sat there, side by side. Norman could feel Pamela's shivering body against his. Every so often she flinched when she heard the report of a gun as Boots or Duke fired blindly down the shaft.

"Keep quiet," Norman whispered. "If they don't hear us they'll think they managed to hit us. Or that we're already dead from the fall."

All they could do was sit in the stinking tunnel.

And wait.

Norman could see by the luminous face of his watch that they'd waited nearly half an hour when he heard Boots calling down to them.

"Normy . . . Normy? I shouldn't be telling you this, Normy. Duke'd get mad, but me and you had a thing, didn't we? We could've been a couple and done nice stuff together."

Norman kept his mouth shut.

"But, like, for old times' sake, I gotta tell you this. Listen, Normy. Duke's gone to get more ammo and a flashlight. He's gonna come down there after you. He said he'd . . . Uh-oh." Her call turned into a whisper that Norman could only just make out. "He's coming back. Run, Normy, while you've got the chance."

Norman found Pamela by sense of touch. He moved forward until her hair brushed his lips. Now he could whisper into her ear without being overheard.

"Pamela. What Boots just said. What do you think?"

Pamela whispered back, "Could be the truth. It will be dark soon. They probably don't want to risk leaving us, just in case we find a way out."

"Stay here; I'll take a look up the shaft."

"Careful, Norman. Could be a trick."

By sense of touch, groping his way over rotting human carcasses, he made it back to the shaft. When he looked up he could see Boots with her halo of short blond hair. She was looking down into the hole. From the way she didn't react when he peeped up he guessed she couldn't see him.

He couldn't see much, either.

Just the entrance to the shaft. A few roof timbers above it. No actual roof. Streaks of red cloud in the sky.

Wait . . .

He could make out the inner rim of the entrance to the pit. Beneath that were the walls of the shaft. He could discern patches of gray rock. Also he could see something that made his stomach drop. An iron ladder was bolted to one of the walls. He couldn't see how far it extended, because just a few feet from the surface the shaft walls were hidden by darkness.

But want to bet the ladder comes all way down here?

Norman crawled back to Pamela.

"Looks as if a ladder extends to the bottom of the shaft," he whispered.

"So Duke's gonna follow us down."

Right on cue Norman heard voices from above.

"Pamela," Norman hissed, "we've got to get away from here."

"How?"

"Chances are this tunnel leads somewhere."

"In the dark? Norman, we can't see anything."

Norman's mind whirled into action. *Gotta think our way out. Find a solution.*

A crash sounded from the bottom of the pit. Too much to hope that Duke or Boots had fallen down. Nice thought, though.

"Sounds likely that they're dropping rocks to spook us into shouting out." Norman touched Pamela's bare arm. "Listen, these sacks are full of stuff. There might be something in there we can use."

Pamela's doubting voice came from the darkness. "Like a gun, or a magic-carpet ride out of here? Get real, Norman."

"Just look. There might be something."

"Okay. It's worth a try."

Norman heard the rustle of plastic. Pamela must be tearing the bags open. He found one by touch. He ripped it apart.

Shoes. A comb? Clothes. A spectacle case? Hard to tell in the dark.

"Try to search the pockets," he told her.

"I'm trying . . . it's not easy in the dark. Ugh, I think I've found a pair of underpants here. Big ones."

"A lady's purse. Feels like lipsticks inside. But then it could be rifle rounds. Shit, this is harder than I thought."

"What are we looking for exactly, Norman?"

"I don't know. I'm hoping we know when we find it."

"Great."

More crashes from the pit. Duke must have hefted some of the heavy machinery over the edge.

"Probably hoping to squash us before he comes down," Norman said. "Aw, crap."

"What is it?"

"Thought it was a flashlight. It's just a cell phone."

"Pass it here."

"Why? You'll never get a signal down here."

"Just pass it, will you, Norman?"

"I don't know where it is now," Norman confessed. "I just threw it to one side."

"Find it. It might help."

"You going to hit Duke with it?"

"No, don't be ridiculous. Just find the phone, will you?"

Norman searched through thighbones, rib cages, moldering assholes, discarded shoes, jackets—all by touch—then . . .

"Here's your phone," Norman told her. "For what good it is."

"There might still be some charge in the battery—"

"I don't see what—"

"There!"

"My God."

"See?"

"Pamela. You're a genius."

With a bleep, as she pressed the power button, the cell phone's screen glowed a green-yellow. It wasn't all that bright, but it was enough.

Norman could see Pamela's grinning face in the dim glow. He looked at the cell phone's keypad and screen glowing in her hand. She moved the phone over the bottom of the tunnel.

The downside was that now they could see the decomposing arms, legs, torsos, hearts, lungs, and spinal cords of dozens of men and women.

"No wonder it stinks." She gulped. "These people are putrefying."

At the bottom of the pit shaft was a rounded mound of more bodies. Norman was beginning to think the illuminated cell-phone screen was brighter than he could have imagined when he realized the light came from above.

Duke was coming down the ladder. He shone the flashlight down to make sure no one below had an unpleasant surprise waiting for him.

"Shit," Norman breathed. "Here he comes."

"Wait, we can't walk by the light of the cell phone. See, it goes off every few seconds." She pressed one of the keys. With a bleep the light came on again. But only for five seconds.

"Shine the light on the bags. There's got to be some matches here."

As quickly as they could they searched the plastic sacks by the feeble light of the phone.

"Wait," she told him. "You go through the bags; I'll keep the light near your hands."

Now they worked together. She helped him by repeatedly depressing a button to keep the cell-phone screen glowing. When it was lit she held the device as close to his searching hands as possible.

"Hurry up, Norman . . . I can hear him climbing down the ladder."

Now Norman saw driver's licenses, pens, combs, car keys, maps, travel itineraries, socks, women's lingerie, novels, music cassette tapes, spectacles, then—*Bingo!*

"Look."

"A cigarette lighter," she said. "Does it work?"

"Here goes."

He rotated the wheel on the top with his thumb. A yellow flame popped up from the metal casing. Norman saw it was a retro model, complete with a cannabis leaf printed on the side.

"As far as I can tell, it's full of lighter fuel," he told her.

"We've gotta risk taking that. Duke can't be far away."

Norman kept the small flame burning as he stood up. To lift himself to his feet he pushed down on a torso, also using the hand that held the lighter. The torso was decomposing in style. There was no head. An oozing hole formed in the cleft between the shoulders. The chest and belly were rounded with gas. Chest hairs stood on end. Even the belly button had popped, going from an inny to an outty. Its internal pressure must have been formidable.

The moment Norman pressed down on the bloated belly the torso farted through the neck hole.

A loud, rich raspberry of a fart.

An instant later the decomposition gas touched the flame of the lighter. Norman flinched as a ball of fire rolled past his face, singeing his eyebrows.

Before the flame died it lit the tunnel in vivid detail. He saw the tool marks of picks on the walls. Saw the rails used by the ore hoppers. They ran into the distance along a dead-straight tunnel.

He saw Pamela's startled face as the gas generated by putrefying internal organs flared off. Her face possessed a strained, tight look. A tightness that trembled. She was wet and shiny all over. Streaks of brown cadaver juice marked her cheeks.

Norman saw that when he'd dragged her over the edge of the abyss he'd torn her sweater. A rent reached down from her collar to her breastbone. It exposed the gleaming upper half of her breast. A smooth globe of perfection.

Norman's flesh tingled. This time the snake venom wasn't to blame.

When the release of flammable gas burned itself out, she said, "Come on. He can't be far from the bottom."

Pamela didn't bother with the cell phone now. It was way too dim compared to the cigarette-lighter flame. Even so, she slipped it into the pocket of her shorts.

"Just for reserve," she told him.

Now they hurried as fast as they could along the old mine workings. In the flicker of the lighter they could see timber supports, plus twin rails that were encrusted with dust.

"Gotta hope there's another way out," he told her.

"Either there is, or we die trying."

"Succinctly put."

A white light reflected from the stone walls.

"Oh, God," Pamela hissed. "He's here."

Norman glanced back. They'd covered close to a hundred yards since leaving the bottom of the pit, with its rich deposit of rotting body parts. Although Norman couldn't see it now. All he saw was a dazzling mass of light.

Duke was shooting the flashlight straight at them.

Not only the flashlight.

A ricocheting bullet went screaming by them.

"Nowhere to run to, old buddy." Duke's voice boomed along the tunnel. "If you stop running I'm gonna promise to make it painless. You won't feel a thing."

Norman's legs weakened. The snakebite was slowing him down again. No . . . that wasn't it. It was another reason.

"We're running uphill," he panted.

"Could be a way out up ahead."

"Pray God there is."

"And Duke might be doing us a favor?" She glanced at the lighter in his hand. "Kill it."

"Right! Duke's flashlight!"

He snuffed the flame. Duke lit their way as well as his. Without having to worry about the burning wick going out they could move faster.

Ahead, they could see an opening cut in the rock. The tunnel had branched into two.

"Rockfall to the right," Pamela said, breathless. "Go left."

This tunnel ran even more steeply uphill. After a few paces it opened into a gallery where the miners had worked the seams. Then they must have loaded the ore into wheeled trucks that ran under the force of gravity to the bottom of the shaft he and Pamela'd fallen into. There, machinery would have hauled the ore to the surface.

The gallery they'd entered was a deep gray that glittered with speckles of ore in the walls.

"Jeez. This is big enough to put a house in." Pamela looked up, awed at the high ceiling.

"Yeah, but I wish they'd ventilated the place. I can hardly breathe."

"It'll be a buildup of gas." Pamela struggled for breath, too.

He noticed the way her lips became pale. When she sucked in breath her breasts rose as her rib cage expanded. He saw the pale curve of them through the rip in the sweater.

"We can't wait here any longer," Norman gasped. "Duke's not far behind. See the light?"

He was right. There was still no need to use the cigarette lighter. Duke's flashlight sent a wash of white light into the miners' gallery.

"Gotta keep moving." She heaved in a lungful of toxic air. "Right."

They walked on. Running was impossible. The stone floor was humped in the middle. A seam of harder rock had forced the miners to dig upward before the seam of rock that formed the obstacle dipped down again. It forced Norman and Pamela to walk up a steep incline before descending the other side. At the top of the mound Norman's throat stung; his eyes watered.

When they'd passed the highest point he spluttered the words, "That's where the gas was densest."

Pamela nodded. Her eyes streamed with tears.

Now they could hear footfalls. Duke must be close now.

All they could do was continue. The roomy gallery narrowed back to a tunnel. They followed the tracks into the gloom.

When they reached an old ore cart on the tracks Pamela stopped him.

"Norman," she said, "I've got an idea."

CHAPTER FIFTY-THREE

Norman stared at the miners' ore truck as it sat on the rails. A block of wood the same shape as a wedge of apple pie had been forced under a rusty iron wheel to stop it from running away. Probably an act by the last miner to walk out of here eighty years ago.

Norman gasped for air. His leg hurt where the rattler venom still saturated muscle tissue. Even his hand tingled where Priest, the crazed cannibal, had chewed on it.

At last he found breath to speak. "Pamela, I hope you're gonna tell me we can get in that thing and ride outta here."

"Nope . . . the tunnel runs uphill. If we climb in the truck and get it rolling it'll take us right to Duke."

Norman glanced back down toward the gallery. The flashlight was growing brighter. "Well . . . Duke . . . Duke's getting closer all the time." He licked his dry lips. "What's the plan?"

"Give me your shirt."

"Huh?"

"Your shirt. Quickly!"

From the bottom of the tunnel Duke sang out, "Fee, fi, fo, fum, I smell the blood of a college bum." The guy laughed. A mad-sounding laugh. The kind of laugh a man made as he sliced a guy into pieces.

"Norman? Shirt!"

"Okay, okay." Norman ripped off his shirt, not bothering to undo the buttons. Quickly she tied the shirt to the front of the ore-hopper truck, around the iron mechanism that would have hooked into the next truck in line.

"Lighter." She held out her hand.

Norman handed it to her.

She rolled the metal wheel to ignite the wick. Then she held the blue flame to Norman's shirt. With a crackle it started to burn.

"Great," he gasped. "You've tied my shirt to a truck. You've set it alight. Now what?"

"Kick the wedge out from the wheel."

"Anything to please a lady." He was light-headed now. These actions made no sense to him. But he did as she asked anyway. With a few kicks of his foot he knocked clear the timber wedge that acted as brake.

"Norman, stand back!"

He stood back against the tunnel wall, out of the way.

Nothing happened.

"The axles will be rusted," he told her. "It's stuck . . . stuck like shit to a baby."

"Norman!" Duke called. "What you doing playing with rusty trucks, bud? Gonna cut yourself."

Norman couldn't see Duke properly, but he guessed he'd just entered the section of tunnel that contained Pamela, himself, and the truck. The resolutely stationary truck.

Pamela hissed, "Get behind it. *Push!*"

"You really think it's gonna run him down?"

"Just get this truck rolling, Norman."

He limped behind the truck to help Pamela, who had her shoulder against the hopper that normally would have contained the mined ore. He helped her push.

Through clenched teeth he panted, "Wouldn't we be better running away . . . rather than doing this?"

"We can't outrun the guy. He's armed. We're not. This is our last hope."

"Gee, some hope."

"Get it moving before the shirt burns out."

"Like that makes perfect sense."

"Listen to me. When you set fire to the gas pooping out of the body earlier—it was methane gas. A by-product of putrefaction."

"So?"

"Methane. It's odorless, colorless. It's lighter than air. . . . Uh, come on, it's starting to move."

The wheels squealed as they turned for the first time in decades.

"Norman?" Duke's voice. "You playing with matches up there? I can see somethin' burning."

"Methane's flammable," she panted.

"Why didn't we blow up when you set fire to the shirt?"

" 'Cause of the hump in the gallery floor down there. Remember when we couldn't breathe? Methane's gathered in a pocket where the floor of the mine rises up in that hump."

"From all those rotting bodies?"

"Yup, those dead people are a regular gas factory."

"It's going!" Norman cried out as the wheels unstuck themselves and began to roll. Axles squealed. He straightened to see the truck moving faster and faster downhill toward the light source that was Duke's flashlight. The thunder of iron wheels against the track filled the void.

"Get back against the tunnel sides!" Pamela shouted above the racket of the runaway ore truck. "Cover your ears with your hands. Keep your mouth open; otherwise the shock wave will pop your lungs."

Shock wave? It sounded as if the truck with his burning shirt tied to the front was about to go nuclear.

The rumble of the truck receded; then came Duke's scornful laughter.

"You really thought you could run Duke down with that heap of junk! Man, you've gotta try harder than that!"

The rattle of wheels faded.

The sense of anticlimax nearly caused Norman to weep. All that effort? For what? Jesus, they would have been better—

Norman didn't so much hear the explosion.

All he really remembered was a blue light of such intensity he could still see it when his eyes were shut tight. Then he was flying through the air. Then he was lying with something soft on top of him.

There was darkness. He seemed to be breathing dust.

Jeez, at least he was breathing.

The darkness seemed to last a long time. He was too dazed to do much other than lie there.

After a spell he heard a noise in the stillness. An electronic bleep.

A green face floated in front of his.

"Are you all right, Norman?"

"Pamela?"

"Yeah, sorry, I seem to be lying on top of you."

"Believe me, that ain't a problem."

She moved the cell phone so she could reveal a little of their surroundings.

They couldn't see much. Dust misted the air. In the light of the cell phone it created an eerie, greenish fog.

"Duke," Norman said. "If we're in one piece, then—"

"Relax," she told him. "When your burning shirt detonated the methane, you could truthfully say that Duke sorta went to pieces."

The light on the phone went out again.

She pressed another key.

Bleep.

The light came on. Norman saw bits of Duke. Big bits. Small bits. Charred bits. Bloody bits. His head lay in the center of the tunnel, looking back at them. He still wore the disdainful sneer, the lip curling up. Only there was no body.

"Appears as if Duke's gone to the bad-boy convention in the sky."

"Yup." She smiled. "Duke. RIP. Rest in pieces."

They stood up. Dusted each other off. Norman had had the good sense earlier to replace the lighter in his pocket. He lit it again.

"Okay," he announced. "Let's find the exit."

CHAPTER FIFTY-FOUR

When Norman stepped out of the mine's ventilation shaft it was night. Even so, he saw the light.

Not that he was suddenly overcome by the sweet love of the Lord.

Nor any revelation concerning Jesus, Buddha, or Shiva.

No.

Norman saw Pits in the moonlight below him, and then he saw the light of his own personal revelation. He thought: *Duke's gone. I'm still here. I'm going to take over.*

That town is mine.

Pamela said, "Take care where you're stepping, Norman. This path runs right at the edge of the cliff."

"Don't worry," he told her. "After what happened tonight I've gotta be indestructible."

"I wouldn't push your luck. That's a sheer drop."

Norman felt good. Duke was dead. Boots wouldn't be a problem. This moon was so bright he could clearly see the narrow path that hugged the edge of the cliff. He glanced down to his left. The rock face plunged down maybe a hundred feet to a scree of rubble at the bottom. Probably old mine waste thrown out of the shafts that pockmarked the hillside here. In the distance a coyote howled in the hills. Some animal part of Norman howled back.

A desire that was nothing less than wolfish began to burn in his belly. He stopped. Glanced back at Pamela, who followed him along the narrow path.

She looks good by moonlight. Skin glows sliver. Hair like gold.

He saw her bare shoulder where her sweater had been torn open earlier when he pulled her into the mine shaft so they could escape Boots and Duke. That bare shoulder burned in the moonlight. Norman burned inside.

He wanted her.

Hell, he'd earned her. He'd every right to take Pamela for his own. After all, Duke promised that Norman could have her first, hadn't he?

"Norman?" Her voice quavered, as if she'd seen something in his expression that worried her. "Norman, we need to go to the house and free my friends. Then we've got to find Boots. She's still armed, remember?"

"Me and you," he breathed.

"Me and you what?" She tried to smile as if he were joking. But even in the moonlight he saw clearly enough that the smile died on her face.

"Me and you," he whispered. "King and queen of Pits."

"King and queen of Pits? What on earth are you talking about, Norman?"

"Pamela, don't you see? We've got brains. We're brighter than the other bozos who live here. We could take over here."

He stared at her as she stood with the rocky hills bathed in moonlight behind her. A shooting star streaked through the heavens, like an omen.

Pamela was stunned for a moment. Couldn't speak. Then: "Norman, you're not being rational. Why do we want to take over Pits? They're nice people here; they saved my—"

"Pamela, listen. We can do it. There are guns in my trailer. We can force Lauren, Nicki, and the rest to do what we want. We can live here like royalty."

"Norman, the shock of that explosion must have confused you. You're sounding crazy. You're talking like . . ." She paused.

"Like Duke?" He felt a smile spread across his face. "Yeah, you could say I inherited the Dukedom."

"Norman, you don't know what you're saying."

"Pamela, come with me. We can rule together."

"Norman—no!"

She turned to walk away from him.

At that moment he couldn't say if he went crazy, or revealed his real character that had been hidden for years, or whether the spirit of bad-boy Duke really did ghost through his flesh to take control of his brain. But he snarled.

Lunged at Pamela.

Grabbed hold of her.

"Once you've been with me," he grunted in her face, "you won't want anyone else. Other men will seem like a heap of wet rags compared to me!"

"Norman. You *are* crazy! You're a nobody who got hooked up with two weirdoes. They've sent you insane."

"Nobody? I'm *not* a nobody. Listen, Pamela." He held his hands up in front of her face, the fingers splayed. "I've killed men with these bare hands. Today I killed Terry."

"Terry . . . you killed him?" She shook her head in horror. "I don't believe you."

"I cracked his skull like a nut. I can show you where I left the body."

"Please, Norman, come down to the trailer. You've got to lie down and rest."

"I'm gonna lie down, all right. With you!" He grabbed hold of her sweater. Started tugging.

Pamela tried to pull away. She put one foot over the edge of the cliff. Her leg swung a hundred feet above jagged stones.

Norman gripped her arms, then dragged her back onto the path.

"See," he told her. "I've just gone and saved your life all over again. You owe me a blood debt now."

She struggled. "Norman, please."

He twisted her around so he could hug her from behind. In a parody of a dance move he embraced her, his chest pressing against her back, his head jutting forward so he could press his cheek against hers.

"Pamela. You see Pits down there, all shining and beautiful in the moonlight? That's ours now. Our dukedom."

"You're holding me too tight . . . I can hardly breathe."

"In a minute I'm going to undress you. Then I'm going to make love to you . . . right here on the path overlooking the town that we're going to own."

"No!"

She struggled. Kicked back with her heel.

Norman laughed. He grabbed her sweater where it was torn. He pulled. The gash in the fabric opened wider, ripping, exposing the upper part of her breast.

This's gonna be good . . . real good. His heart thudded. His groin tingled. He could even hear Duke's voice inside his head urging him on. *"Way to go, Normy, old buddy. Nail her for me. Screw her so hard she can't walk for a week."*

"Norman, please don't do this . . . please!"

Then a calm voice. "Pamela's right, Norman."

"Uh . . ."

Norman looked up at the boulders on the hillside. Standing there was a figure. Norman blinked. Moonlight played tricks on him, for the human figure appeared to possess wings that jutted from its sides.

"Sharpe." This was Pamela crying out in relief. "Sharpe, thank God."

"Sharpe. That really you?" Norman asked. Suddenly his sense of macho power vanished. His legs took on a rubbery aspect.

Easily now, Pamela wriggled free of him.

She moved to one side until she stood maybe ten feet from Norman.

Meanwhile, Norman stared at the man with the wings. It was Sharpe standing there in the moonlight. Norman blinked. Looked harder.

No. Those *weren't* wings. Sharpe stood with his hands on his hips. Moonlight did the rest to create the illusion of angel wings jutting out from either side of his torso.

"Norman, you were hurting Pamela. No real man would force himself on a woman."

"I wasn't," Norman protested. He stared up at Sharpe's face veiled by shadow. His flattop haircut made his head look almost square in silhouette. His white short-sleeved shirt seemed to glow with its own light in the radiance of the moon.

Sharpe was motionless.

Sharpe was calm.

And Norman sensed that Sharpe had passed judgment on him.

Norman's heart pounded in his chest. "You're going to kill me, aren't you?"

"Worse," Sharpe said.

"Worse? What can be worse than killing me?"

"I'm gonna put you on my bus; then I'm going to take you home to your family. And then I'm going to stand there while you confess to your mother and father all the bad things you've done."

"No, you can't . . . *you can't!*" Norman's voice rose in a scream as he imagined the scenario.

Him quaking there in the living room. Admitting to his mother and father how he killed the cops. How he killed Terry.

Then tried to rip off Pamela's clothes.

Oh, Jesus. No may.

Guilt came in dark, sickening waves. Remorse was as bitter as bile rising in his throat.

He had to escape. He couldn't let Sharpe take him back home to face that kind of shame.

Norman turned, ran.

Ran blindly. Straight over the edge of the cliff.

Fell.

Fell a long, long way.

The cool night air rushed by him. In the moonlight he saw the ground come speeding upward to meet his falling body.

I'll be fine, he told himself. *Sharpe will save me. Sharpe's got wings. . . .*

Then he remembered that the wings he'd seen were a trick of the moonlight. Just an illusion.

Not like those hard rocks just seconds away.

Norman wanted to cry.

But he didn't have time.

CHAPTER FIFTY-FIVE

APPETIZERS

Pits enjoyed its celebration party.

Their personal thanksgiving that the danger to them was passed.

All the people of Pits turned out. All seven of them. Sharpe, Priest (in his wheelchair), Lauren, Nicki, Wes, Hank, and Pamela.

They lit a big fire under the summer stars, where they flame-cooked delicate little blood sausages as an appetizer for the main course. Then Lauren broiled steaks on the barbecue. In tubs of ice were about a hundred bottles of beer and sodas of all different varieties.

"You ready for your steak, Wes?" Lauren asked.

"Could eat a horse," he replied.

"Horse is one thing that isn't on the menu."

Wes sat beside Pamela at a long wooden table. Sitting opposite were Nicki and Sharpe, with a space beside him for Lauren. Priest sat at one end, his baldhead gleaming like a silver dome in the firelight.

At the other end—at the head of the table—in his rightful place as mayor was Hank, looking quite the gent in his best Stetson. Everyone was in good spirits. All were having fun.

Just one week ago the madness had ended.

Of course, this might be another kind of madness, Pamela thought. *But it's a peaceful, well-ordered madness. A happy madness.*

After Pamela and Sharpe had walked down from the cliff top that had claimed Norman's life, they'd circled around the hill to Boots, who still guarded the pit shaft, gun in hand. Sharpe had distracted her while Pamela introduced the woman's head to a piece of lumber. The hard way.

When Boots woke up she was almost relieved that Pamela had survived. She was full of optimism for a future without Duke and Norman.

"I always thought they was gonna be trouble," she'd confided.

"How's the steak?" Pamela asked with a wink. "Tough as old boots?"

"Hey, I heard that," Lauren protested as she sat down beside Sharpe. "Only kidding."

"You know," Wes said, "it really does taste like pork." He smacked his lips in appreciation of the meat's flavor.

Priest sang out, "Now, didn't I always tell everyone? You've not lived until you've eaten your fellow man . . . or in this case . . . woman."

Hank raised his bottle of beer in a toast.

"*Haw!* Here's to Boots. A woman who can satisfy the inner man."

They all hoisted their bottles. "Boots!" Spontaneous applause broke out around the table.

Meanwhile, Boots—or what little remained of her—sizzled over the hot coals of the barbecue.

ENTREES

A week after that meal, with Boots as dish of the day, there was another celebration, when Hank did his rightful duty as mayor and conducted a marriage ceremony that the good people of Pits had been awaiting for a long time. Across the town's two main buildings—the gas station and the café—were banners that announced:

LAUREN & SHARPE
CONGRATULATIONS ON YOUR SPECIAL DAY!

Pamela smiled as she flipped the special-recipe Pits Burgers for the wedding feast. Then she slipped them onto buns for Nicki to distribute. It wasn't every day that Pits celebrated a wedding of two of its townsfolk.

People came from miles around to watch Sharpe slip that band of gold on Lauren's finger. Many of the well-wishers were men, women, and children whom Sharpe had saved in the past.

Pamela's smile broadened. She'd never seen a couple more in love.

"Ouch." The final burger on the skillet spit a drop of hot fat onto the back of her hand. Shaking her head, she used a pair of long-handled kitchen tongs to grab the offending burger. As she did so, she couldn't resist scolding the meat that had stung her. "That's the last time you ever hurt anyone, Norman Wiscoff." She laid the Pits Burger on a bed of lettuce, then dropped a slice of cheese on top of the steaming patty of meat.

Norman meat, to be precise. After all, Priest had insisted it would be a waste of perfectly good eating to leave Norman at the bottom of the cliff for the vultures and the coyotes.

Norman had always wanted to be cool. In the end he got what he wanted. He wound up in the café's deep freeze.

That is, after he'd been expertly rendered into cutlets, filets, chops, spare ribs, and burgers.

"Pits Burger to go!"

"Is that the last one?" Nicki asked as she collected the plateful of food.

"The *very* last one," Pamela announced, beaming.

"Well, come out and join the party."

They walked out into the sunshine, where the party was in full swing.

JUST DESSERTS

That evening, after everyone else had gone home, Pamela joined the other residents of Pits as they waved Lauren and Sharpe off on their honeymoon. The setting sun hung low, flooding the Mojave Desert with a light of pure gold. Cacti stood in the sand; they looked as if they were waving, too.

When the bus pulled away, with Sharpe at the wheel, and Lauren sitting right behind him on a bench seat, the good folk of Pits cheered and whistled and waved.

Lauren glanced back into the body of the bus. Okay, it might be unusual to take a busful of passengers on your honeymoon.

But Sharpe was different, she reflected.

Come to that, the bus's passengers were different, too.

Sitting silently upright were the mannequins in their summer clothes. Right in the front two seats were three newcomers.

Sharpe had unique ideas. Some might call him a visionary. Though not everyone understood his motives. But Lauren did.

Because the three new passengers on the bus were Boots, Duke, and Norman. Or at least, they were three plastic clothing-store mannequins that Sharpe had artfully made to *look* like Boots, Duke, and Norman.

Boots sported her short bleached hair, wearing her skimpy tank top and white cowgirl boots.

Norman sat beside her, in a white T-shirt and beach shorts, his eyes staring glassily ahead.

Duke lounged by himself in the middle of a seat designed for two. He wore a white T-shirt like Norman's, blue jeans, motorcycle boots. Sharpe had painted his features well. The bad-boy upper lip still curled. One plastic arm reached back to rest on the seat back. On that arm a tattoo read, BORN TO RAISE HELL. Even though the body was synthetic, he still looked cool.

Why had Sharpe brought replicas of these three onto his bus? Lauren had wondered about that. The other mannequins were Sharpe's reminders of the people he'd saved from the killing heat of the desert.

At last she realized these three dummies were a warning.

They were saying:

If you ever come to Pits, California, pop. seven, you'll be greeted with the warmest of welcomes. But take care. If you arrive with the intention of causing hurt, then you might end your days just like Boots, Norman, and Duke here.

Out on the desert highway.

Riding the Glory Bus until the sweet by and by . . .

And that, my friends, means until Judgment Day.

AFTER MIDNIGHT
RICHARD LAYMON

Alice has quite a story to tell you. That's not her real name, of course. She couldn't give her real name, not after all the things she reveals about herself. All of her...*adventures*. She wouldn't want the police to find her, now would she?

It started out so nice. Alice was house-sitting, enjoying having the whole place to herself. But everything went wrong that first night, when she looked out the window and saw a strange man jumping naked into the swimming pool. Alice just knew he would be coming to get her, like all those other men before. But she would never be a victim again. Not after she remembered the old Civil War saber hanging in the living room...
